CHRISTINA DODD

Priceless

AVON

An Imprint of HarperCollins*Publishers*

This is a work of fiction. Names, characters, places, and incidents are products of the author's imagination or are used fictitiously and are not to be construed as real. Any resemblance to actual events, locales, organizations, or persons, living or dead, is entirely coincidental.

AVON BOOKS
An Imprint of HarperCollins*Publishers*
10 East 53rd Street
New York, New York 10022-5299

Copyright © 1992 by Christina Dodd
Excerpts from *Confessions at Midnight* copyright © 2008 by Jacquie D'Alessandro; *Priceless* copyright © 1992 by Christina Dodd; *The Perfect Wife* copyright © 1996, 2008 by Victoria Alexander; *The Seduction of an Unknown Lady* copyright © 2008 by Sandra Kleinschmit
ISBN: 978-0-06-104153-2
www.avonromance.com

First HarperCollins special paperback printing: September 1998
First HarperCollins paperback printing: August 1992

Avon Trademark Reg. U.S. Pat. Off. and in Other Countries, Marca Registrada, Hecho en U.S.A.
HarperCollins® is a registered trademark of HarperCollins Publishers.

Printed in the U.S.A.

10 9 8 7 6 5 4 3

To Shannon
Thank you for helping me plot my stories,
For being proud of me,
For loving me as much as I love you.
You'll enjoy this book
As soon as Mommy decides
you're old enough to read it.

And a special merci beaucoup *to Susan*

Bits of Wisdom from Eighteenth-Century England

*She drank good ale, good punch and wine
and lived to the age of ninety-nine.*
> Tombstone of Rebecca Freeland (d. 1741)

*I deplore the unpopularity of the married state,
which is scorned by our young girls nowadays,
as once by young men. Both sexes have discovered its inconveniences, and many feminine lib-
ertines may be found amongst young women of
rank. No one is shocked to hear that, "Miss So
and So, Maid of Honour, has got nicely over her
confinement."*
> Lady Mary Wortley Montagu

*Sir, I mind my belly very well, for I look upon it
that he who will not mind his belly will scarcely
mind anything else.*
> Dr. Samuel Johnson

*One night as I came from the play
I met a fair maid by the way;
She had rosy cheeks and a dimpled chin
And a hole to put poor Robin in.*
> Traditional English song recorded by Francis Place

*Conceal whatever learning you attain, with as
much solicitude as you would hide crookedness
or lameness.*
> Advice to her daughter from
> Lady Mary Wortley Montagu

Chapter 1

London, England
1720

"Bronwyn, someone's going to see us."

"Just keep watch." Bronwyn Edana worked frantically at the keyhole. "I've almost got it."

Olivia wiped tears of fright from her cheeks and peered down the darkened hall of the Brimming Cup Inn. "We shouldn't be doing this. If the landlord should find us here—"

"Listen to that moaning." Through the locked door there came the sound of whimpering. Bronwyn whispered, "That person in there is sick or hurt somehow. Do you want to abandon a fellow human being in agony?"

"No. . . ." Olivia didn't sound too sure.

"Of course not."

"But Maman and Da placed us in the care of the landlord while they went into London, and the landlord said—"

Bronwyn wiggled the heavy iron nail in the hole and caught the locking device inside. "I've got it!" she crowed, then groaned when the nail slipped off. Sinking back on her heels, she answered her sister. "The landlord ignored this lady's cries for help. He said the gentleman who rented the room was respectable and paid a great price. He only cares about the money, and about making sure that we stay in our rooms like proper young ladies."

"What if Maman and Da discover what we've been doing?"

"They would say we're doing the right thing."

Olivia stared at her impetuous sister.

"All right. They'd say to ignore it." Wiping her sweaty palm on the skirt of her riding costume, she tried to still the tremble in her fingers. "We wouldn't be at this nasty little inn if Maman and Da hadn't wanted to visit the moneylender. Once they receive my dowry from Lord Rawson, they'll be flush with coin once more, and we won't have to stay in these terrible places."

"Oh, Bronwyn." Olivia sighed. "Once they receive your dowry, you'll be wed and you'll not be with us in these terrible places."

A mutinous defiance steadied Bronwyn's hand. "So Maman and Da will live with the consequences of our adventure—if they find out."

"But I'm frightened," Olivia admitted.

The love Bronwyn felt for her eighteen-year-old sister tempered her aggravation. She'd always taken care of Olivia, from the day her parents first presented her four-year-old self with the pretty baby. Still, Olivia was the epitome of conformity.

Right now Bronwyn didn't have time for conformity.

"You can go back to our room if you wish. I'll

handle this without your help," Bronwyn said in a hurt tone.

"No!" Olivia took a frantic breath. "No, I wouldn't leave you, you know that. But—"

Rallying with telltale swiftness, Bronwyn said, "Good. I'll need you if this is as bad as it sounds." Leaning her weight against the metal clamp, she heard the click as the bolt shot back. "I've got it!"

Her hand on the doorknob, she prepared to enter the room.

"I'll guard the door," Olivia whispered.

Bronwyn paused and smiled at her affectionately. "I know you will. I trust you." She slipped inside the room and moved to the bed. A soft weeping led her, but nothing prepared her for the young, badly battered woman tangled in the sheets. Bronwyn's resolution faltered a moment, and she fought the faintness threatening to undermine her. She leaned close to the woman's face. "Let me help you."

One eye struggled to open and focus; the other was swollen shut. The bruised mouth worked, and at last the woman said, *"D'eau."*

Bronwyn stared. "What?"

"D'eau," she whispered again.

The woman spoke French. Searching her meager knowledge of the language, Bronwyn translated, "Water." On the stand she found a pitcher, cup, and basin. She called Olivia as she filled the cup, and reluctantly her sister stepped in. "You'll have to give her the water as I hold her up," Bronwyn instructed.

"Oh, Bronwyn, I wish we'd driven right through to Lord Rawson's. I'm so scared." Olivia almost sobbed in her distress, and Bronwyn struck her lightly on the shoulder.

"Brace up." She handed her the cup. "I need you."

At the bed, Bronwyn lowered herself onto the mattress. As she slid a hand behind the woman's head, the invalid groaned pitifully, as if every movement, every breath, hurt. Bronwyn's eyes filled with tears, but when she looked up, Olivia had done as instructed. She'd put the cup to the woman's mouth.

The woman drank greedily between gasps until at last she stopped. *"Merci,"* she said, gazing at Olivia. "An angel."

"So she is," Bronwyn agreed, relaxing. French might be this woman's native tongue, but she spoke English well. "She's an angel come to rescue you. She'll go and find a doctor to help you now."

"Non!" A frail hand clawed at Bronwyn's arm, then fell away. "Tell no one. He will kill me . . . if you do."

Bronwyn glanced back, expecting to see a menacing figure. "Your husband?"

"Non! I am not so foolish." Her vehement denial seemed to sap her strength.

As Bronwyn had known it would, her sister's natural nursing skill took over. Olivia wet a towel and smoothed the hair back from the invalid's forehead. "What's your name?"

"I am Henriette." Her eyes opened, closed. "Does he have you, too?"

"No, no one has me."

"Bon. So beautiful a woman . . . should not be in brutal hands." She twisted as a spasm tore through her. "Run away. Do not let him get you."

"I won't let anyone get her." Bronwyn picked up one fragile hand as it lay on the covers. "She's my sister."

"Sister?" Henriette gazed at them. "Nothing alike."

"We're alike in our spirit," Bronwyn insisted. "We'll help you escape."

"Too late. Light candles . . . for my soul, I beg."

"Of course," Olivia agreed.

"The wicked man murdered me. Promise me you will light"—Henriette caught her breath against the pain—"light candles to guide me." Her hand plucked uselessly at the air. "Promise."

Olivia smiled, as sweet as the angel Henriette called her. "I promise."

Satisfied, Henriette closed her eyes. "*Allez*. Go. He is coming back."

Bronwyn shook her head. "No one is going to get me, and I can find someone to help you—"

"They will accuse me, because I am French. They will say I did it, but I did not."

"I don't understand," Bronwyn said.

"He murders someone and blames me."

"What? Who?"

"I do not know who. He says to his servant . . . he would kill a man by dropping a stock on him."

"A stock? A stump?"

"*Non*." Wagging her head back and forth on the pillows in an exhausted effort, Henriette insisted, "Stock."

Such garbled nonsense made no sense to Bronwyn. "Surely there are better ways."

"*Non*. . . ." Henriette coughed, and blood trickled from the corner of her mouth.

Olivia sprang forward with the cloth to wipe Henriette's lips. "Don't talk," she urged.

Henriette waved her away. "When he realized I had heard, he took me. Beat me until I die."

Bronwyn soothed her with a stroke of the hand. "We can't leave you here."

"Can't we tell the landlord?" Olivia asked. "If he knew how badly this woman was hurt—"

Bronwyn exploded as if she had been holding in her exasperation. "This is London, he said, and if I extended my hand in friendship to everyone in need, I'd get it chopped off. He said to sew and take my mind off her moans."

"This is so awful." Olivia hid her face in her hand. "What can we do? We're just two girls. We're not even married."

"I'm betrothed. Does that make me reliable?" Bronwyn reached up to her taller sister's shoulders and shook her slightly. "There's a way. I have a plan."

"Not one of your plans," Olivia wailed.

Bronwyn ignored her, asking Henriette, "Is there somewhere I can take you?"

Intense longing swept Henriette's face. "If you could, *le bon Dieu* would bless you."

"Tell me where you would go," Bronwyn coaxed.

"Madame Rachelle's salon. Do you know where . . . ?"

"I'll find out. Olivia, go to the footman downstairs and tell him we want a coach for our mother."

"Go by myself?"

"Would you rather stay with Mademoiselle Henriette and I'll go?"

Olivia glanced at Henriette's swollen face, then at the door. "I'll stay."

Staggered by the uncharacteristic bravery, Bronwyn asked, "But, Olivia, what if that man comes back?"

"I'll put a chair against the door. I don't like to talk to strangers. I can't order a coach. Henriette needs me, and I'm better in sickrooms."

Bronwyn stuck out her jaw. "I've been fine so far."

"You've been very brave, but you're white as a new-bleached petticoat." Olivia gave Bronwyn a little push. "Hurry."

Bronwyn smiled at her tenderhearted sister. "I'll rap three times when I come back, and you let me in."

Dashing out the door, she clattered down the dark stairs, then halted at the bottom. She was the daughter of an earl, and she should act like one. She straightened her expensive brown wig and pinched her tanned cheeks to bring up the color. With excessive nonchalance, she strolled through the taproom and to the front door. She peeked out and spied a young man, the kind who would call for transportation for her if tipped with a copper. Stepping over the threshold, she called, "You! I need a coach for my mother. She wishes to go into London proper. My mother is an invalid with gout and"—she took a deep breath—"she needs a coach."

The boy responded to the glitter of her coin. "Aye, m'lady, be glad t' call a coach.

She backed through the door. "Don't let it get away. Keep it here." She turned and hurried back to the room, knocked three times, and listened as Olivia dragged pieces of furniture away. "Hurry," she urged when Olivia got the door open. "I've got her a coach."

Olivia looked as if she'd been crying. "Henriette can't walk downstairs. She's bleeding badly."

From the bed, the hoarse voice of Henriette interrupted. "Do not let me die here, *je vous en prie*. Take me to Rachelle. To peace."

"Oh, God." The large stain of red against the sheets made Bronwyn clutch the door. All Henriette's blood was seeping away, robbed by some ghastly internal injury. Olivia reached out for comfort; Bronwyn pulled her into her arms. This was so much worse than they'd ever imagined, so much worse than anything they'd seen in their sheltered lives. Yet their sisterly affection fortified them, and Bronwyn mumbled into Olivia's shoulder, "We can't give up now. Help me wrap her in the sheet."

Bronwyn stripped the top sheet from the bed, and they slid it beneath Henriette. Assisting Henriette to sit up, they bundled her into the cloak. As they tucked her veil over her face, Bronwyn realized she and Olivia would have to support her all the way to the street. Bronwyn was grateful for the functional riding costumes they wore for traveling, and for the first time in their lives she thanked God for Olivia's tall and graceful strength.

Arranging Henriette's arms around their shoulders, they put their arms around her waist and edged out the door. Henriette took her weight on one foot while the other dragged. At the head of the stairs, Bronwyn instructed, "Don't forget to watch her skirts as well as your own, Olivia. Henriette, you're to let us carry you down the steps. Look pleasant, Olivia. We're going on an outing."

Henriette relaxed. Olivia showed all her teeth in a contrived smile. Bronwyn did the same. When the landlord of The Brimming Cup hailed them, she turned with a heavy heart.

"Well, ladies, I see ye found a way t' entertain yerself while yer parents is gone. That's better than stickin' yer nose in other folks' business." The balding man seemed anxious to make up for his previous rudeness. No doubt Da hadn't paid him yet, and he didn't want her to complain. Peering at the veiled lady, he asked, "Yer grandmother? I 'adn't realized she was 'ere with ye."

"Why, yes," Bronwyn agreed, "we brought her in this afternoon while you . . . handled our luggage. She travels with us."

"Good. I worried that yer parents would go gallivantin' into Lunnon proper without leavin' someone t' chaperone two such beautiful women." He spoke to Bronwyn, but his gaze lingered on Olivia. "Quite a 'eavy duty t' place on a landlord."

The tense figure under Bronwyn's hand relaxed infinitesimally. Bronwyn sighed wistfully and widened her eyes with what she hoped would be taken for innocence. "Maman and Da know we're always safe with Grandmama. She wishes to visit a few of her haunts in London town."

The landlord held the outer door as they struggled through it three abreast. "It's a grand city. Ye'll enjoy yer tour."

The coach waited, the boy holding the door. The landlord reached out to help them maneuver Henriette inside, but Bronwyn snapped, "Don't touch her!" The landlord stepped back, offended, as they hoisted Henriette up the step and placed her on the seat. "Grandmama doesn't like strangers."

"Grandmama?" The boy scratched his head. "I thought ye said this was yer mother."

The landlord's long features sharpened with curiosity. "No, their mother is a younger lady."

Accusing, the boy insisted, "Ye said it was fer yer mother."

"Yes . . . well . . ."

From inside the coach, a creaky, weak voice said, "Their mother is so flighty, I have raised these girls. They call me 'Mother.'"

Reminding herself what was at stake, reminding

herself that she was the aristocrat and the landlord her servant, Bronwyn said, "Come, my good man, get these horses moving." Her imperious air faltered when the beauty patch above her lip dropped to the floor. As the boy shut the door, she glanced out to see him hiding a grin.

At the grand house on Curzon Street, Bronwyn knocked and shifted nervously. What kind of explanation would she give to whoever answered the door?

The door opened, and a young woman with ink-stained fingers stared absently at Bronwyn and asked, "Have you come to see Rachelle?"

The French accent, so similar to Henriette's own, impressed Bronwyn, and she said urgently, "I have a friend of Madame Rachelle's. Her name is Henriette—"

The door swung wide. "Henriette?" The woman turned and shouted, "Henriette is back."

From inside in the shadows, the call echoed, and three women, none more than twenty-five, surrounded the coach.

"Take care," Olivia ordered in a rare display of authority. "She's in pain."

The women looked startled, and Olivia gently shouldered them aside. "Are you ready, Henriette?"

A mumbled affirmative, and Olivia and Bronwyn supported her up the stairs. The woman's strength had disappeared; they carried her into the entry.

"She must lie down," Bronwyn said. "Where can we put her?"

"On the sofa in the drawing room," came an order from the foot of the stairs.

Intent on maintaining her balance, Bronwyn barely glanced at the owner of the authoritative French voice.

Henriette's head flopped back as they laid her down, and she whispered, "Rachelle."

A spare, older woman with a widow's cap knelt beside the sofa and pushed Henriette's veil aside. The young women gasped when they saw Henriette's condition, and Bronwyn felt sickened, exposed once more to such brutality.

Rachelle's gaze never left Henriette. "Can you help, Daphne?"

One young woman stepped forward, performed a quick, deft examination, then touched Rachelle's rigid figure. "I would do anything for you, Rachelle, you know that. But there's nothing I can do here." Fingering the fringed shawl that rested on her shoulders, she muttered, "If you wish to have another observe her, I will not be offended."

"No." Rachelle pressed her hand on the pulse at Henriette's neck. "She is dying."

Olivia slipped her hand in Bronwyn's; they clung to each other. Only Rachelle didn't flinch. "Who did this to you, *ma mignonne?*"

Henriette's lips moved, but no words escaped. Bronwyn poured sherry from a carafe and offered it to Rachelle. Without looking up, Rachelle placed it at Henriette's lips, but Henriette couldn't drink. Dipping her finger into the liquid, Rachelle ran it over Henriette's lips. "I thought you had run away with your young lord. You did not?"

Henriette shook her head.

"So he said. Does he know about this?"

Another negative, and Henriette's consciousness slipped away.

Standing, Rachelle swung on the sisters. "How did you find her?"

Bronwyn wet her lips. "She was imprisoned in the room next to ours. We broke in and—"

Rachelle surged forward, and Bronwyn found herself pressed against a bony chest. "Of course. I should have recognized your courage at once." She drew Olivia into the embrace. "And your courage was the greater, for you were petrified. Go with my friends. They will offer refreshments."

Following the gestures of the young women, Bronwyn and Olivia left the room. Bronwyn glanced back to see a ravaged Rachelle cradling Henriette in her arms. The portrait of Rachelle's grief burned into her brain.

Clasping hands with Bronwyn and Olivia, Rachelle drew them to the drawing room. "I care for all my charges, but Henriette was my daughter. Rebellious, headstrong, but my child nevertheless. And at sixteen, who is not determined to get into trouble? I barely held her in my arms, and she was gone." The narrow, veined hands tightened on theirs in a convulsive grasp. Her head dropped as if it were heavy, and Bronwyn's heart ached.

Bronwyn stammered, "I'm sorry. I wish we could have helped."

"But you did help. You brought her home to me."

"Madame Rachelle," Olivia said, "I must tell you I promised Henriette I would pray for her. This is a sacred trust. Do you know the placement of the nearest Catholic church?"

"Your prayers will be answered as well if you pray in an Anglican church," Bronwyn suggested.

Olivia turned her reproachful gaze on her sister. "I promised her I would light candles for her soul, and I will do it in the proper circumstances."

Bronwyn recognized her sister's—for her—rare determination. "Of course. We'll stop on the way back to the inn. If Madame Rachelle would direct us?"

Rachelle considered Olivia thoughtfully. "You are a dear child. In England, it is not easy to find a place to worship in my faith, so I have a chapel in my home." She lifted a silver bell and rang it. One of the women answered the summons and led Olivia away.

Rachelle pulled a handkerchief from the pocket of her skirt but did no more than dab her reddened nose. "You think I am heartless, do you not?"

"No," Bronwyn stammered. "No, I—"

"Would your mother take the death of you or your sister as calmly as I am?" Her accent was stronger than Henriette's; her character was forged in fire.

"No . . . No, she would be devastated. Loudly devastated."

"I fled France to avoid just the same sort of nightmare that has now taken my daughter from me. It seems I have lived with this kind of pain every day, and pain has calloused me." Rachelle pressed her flattened palms together and leaned over them, as if she fought a spasm. "Yet sometimes this anguish stabs me. I will have my revenge. I will find this brute who murdered her."

"If I think of anything else Henriette said, any other clue, I will contact you," Bronwyn vowed.

"I know you will." Madame straightened and studied Bronwyn. Gesturing at her wig, Madame asked, "May I?" Before Bronwyn could reply, she whipped Bronwyn's elaborate hairpiece away.

Clutching her head, Bronwyn protested, "Madame Rachelle—"

"Rachelle." The lady lifted an admonishing finger. "I am Rachelle to my friends."

Bronwyn stood silent as the bands holding her hair slipped. She couldn't call this contemporary of her mother's by her Christian name. That would indicate disrespect.

As if anxious to escape their confines, her curls leaped from between her fingers. "My hair is unmanageable without my wig. I would cut it, but my father—"

"Cut this?" Rachelle pushed Bronwyn's hands away, pulled off the bands, took one lock in her fingers. "Cut this? It is so fair it is almost silver. It is *clair de lune*—moonlight."

"No, I can't cut it. My father won't hear of it."

"I would not allow Henriette to cut hers, either, and I spent hours combing it. . . ." Two tears, like twin jewels, brimmed in Rachelle's large eyes and ran down her faded cheeks. She put her hand over her mouth to contain her sobs. Her bones poked at her flesh and made her appear fragile in her sorrow, and when she spoke again her voice quavered. "Do I know your father?"

"He's Lord Rafferty Edana, earl of Gaynor."

"No, I do not believe he has ever joined our evenings." Rachelle used her lacy handkerchief to catch the last tear. "Gaynor? Where is that?"

"On the wild north coast of Ireland, where the seals play and the seagulls call."

"You were raised there," Rachelle observed. "I hear a faint brogue in your voice."

"My father insisted we be brought up on his ancestral estate. We all stayed there until the age of ten. Then we were brought to England." Bronwyn sighed. "My mother insisted we all be educated on *her* ancestral estate."

"All?"

"There are eight of us sisters. Linnet, Holly, Lucille, Edith, Duessa, Wallis, Olivia, and me."

"Wait. Wait." Rachelle lifted a finger. "Do you mean you are one of the so-called Sirens of Ireland? Your sister is Linnet, countess of Brookbridge?"

Bronwyn nodded.

"Your sister is Holly, viscountess of Sidkirk? Lucille, marchioness of Cumrith?"

Bronwyn nodded and nodded.

"Edith, marchioness of Kenilcester? Duessa, duchess of Innsford?"

"The Duchess Duessa." Bronwyn grinned. "She's the first one to capture a duke. Wallis captured only a baron, but his fortune makes up for his lack of consequence. I am next in the matrimonial line, then Olivia."

"When will you be wed, then?"

"My father refused to consider any of my previous offers. Either their titles or their fortunes proved lacking."

"But now?"

"I'm betrothed to the Viscount Rawson."

Rachelle tossed aside the hated wig. "Adam Keane?"

Bronwyn asked, "You know him? Is he good-humored? Obliging?"

"Good-humored? Obliging? *Non!* Good-humored is not the word I would put to Adam Keane. He is *sombre* and . . . brooding, and too intelligent for his own good. No, definately not . . ." Rachelle's words trailed off, and her eyes sharpened. "You have never met him?"

The intricate pattern of the sofa's upholstery attracted Bronwyn's consideration. With a careful finger, she traced each stem and flower. "He took me sight unseen. Isn't that sweet?"

"Adam Keane is never sweet," Rachelle said flatly.

"He is a man with a chip on his shoulder. Is he expecting you to look like one of your sisters?"

"I suspect."

"What will you do when he sees you?"

With a flash of humor Bronwyn said, "My parents will be there. He can't kill me."

Rachelle remained serious. "No, but his sarcasm can be withering."

"My father says I'm pleasant enough to look upon," Bronwyn said defensively.

Standing, Rachelle fluffed Bronwyn's hair until the long tresses stood in wild array about her shoulders. "My dear, you are *magnifique*—"

Bronwyn snorted.

"—but in the typical English way, your looks have been ruined."

"Maman does the best she can."

"Your mother looks like your sisters, I suppose?"

"My sisters can't hold a candle to her." Bronwyn's affection and pride shone through her embarrassment. "Tall, elegant, cool, with long black hair like Olivia's, but hers has a white streak at the temple. Her skin is pale and pure. For her, for my sisters, the family resemblance is strong."

"You, my dear, are a changeling, but nevertheless *frappant*. Striking."

"My father calls me 'Pixie' because I'm so short and I'm always going out in the sun and turning brown. See?" Bronwyn pointed to her nose.

"A charming contrast with your wild curls and your startling eyes." Rachelle turned Bronwyn's head. "What color are they?"

"Brown, for lack of a better word. Da says they're pretty."

"I think I like your father."

The flowers in the upholstery design attracted Bronwyn's attention again. "Most women do. He's an Irish charmer."

"Perhaps I shall invite your parents to join one of our gatherings some evening. It would be fascinating to speak to the mother and father of such pillars of society."

"My mother? You want my mother to come?"

"Would she not?"

"I don't know. I never thought—" Bronwyn gulped. "Madame Rachelle—"

"Just Rachelle, *s'il vous plaît*."

"I have wondered . . . what kind of place is this? I've heard that sometimes . . ." Bronwyn plucked at her skirt, creating little pyramids. "Well, not that anyone tells me about anything, but there are rumors of places where only men . . ."

Rescuing her, Rachelle patted her hand. "Too many Englishmen think as you do. This is a salon. My friends, the girls who live with me, are *jeune filles de bonne famille*."

"Gentlewomen?"

"*Oui*, gentlewomen who have met with hard times. One of them studies the skies, seeking the answers of life in the movement of the stars. One sings with a pure and beautiful voice. Daphne—you saw her—studies the human body, wishing all the time she could become a *docteur*."

"You . . . do this for friendship's sake?"

"So suspicious," Rachelle chided. "I have money. Who else would help these girls? In France, *salonières* assist the worthy with pensions. In France, salons are an institution, a place where men and women of the intellectual, social, and artistic elites can converse freely."

Dazed with relief, Bronwyn sighed. "Then the Edana reputation is still unblotted."

"Perhaps not. I am a widow of a French nobleman, a chaste woman. Yet there are always *les saintes nitouche* who assume any platonic relationship between a man and woman is destined to fail. There could be talk if it is discovered you were here." Rachelle laughed with a catch in her voice as Bronwyn's face fell. "I will send you back to the inn in a covered carriage."

Recalled to her duty, Bronwyn stood. "I'm afraid we should be returning. My parents don't know where we are."

"I do not mean to criticize them, but they should not have left their most precious treasures alone in such a place." Remembering her own treasure, so recently stolen, tears brimmed in the corners of Rachelle's brown eyes.

"My parents are a law unto themselves," Bronwyn assured her, "but none of my sisters have ever been the object of violence."

Rachelle took her arm and led her into the hall. "Perhaps your sisters have not your kind and impetuous nature."

"If you mean they aren't given to mad impulses, I'm afraid that's true." They turned into a tiny chapel at the back of the house, rich with the scent of flowers and candles. The women of Rachelle's household knelt there with Olivia in their midst.

As accustomed to her sister's beauty as Bronwyn was, she started at the sight of that pure profile. Olivia's serenity seemed sublime, her devotion frightening.

Bronwyn hurried forward and touched Olivia's arm. "Come," she whispered. "It's time."

"Of course," Olivia said. "But first, won't you light a candle for Henriette?"

The memory of Bronwyn's days in Ireland remained. There she had learned the rudiments of the Catholic religion. Her mother, her feet firmly rooted in English tradition, would have been horrified, but some childish wisdom had kept her daughters from telling her of it. Now Bronwyn lifted the scarf from around her shoulders and covered her head. Under her sister's approving gaze, she said a prayer for Henriette's soul. Standing, she ordered, "Come, Olivia."

With one last, lingering glance at the altar, Olivia obeyed.

"I called a carriage for you," Rachelle said as they hurried to the door.

Olivia pointed to her own head, then to Bronwyn's. Bronwyn's hand flew to her hair. "My wig! I forgot it." Changing direction, she returned to the salon and rescued the hairpiece from its place beside the fireplace.

"Will you put it on?" Rachelle asked.

Frowning at the brown wig draped across her hand, Bronwyn said, "No, I'll go like this."

"As you wish. *Encore, merci beaucoup.*"

This woman had lost her daughter today, and "You are welcome," seemed an inadequate answer. Bronwyn said it anyway, in admiration and homage.

With her hand on the doorknob, Bronwyn looked back into the salon. She could imagine this room crowded with literary and political giants. She could hear soft feminine voices speaking of politics, of literature, of music. She could feel the heat of the debates. Longing surged through her.

A hand touched her arm, and she swung to see Rachelle beside her. "Anytime you wish, come to me. I am indebted to you for your brave rescue of my child, and besides . . . I like you, Bronwyn Edana."

"Thank you for your offer, Madame—"

"Call me Rachelle."

"Thank you for your kind offer"—she took a breath—"Rachelle, but I could never do what you suggest."

"Never say 'never.' Just remember." Rachelle withdrew into the shadows of the house. "Remember if you are ever in need."

Chapter 2

I'm sorry, Da. It's all my fault."

"I know it's all your fault, Bronwyn. No other thought ever crossed my mind." Lord Rafferty Edana, earl of Gaynor, paced across their room at the Brimming Cup Inn. "Your shenanigans will be the ruin of ye someday. I don't know where ye got your fecklessness."

Bronwyn peeked out from the wig her mother was tugging on her head. "From you?"

Lady Nora tugged hard on a loose strand of hair. "Don't be impertinent, young lady."

Bronwyn chose discretion. "No, Maman."

Lord Gaynor stuck his fingers in the pockets of his embroidered waistcoat and rocked back on his heels. "I can't believe ye simply decided to explore London on your own. What madness swept ye to such depths?"

"I was bored."

Impatient, he waved her excuse away. "Ye tried that already. Let's hear the truth."

She could never fool her papa, Bronwyn reflected. The man knew her inside and out. For all her mother's denials, she was exactly like the audacious man she called her father. She hadn't his looks or his charm, but when it came to split-second decisions, his daring had found a home in her. Staring at him boldly, she said, "We went to visit a salon."

"That is the silliest thing I ever heard," he roared. A burst of moist, nervous laughter shifted his attention to Olivia. "Olivia, me darlin'," he crooned, his Irish accent thick enough to cut, "tell your ol' da the truth. Where did Bronwyn drag you off to?"

Olivia gulped. She looked to Bronwyn, who lifted her eyebrows. Transferring her attention to Lord Gaynor, Olivia laced her fingers in her lap. "Bronwyn told you, Da. We went to visit a salon."

"A salon?" He circled the trembling Olivia. "What did ye do there, darlin'?"

"We, ah, we drank tea and talked with the lady who ran it?" She checked Bronwyn, relaxing under her sister's approval. "Aye, Da, that's what we did."

"What was this lady's name?" he queried, all charm and sweetness.

"Madame Rachelle," Bronwyn answered promptly, and he swung on her in irritation.

"I wasn't asking ye, colleen. Ye just tend to your business."

"I was trying to help," Bronwyn protested, her innocence as false as his.

"I know your kind of help." He turned away, muttering, "Help indeed."

Always quick to head off a quarrel, Olivia agreed,

"Her name was Madame Rachelle, and she fed us cakes."

"Drank tea, did ye? Ate cakes, did ye?"

"Yes, Da, cakes too."

"Then ye two won't be needing the dinner we've kept back for ye." He nodded at their dumbfounded expressions. "I've already paid the shot."

Seeing her chance for a meal slip away, Bronwyn snipped, "Then you got money from the moneylender, Da?"

"Mind your tongue, lass," he answered. "Money is of no concern to m'daughters."

"Were that that was only true," Bronwyn said.

Lord Gaynor put his hands on his hips. "Not two months ago, lass, I invested in a concern that will be the making of us."

"The moneylenders loaned you enough to invest?"

"The moneylenders loaned us enough to keep us until the coin overflows my copious pockets." Faced with Bronwyn's skepticism, Lord Gaynor remembered he never discussed finances with his womenfolk but he couldn't resist bragging, "Keep yer eye on me, lass." To Lady Nora he said, "We'll be on our way to Lord Keanes's immediately. Are you finished with Bronwyn's wig, m'dear?'

Like a ship in full sail, Lady Nora stepped around Bronwyn to join him. "I am." Studying Bronwyn critically, she said, "I've done the best I can. Little Bronwyn must do the rest. Girls, ready yourselves and meet us downstairs."

As the door closed behind them, Bronwyn complained, "I wish Maman wouldn't call me, 'little Bronwyn.'"

"I suppose they got the money."

"Of course they did." Bronwyn rubbed her rumbling stomach. "What moneylender would refuse Da now, with the prospect of Lord Rawson for a son-in-law?"

"I'm hungry," Olivia complained.

"Well, I'm not."

Olivia's eyes flashed. "You are too."

"You always get peevish when you're hungry," Bronwyn said. Before Olivia could retort she added, "Will Lord Rawson have a very large supper, I wonder?"

Diverted, Olivia suggested, "Breads and jellies, and those little apples draped in cinnamon pastry?"

The sisters stared at each other.

"You wash first," Bronwyn commanded. "And hurry."

As they left the room, the landlord's voice echoed up the stairs. "Yer Ludship, they tol' me they was goin' out with their grandmother. I can't 'elp it if their idea of 'onesty don't square with mine."

"Be careful what you say, my man," their father said, hostile with the insult to his daughters' integrity.

Bronwyn and Olivia exchanged glances and descended in a silken rush. The landlord, red-faced and indignant, was saying, "They even tol' me footman they was goin' about with their mother, but the lady they brought down was old. Couldn't hardly walk."

As Lord Gaynor's eyebrows climbed, Olivia slipped her hand under his arm. Bronwyn took the other. Together they wheedled, "Da, we need to go."

He tried to shake them off. "This lowlife of an innkeeper—"

"We won't get to Boudasea Manor until after dark if we don't hurry," Olivia insisted.

"I need to hear—"

"It's only in Kensington, Da, but we'll not be safe from highwaymen if we don't leave soon."

Lord Gaynor glared. "Anxious to go, aren't you, dearies?"

Olivia tugged his elbow. "The horses are in the street, Da, and I'll wager Maman's inside the carriage."

Weakening, he took a step toward the door. "I'll get the truth of this soon, me dear little colleens."

The sisters herded him outside before he could argue further. "Da, we told you the truth," Bronwyn insisted.

He snorted but asked only, "Will you ride in the carriage, Bronwyn?"

"We'd rather ride our horses, Da, like you. Can we?" Olivia hung adoringly on his arm.

"You know I can never deny you two minxes anything."

The voices faded as the equipage rattled away, and the footman came in, pocketing the large vail he'd received from Lord Gaynor. "A generous man," he informed the landlord, "but a fool fer 'is daughters."

"I could not help but watch that scene with great interest." A gentleman's gentleman stepped forward. His wig was pulled back in a ribbon and well dusted with gray powder; his large brown eyes rested deep in his sallow skin. His musical voice rang with the accent of Italy. "The girls have got Lord Gaynor wrapped in pink embroidery thread."

Not pleased to be providing shelter for the foreign-looking servant, yet unable to express himself with the vehemence he longed for, the innkeeper contented himself with a sniff. Grudgingly he agreed, "That they do, Genie."

"Gianni," the valet corrected.

"What?"

"Gianni." The valet smiled reproachfully. "My name is Gianni."

"Whatever." The landlord raised his voice to speak to the whole taproom. "If they was mine, they'd be nursin' their backsides, not ridin' merrily away t' some fancy estate."

Gianni ignored the landlord's words. "They were in the room next to my master's, were they not?"

"Yes, an' a whinin' couple of females they was. Complainin' about yer master's, er, lady . . ." The landlord trailed off under the valet's liquid eye.

Jumping in with a youth's eagerness, the footman said, "First they say that veiled woman is their mother, then they say she's their grandmother. Ye know what I think? I think she weren't even related t' them. Their father certain didn't know nothin' about it."

"Ye don't suppose . . . ?" The landlord gaped at Gianni in dismay, but he only nodded regally.

"I must ready my master. We'll be leaving immediately." He ascended the stairs with stiff-necked dignity, rapping at the door at the end of the hall.

Letting himself in with a key, the valet eagerly reported, "Just as you suspected, my master, the girls in the room next door helped Henriette escape while we were out."

"Damn." The man called Judson sat before the mirror, studying his pockmarked face with little pleasure. "I'm ready for my wig."

Gianni hurried to his master. After arranging a cloth across Judson's shoulders, he lifted the large, full-bottomed wig from its stand. He settled it on his master's hairless head and shook powder over it.

"Who are they?" Judson inquired.

"Two young ladies of quality, although I caught only the name of the elder."

Judson lifted his handkerchief and dusted the excess powder from his face. "Yes?"

"Bronwyn Edana."

Turning on Gianni like a tiger on his prey, Judson whispered, "Of the famous Edana sisters?"

"Yes, sir."

"That's bad." Holding a soft brush dipped in color, Judson leaned close to the mirror and painted eyebrows where there had been none. "Those Edanas are integrated into society, and not easily eliminated. I suppose she looks just like the rest of her sisters?"

"Not at all. Most unattractive."

"Ah." Judson studied his results. The wig covered his baldness, the paint gave him brows. Yet nothing could replace his eyelashes, or give him back all he'd lost to the smallpox. "Do you think anyone notices I have no hair on my body?" he fretted.

With a well-rehearsed sound of disbelief, Gianni denied it. "Women don't like men who are covered with fur, like an animal. You know how the ladies fawn on you. Asking your advice about their cosmetics and their wigs, praising your sense of color . . ."

His vanity appeased, Judson asked, "Where was this creature going?"

"To Boudasea Manor."

"That's the new home of Lord Rawson."

"Yes, my master."

At the valet's obvious relish, a half smile cocked Judson's mouth. "Tell me, Gianni. What do you know?"

A half smile answered his. "You know how I hate to repeat rumors—"

"Of course."

"But word is that the girl is to wed the noble Adam Keane."

Throwing back his head, Judson burst into laughter. "Adam Keane?" He laughed again. "The viscount of Rawson? That sour seaman? Oh, that's too good."

Pleased with his master's merriment, Gianni laughed, too. "Yes, my master."

"I was raised with him, you know, and I hated him even then." Judson stared in the mirror, but he saw into the past. "Wretched man. So self-confident. So *handsome*."

"Not more than you, my master," Gianni assured him.

"Oh, yes," Judson hissed with malevolent envy. "Even before the smallpox, he turned heads where I did not."

Gianni wrung his hands at his master's unhappiness.

"But how delicious. An ugly bride. What distress that will cause him." Carroll Judson dusted his fingers. "I'll not have to worry about her, then. He'll never let her off his estate, never speak to her, do no more than give her children. Let's leave this place." Having lifted the leather pouch that hung around his waist, he opened it with care. Gianni turned his back as his master fumbled with the coins, waiting as he always did for the largesse Judson dispensed. "Here." Judson thrust the money at Gianni and glanced disdainfully at the bloody bed. "Give this to the landlord and tell him he needs to clean."

"She's just as beautiful as rumor said." Adam Keane kept his horse under restraint with a strong hand on the bridle.

Northrup swallowed. "Sir?"

The setting sun shone toward the riders, and Adam stared through his spyglass across the green sweep of his lawn. "Look at that black hair, that fair skin. See how gracefully she sits her mount. No doubt she'll be just like the other Sirens of Ireland—none too bright, a good breeder, a good manager. That woman is worthy to be the mother of my children."

Tugging at his cravat, Northrup said, "Sir, I believe there's some mistake."

"True, she looks younger than her twenty-two years." Adam scraped his thumb across his chin, already darkening with the shadow of his beard. "If the marriage contract hadn't assured me she was of a suitable age, I would have never thought it. The Edanas wouldn't be fools enough to try and cheat me?"

"No, no," Northrup burst out, horrified. "I met Lady Bronwyn during my days at court, and assure you her family isn't trying to cheat you."

"Good man. I knew I could depend on you." Adam nodded briefly. "For all that she's an Irishwoman, I'll have no trouble bedding her."

"Sir, I believe you're looking at Lady Bronwyn's sister." Once he'd spit out his message, Northrup sighed with relief. When Adam folded the spyglass together and turned his gaze on him, the secretary gasped at the dash of cold. He'd forgotten how frigid those gray eyes could be.

"I beg your pardon?"

Adam's grammar was as fine as Northrup's, but in his speech Northrup could hear the distinctive meter of a seaman. That betrayed Adam's perturbation more than the tightening around his mouth. A high note colored Northrup's reply. "I said, my lord, that you're looking at Lady Bronwyn's sister."

"I heard you."

Northrup cleared his throat and lowered his voice. "Yes, sir. Lady Bronwyn is the woman next to the . . . girl you described."

Adam glared at the wedding party as it rode closer. "That's the maid."

"No, sir. That's Lady Bronwyn. If you will recall, I told you of her distinctive features when I returned from my trip to Amsterdam."

Adam's grip tightened on the reins, and beneath him his horse stirred. "Now I remember. From now on, I'll have to listen more closely to my esteemed secretary, shan't I?"

His smile froze Northrup's bones. Lord Rawson seldom took advantage of his position as master, Northrup mused, but when he did, it always made Northrup unhappily aware of his own privileged upbringing.

"She looks like a King Charles spaniel, beribboned and curled." Adam tucked his spyglass into its leather case. Guiding his horse down to the curved gravel drive, he suggested, "Shall we go greet my bride?"

What sort of symbolism prompted the two gentlemen to watch their guests' arrival from the top of the rise? Silhouetted against the setting sun, the horsemen and the partially finished chapel offered a sight that chilled Bronwyn. One of those men was her fiancé. One of them would have the right to control her behavior, her dress, her body.

Olivia divined Bronwyn's chaotic emotions and offered compassion without succor. "It won't be so bad. Many men are affectionate with their wives. Look at Da. He dotes on Maman."

"Yes, and look at our King George," Bronwyn

snapped. "They say he divorced his wife, locked her up in a German castle, ignored her pleas for clemency. She hasn't seen her children in twenty years."

"He divorced her for infidelity."

"His crime was the greater. He lifts every skirt he can, they say, and he had his wife's lover assassinated." Grimly Bronwyn contemplated her fate. "I tell you, sister, I wish Da hadn't insisted we be married from oldest to youngest. Lord Rawson would much rather have you, I'm sure."

"Don't say that!" Olivia cried. "I don't want him."

Startled, Bronwyn faced her sister. "Have you heard something I haven't?"

"No!" Olivia placed her hand on her breast and took a calming breath. "No. I just . . . I don't want to marry yet."

"You shouldn't have to," Bronwyn assured her. "The marriage settlement Lord Rawson offered should keep Da and Maman in silks for another few years. Who knows, perhaps Da will invest in something useful this time and make his fortune."

"Perhaps." Olivia's hopeless tone clearly told her opinion of that. "Here they come. Which one is he, do you suppose?"

With one glance, Bronwyn knew. He was the gorgeous one. He was the one whose sculptured face was the epitome of male beauty. He was the one with the fashionable sneer. One glance, and she looked at him no more. As her father, with his good-fellow-well-met voice, greeted Adam, she kept her eyes trained below his collar.

The talk washed over her, but she could no longer ignore him when he took her hand. "Lady Bronwyn. You're a breath of fresh air in my unexceptional life."

Her stomach twisted. It wasn't a compliment, for all he made it sound as smooth and charming as a sonnet. She looked at him then, and his remote disapproval stole her breath. His glacial eyes rested on her regally. His lips pinched into a tight line, and his nostrils quivered with disdain.

Chiming like a bell, her mother said, "Thank His Lordship, Bronwyn. Greet His Lordship! After all, you'll have years of marital bliss ahead. You must begin correctly."

"Lord Rawson, I'm well aware of the honor you confer on me with your"—the words stuck in her throat—"your offer. I'm sure I'll never forget it."

The last sentence sounded a little sarcastic. She smoothed her expression into that of a placid sheep—no small achievement, for he still held her hand. She wanted to adjust her wig, to press her velvet beauty patch more firmly on her cheek. She settled for licking her lips. He watched her, close and attentive as a prospective bridegroom. Which he was, she reminded herself.

He gave her a chilly smile. "All is in anticipation of your coming. The manor gleams from top to bottom. The housekeeping staff is assembled by the door, waiting to meet you."

She stared at him, jolted with the reminder that the worst of her ordeal remained. With a twist of her wrist, she tried to retrieve her hand, but he refused to allow her even so small a retreat.

He said, "My mother can barely restrain her impatience."

Her palm began to sweat.

"She's a most opinionated lady, used to having her own way. I'll be anxious to hear her verdict on the bride I bring her." He lifted her hand, kissed the back, turned it over, examined it. The gleam of his eyes reveled in his victory, and he released her. "Come and see the house."

Set among towering trees that seasoned it, Boudasea Manor sparkled with marble and soared with columns. The butler pointed out its contemporary improvements, as did the housekeeper and various retainers. With running water in the kitchen and a private sewer to the river, the manor was a miracle of the modern age. The room Bronwyn shared with Olivia held everything a young woman would want. The room adjoining Adam's, into which she would move only too soon, combined taste with comfort. Quality was stamped on every item; quality, Adam said, was his overriding concern.

He meant, she knew, that she hadn't come up to his definition of quality.

Going now to dinner, she wished she could sink through the floor and drown in one of those conduits of running water. She'd imagined horrors, but this evening had put her nightmares to shame—and the worst was yet to come. Adam had a guest. In for a cozy dinner, he'd said, but she knew why this "guest" visited now. He was a friend, come to inspect the recently purchased goods.

Like a buzzing in her ear, she could hear her mother giving advice as they strolled the mirrored hallways to her doom.

"Don't gawk about you. Keep your head lowered and a modest demeanor. Don't interrupt the men's conversation, especially if you're sure they're wrong."

Bronwyn shot a look at her mother, but Lady Nora

never noticed. "Remember what I've taught you. Men prefer women who are useless and decorative." She arranged the silk of her skirt with a series of little jerks. Her blossoming panniers held the glowing scarlet of her underdress out to the sides. The costume enhanced her coiffure, an artful arrangement of her own black curls, and the cream of her skin. Retrieving her patch box from her voluminous pocket, she placed a heart-shaped bit of black velvet above her upper lip and perfected her seductive smile.

It would hardly do to compare herself with her mother, Bronwyn thought, but with so many mirrors around them . . . Overwhelmed by a profusion of laces and ribbons, the formal white dress did nothing to enhance her tanned skin. The fashionable décolletage should reveal the curve of her bosom, yet she had little to reveal, and that was bolstered by a stuffing of linen beneath. Her brown wig towered above the top of her head, and a ringlet trailed over her shoulder. On a woman as petite as she was, it had a crushing effect, and the high heels she wore didn't help.

How women ever learned to walk in them, she didn't know. She stopped and shook her foot, but nothing could ease the cramp. She sighed, and Lady Nora jerked her attention from her own fascinating reflection and back to her daughter.

Putting her patch box away, she said, "Lord Rawson seemed most impressed with you."

Bronwyn plucked at the silk of her white fan. "Maman, he was stiff as a stick."

"La, child." Lady Nora touched Bronwyn's cheek with her finger and smiled. "He's capable of much worse. I didn't want to tell you, for fear it would worry you, but the man has a nasty temper, and has been known to give vent to it rather loudly in public. You can imagine my relief when he was gracious."

Could Lady Nora be so obtuse? A hard look at that enchanting face convinced Bronwyn. Lady Nora could. A glorious butterfly who'd never had to look beyond the obvious, she took Adam's artistically phrased insults as plaudits. Bronwyn ignored the stab of envy such oblivion caused her. "Why didn't Da tell Lord Rawson that I don't look like the rest of you?"

Lady Nora shrugged, her white shoulders rising and falling in a move she had practiced many times. "What difference will it make in the end? We needed the money, and his was the best offer we'd obtained for you."

"I wouldn't be surprised if he cried off," Bronwyn said.

Laying the back of her hand across her forehead, Lady Nora cried, "Don't be silly, child. You are *betrothed* to him. He can't cry off. It would be an insult to you, and more serious, it would be an insult to our family. Your da would be justified in calling him out, should Lord Rawson do such a mad thing." She shook her head. "No, he won't cry off."

"He's sorely disappointed."

Something in Bronwyn's face must have spoken to Lady Nora, for she said petulantly, "Oh, really, he's going to be your husband. He'll look for his pleasure elsewhere. Your function is to bear him two healthy heirs."

"One for the heir, one for a spare," Bronwyn intoned.

"Exactly. Then you'll find your own lover. In the meantime, this future husband of yours positively glows with health. There is that distressing limp, of course, but his shoulders strain against his coat. And you know"—Lady Nora tittered behind her fan—"the dandies of London must envy him his thighs and calves. *His* stockings aren't stuffed with cotton."

"Maman, it sounds as if you're selling me a horse. Have you checked his teeth?"

Lady Nora snapped her fan closed. "I want you to realize the advantages of this match."

Prodded by the cold analysis of her bridegroom, Bronwyn asked the question she'd always wanted to. "Why don't I look like the rest of you, Maman? Am I a product of a lover?"

"A lover?" Lady Nora stopped and stared at her daughter. "How can you ask that, when all of London buzzes with my devotion to your father?"

"Perhaps I'm the product of Da's misalliance?"

Two bright red spots bled through Lady Nora's rouge. "Not at all," she said, but she didn't deny Lord Gaynor's wanderings. "You are the image of your da's great-aunt. The wild hair, the height, the dreadfully tanned skin."

"I don't remember her," Bronwyn said doubtfully.

"Of course not. She died before you were born. A wizened old maid who spoke her mind without respect to station or relationship."

Bronwyn liked Da's great-aunt already. "You met her?"

Touching a scented handkerchief to her nose, Lady Nora sniffed delicately. "Heavens, yes. Your da had a fondness for her. I remember those great eyes staring, and that frazzled white hair flying. She rattled on about the circle stones of Ireland, and how some magician had set them up." She strolled down the hall, waving the handkerchief in front of her face.

Tagging along after her mother, Bronwyn said, "I

wonder if she read the Gaelic manuscripts of the monasteries."

"Probably." Lady Nora sighed with indifference.

"She does sound like me."

"Never say so." The trembling of Lady Nora's feathers betrayed agitation. "You're not like that ridiculous spinster."

"She doesn't sound ridiculous to me. Just learned and eccentric."

"Learned and eccentric! How much more ridiculous can a woman be?" Lady Nora's expression was reflected in the endless mirrors as she passed. She seemed puzzled by the child fate had bestowed on her. "You've always been a trial to me. Asking odd questions. Reading books. Begging that dreadfully erudite governess to teach you Latin instead of French. French is a civilized language, and you refused to learn it. I never understood you. You aren't like the other children, but I've done my best."

In the face of her mother's distress, Bronwyn conformed once again. "Yes, Maman. No one could ask for more."

Lady Nora turned to Bronwyn and fussed with her gown. "I've dressed you in the best of clothing. It's not my fault that your appearance doesn't lend itself to the fashions of the day."

"No, Maman."

"Stop ripping at your fan. You shred all your fans with that distressing habit of yours."

Stilling the nervous movement of her fingers, Bronwyn agreed, "Yes, Maman."

Lady Nora's glorious violet eyes met Bronwyn's for the first time. "I always loved you. Never doubt that."

How could Bronwyn question her mother's fervency? "I know you love me, Maman."

Lady Nora placed her cheek against Bronwyn's in a brief gesture of affection. "There! That's taken care of." She drew back and adjusted Bronwyn's wig with an expert hand. "I don't want you to get hurt. This is marriage. Lord Rawson gets his entrée into respectable society again, you get the husband you so badly need, and your father and I get money." Lady Nora took Bronwyn's arm with more force than was necessary and shook her sharply. "Don't ask for more."

"No, Maman."

With a smile and a trill, Lady Nora swept into the drawing room. "Here we are. Have we kept you waiting?"

Lord Gaynor, Adam, and Adam's friend abruptly ended their discussion; Olivia stood up from her chair beside the window.

Adam bowed, his gaze on Bronwyn. "To feast my eyes on such beauty, I'd easily wait twice as long."

Her mother's sharp elbow in her ribs prompted Bronwyn to simper and hide her face behind her fan. A few loose threads waved before her nose. "You flatter me, Lord Rawson."

He didn't deny it. She stuck out her tongue before she lowered the concealing silk. Batting her lashes at Adam, she asked, "Who is this gentleman?"

He blinked as if her flutter bothered him but introduced her to Robert Walpole. "A member of the House of Commons," Adam concluded as the gentleman, stout and on the better side of forty, looked her over frankly.

Bronwyn had been made to feel like a commodity too many times that day. Gritting her teeth, she asked, "Is that a great thing?"

Walpole's gaze snapped from her bosom to her face. Too offended to cover her resentment, she stared back at him until he roared with laughter.

"Not at all, my dear. It's nothing when placed beside the conversation of a scintillating lady." Offering his arm, he said, "I'll take you in to dinner."

Adam intervened when she would have accepted. "She's my fiancée, Robert. I take her in to dinner." Realizing, perhaps, he'd sounded less than gracious, he added lightly, "It is, after all, my privilege."

So, Bronwyn diagnosed, he didn't want his friend Robert to discover he was disappointed with his betrothed. Her mouth curved. How interesting. Her brief euphoria faded when he continued, "Lady Bronwyn hasn't met my mother, yet."

Her gaze brushed Robert Walpole's, and his expression revealed a comical horror. He dropped his offered arm, backed away as if she'd been contaminated. "Well, yes, of course. Haven't seen hide nor hair of the, er, dear lady since I arrived. Go on, go on." He made shooing gestures. "Meeting Adam's mother is an experience you should, er, experience."

What fear made the statesman blench and retreat? Was Adam's mother as dreadful as that? Bronwyn wanted to plead for clemency, but there was none. With his walking stick held at a jaunty angle, Adam waited for her to proceed him. Clenching her fan, she did. In an awesome silence, they traversed the mirrored hall to a small door set in the wall.

The parlor beyond was decorated in crimson and furnished with delicate-looking furniture. Heavy drapes covered the windows, and candles lit the room. Their dancing light found the face of the woman seated on a settee—an immense woman, dressed in a loose, flowing robe. Her chins stair-stepped from her chest to her face with nary a glimpse of her neck. Her tiny, red rosebud mouth stretched in a smile. Her cheeks flowed on for acres. Her nose was an indeterminate blob, but her eyes—

Enigmatic, Bronwyn thought, her startled gaze fixed on the immobile lady. When their eyes locked, she realized, *And so sad*.

Adam advanced on the woman and kissed her cheek. "Mab, this is the lady who has consented to be my bride. This is Bronwyn."

One pudgy hand was extended. Bronwyn took it warily.

"I'm pleased to meet you, child. I am Lady Mab, as my disgraceful son failed to tell you."

"Lady Mab, dowager viscountess of Rawson," Adam insisted.

"A title to impress the insolent." Without moving her head, Mab transferred her attention back to Bronwyn. "Are you insolent?"

Bronwyn was stricken dumb. With a privileged few she was dreadfully insolent, yet she couldn't admit that.

Tiring of waiting for her answer, Mab said, "I believe you've found the girl you desired, Adam."

"Yes, Mab."

Unspoken messages lurked beneath the surface, but Bronwyn was too befuddled to decipher them.

Adam asked, "Mab, will you come to dinner?"

"I wouldn't miss the first meal with my future daughter-in-law." Mab hoisted herself to her feet.

"I warn you, Robert Walpole is here," Adam said.

An anticipatory smile spread across Mab's face. "Perhaps you should warn him, not me."

Chapter 3

*B*ronwyn's my girl, she is." Lord Gaynor leaned back in his chair, his supper pushed away and his wineglass tilted. "She's got all the Edana daring and intelligence. The other girls took after m'wife"—he lifted his goblet in salute—"but Bronwyn's all mine."

Lady Nora's smile strained to remain pleasant. "Dear, surely you jest! You're not trying to say Bronwyn is intelligent. Why, she's just a girl who enjoys nothing more than a fancy needlework and a canter on a gentle horse." She patted Bronwyn's hand. "Isn't that the truth, dear?"

Lord Gaynor snorted, ready to disagree. Intercepting a poisonous stare from his wife, he subsided with a cough. "Good dinner, Rawson."

"My thanks." Adam wondered if the interminable supper would ever end. He'd had enough of Lord Gaynor, singing his plain daughter's praises, and enough of Mab's sorrowing glances. He wanted to get down to the business of the evening, and that he couldn't do while the ladies remained. His mother, the official hostess, refused to lead the exodus from the table so the men could drink their brandy and smoke their cigars. Stricken with an inspiration, he said, "Since my future wife is seated at the table with us, perhaps she could take the ladies into the parlor for conversation." His eyes flashed triumph at Mab. "Would you do that, *Bridget*?"

The insipid girl he'd contracted to never blinked an eye. She rose with a gracious smile. "Shall we depart, ladies? The gentlemen wish to discuss important matters unsuitable for feminine ears. Will we see you later, *Abel*?"

He almost missed it, she slipped it in so easily, and when he did react he saw only the backs of three skirts as the women abandoned the dining room. Dismissing her dig as a slip of the tongue, he glared at his mother and prepared for verbal battle. To his surprise, she stood.

"As my daughter-in-law wishes, I'll leave you gentlemen." Before she exited, she turned back. "So good to see you again, Robert. Do return soon."

As the footman shut the door behind her, Robert Walpole was pulling at the scarf that bound his neck. "I tell you truly, Adam, your mother terrifies me."

"She knows it, too," Adam confirmed.

"She's so big and"—Walpole gestured with his hands—"big."

Adam smiled fondly. "Most people find my mother a gentle soul, kind to a fault."

"She's nice to everyone but me."

"I think, Robert, you disgust her with your boasting and your licentiousness."

"Who could be offended by me?" Walpole adjusted his wig. "Besides, women should be womanly. Silly, vain, seeking a man's attention. Not watching a man with wise gray eyes until he squirms, or pricking his little fantasies with the sharp end of her tongue."

"She does do that, doesn't she?" Adam smiled with wicked pleasure at his friend. "Why do you think she enjoys having you for supper?"

"Cannibalism?" Walpole quipped.

Adam relaxed. "Have you lost your pound of flesh?"

Unbuttoning his waistcoat, Walpole rubbed the expanse of belly beneath the linen shirt. "I'll have my mistress check later."

"Not your wife?" Lord Gaynor asked with interest.

"Not tonight. My wife's not scheduled for tonight." A leer spread across Walpole's broad face. "Nor for tomorrow night, either."

"You didn't get those five children with Catherine by ignoring her," Adam interposed.

"There's enough between my legs to satisfy all the ladies," Walpole boasted, "and keep the prostitutes of all London in business, too."

Adam reached for the brandy decanter. "I'll need a drink to wash that down."

Walpole's hearty laugh rang out. "Never had the stomach for whoring, did you, Adam?"

"A seaman gets enough of whoring when he puts into port." Adam passed a glass to Walpole.

"Admit it, it was a liberal education," Walpole teased.

"Education? Well, perhaps. I learned how to make love in four languages." Adam poured for Lord Gaynor and himself, then set his glass on the table and stared through the amber liquor.

Lord Gaynor, too, lifted his glass and stared through it. "Looks almost like my Bronwyn's eyes."

"Mm, no," Adam said absently. "Her eyes have a tinge of auburn to them. More like sherry."

"So I've always said." Lord Gaynor downed his drink in validation.

Walpole pushed back his chair. "How are your stock investments proceeding, Adam?"

"As usual."

"Making a fortune, are you?" Walpole shoved his feet on the table with a sigh.

"I've managed to escape the buying frenzy that's attacked the rest of the London populace."

"Bless the fools, they'll fling their money after any ludicrous venture," Walpole agreed.

"Did you hear the latest?" Adam sipped his brandy. "Some man sold stock in a company to create perpetual motion."

Lord Gaynor looked from one to the other with wide eyes.

Walpole nudged the plates before him with the toe of his boot. "I'll go one better. A fellow sold stock in a company to import jackasses from Spain."

"As if there weren't enough of them on Change Alley already." Adam signaled to the footman, and the footman rushed to remove the offending china.

Lord Gaynor chuckled nervously.

"And there was the scheme for extracting oil from radishes."

"Why?" Adam loosened the ribbon tied at the back of his neck and shook his dark hair to free it.

"Lamp oil?" Lord Gaynor suggested, and Walpole laughed at the wit.

"A good joke. The amazing thing is, there are jackasses"—he lifted his glass to Adam—"who bought stock in these companies."

"My favorite," Adam said, "is the promoter who announced he was selling stock in a company for carrying on the undertaking of great advantage, but nobody is to know what it is."

"And?" Walpole asked with interest.

"And he received a thousand subscriptions of two pounds by midday."

"And?" Walpole insisted again.

"He disappeared in the afternoon," Adam reported, his eyes alight with amusement.

Contagious amusement, for Walpole chortled and Lord Gaynor smirked.

Walpole grimaced in disgust. "I tried to tell them. Didn't I try to tell them?"

"You tried to tell them, Robert. You gave an elegant speech in the House of Commons about the fallacy of assuming the South Sea Company would pay off the national debt." Adam grinned with false sympathy. "Too bad all the Members of Parliament left while you were giving it."

"Damned MP's. Think I'm a common squire, too stupid to see what's as plain as the nose on my face." Walpole touched the bulbous growth with his finger.

Adam shoved aside his glass. "How could you fight those bribes? The directors of the South Sea Company spread money so thick, every politician stubbed his toes on the coinage."

"The South Sea Company?" Lord Gaynor asked

with interest. "But aren't they a legitimate company, authorized by Parliament and the king?"

"That they are. But with so many small companies mucking about, siphoning the investments from the South Sea Company, George Hanover is getting alarmed." Walpole's familiarity mixed with contempt for the German ruler who'd accepted the English throne.

Lord Gaynor looked puzzled. "The king? Why should the king care about the South Sea Company?"

"Investments, my dear man. Investments." Adam stretched out his leg, rubbing his thigh. "How do you think the South Sea Company received permission to push itself on the gullible public with such abandon? John Blunt, the director of the whole nefarious scheme, presented the king with a massive portfolio of stock. As of June eleventh, Parliament will outlaw stock issued by any but companies licensed by . . . Parliament. The king threw his considerable weight behind that proclamation, you may be sure."

Lord Gaynor slapped his glass on the table, slopping wine on the polished surface, objecting, "Fortunes have been made with the South Sea scheme."

"Of course. *I've* made a fortune with the South Sea scheme." Adam propped his leg on the ottoman his footman brought him. "The directors of the company have shown a remarkable talent in manipulating the market. But mark my words, Lord Gaynor, this is a short-term investment. There's no profit within the company to back such wild speculation. The project will burst in a while and drag down every poor sop who's invested with it."

"If you've invested in the South Sea Company, best to listen to your son-in-law," Walpole advised. "The man has his thumb on the pulse of the stock market in London. No one knows more than Adam."

His interested gaze on some distant object, Lord Gaynor nodded.

Satisfied, Walpole asked, "How long do you give the company before it goes down, Adam?"

"I'm watching it."

"Adam. . . ." Walpole laughed. "Cautious man. I say November."

Adam shook his head in negation.

"Longer?"

"No."

"Oh, come, Blunt will keep it together until the cold weather, at least."

"If you say so, Robert." Adam stood, wincing. "Shall we join the ladies?"

Knowing he'd not pry any other commitment from Adam, Walpole stood and jostled Lord Gaynor's shoulder. "Come on, man. Must join the ladies. Leg bothering you, Adam?"

"A bit." Adam straightened and reached for his malacca cane.

"That's what you get for catching a Spanish cannonball."

"Nothing so dramatic," Adam said. "Only the bits of deck where it hit."

"Damned Spaniards."

"Not at all." After leading them to the drawing room, he stood aside to let them precede him. "The wealth carried on that one Spanish ship was the hen that laid my golden egg."

Walpole slapped Adam's back as he passed. "Yes, and you've been squeezing the poor chicken ever since. I can hear it squawking clear down at my country home."

"Norfolk's so dull, a little squawking would . . ." Adam's voice trailed off as he surveyed the placid occupants of the drawing room. "Where's my mother?"

Walpole lifted his hands in wonderment.

Alarm shot through Adam. "My God, where's Bronwyn?" Not that he cared for the silly twit, but his genteel mother disapproved of his cold method of choosing a bride. He'd seen her strip Walpole of all dignity and courage, and he feared it would be a poor start to a marriage should she do so to Bronwyn.

Olivia lifted her frightened gaze from her hands, and Lady Nora demanded, "Why?" Ignoring them both, Adam wheeled around, the nagging pain in his thigh forgotten, and headed for Mab's study. The sight that greeted him there brought him to an abrupt halt.

The two women sat in the light of the candles, sewing. Low and sweet, their voices spoke in harmony. No impatience turned Mab's mouth down. No fear made Bronwyn's hand tremble.

He couldn't believe it, and his eyes narrowed as he considered the domestic scene.

His mother saw him first. "Abel! Come and visit with us."

Cautious, suspecting a trick, he limped into the room and sat down on the far side of Bronwyn's settee. "It's Adam," he corrected pleasantly.

"So it is." His mother chuckled like the traitor she had proved to be. "So it is. We're just working on the clothing for the Boulton boy. His parents died of the typhus last year, if you'll recall, and I've arranged to have him apprenticed to a candlemaker."

"Is he old enough?" Adam asked, his hands placed precisely on the amber knob of his cane.

"He's ten, and the people who have taken him are kind." She placed a stitch with precision. "I make sure of that. Did you need something?"

"No, I . . . missed Bronwyn in the drawing room and feared she might have lost herself in the corridors."

"Not at all," Bronwyn said. "Mab invited me to visit her, and I was honored to comply."

Incredulous, Adam said, "You call her Mab?"

Bronwyn glanced at him, at her hostess. "Isn't that right?"

Adam's eyes narrowed. "Of course, but she only allows—"

"My beloved relatives to call me 'Mab,'" his mother interrupted. "And as my daughter-in-law, you're welcome." Her rebuke stripped him of his indignation. "That's why I requested that you call me by my first name."

She invested the phrase with significance, she spaced each word individually, and he registered her meaning. For some reason Mab had decided to extend her protection to his intended. He would seek her reasons later; for now he must play host to his guests. He stood and bowed. "If you're ensconced so cozily, then, I will leave you and attend to my business."

Mab waved a hand in dismissal. "A sound idea, son. After all, you'll be starting a family soon. You'll need to be on sound financial footing."

Adam glanced at the girl who would be his bride and shuddered. It did his vanity no good that she looked at him with equal horror.

Bronwyn still stared at the doorway after Adam had vanished.

He had his mother's eyes. But while his mother's gave comfort with their warmth, the man's eyes were anything but comforting. Disturbing, yes, and intense—vividly gray, with long, black, curly lashes that emphasized the lazy droop of his lids.

"You don't like him," his mother observed.

"Not a bit," she answered absently, then swung her appalled gaze on Mab.

Mab didn't appear perturbed. She sat on the mammoth chair designed for her contours and sewed a pair of boy's pants. She seemed so placid, so peaceful, a large, amiable queen in her home. Only her hands betrayed the lie. They wielded the needle faster than Bronwyn's eye could follow.

Wishing she could swallow her words, Bronwyn stammered, "That is, Lord Adam is an unknown quantity to me, and I'm unable to declare whether I like him or not. He's a kind man, I'm sure."

Mab's gaze stabbed her. "Kind? He's the kind of man who can make a woman feel stupid and ugly."

Bronwyn gaped at her, then decided, *In for a penny, in for a pound.* "And unwanted," she said defiantly.

"Surely unwanted. However, if you continue to keep silent, keep house, keep out of the way, he'll soon learn to tolerate you."

Picking up the shirt Mab had given her, Bronwyn nodded and stabbed the material with her needle. "That's the best I can expect from marriage."

Quiet reigned, but Bronwyn realized she had distressed the big lady with the sweet face.

"You hold yourself so cheaply?"

"Not myself. But men want beauty, wit, a gracious way with the harp. Nothing more."

Mab sighed. "You're a parrot, repeating your lessons."

"Mab"—odd how Bronwyn felt so at home with the name—"your son offered for me because he believed I was like my sisters."

"And how are they?"

"Beautiful and empty-headed." Bronwyn nibbled her thumbnail. "To marry into the Edana family guarantees a man will have a wife who'll pull him to the top of the social heap. My sisters are, without a doubt, the best hostesses in London. An invitation to one of their parties is a privilege much sought after."

"Then you'll be giving parties like that?"

"No doubt."

"And the ton will fight for your invitations, as they fight for your sisters?"

"I'd better pull it off, or Lord Rawson will be disappointed again." With a shrug of sorrow for her ragged nails, Bronwyn demolished her manicure.

"How else is Adam disappointed?"

"I'm not witty. I don't play the harp." Sweeping her hand along her length, Bronwyn explained, "I'm certainly not beautiful."

"Ah." Mab's head went down, and she hid the expression in her eyes while she stitched. "Of course, your sisters' beauty has made their lives perfect."

"Well, no." In her mind, Bronwyn drifted out of the room. Mab's constant probes made her remember the dream she'd had as a child. The dream of a man who'd laugh with her, talk with her, love her for herself. But the picture of Adam, scowling, sarcastic, intruded into her imagination, and she sighed. "Actually, their husbands keep mistresses, and some of my sisters have their lovers, too."

Satisfied, Mab said, "Their beauty hasn't kept their husbands by their sides. But there is another way."

On Adam's return to the drawing room, he found Walpole taking his leave. "Must you go, Robert? This is going to be a deadly bore without you."

"Love to help you out"—Walpole's grin denied his concern—"but indeed I must leave. The actress who is my trollop has made a small fortune on Change Alley and is retiring. Tonight, she insists, is her farewell performance. You don't expect me to miss it, do you?"

Adam walked with him toward the door. "What was her name again?"

"Mrs. Ash," Walpole said.

"Mrs. Ash is such an exhibitionist, she'll return to the stage regardless of her wealth."

"Oh, it's not her farewell performance on the *stage*," Walpole corrected.

Adam digested that. "Then you must not be late. How would she perform without you?"

"My thought exactly. But I did want to speak to you." Walpole glanced about him. "Where can we be alone?"

Adam led the way into his study, and Walpole shut the door behind them.

With lifted brow, Adam studied him. "If you're going to tell me a state secret, I don't want to know."

"The only state secret I know is that the Prince of Wales hates his father," Walpole said absently.

Adam snorted. "Quite a secret."

"It's quite a state." Walpole took a turn about the room while Adam leaned against the edge of his desk. "It's this South Sea Company business," Walpole burst out. "There's something wrong with it."

"Indeed there is," Adam agreed, "but I thought we'd covered that."

"There's something more." The normally placid man tapped his fingers against the elaborate marble fireplace mantel. "My spies are bringing me some damnable rumors, and I don't like them. I can't confirm them, but I don't like them."

"Such as?"

"There's more here than a simple swindle. The directors are too smart for their own good, and I believe they have plans for the government."

"The government?"

"You know I used to be first lord of the Treasury and chancellor of the Exchequer." Walpole rolled the title off his tongue, and Adam grinned.

"A very able chancellor, too."

Settling his shoulder against the mantel, Walpole shrugged without modesty. "I tend to agree. Now I'm merely a lowly Member of Parliament."

"Hardly lowly," Adam observed. "You may pretend to be a country squire, you may be the lewdest man I've ever met—"

Walpole beamed, not at all offended.

"—but there's none more competent than you when it comes to steering the government. Someday, God willing, you'll direct this country to its proper glory."

Scratching the stubble on his chin, Walpole said, "I'll not argue with you. England just needs a good, long peace and she'll be the greatest nation this world has ever known. I tell you the truth, Adam, I'm planning to direct her." His shrewd gaze met Adam's. "Nothing will stop me."

Such a clear declaration didn't shock Adam, but he

wondered, "To how many other men have you confided your ambitions?"

"No one."

"Not even when you'd spliced the main brace and were so drunk you couldn't see straight?"

"Perhaps once," Walpole admitted.

"In your usual shy, retiring manner, you told an entire dinner party you planned to run the government, is that correct?"

"I detect sarcasm in your voice."

Adam placed his fingers on his chest and pulled a long face. "I? Sarcastic? Good God, Robert, you're lucky no one has shot you."

"I told you, I'm nobody."

"Who's clever enough to be somebody." Adam shook his head. "Robert, Robert, Robert. What will I do with you?"

Fingering the design of the marble, Walpole demanded, "Spy for me."

"What?"

"You heard me. There's some plot afoot, and I want to know what it is." Earnest and inquisitive, he peered at Adam. "There's a buzzing that fades whenever one of my informants gets close."

Adam covered his sense of savage frustration. "And you thought perhaps I would be well suited for the nasty business of spying?"

Swept away by enthusiasm, Walpole paid no attention to the warning signs. "Particularly well suited. You know the coffeehouses on Change Alley as well as any man on earth. If there's a way to discover this intent—or even the source of the intent—you can do it."

"What makes you think I can do you any good? Everyone knows you're my friend."

"Perhaps you can't, but it's worth an effort. Spying pays well," Walpole hinted. "Court appointments, favors, even cash."

Adam's fury abruptly sprang out of control. He leaned forward, his breath rushing between his teeth as he fought to keep his hands from around Walpole's neck. "If that's what you think of me, get out of this house and never come back. My father stooped to every dishonest endeavor that came his way and was damned proficient, but to you, at least, I thought I'd proved—"

"Damn it to hell!" A string of ever-stronger expletives, notable for their variety and description, clouded the air around Walpole. "Do you still fret that old scandal? No one remembers it—there's nothing older than last year's news, and that was years ago."

"My father dishonored this family so thoroughly, the stain will never be wiped away. Do you honestly believe no one remembers?" Adam asked with a sneer. "The ladies titter behind their fans, while the men step back from me as if they will be contaminated by my presence."

"Maybe, just maybe, that's because you stalk around like the devil seeking new souls." Walpole strode toward Adam, poking his finger into the air like a schoolmaster about to cane a boy. "Social gatherings are frivolous conversation, flirtations, deep drinking, revelry. Then you come in and glower at the assemblage— just as you're glowering now—"

Adam tried to lighten his expression, and Walpole shook his head. "Better to cover your eyes, Adam. You go to a party and the hostess sighs. She knows if you join a casual game of cards with the gentlemen, they'll all find excuses to leave. Not because you'll contaminate them, but because they know they'll be solving the world's problems before the first hand is done. Can't discuss their fancy women, can't talk horses, can't talk about their newest shipment of smuggled brandy, just have to be somber. Talk finance, or farming methods, or some other deadly dull subject."

"Come, I'm not that bad," Adam objected.

"Put a damper wherever you go," Walpole insisted. "And with the ladies, it's worse. You subject those fragile flowers of the ton to that stare of yours, and they either want to get in your breeches or faint. Or both. The fire of your gaze, the ice of your personality, fascinates them. No wonder you had to seize on a fiancée who hadn't met you. I don't understand why that young woman hasn't run from the house screaming."

Adam snorted, but his temper began to fade, and Walpole flung his arm about Adam's shoulders. "I meant nothing by offering you a bribe. How the hell do you think the nation runs? Corruption's the backbone of the English system, and it's the best in the world. Why cavil at success?"

Steady as a rock, Adam answered, "I don't give a damn if the whole world does it, it doesn't make it right."

"Self-righteous bastard!" Walpole glared right into Adam's eyes. "If you think I'm going to work my arse off for a pittance, you're mad! Why take a government appointment if you can't feather your nest?"

"Mayhap you should do it for Mother England," Adam suggested.

"Mayhap *you* should do it for Mother England," Walpole repeated right back at him.

Understanding came quickly. "Spy, you mean?"

As Adam's reason returned, Walpole grew bold. "For God's sake, man, think. If I don't take the reins of the government, who will? The king just wants to return to his beloved home in Hanover to swive his dirt-ugly mistresses. The Tories are in total disarray. My Whigs have no well-defined leadership, and when this South Sea bubble bursts, every man and woman who bought stock will riot. You've been in London when the rabble riots. You know they'll overturn the carriages of the rich and break every shop window between here and Islington." Walpole's earnest appeal lost nothing by being self-serving. He was right, and Adam knew it. "This rumor could be my key to the most influential post in England."

"And it could be a chimera."

"And it could be a chimera," Walpole conceded. "In that case, you aren't spying, are you?"

A disgusted smile curved Adam's lips.

Encouraged, Walpole coaxed, "Say you'll do it."

Adam lowered his head. The role of spy tasted foul in his mouth, but what choice did he have? When he'd been sick unto death with the infection in his leg and the ship's leech had threatened to amputate it, he'd thought he would never again see the green shores of England. He'd vowed to kiss the sweet earth if ever God allowed him to return. He would do anything to preserve this country, and he believed Walpole was the man to carry England to its greatest heights. Fixing Walpole with the intense stare he was still unaware of, Adam said, "I'll do it."

Chapter 4

"D a, let me go." Desperate to escape, Bronwyn tugged at her hand, her ruffled silk apron fluttering about her waist.

Lord Gaynor paid no attention as he dragged her along the tended paths toward the study where Adam worked. "Ye'll have to talk with him sooner or later, me darlin'," he advised. "Saying 'How de do?' on your wedding night's not decorous at all."

"Maman doesn't care," Bronwyn protested.

"Your mother's an excellent woman, but she's a bit of a cold fish when it comes to matters of the heart. A little practical, if ye follow me meaning." He stopped on the wide terrace and patted her hand. "Just leave this to your ol' da. I'll have Lord Rawson supping from your plate before the day is over."

Her gaze on the open windows, she whispered, "I

don't want him supping from my plate, or even"—she groped for words—"drinking from my glass."

"Nonsense, girl, of course ye do. Every woman wants her husband to be enthralled by her, and ye're the only one of my girls who's capable of such a feat." Lord Gaynor's booming voice made her cringe as he added, "It won't hurt to talk to him, now will it?"

In a way, Lord Gaynor was right, but she didn't want to talk to her betrothed. When Adam turned his intense gaze on her, she felt just as giddy as any schoolgirl. She didn't know why, but she wanted to faint from fright or fling her arms around his neck, and both reactions made her nervous. Avoiding him seemed the best course of action, easily followed, for he'd made no attempt to seek her out in the few weeks she'd been there.

Yet her da, the eternal matchmaker, seemed determined to bring them in contact. Lord Gaynor pinched her cheek with his well-tended hand, then pinched her other cheek to even the color. "There now. Ye look lovely."

Hopeless as a prisoner on Tyburn Hill, Bronwyn followed him through the doors to the study.

Adam lifted his head from the papers he'd been filling with the scribble of numbers and observed them without emotion. "Yes?"

Lord Gaynor shoved Bronwyn onto a chair in front of the huge expanse of desk. As he strolled to the decanter, she miserably knitted her fingers in her lap. All of her fingernails were stripped, she noted. She risked a glance at Adam. If he'd heard her father's proclamations on the terrace, he gave no sign. But that meant nothing. He never gave a sign of his sentiments, never gave any of himself away.

Pouring an ample measure of his morning libation, her father said, "Been meaning to ask ye, Adam, about the date for the wedding. Need to set it. Need to start the whirl of parties."

Bronwyn closed her eyes. Trust her da to attack the situation with a vengeance.

From too close, she heard Adam answer, "The wedding? I assumed we'd take this time to get to know each other, and marry in, say, October?"

"A sensible plan," she approved, opening her eyes and preparing to rise.

Her father's heavy hand pushed her back down. "A wretched long wait," he complained. "Surely a summer wedding would be better?"

"No."

Adam's blunt refusal barely fazed Lord Gaynor.

"When the roses are blooming—"

"No," Adam said again.

"M'wife brought a wedding gown made to Bronwyn's specifications."

Adam leaned back in his chair and studied her father. "It occurs to me, Lord Gaynor, that perhaps you're bored in my home."

Dismay slid across Lord Gaynor's face. "No, no! Not at all. Your home is one of the newest and best in Kensington. Convenient to London, yet with the charms of a country estate. There's a darlin' country village with a quaint shop . . ." A rueful Irish smile tilted Lord Gaynor's mouth as Adam pulled a disbelieving face. "M'wife and I do find it a bit quiet," he admitted.

"And you can't leave until the wedding is performed," Adam speculated.

"Of course not. Wouldn't be proper."

"If I could perhaps sweeten the deal with a little

loose change." Having opened the drawer beside him, Adam pulled out a slip of paper and wrote a few words. Presenting it to Lord Gaynor, he instructed, "Give that to Northrup, my secretary. He'll get you a draft on my bank. Of course you have use of my carriages—they'll convey you where you wish. My mother is here to act as chaperone, and Olivia will be happy as long as her sister remains, I suspect."

Bronwyn's heart plummeted to her toes. He meant to keep her. She'd been hoping he would sink his honor and hers, too, and dismiss the marriage contract. But no, it seemed he would not, and she knew her father too well to think he'd refuse the money. Every penny produced by his Irish estates slipped through his fingers as easily, as relentlessly, as sand through an hourglass. Indeed, the need for money had been his reason for urging an early wedding, she was sure. He wanted the dowry Adam had agreed to settle on her.

Fingering the paper, Lord Gaynor protested, "I couldn't take such a loan."

"Consider it a gift," Adam urged. "Lady Nora would be glad of a visit to the city, I'm sure."

As Bronwyn expected, Lord Gaynor pocketed the voucher. Yet he frowned and queried, "Is it true what your friend said?"

"My friend?"

"That fellow Walpole." Lord Gaynor tossed back his liquor and refilled his glass as if he needed fortification. "Is it true about this money business? Are ye as clever as he says?"

Adam said nothing for a few beats, then admitted, "Yes."

"Rather disreputable, isn't it? Making so much money?"

Bronwyn moaned so faintly she knew they couldn't hear it. Still, Adam bent a glare on her, and she thought the temperature of the room dropped appreciably.

"Not so disreputable as being poor."

The chill didn't seem perceptible to Lord Gaynor. "Good thing your family's an old and noble one. Don't know how ye'd stand the disgrace, otherwise. Ye're acting like a merchant."

"So kind," Adam murmured.

"Just keep it quiet," Lord Gaynor said. "If ye don't rub society's nose in it, ye'll keep their respect. I'd hate to have it known my daughter married a *clever* man."

Adam's quiet voice agreed, "Most humiliating."

Wishing she were anywhere else, Bronwyn closed her eyes again.

"I'm going to be your papa-in-law, and as your own father is dead, I thought ye'd appreciate a little advice." Lord Gaynor sipped his drink and nodded. "Thought ye'd appreciate it. Not that I mind your head for business. Why, I'd even take a bit of advice from ye and not feel besmirched."

Adam leaned back in his chair and pulled the feather of his quill through his fingers. "Of course, I'd be glad to advise you, but I doubt Bridget—"

She looked up at him.

"—Bronwyn"—he corrected himself—"would be interested."

Lord Gaynor drained his glass, then squinted across the breakfast room at Adam. "She's a clever miss. Ye'd be surprised."

Adam lifted an eyebrow at her, as if he were questioning her. She looked back down at her hands and wished her da would keep his mouth shut. If he believed cleverness was unacceptable in a man, what madness made him think it should be acclaimed in a woman?

Adam sounded almost amused as he said, "I've been down at Change Alley, and the stocks are frenzied as ever."

"Has the proclamation against the stocks not licensed by Parliament taken effect?" Lord Gaynor asked.

"Enforcement will begin on Midsummer Day—June twenty-fourth." Foreseeing a long conference, Adam capped his inkwell with a cork. "The rumor of it has burst a few of the bubbles. The owners have packed up shop and left without a whimper. There are others, however, who say they'll ignore the proclamation, or claim their obsolete charters are legal."

"Will they succeed in fighting the proclamation?" Lord Gaynor asked.

Bronwyn wrinkled her forehead. When had her feckless da learned enough to comprehend the intricacies of the stock market?

"If I knew that, I could make a lot more of that money which so embarrasses you," Adam said acidly. "Enforcement will be spotty at first, but it should be efficacious eventually."

"And when it is?" Lord Gaynor's eyes glowed.

"Stocks will drop like rocks." Adam dropped a paperweight as illustration. "Anyone holding the burden of stock will be crushed. Bankrupt."

A thought as dramatic as it was illuminating streaked across Bronwyn's mind, and boldly she asked, "Will men be killed?"

Adam looked startled. "Perhaps."

Lord Gaynor patted the top of her wig. "'Tis not something ye should worry your pretty head about."

She looked to Adam, and he replied to the demand

in her face. "Certainly the rabble will riot, for they'll no longer have the illusion of being rich. Men will be killed then."

"Is there another way to kill a man with this stock?"

Adam tugged at his ear as if he couldn't believe her questioning, but he answered steadily, "An interesting turn of phrase—killing a man with a stock." He looked at her inquiringly, but she said nothing. "I have no way of knowing for sure, but I believe there will be suicides."

"Suicides," Bronwyn said. "Riots. I think I understand."

As bewildered as Adam, Lord Gaynor asked, "Understand what, Bronwyn, me colleen?"

Reawakened to her surroundings, Bronwyn bit her lip. "Nothing, Da. Lord Rawson just explained something I had heard but didn't understand."

Her father stared at her oddly but asked Adam, "Should I be selling me South Sea stock?"

"You do own some, then?" Adam asked.

"I bought before I came," Lord Gaynor said without elaboration.

"For how much?"

"For three hundred."

Adam nodded, satisfied. "You'll do well. Don't sell yet. I'll warn you."

"I'll depend on it. 'Twould be a good thing to have a bit of loose cash." Lord Gaynor strode toward the door. "Are ye coming, me colleen?"

Bronwyn glanced at Adam, then half rose. Yet she had to confirm her suspicions; the dead Henriette's words haunted her. *Kill a man with a stock*, Henriette had said; was this stock an investment in a company? She reseated herself. "Not yet, Da."

His mouth dropped. He appeared as shocked as if she'd declared she'd visit a dragon in his cave, but he couldn't imagine she would stay to discuss finance. Beaming at her, he said, "There's me lass."

Bronwyn writhed under his heavy approbation, so thick it hung in the air like a skunk's scent. After he left, silence blanketed the room; Bronwyn looked around her with false interest. "You certainly have a large study," she said brightly.

Adam gave no response.

"With . . . with the most modern of furniture." She craned her neck to look up. "And the whole house is constructed in the Palladian style, is it not?" Still no response, and she found Adam's gaze unblinking on her face. She gave up. She would never be clever with small talk. Clearing her throat, she pursued her topic with less tact and more interest. "Da seems quite enthralled with this stock business. Do you think you could explain it to me?"

Adam steepled his fingers. "What would you like to know?"

She asked the first question that popped into her head. "How did my da get enough money to invest in such a venture?"

"First he had to have a little capital, some money to invest."

She thought about it. The moneylender again, no doubt. "He had it."

"The South Sea Company is loaning money to investors so they can buy their own stock, ensuring a flow of money to their coffers from even those too poor to invest properly."

"And stock is . . . ?"

"A certificate of investment in a company by an

individual which gives him the right to a percentage of the largess."

Bronwyn blinked. "So my da took a little cash down to Change Alley, found someone from the South Sea Company, told him he wished to loan them money. The man took the money, gave Da some vouchers, and if the company makes a profit, Da is entitled to some?"

Adam pushed back his chair and stood. He leaned across his desk, supported by his fingers, and searched her face as if he had discovered gold where he expected only clay. "Extraordinary." Pushing away his large chair, he dragged two smaller ones to the kneehole and commanded, "Come around here."

She gaped, horrified by the invitation.

A flash of impatience, then he schooled himself to geniality. "Please come here."

Cautiously she stood. The desk was massive, new, made of walnut and polished until it shone. It was a very long walk around the edge; she thought she would trip on the fringed rug if she attempted it. But Adam waited on the other side, and for some reason she didn't want him to think her a coward. Using her mother's mincing steps, she trod the long loop to his side. He held one of the chairs; she seated herself. He scooted himself in beside her, so close their knees touched. So close she could smell the scent of mint that clung to him like an Irish breeze.

An odd paralysis gripped her, and she held the desk's scalloped edge until the decoration dug into her palm. Adam made no attempt to ease her discomfort. His coat had been discarded, his throat bare of a cravat. She'd never seen him in such disorder. Always before he'd been formal, proper, fashionable, if severe. She'd refused to consider how he'd look in the marriage bed.

A glance at his chest, clad in only his shirt, made her realize why. The fullness of the soft cambric couldn't disguise the muscles beneath, and she was too aware of his arm as it rested on the back of her chair. Tight against her bared shoulders, its warmth seeped into her skin.

She sat up straight, so her back didn't touch the chair. "Credit!" She attacked with vigor. "I don't understand credit."

He bent his dark gaze on her face, observing, "Nor does most of the country."

Why was he staring at her so closely? Was there a mark? Did the beauty patch above her upper lip hang loose? She'd been uncomfortable before; now she hung on the hook of suspense. Her fingers fastened on the ruffle of her silk apron, and she plucked at the hem. "How does one buy stocks on credit?"

"With a payment that locks one into a certain number of stocks."

She wanted to scrub at her skin. "How does one make money? If one tries to redeem the stocks at the office of the South Sea Company, and they're not completely paid for—"

"What one tries to do is sell them to another investor, leaving him with the debt and taking the profit," he explained, patient with her ignorance.

"Why would an investor buy a debt?"

"Because he's—"

"Betting the stock will rise even higher," she interrupted as the light dawned, "and he'll be able to make a profit, also."

For the first time since she'd lived in his house, he smiled. He smiled at *her*. Her breath caught. She froze. The man she'd thought of as severe, austere, a maiden's vampire fantasy, transformed himself into a wicked highwayman, waiting to rob her of her good sense. Their eyes locked.

"Is something wrong?"

She thought his voice had deepened, and the smile she found so appealing became a knowing stare.

"No, you . . . were explaining how the sale of stock worked." He had grooves beside his mouth, she saw, that deepened with his pleasure. The hem of her apron came loose; she pulled at a thread. "Is there an unlimited amount of South Sea stock to buy?"

"No."

"That keeps the stock in demand," she guessed.

"There is more to you than meets the eye." His fingers touched her cheek, and she jerked back from the contact. His lids drooped; he appeared to know a secret. "I won't hurt you. I just wanted to see if your skin is as soft as it looks."

Confused by his attention, she shrugged. "It's just skin. Like your skin."

"Not at all like mine." He lifted her hand away from the ruffle and brought it to his face. "See? The wind and salt of the sea have toughened me."

He pressed her palm to his chin. She wanted to pull away, but that would be foolish. For some reason she didn't want him to think she was foolish. Instead she avoided looking at him and felt the stubble of his beard with an increased awareness. Why was she noticing his features in such detail, when she had stayed in his study to speak of stocks?

"And I'm tanned dark by my constant rides into London," he murmured.

"I'm tanned, too." Retrieving her hand from his grasp, she flashed him a grin to prove she didn't care.

"But no freckles. Your complexion is clear as a sunny day."

Her chin dropped with her surprise, but she thought she recovered before he noticed. "Do you buy stocks from the South Sea Company proper, or do you buy from the other investors?"

"Northrup goes to the South Sea Company when the directors have a consignment to sell. For instance, on April fourteenth, he bought shares at the quoted price of three hundred pounds."

"Each?"

"Each. On April thirtieth, he bought shares for four hundred pounds." He paused. "Each."

Was that humor? Spying the twinkle in his eye, she smiled timidly. Understated and rusty, perhaps, but it *was* humor. "Have you sold that stock?"

"No. In fact, I've bought more."

She smiled more widely, hoping to coax another of those heart-stopping grins from him. "How do you know when to sell?"

"The coffeehouses on Change Alley are a lively place for information, if a man knows what to listen for. There are informants, some reliable and some not, who'll sell their knowledge for the right price. There are rumors to sift through."

Her glow broke through to him, and his teeth gleamed in another evidence of his pleasure. His smile sapped the strength from her spine, and she slid against the chair back.

He continued, "An astute man knows what to listen for, and I'll sell when it's time. Are you worried about your father's investments?"

Intent on the arm he wrapped around her shoulders, on the pressure of his knees against hers, she said, "I didn't even realize he'd made investments. It's so unlike him to be wise."

"The stock-buying madness has struck the whole country. I would have been surprised if he were exempt."

He watched her closely, and she wished she hadn't revealed so much about her father. She tugged at a loose seam along the ruffle.

Abruptly changing the subject, Adam asked, "Why were you so startled that I noticed you are attractive?"

"Attractive?" She mulled over his choice of adjectives. "I think I have reason to be startled that you now think I'm attractive."

His half smile acknowledged his guilt. "Haven't your other admirers been as observant?"

"No," she faltered. Should she tell him she'd had no other admirers? Should she ask if he were an admirer? She watched him as he picked up his quill and turned back to her. "No," she decided. He ran his finger along the edge of the feather as if testing its sharpness, and she gripped the apron in a stranglehold. The small sound of tearing silk dismayed her, and to cover it she asked, "Is the whole world gaining wealth?"

"Did you wish to speculate?" He touched the tip of the quill to her neck.

That tiny contact seemed to burn her. As he trailed it along her collarbone, she lost her will to speak, to move, even to breathe.

"If you wish to trade stocks"—the feather meandered down to the cleft of her bosom—"you'll find my help most valuable."

She swallowed audibly.

"But of course there is a fee." His free hand grasped her bare shoulder. "To be paid on demand." Tossing the quill aside, he leaned closer. "How large your eyes are," he marveled. "How you stare at me."

"I don't understand half of what you say," she whispered.

"Too late to gammon me. You've proved you have an unusual intelligence for a woman." Now both callused palms cupped her shoulders. "I want a kiss."

Incredulous, she said, "But you think I'm ugly."

"Do I?"

"You, uh . . ."

"Your eyelashes are so long, they must tangle together." He brushed her lashes in a butterfly touch.

She closed her eyes and let him embrace her. As he massaged her shoulder blades with his hands, the knots in her muscles eased. He kissed the corners of her mouth, tasting her as if she were a delicacy. "You're uneasy with me," he murmured. "I've noticed that before."

His lips brushed hers with each word before they settled over hers. The contact made her giddy, made her seek air where there was only his. Yet when she opened her mouth, he was there, sliding his tongue in to explore hers. That was odd. She tensed, but his fingers on her chin kept her in place. Was he mocking her?

No, he seemed to be encouraging her. Shyly she reached out with her tongue and engaged in a miniature struggle. When she lost, she was glad, glad to have him so intimate with her, glad to have him gather her close.

Yet when his nimble fingers found her breast, caressed it through the silk of her bodice, her eyes sprang open and she pushed at him.

His face was too close: his eyes were unreadable, his heavy brows a single line across his forehead. His mouth was too close: an instrument of torture and enchantment. She could still taste him, savor the roughness of his perfect teeth. She could still inhale his breath, still tingle with the brush of his hand to her body, still bathe in the warmth of his flame.

Reality arrived in a rush.

She dragged air into her lungs and clamped her fingers around his wrist. "Let me go."

That man was smiling again, and never had she seen a charm to melt her resistance. He cupped her breast for one last moment, just to prove he could, and then dropped his hand. "Your eyes are shining."

More insistent, she said, "Let me go."

"Ye heard her, ye cad." Lord Gaynor posed in the doorway, looking all the world like an outraged English aristocrat. "Let me daughter go!"

Mortified, Bronwyn tried to stand, but her knees were crammed too tightly beneath the desk. She couldn't move the chair back on the carpet. And Adam blocked her retreat. Not the genial Adam who'd been her companion this last half hour, but the austere lord who had frightened her before.

Unperturbed, he queried, "Lord Gaynor, did you forget something?"

Lord Gaynor strode forward. "Yes, I forgot to remove me daughter from your lascivious clutches."

Adam lolled back in his chair. "We're to be married."

"Ye go beyond the bounds of what's proper," Lord Gaynor insisted.

"Oh, come." Adam dusted an imaginary mote from his sleeve. "Bronwyn can't just say 'How de do?' on our wedding night, can she? It's not decorous."

Bronwyn moaned as Adam repeated Lord Gaynor's own words. The sweetheart who'd kissed and caressed her so delicately had heard every word out there on the veranda. He hadn't kissed her out of desire or kindness or mutual pleasure. He was angry. Angry at her father for his clumsy attempt at matchmaking, angry at her for plotting against him.

And she'd fallen into his revenge like the love-starved creature she was. Embarrassment, like a great wave, lifted her from her chair. She shoved it out from under the desk. When Adam reached out for her, her elbow struck his chest smartly. He fell back as she drew herself up. With her hand gripping her apron, she said, "Nothing happened, Da."

Lord Gaynor stopped his dramatic performance and became her concerned Irish father. "Don't lie to your old da, me darlin'. That man was kissing ye."

"Not at all. I had something in my eye." Stepping out from behind the desk, she swept past Lord Gaynor. At the door she turned. In her hands the apron ripped loose from the waistband as she glared at Adam. "But it turned out to be nothing."

Lord Gaynor stared at the spot where his daughter disappeared, then at Adam, who sat rubbing his chest. Like a hound on the scent, he thrust his head out and crept toward Adam, his gaze fixed on his future son-in-law's face. He leaped forward, his hand outstretched to Adam's lip. Adam flinched back, but too late. Lord Gaynor said, "Ah-ha!"

"Ah-ha?" Adam drawled.

Lord Gaynor turned over his hand, and there on his outstretched index finger was the heart-shaped patch Bronwyn wore above her mouth.

Chapter 5

"My lord, London has gone mad." Fresh from Change Alley, Northrup discarded his overcoat with a flourish.

Adam closed his hand over the beauty patch, hiding it from view. Lord Gaynor had pressed it into his palm with an admonition not to move so quickly with his "darlin' Bronwyn," then swept from the study, the portrait of the offended parent. Except for the smirk on his handsome face.

Adam wondered about the Irishman. He couldn't help but like the spendthrift, yet why would he barter his daughter—his favorite daughter, it appeared—to a man whose family name was synonymous with corruption? Robert Walpole insisted Adam's integrity was unblemished, but Adam knew better. His father had stained the family honor, and nothing could cleanse it.

Northrup continued as if he didn't notice Adam's distraction, "It's as if a great midsummer madness has swept the city."

"How so?" Adam pulled out a trash container to toss the bit of velvet, then hesitated and placed it in the desk drawer instead. What about this woman he was betrothed to? She'd been so nervous when first they met, he'd believed she would try to cry off. Indeed, he'd heard her beg Lord Gaynor not to make her speak to him, seen her look of desperation when Lord Gaynor pressed to set a wedding date.

Setting his new hat gently atop the overcoat, Northrup turned back to Adam. "The South Sea Company has offered fifty thousand shares to be put on the market for one thousand pounds apiece."

Adam stared into the desk drawer. Yet her appearance wasn't so dreadful, he thought. A discerning eye revealed a wide and merry mouth, given to smiles and ripe for kisses. Life, her gaze told him, was a serious business, but still she found humor in her father's posturing and his own too serious manner. And regardless of the fashion, he liked the golden tone of her skin. So she had no reason to be nervous with him.

"Lord Rawson?" Northrup said.

Maybe she was nervous because he'd been less than gracious when presented with her. Maybe she was nervous because she feared the marriage bed. Maybe she didn't know about his father and the disgrace.

"Lord Rawson?"

"What? Oh." Adam leaned back in his chair. "One thousand pounds apiece? That's over the current market price."

"Twenty-five percent over the market price," Northrup said. "But the terms are attractive. All they're demanding is a down payment of ten percent, and the rest is to be paid in installments."

"No more than I expected." Adam templed his fingers at his lips, and their sensitivity reminded him of the kiss he'd shared just a few moments ago. Bronwyn stirred the fires of his passion, if not his sentiment. His mother complained he armored himself against emotion, and indeed he did. It was safer, cleaner, less painful, and he'd had enough pain to last a lifetime. "Have they sold it out?"

Northrup's boyish face lit. "Not yet, but they soon will."

His enthusiasm at last focused Adam's attention on the business at hand. "Did you buy any?"

"No, sir," Northrup said earnestly. "I followed your instructions and didn't buy you any."

Adam's mouth tightened. "I meant, did you buy some for yourself?"

Northrup flushed.

"That's a new overcoat, is it not?"

"I needed a replacement for my cloak." Northrup's hauteur came tardy and with too little conviction.

Adam regarded his secretary thoughtfully. "It's been a hard comedown, working for me, hasn't it?"

"Oh, no, sir," Northrup hastened to reassure him. "It's been a . . . a learning process."

Not believing it, Adam snapped, "Perhaps you should remember you're no longer the prospective marquess of Tyne-Kelmport."

"I never forget it," Northrup said, stiff with dignity. "Nor do I complain."

"That's one thing in your favor." Wielding his knife, Adam trimmed the tip of his quill. "I suppose I understand your eagerness to invest in the South Sea

Company. Just sell your stock when I tell you, and you'll stand to make a profit."

"I've worked for you for two years now, my lord. I've picked up on your methods, and I believe I'd best handle my stock by myself."

Adam studied the young man. Hands on waist, Northrup tried to look mature and brave, but he betrayed his agitation when he licked his lips. "A bit independent, aren't we, Northrup?"

Something in Adam's gaze seemed to remind Northrup of his place. "I beg your pardon, my lord."

"I took no offense." And he hadn't. His secretary was a useful young man, no more, no less. If he wished to wreck himself on the rocks of finance, Adam felt no responsibility, only a vast irritation. Northrup worked hard, understood the system, and anticipated Adam's needs. To replace him would be almost impossible. Pointing to the pile of paperwork on his desk, Adam said, "If you're ready, let's go to work."

Northrup looked around for his chair and saw it beside Adam. He frowned, puzzled, until he retrieved it. Then, with a smile, he said, "Ah, Lady Bronwyn was here."

Adam jumped guiltily. "How did you know that?"

Northrup dusted a pile of silk threads from the seat. "Was she dismantling one of her fans again?"

"No, I believe it was . . . an apron of some kind. One of those little garnishes women hang on themselves." Adam contemplated Northrup. How much did he know about the dauntless Bronwyn? An odd curiosity gripped him, a need to know about his fiancée. Yet should he discuss her with this young man? What protocol governed such a conversation? Northrup no doubt knew, but Adam had never learned the refinements of proper society gossip. Tentatively he asked, "Does she do that often? Dismantle her fans?"

Northrup laughed. "Haven't you noticed? When she's nervous—and that's almost always in company— she picks at her fan."

Precise, scrupulous, Adam insisted, "She wasn't carrying a fan."

"If nothing else, she chews her fingernails. She told me her mother scolds her."

"She told you?" Adam asked in astonishment.

"She's such a friendly young lady, and we've chatted." Northrup seated himself and uncorked his ink. "Do you have letters you want sent, sir?"

"I have some figures I want copied and checked." While searching through the papers before him, Adam asked, "That's right, you'd seen her at court, hadn't you?"

"Lady Bronwyn? Briefly, sir." Northrup picked up his quill and held it in readiness.

Something stirred in Adam. "You're about the same age, aren't you?"

"Yes, sir."

Adam stared at the paper in his hand until the numbers made sense. "Here it is."

Northrup accepted the figures.

"She's not as plain as she looks."

Northrup looked up in surprise. "Sir?"

Realizing how silly that sounded, Adam said, "What I mean is, Lady Bronwyn has pretty eyes."

"I quite agree." When Adam said nothing else, Northrup went back to work.

Adam gazed out the window at the sculptured gardens until Northrup's words sank in. "You agree, do you?"

The quill scratched across the sheet. "Yes, sir. And I like her smile. She has dimples."

"A dimple," Adam corrected. "In her left cheek."

"Ah, of course. . . . These columns are correct." Northrup passed the paper back.

"Add these, if you would." Adam pushed another sheet across the wide desktop. Tapping his fingers, he said worriedly, "If she's not careful, she'll get the reputation of a learned woman."

"A dreadful thought." Northrup shuddered with genuine revulsion. "Is there anything worse than a learned woman?"

"It's not so dreadful," Adam objected quickly, then blinked. How odd. He wanted to defend Bronwyn, the woman he had been treating so rudely. Northrup's incredulous store made him add, "At least a man can talk to her."

Northrup gave up any pretense of working. "Lady Bronwyn? Yes, I've always been able to talk to her. She's one of the kindest women I've ever met."

"Kind? I don't know about kind."

"You've been avoiding her. How could you know?" Northrup asked.

"Getting daring, aren't you?" Northrup refused to apologize, and Adam smiled with grim appreciation. "You're right, of course. I've been sulking like a man unable to make the best of a situation, when that quality is one I've always prided myself on. Well, that will change. From now on, I'll court Lady Bronwyn with all the finesse a young woman could wish for."

"Good for you, sir," Northrup said warmly. "Lady Bronwyn deserves a little of the admiration her sisters drown in."

"Precisely."

"She's worth more than all seven of her sisters."

"Even Olivia?" Adam teased, aware his secretary had been stricken with Cupid's arrow with his first glance at Olivia's perfect features.

Northrup grimaced. "Olivia's beautiful. Probably the most beautiful of the Irish Sirens."

"I've noticed you watching her."

"It was never more than admiration," Northrup said defensively. "She inhabits a dream world, removed from day-to-day life."

"She's like a precious glass," Adam said. "Too fragile to use."

"Exactly. Olivia's so heavenly minded, she's no earthly good, if you know what I mean."

"Um-hum." Adam's mind drifting back to Bronwyn. He tickled the palm of his hand with his quill. She had liked it when he'd trailed it over her skin. She had enjoyed the touch of his hand. When he kissed her, her eyes had blurred, softened, gone sweet and warm—yet she reacted as if she'd never been kissed before. He glared at Northrup. Surely some young buck had cornered her sometime to press his attentions on her. After all, she was twenty-two. "What was her reputation at court?" he snapped.

"Olivia's?"

"Bronwyn's!"

Northrup shook his head as if he were dizzy. "Lady Bronwyn lived at court only a few days for her sister's wedding. She had no reputation. Few even recognized who she was."

Cheered, Adam queried, "Did she look similar to the way she does now?"

"She was gawky, like an overgrown child. She tripped on her train during the wedding procession.

She dropped her sister's ring." Northrup winced at the memory. "She insisted on speaking some kind of broken German to King George, and he adored it."

Adam covered his eyes. "Did he pinch her?"

"Worse. He introduced her to the Maypole."

"His mistress?"

"Everyone has forgotten, I'm sure," Northrup comforted. "Just as they've forgotten her excitement about that medieval Irish manuscript displayed at the cathedral."

"Excitement? You exaggerate," Adam scoffed.

Northrup looked grim. "She could *read* it, sir."

Adam laid down his quill. "Read it? Wasn't it in Latin?"

"In Latin and that other"—Northrup pulled a face—"that other language they speak over there."

"Gaelic? Where did she learn Gaelic?" Adam could hardly believe it. "In Ireland, only the peasants speak Gaelic. Why, she's the daughter of one of our noblemen."

"She said the nuns taught her Gaelic."

"The nuns?" Adam asked, alarmed. "Is she a closet Papist?"

"No, sir. No, no, I would have warned you. I owe you that much loyalty," Northrup said. "She claimed she was sent to the convent on a regular basis to learn needlework."

"A tricky business, that." Adam shook his head. "She could have been imbued with all sorts of disloyal teachings."

"Rest assured she was not, at least not by the nuns. However, she also claimed her governess taught her Latin."

Alarmed all over again, Adam barked, "Her governess?

What was the woman thinking of, teaching another woman Latin?"

"You'll have to ask Lady Bronwyn," Northrup said meaningfully. "During one of your private, tender conversations."

Adam didn't care for the insinuation that he needed to be instructed in matters of love. "Other men court women. I'm sure I'm capable of it."

"Flowers," Northrup suggested. "Little gifts. Watch her with appreciation. Touch her waist as you guide her into dinner."

"I know what to do," Adam said with irritation: "I'll show her my desire in subtle ways."

"I'm sorry." Bronwyn said it even before the wine, like a great red tide, spread across the lace draped over the end table. She grabbed for the glass as it rolled, but it fell and broke with the refined shatter of leaded crystal. The wine stained the exquisite Chinese rug in the middle of the drawing room, and she said again, "I'm sorry."

As the footman rushed to clean it up, Mab assured her, "It's of no consequence. The gentlemen Adam calls his friends break more glasses in one evening than you've broken since you've been here."

But not by much. Bronwyn could almost hear Adam thinking it. She avoided his gaze and found herself nailed to her chair by her mother's glare. With a fix from those fine violet eyes, Lady Nora made it clear that Bronwyn should purge herself of such reprehensible clumsiness.

The problem was, Bronwyn couldn't seem to help it. Ever since that afternoon in his study, Adam had treated her to an intense regard that shattered her composure as absolutely as the glass was shattered.

She thought she was angry with him. Such cavalier treatment deserved anger. To toy with her emotions so coldly boded ill for their marriage. Boded ill for her.

But his kiss hadn't tasted vindictive, and his later attentions hadn't been scornful. He acted like a man courting a maid, but his courting wasn't of the fashionable variety. He knew nothing of teasing, of a light-hearted pursuit. When he kissed her hand, his mouth lingered. When he took her in to dinner, his palm burned through the cloth at her waist. When he presented her with a flower, he placed it intimately and with such ardor that it wilted in her hand.

She didn't know which frightened her more—the idea that he was seeking some kind of revenge or the idea that he wasn't. Even now, she thought her wig would ignite spontaneously as he considered her.

"I've been invited to attend the St. John's Eve celebration in the village." The words of the invitation were polite; Adam's tone betrayed a passionate objective. "I hope Bronwyn will attend with me."

Apparently Lord Gaynor read Adam's intentions, for he asked, "Isn't St. John's Day also Midsummer Day?"

Adam caressed the slope of his brandy glass with his fingers. "I believe so."

"Quite a pagan celebration among the peasants, isn't it?" Lord Gaynor suggested.

Adam lifted his brow, smiled blandly.

"That would be an interesting outing for the entire family. Thank ye for asking us," said Lord Gaynor.

Bronwyn grinned at him gratefully, but Lady Nora cried, "Impossible! We're promised to Lady Hogarth's party that night."

"A trifle, me darlin'. They'll never miss us."

"Not true, dearest." Lady Nora simpered, but her

mettle shone through. "Lady Hogarth is one of my dearest friends, and she's depending on us. Our daughters will be there, and Lady Hogarth is noising it about as the 'return of the Sirens of Ireland.'"

"The most beautiful women in London society, together at one party." Lord Gaynor puffed out his chest. "We must go."

Bronwyn snapped the hinges of the patch box hidden in her pocket. Her father's easy dismissal of her as a Siren rubbed at a wound so old she scarcely noticed it. But she didn't want to be alone with Adam, and so her precious father knew well. "Da," she protested.

Lord Gaynor shrugged. "Ye'll have a good time with His Lordship. Olivia can go with ye."

From the depths of her chair where she hid, Olivia squeaked. Bronwyn sank back on the settee. What good did her absurd da think Olivia would be? Adam alarmed Bronwyn; he frightened Olivia into fits.

"What kind of wholesome entertainment is in store for my daughters?" Lord Gaynor asked, wanting to display interest in the activities. "Do the local folk have a hearty celebration?"

"I don't know. I bought this property only two years ago," Adam said.

"That's right." Lord Gaynor drew out a long, curved pipe. "This property was the estate of Lord Wilde and his family. They lost it in a reverse of fortune, did they not?"

"Damned fool Wilde thought finance the province of the middle class." Adam's mobile mouth curled with scorn. "He's found that without financial sense, even a noble family can be destroyed."

Fumbling with his tobacco pouch, Lord Gaynor objected, "One must have charity."

"No one had charity for me," Adam retorted coolly.

"No matter how reprehensible your father's behavior was, ye retained your title." Lord Gaynor waved an agitated hand. "Surely ye agree the elite of this country need to be preserved."

"Do I?"

It didn't sound like a question to Bronwyn, and she watched Adam with big eyes. What kind of background did Adam Keane come from? When her parents informed her of her betrothal, they told her Adam was a viscount from an old and noble family. Plainly they hadn't told her his entire history, for his brittle scorn for the unfortunate Wilde family told a story of its own.

Lord Gaynor poured a measure of tobacco into the pipe and tamped it with a silver utensil. "The nobility are the living reminders of England's mighty past."

"England's future is brighter than its past could ever be." Waving his footman forward, Adam declared, "Let each man make his way on his own, and let the best man succeed."

Lord Gaynor dropped his tobacco pouch. "Good God, that would be chaos."

Mab interposed, "Chaos is a strong word, but my son has traveled a road few can imagine. From the depths of bleakest poverty, he raised himself using only his luck and wit."

"Mab," Adam interposed. "My bleak past is of even less interest than England's mighty past."

Bronwyn didn't agree. She desperately wanted to know the details, but Adam told the footman, "Have the maid clean the tobacco and finish picking up the glass. Lord Gaynor needs a flint for his pipe." The man hurried from the room as Adam continued, "I had this house built last summer. Mab and I moved in at Christmastime."

As Adam spoke, Bronwyn leaned forward and touched Olivia's hand. Olivia nodded, and the girls rose. "We will retire now," Bronwyn announced.

Adam rose at once and came to her side. He lifted her hand to kiss it, and somehow his mouth found the pulse beating at her wrist. It leaped beneath his lips, and his gaze found hers. The tide of crimson rose from her toes, dying her chest, her neck, her face.

He murmured, "I look forward to Midsummer's Eve with a fervency I never felt before." After she choked out some vague reply, he turned to Olivia. His voice softened, he smiled kindly. "We'll provide you with a pleasant evening, also." His courtesy for Olivia was all the more obvious after his ardent handling of Bronwyn.

It made no difference. Olivia scurried from the room as if she were threatened by his masculinity. Although Bronwyn experienced the same reaction, it irritated her to see Olivia behave in such a manner, as though Adam were a satyr.

Bronwyn hurried after her sister and caught her elbow. "Olivia, stop running like a scared rabbit. He won't harm you."

Olivia grabbed her in a crushing grip. "He frightens me so. Bronwyn, he looks as if he's about to gobble you up."

"After he got over his first disappointment with his homely bride, he's been all that is considerate." It was true, she supposed. One couldn't—or shouldn't—complain about too much attention. Unbidden, Rachelle's invitation to join her salon sprang to her mind. "Sometimes I think life would be easier if I were shut away from all this nonsense. If there weren't any men to fret me with their tantrums. If I could live as I wished without worrying about what society thinks."

"I wish I could, too. Oh, I wish I could, too." Olivia cast a fearful glance down the hall to the open door of the drawing room. Pulling Bronwyn along with her, she said in a tone of accusation, "You said he kissed you."

"Men are supposed to want to kiss their fiancées."

Olivia shuddered and climbed the stairs. "A man's baser instincts lead to dreadful acts."

Bronwyn raced to pass her, stopping her at the landing. "How do you know?"

"Sister Mary Theresa told me." Olivia folded her hands in front of her.

"Sister Mary Theresa?" Bronwyn was flabbergasted. "That was years ago!"

"I remember," Olivia said primly.

Bronwyn stepped aside and let Olivia pass, then tagged along behind. "You'll be along to protect me from his baser instincts when we visit the village."

Reaching her room, Olivia said, "I'm sorry, but I'm not coming."

"What do you mean you're not coming? Da said—"

"I heard what Da said. He said St. John's Day is actually a pagan carryover from Midsummer's Day." Olivia stepped through the threshold and prepared to shut the door in Bronwyn's face. "I won't pollute my soul by attending a pagan ritual."

Bronwyn pushed the door wide and barged in. "Da didn't say anything about the pagan carryover. Where'd you hear that?"

"Sister Mary Theresa told me to be careful, that the Devil still seeks to reclaim his lost holidays by masking them as Christian saint days."

Bronwyn took her sister by the shoulders and shook her. "Be careful. We're Irish, and members of the Church of England, but if any hint that we were Papist came to the attention of society, we'd be pariahs."

Olivia gulped and whispered, "I know." Her big blue eyes pleaded for understanding. "I know you want me to come, but my soul would be in peril."

"What about me? When Adam looks at me, I know it's not my soul that's in peril."

"You shouldn't go, either."

Exasperated, Bronwyn paced away. "I can't tell him no!"

"But that creature will take the chance to kiss you again"—Olivia acted as if the thought could never have occurred to Bronwyn—"and how can you stand it?"

"I stood the last kiss very well," Bronwyn confessed. "He kissed me until my garters smoked."

"Bronwyn!"

Not wanting to gaze on her sister's shocked countenance, Bronwyn studied the toe of her shoe digging against the carpet. "Well, he did."

"Oh, Bronwyn, this is tragic." Olivia collapsed onto a chair. "You're not in love with him, are you?"

"I don't know." Bronwyn waved her arms. "I don't know. I like it when he kisses me, and sometimes when he looks at me, I feel this sinking in my stomach."

"Because you're frightened?" Olivia guessed.

"Maybe sinking isn't the correct word. More like . . ." Faced with her sister's blank stare, Bronwyn gave up trying to describe it. "It's not a bad feeling. Just anticipation, I suppose."

Putting her fingers to her temples, Olivia whispered in dire tones, "You are in love with him."

"In love. That's such a strong term." Bronwyn meditated. "Probably it's only infatuation."

Olivia pressed her lips together in a tight line, then

said, "Think of Maman. You don't want to be like Maman, do you?"

"Da loves her," Bronwyn answered. She didn't like the way Olivia made her feel—defensive and alarmed about her own common sense.

"And she loves him. With her looks, she could have married any man, but she ran away with Da instead."

Protective of her dearest father, Bronwyn said, "There's nothing wrong with Da!"

"Nothing, except he hasn't any money, and he's more Irish than English, and he follows his heart." Olivia counted his deficiencies on her fingers. "Maman's had to be the brains of the family, and she's ill suited to that."

"Yes," Bronwyn acknowledged.

"Maman could be living in luxury right now, rather than staying in the home of her daughter's betrothed."

"It's not been so awful."

"Pretending she's living here because Adam asked her to, when she actually hasn't the money to open their London house." Olivia clenched her fists. "She could be a duchess."

"I know," Bronwyn agreed miserably.

"And what does she get for all her sacrifices? Da still finds other women to amuse him. She always knows, and she always eats her heart out."

Bronwyn shrugged, not indifferent, but very uncomfortable.

With full-blown indignation, Olivia queried, "Don't you remember when Holly fell in love with her fiancée? They were married and rapturously happy until another pretty face caught his attention. And then another, and then another—"

"You don't have to harp on it."

"And poor Holly still loves that man, and every time he finds another mistress she cries and cries."

"I couldn't love a man like that," Bronwyn said with emphasis.

Olivia laughed a little hysterically. "The women in this family don't have a choice. None of our other sisters love, because they've never found the right man. But when one of the Edana women does love, it sticks like tar. Nothing scrapes it off, nothing remains the same. No matter what that man does, we Edana women can't escape the awful trap."

Bronwyn turned away from Olivia's certainty.

"Maman's beautiful. Holly's beautiful. Neither one of them can keep the man she loves. Worst of all, Adam is by far the most attractive of the husbands."

"You noticed, did you?" Bronwyn said dryly.

Olivia leaped to her feet and came to embrace Bronwyn. "I love you dearly, but your looks won't keep a man by your side. With those mesmerizing eyes, he must have women throwing themselves at him. If you love this viscount of Rawson, you'll have nothing but heartache in store."

Olivia's words struck deep at Bronwyn's precarious poise, but she seized the moment to declare, "That's why you must come with me tomorrow night."

"No." Olivia shook her head. "I will not."

"Yes, you will."

"No, I won't."

Chapter 6

Olivia wouldn't come." Seated in the horse-drawn cart, her skirts spread in a great pile of yellow dimity that draped over Adam's legs and dangled off the side, Bronwyn bounced along the road to the village.

"Olivia is delicate, isn't she?" Drawn by his dark magnetism, the setting sun kissed Adam's face and acquainted itself with his features.

Bronwyn's fingers itched to touch the spark of gold in his black hair. "I don't know if delicate is the correct word." Still peeved at Olivia's defection, she strove for a pleasant tone; his sidelong glance told her she hadn't quite succeeded.

"Did she have the headache?"

Bronwyn examined her thumbnail. It had grown out to an acceptable length, and she rubbed the smooth edge with her index finger. "I believe she's suffering, yes."

"Your sister seems almost ethereal, untouched by the world." His carefree handling of the ponies matched his casual outfit of brown breeches and a snowy shirt. His rough stockings and sturdy shoes told the story; tonight he cared nothing for formality.

His carefree demeanor made her yearn to discard the panniers that held her skirts out so stiffly, to toss aside the decorative petticoat, to remove the stomacher that cinched her tight. Her full and formal wig she'd relinquished for a smaller one topped with a cap. She wished she could run barefoot as she'd done as a child, feeling the grass between her toes.

He continued, "Olivia's skin is so fair, her hair so dark, she looks like the princess in the old fairy tales."

Bronwyn smiled, a mere curving of the lips, and touched the modest wig covering her own scorned locks. "She looks like the rest of my sisters."

"You're different."

"So I've been told," she said in brittle agreement. In the silence that followed, she scolded herself. Adam admired Olivia; who did not? For the first time in her life, she didn't want to hear someone praise her sister, and that only because of this inconvenient emotion stirring in her.

"Will your father be angry with you for coming with me?" She didn't answer, and he added, "Alone?"

She almost laughed aloud. "I can handle Da." Seeking to mend her bridges, she waved at the village cuddled into the hollow before them. "Olivia's going to be sorry she missed this. I can smell the food cooking."

"See the bonfires on the hills?" He pointed his whip. "That's a tradition on Midsummer's Eve. The villagers believe it welcomes summer."

She grinned as they rattled into the village square. "So this really is a pagan celebration?"

"Let's say it's a Christian celebration with pagan roots."

One of the villagers standing in the doorway of the tiny inn hailed him. Adam greeted the man by name and came to a halt.

"M'lord, a pleasure." John wiped his hands on his apron. "We was hopin' ye was comin', but ye missed th' cheese rollin'."

"My misfortune," Adam said, grinning.

John agreed solemnly. " 'Twas a hearty sight."

"What is a cheese rolling?" Adam quizzed, echoing the question in Bronwyn's mind.

"Ye've never attended a cheese rollin'?" John studied them as if they were strange creatures. "We take a big wheel o' cheese, see, an' roll it down th' hill, an' th' boys chase it, an' th' winner gets th' cheese." Seeking to comfort them, he added, "Still an' all, ye're here in time fer plenty o' games. Th' men are playing marbles now. Th' boys'll be tacklin' a greased pig. We've got wrestlin' with some o' our best men t' bet on, an' this before 'tis total dark an' we can light th' bonfire in th' square. Son, take th' lordship's horses an' put them in me stable." A ten-year-old ran to the ponies' heads, and Adam descended to help Bronwyn down.

"Is this yer lady?" John asked, not bothering to hide his fervent interest. "The lady ye would wed?"

"Indeed it is." Adam wrapped his hands around Bronwyn's waist and swung her down. He kept his hands there while he gazed at her, and a hot blush worked under her skin. "Lady Bronwyn Edana, daughter of the earl of Gaynor."

"A fine lady t' come t' our humble celebration," John said.

Crowding close under the villager's arm, a woman Bronwyn suspected was his wife asked, "But did ye come without a chaperone?"

Adam let Bronwyn go, and she turned to the woman. "My sister was ill. Mab will be along later, and for this brief visit I decided to trust Lord Keane."

"Did ye now?" The woman examined Adam with a critical gaze. "No doubt ye could trust him with yer life. But with yer virtue?" She twisted her thumb down and turned profile in the doorway. Her belly, swollen and waiting to be delivered of its burden, gave a visual warning more potent than words. "Don't let yer trust carry ye too far."

Nudging his wife behind him, John sputtered and apologized. "Ye'll excuse Gilda, m'lord, she's in th' last stages an' taking advantage o' me soft nature."

Adam grinned again and without words invited Bronwyn to share his amusement. She couldn't help herself. She responded. In the radiance of his pleasure, she realized Gilda's warning came too late. Bronwyn would trust Adam. Trust him with her life, trust him with her virtue, for no better reason than an instinct that claimed him as hers.

"Look at the flames licking out of those barrels." Standing on the top of the knoll, on top of a rock, Bronwyn clapped her hands like a child given a sugar plum. "Why do they roll them down the hill?"

Adam stood below and watched her excitement in the flickering light of the bonfire. "It's a tradition," he said, as he'd said so many times this evening.

"Have they always done so?"

Smiling faintly, he said, "I suppose. You'll have to inquire."

The idea was parent to the action. Holding her skirts, she leaped from the rock. Adam thought he heard a ripping sound, but, unperturbed, she bounded to the fringe of the bonfire. Giving way good-naturedly, the villagers closed behind her. They'd come to like her as she cheered the marbles and the wrestling. She'd laughed until she cried as the boys struggled to hold a greased pig, and she'd not taken offense at the curiosity of the villagers for Adam's betrothed. She'd drunk ale with them, chatted with them, thanked them for inviting her, and she'd made them her adoring disciples.

Now she had to yell to have herself heard above the roar of the conflagration, and Adam moved closer to hear her say, "You make a bonfire. You fill barrels with flame and send them down the hill. What other things do you do at Midsummer?"

To his surprise, the villagers laughed in a knowing fashion.

One of the men, well fortified with liquor, said, "Well, this is a great time t' drink ale."

"How so?" she asked.

"'Tis church ale, an' all th' profit from th' brewing goes t' th' church." His bushy eyebrows wiggled. "'Twouldn't be reverent t' refuse a drink."

He staggered sideways. "I can see you've done more than your share to support the church," Bronwyn teased.

One of the unmarried girls pushed forward. "M'lady, see that moon?"

Bronwyn stared up at the round globe lifting just above the horizon.

"That's the Midsummer moon, an' it brings a turrible

madness," the girl explained. "A love madness. Any girl seeking t' know her future husband should place a garland o' flowers under her pillow. Whoever she conjures will be th' man."

The villagers laughed and clapped as she removed her garland and placed it on Bronwyn's head.

Adam pushed forward to his betrothed and settled the flowers closer against the itchy wig. "It gives me pleasure to know you'll dream of me."

Bronwyn's eyes fell beneath his gaze; the villagers snorted and coughed. John presented them with two tankards. "This round of ale's on me. Come down th' hill now, m'lord an' lady, an' start th' dance fer us." He pulled his forelock. "When ye want t', a' course."

Adam looked at Bronwyn inquiringly, and she nodded. "Let's go," she agreed, accepting the ale. "I've never been to a Midsummer's Eve dance before."

"Nor I." He offered his arm, and she took it without hesitation. She stumbled and would have tumbled down the hill, and he noted that his lady seemed the worse for the drink. Mentally he tallied the tankards and asked, "Bronwyn, would you like to refresh yourself?"

"Take me to the inn," she answered instantly, and grinned at him.

How could he have ever thought her homely? That smile of hers lit her face like a fairy light. Her body moved with a grace that made a man think of long, slow loving. When he'd been beside her in his office he'd been unable to keep himself from touching her. As he'd expected, her shape had been augmented by stuffing, but not totally. Above the wad of cloth dwelt a breast, round and sensitive, and he'd liked its shape. Finding it had ignited his curiosity, and now he wondered what other mysteries his fiancée concealed.

His own curiosity had brought him too many sleepless nights.

Mimicking his thoughts, although she didn't realize it, she said, "You've fulfilled a great curiosity of mine."

"In what way?"

"I had read about Midsummer Night and the Irish celebrations in the Gaelic manuscript I was translating, and—"

"Translating?" He recalled the tale Northrup had told him. "You mean reading."

Her hand flew to her mouth, her gaze to his face. She looked the picture of guilt, and she agreed, "Reading! I meant reading."

She lied. There was no doubt. He'd questioned enough cabin boys and seamen to know shame when he saw it. Lesser men than he could decipher her gestures, but what did it mean? Surely his little noblewoman couldn't read Gaelic. Elaborately casual, he asked, "Where were you reading such a thing?"

"In Ireland," she answered. "Look at the stars. They're big and bright, without a cloud to hide them."

Trying to distract him, and none too cleverly, he diagnosed, "That's right, you lived in Ireland as a child. That's one island I've never visited."

With the mood swing of the tipsy, she twirled around, laughing. "You should go. It's the most beautiful place on earth."

Without exerting his imagination, he could imagine the urchin she had been. "Did you run free during your time there?"

"No. No, no." She shook her head so hard that her wig slipped, and a bit of moonlight gleamed close by her hairline. "We had a governess, a Miss O'Donnell.

In that lovely brogue of hers, she called herself a distressed noblewoman and made it sound like an honor. Da paid her to teach us, and teach us she did."

Homing in on the information he sought, he put a foot upon a boulder and propped his arm against his knee in a nonchalant gesture. "What did she teach you?"

"Everything. I thought my head would burst before she was done stuffing it."

"Embroidery? Harp? Deportment?"

"Miss O'Donnell? Not at all. Well, deportment," she allowed. "Miss O'Donnell believed in deportment. But mathematics, languages, history mostly."

"Languages?" He slid her a keen glance, but she had turned her face into the breeze and didn't see it. "Is that where you learned to read Gaelic?"

"No, that's where I learned to read Latin," she corrected, not suspecting how she betrayed herself. "The manuscripts were at the convent where we—Olivia and I—went to learn harp and embroidery. I found one old manuscript written in both Latin and Gaelic. I'd heard the peasants speak Gaelic, of course, but this wasn't the same kind of Gaelic. This was"—she struggled to define it—"archaic. I would have never battled through, but the text was interesting."

"About Midsummer Night?"

"About Druids, bards, and a world long vanished." Solemn, she shook her head. "Gaelic is difficult."

"What did Miss O'Donnell think of such a thing?"

"She'd had brothers, you see, and learned everything they'd learned. But she said if I were to get an education, I'd have to do it myself. She said as soon as I came to England, all I'd learn is how to dance and simper and use a fan." She drooped. "She was right."

He wrapped his arm around her waist and started

them back down the hill. "Is that such a dreadful thing?"

His touch seemed to wake her to her circumstances, and she tensed. "Not at all," she said.

She sounded silly and feminine, but her own natural intelligence made it a parody. Tomorrow he would worry about it, about her intelligence and how it clashed with his own needs. For now, satisfaction struggled for dominance. Another bit of the mystery surrounding this Edana changeling had been solved.

At the inn, Gilda greeted Bronwyn with another tankard of ale. "Havin' a good time, m'lady?"

"Marvelous." Bronwyn sipped the rich brew and queried, "Have you got a room where I can repair a little of the damage this good time is inflicting?"

"A' course. Give way fer m'lady. Don't crowd m'lady." Gilda pushed through the throng of curious, thirsty revelers to an upper-level hall. Opening a door, she asked, "Will this do, m'lady?"

"It will do nicely, I'm sure." Bronwyn glanced around at the simple decorations. "What a homey place."

Pleased, Gilda said, "It's our room, John's an' mine."

"I recognize your light touch," Bronwyn praised. "I could use a little help, too, if you would?"

As if she'd been waiting for the invitation, Gilda stepped inside and shut the door.

"Do you have a pin?" Bronwyn lifted her skirt, revealing a silk petticoat beneath. "I stepped on my hem and it ripped at my waist. Look." She stuck her finger through the hole and wiggled it.

Gilda giggled and opened a drawer in the dresser. "I can sew it on ye easier than I can pin it. I was a seamstress before I married John, an' I'm handy with a needle."

"A fortunate circumstance for John."

"I sew his shirts better than he's ever had them sewed before, an' I stitched all th' clothes fer th' babe," Gilda agreed, placing a stool beside Bronwyn and kneeling on it. "Since John got t' keep th' inn, it's been a happy time fer us."

"Keep the inn? Were you about to lose it?"

Gilda pinned the hole firmly before she answered. "Last year's Midsummer celebration wasn't nearly as cheerful, I'll tell ye."

"Why?" Bronwyn asked.

"All th' lands had just been sold t' Lord Keane, an' we didn't know what kind o' landlord we were getting. Everyone was afraid they'd have no homes." She glanced up and winked. "I got married because o' His Lordship."

"Why do you say that?"

"We wanted t' get married, John an' I, but we couldn't do it until we knew if we'd have a way t' feed our babes. Why, His Lordship could have been one o' those men who don't want a village cluttering up their lands." Gilda threaded the needle. "A lot of these merchantmen who buy a manor don't understand about families who've lived in one place fer generations. They just say th' village is wrecking their view, or some other silliness, an' throw everyone out without a by-your-leave."

"How frightened you must have been when you heard the manor had been sold," Bronwyn sympathized.

Gilda waved the needle and thread through the air. "An' how relieved we were when we found Lord Keane wasn't one o' those high an' mighty gentlemen."

Bronwyn remembered the formidable lord who'd greeted her on her first day. In surprise, she agreed, "He's been very pleasant tonight."

"Pleasant?" Gilda snorted. "Pleasant's not th' word I'd put t' him exactly, but he's a doer all right. Soon as he started t' build that big house, he had th' road improved. Ye can imagine th' difference that made t' th' inn."

"He did it to hurry the construction," Bronwyn said.

"A' course, but he didn't have t' improve it clear down here, did he?"

Bronwyn watched as Gilda's nimble fingers whipped through the material. "No, I suppose not. What else has he done?"

"Him an' his mother are building a school, right here in th' village, t' teach th' little ones until they're ten. Doesn't even matter whether they're poor folks, he says, th' boys are not t' work until they're eleven an' got their growth. Have ye ever heard o' such a thing?" Gilda shook her head in wonder.

Impressed, but not wanting to show it, Bronwyn agreed, "Quite radical."

"Quite scatterbrained, if ye ast John. But me, I like it." Patting her belly, Gilda said, "This child will go far with such learning."

"What if it's a girl?" Bronwyn asked.

Gilda pulled a face. "Then I'll teach her t' sew. No use her learning anything else."

"We wouldn't want the girls to improve themselves," Bronwyn said sarcastically.

Sensing Bronwyn's disappointment, Gilda insisted, "Even fer girls, Lord Keane says th' little ones aren't t' be apprenticed until they're eleven."

"I suppose he has a care for his people."

Gilda finished with her stitching and bit off the thread. "That he does, an' there isn't one of us who wouldn't lie down an' let him drive his fine carriage right over us."

Bronwyn helped Gilda to her feet. "I doubt he'd ask so much of you."

"A' course. That's why we'd do it."

Much struck, Bronwyn thanked her.

Adam waited in the taproom, chatting with the men pressed close against him. Yet something brought his head up, and he watched her descend the stairs. Their eyes locked; the intensity of his gaze burned her, and all around the noise died. She reached his side without being aware of it, gave him her hand without knowing why. "My lord," she whispered.

He lifted her hand to his lips, and she felt the expiration of his breath as he said, "My lady."

She couldn't maintain eye contact at such close quarters, and when she glanced about her she saw grins and nudges. They should have mortified her, but they didn't. It just seemed pleasant that these people who thought so much of Adam should approve of her.

John interrupted the mutual admiration society. "We're ready to start the dancing, m'lord."

"Our signal to proceed, my dear." Adam offered his arm.

When she laid her hand on it, he captured her fingers in his. He held her hand like a man with his sweetheart, fingers curled, palms together. The simple contact brought her gaze to his again. Again she found herself unable to breathe, to move, to think. Something about this man made her common sense collapse like a house of cards.

"The dancing?" John urged.

Adam drew her outdoors, into the heated darkness. A great bonfire leaped in the middle of the square, answering the flames atop the hill, calling in the summer.

On a platform, a swarm of instruments—violin, flute, and harmonica—squalled. The players cajoled off-key bits of melody, then whole bars of music, and at last, inspired by the occasion, a rollicking song. Although Bronwyn had never heard it before, its concentrated rhythm set her foot to tapping.

With a tug of his hand, Adam had her in the center of a circle of clapping villagers. "I don't know how to dance to this," she warned.

"Nor do I," he answered, placing his hands on her waist. "Have a care for your toes."

She had no need to care for her toes, for Adam led with a strength that compensated for his limp. He kept his hands on her waist as he lifted her, turned her, swung her in circles. Under his guidance, she relaxed and began to enjoy the leaping, foot-stomping gambol. The community cheered, not at all distressed by the innovative steps, and the whole village joined them around the bonfire.

Girls with their sweethearts, men with their wives, old folks with their grandchildren, all whisked by as Adam twirled Bronwyn around and around. Bronwyn laughed until she was out of breath, and when she was gasping, the music changed. The rhythm slowed, the frenetic pace dwindled.

She saw Adam's amused expression change as he drew her toward him. His heavy lids veiled his gaze, and she knew he'd done so to hide his intention. She wondered why, then felt only shock as their bodies collided.

Shutting her eyes against the buffet of his heated frame against hers, she breathed a long, slow breath. The incense of his skin mated with the scent of the burning wood, and beneath the shield of her eyelids fireworks exploded. She groaned as her own body was licked by the flames.

Before she was scorched, he twirled her away, then back, in accordance to the rules of the dance.

There were people around, she knew, but she pretended they weren't watching their lord and lady. She pretended Adam and she were alone.

Ignoring the proper steps, Adam wrapped himself around her, one arm against her shoulders, one arm at her waist.

Her hands held his shoulders. Her fingers flexed, feeling the muscles hidden beneath the fine linen. She could hear his heart thudding, hear the rasp of his breath and his moan as she touched his neck with her tongue. She only wanted a taste of him, but he mistook it for interest, for he scooped her up.

Her eyes flew open. He'd ferried them to the edge of the dancing figures, planning their escape like a smuggler planning a landfall. A whirl and they were gone into the trees. Looking back, she could see the sparks of the bonfire, like a constellation of stars climbing to the sky.

This was what she wanted, what she dreaded, what she longed for. Since she'd met Adam, she didn't understand herself. His gaze scorched her, and she reveled in the discomfort. His hands massaged her as if he found pleasure in her shape; they wandered places no one had touched since she'd been an infant, and it excited her. Even now, as he pulled her into the darkest corner of the wood, she went on willing feet.

He pushed her against the trunk of a broad oak and murmured, "Bronwyn, give me your mouth."

She found his lips and marveled at their accuracy. His arm held her back, his hand clasped her waist; all along their length they grew together, like two fevered creatures of the night.

He exalted at the explosion of heat. This little virgin kissed like a dream. Willing, whimpering just for him, she created impulses he'd believed stifled by maturity. He wanted to pull her onto the grass and lift her skirt and plunge into her. He wanted her breasts in his mouth, his hands on her thighs, and a long night ahead. Was this midsummer madness, as the villagers claimed? No doubt, for madness pounded in his veins and brought him pushing at her like a stag with a doe in heat.

Lifting his head, he looked down on her face, dappled with moonlight, and knew he'd never forget this moment. The angles of her face, the pale brows, the sensitive mouth—they were engraved on his mind. Propelled by need, his hand caressed her throat, then slipped to the ruffle that teased her bosom. She didn't move; he wondered if she were too stunned. Wanting to weave the magic around her, he whispered, "Don't stare at me with those big eyes. I won't hurt you." Delving below her corset; he found what he sought.

Her breast felt smooth, firm, topped with a nipple already tightened by his kiss. He groaned aloud and couldn't believe his own unbridled reflex. His response recalled adolescence: the clumsy fumblings, the unrestrainable passion, the wholehearted delight. What had this girl given back to him?

What had she taken? Where was his restraint? She *was* a girl, in experience if not in age, and a gently bred girl at that. He was a cad to press her. Obviously she didn't understand the ramifications of his actions—of her pleasure. Obviously he'd taken her far beyond her experience. But temptation whispered in his ear, telling him they'd be married soon. That the wedding could be moved up if this night bore fruit. That the wedding would have to be moved up, for he couldn't wait to have this girl in his bed every night. Couldn't wait to sample her without hurry or secrecy.

"Dear, let me—" He swooped before he could finish his plea. Lifting her, balancing her on the knee he'd thrust against the bark, he licked her throat, covered her collarbone with a trail of kisses. Artfully he freed her breast; whether so artfully she didn't realize it, he didn't know, or care.

Ah, she knew, for she moaned as his mouth closed on her nipple, and when he suckled she went wild in his arms.

She wasn't fighting him. Thank God, she wasn't fighting, for she'd roused the hunter in him, and he would have been out of control. But perhaps the way she wiggled against his leg was worse. Hampered by her skirts, she tried to slide close to his loins. When she couldn't, she rode him like a horse, moving toward some ever-closer goal. Her eager fingers hugged his head, combed through his hair, discarded his ribbon. When he nipped her, she wailed, "Oh, Adam," and his name never sounded so good.

Keeping his arm around her waist, he let her down and ordered, "Let's go."

"Where?" she asked, but her question didn't interfere with her headlong flight beside him.

"To the house. To my bed."

Chapter 7

To your bed?" She jerked him to a stop. "I would be ruined in your bed."

With a stately nod, he agreed. "That's true."

"My reputation would be destroyed."

"No doubt. And no doubt, too, you've lain awake in your virgin bed, dreaming of the sweetness of love." He leaned close, so close that the scent of him mixed with the scent of new leaves and new life. "There'll be little sweetness between us. In my bed, it will be hot and sweaty. There'll be a stab of pain and endless craving. Little mercy, but a wave of passion. Once you're in my bed, you'll never forget it. You'll never leave it."

Faint with the promise of desire, she whispered, "I won't want to leave it."

Even in the dark she could see the fire in his eyes. "Promise me something."

"Anything." She couldn't believe she'd said it, but she had no second thoughts.

"Promise me you'll stop padding your bosom."

Her jaw dropped.

He lowered his face to hers, and nose to nose he said, "You don't need it. Your breasts are round and sweet and need no augmentation. Promise me."

Whatever she'd expected, it wasn't that, and she contented him with one numb nod of the head. As if he couldn't resist, he snatched a kiss and led her on. The house loomed before them, all the windows lit with the glow of candlelight. Her feet faltered as it reached out to illuminate their disorder. The extravagance of their hunger seemed more at home in the woods, in the dark, with the sky above them and the ground below. The civilization implied by four walls and a roof oppressed.

He felt her hesitate, for he caught her close. Chest to chest, he kissed her until her knees buckled and logic flew away. Then he urged her with his arm around her waist. "The servants will be in bed. We'll go around the back by the stables."

She glanced at him and blushed. He looked almost savage in intent, like a great dark lion protecting his mate. His hair swung untamed about his shoulders, his skin taut across his cheekbones. His mouth looked ready to devour her, and a shiver ran up her spine when she considered it.

What a willing sacrifice she would be.

They crept onto the wide veranda. Adam tried the door into the darkened parlor. It opened with a click. Putting his finger to his lips, he signaled her inside. Once there, she didn't know if they'd ever go any farther. He kissed her, and she wanted his knee between her legs again. She didn't know why she liked that so much, why something magnificent had almost happened, but he incited her curiosity.

With every step toward the hall he touched her, caressed her. Yet a whinny through the open outside door struck her with horror and she burst out, "We forgot the horse."

"What?" He stared as if he were as lost to the world as she.

The fire in his gray eyes almost made her forget, but she gasped, "The horse. The cart."

"The horse? My God, the horse!"

He looked so amazed, she laughed. He laughed. It was the exhilaration of the night, quickly roused, quickly extinguished, and that was how Northrup found them.

"Sir?" Northrup lifted his candle. "Can I help you?"

Appearing as astounded and guilty as she felt, Adam stammered, "Northrup!" He recovered and stepped in front of her. "Northrup, what are you doing up at such an hour?"

"It's not late, sir. Almost midnight. I was working on the figures you requested for the South Sea Company." Northrup craned his neck to see Bronwyn, and his mouth tightened. "I think you'd be interested in them."

"In the morning, Northrup," Adam said.

"Now, sir." Lifting his candle high, Northrup displayed a stubborn streak Bronwyn had never noted before. "I must insist you see the figures now."

As if he couldn't stand to let her go, Adam's grip on Bronwyn's wrist tightened. His fingers trembled, then relaxed. "Of course. If you would give me a moment to wish Bronwyn a pleasant sleep."

Northrup didn't move.

"I'll only be a moment," Adam insisted.

Surprised to find Adam complying with Northrup's demand, Bronwyn watched Northrup's retreat with accusing eyes.

Adam reached out one hand to touch her lower lip, and it lingered there. "I can't take you upstairs now. You must see that."

She couldn't see any such thing.

"Dearest, Northrup would come after me with a gun if I laid another hand on you."

"It's not Northrup's business." Her shaky voice betrayed her indignation.

"He's a gentleman. He's made it his business." His mouth twisted in a self-deprecating grimace. "What's more, he's undoubtedly right, damn him."

His regret soothed her, if only a little. "Come later," she urged.

He laughed as if he were in pain. "Little devil. You stand there and tempt me with yourself, then you tempt me with your words." He took her hand, then dropped it as if her flesh burned him. "No, I won't come later. Come." He led her into the hall and to the staircase. "Allow me my good sense."

She followed reluctantly. "Why?"

Lifting her onto the first step as if she were too fragile to climb it herself, he smiled tenderly at her. "Because I'm the man and men are more pragmatic than women."

Under the prod of lights and frustration, her tumult faded just a little, and she grumbled, "You jest."

He seemed not at all offended. "Allow me my illusions." He whipped the forgotten garland off her head and presented it with a flourish. "Dream of me."

Eyes locked with his, she stumbled up a couple of steps and turned. She walked up two more, glanced back. He observed her with such interest, she wanted to roll down onto his feet. She restrained herself, watching instead as he strolled in through the open door to his study. Then she withered down onto the staircase and pressed her face against the banister.

What a man! If what she'd experienced in his arms was half what her wedding night would bring, she'd give him a child to force his hand. Giggling softly at such whimsy, she didn't listen at first to the murmur of male voices.

But the murmur grew, and she had to listen when Northrup's voice rang out. "Sir, she's a gentlewoman! You can't treat her like a trollop."

Adam's cool voice answered, "Apparently I can."

Stiffening, she wanted to go upstairs, but a dreadful inquisitiveness held her in place.

"I saw her," Northrup said. "She had stars in her eyes. I know you're a cold bastard, but even for you your actions are dastardly."

"What, exactly, are my actions?"

"You're creating false hopes in that girl. I heard what you said about her when she arrived, I saw how angry you were at being cheated out of your beautiful bride. Are you seeking some kind of revenge? Bronwyn can't help it if she's homely."

"I wouldn't call her homely," Adam interposed.

"Good," Northrup said sarcastically. "Call her ugly, you bastard."

From inside the study, Bronwyn heard the rattle of cut glass against a decanter and knew Adam poured himself a drink.

She didn't want a drink. All the ale she'd consumed came back to haunt her now, and she felt sick when Northrup continued, "I know why you're marrying her.

She's an Edana. She'll open doors for you, assist you as you join the cream of society. She'll keep out of your way. Aren't those reasons enough to be happy with your bargain? Do you have to seduce Bronwyn, too?"

"But it's so easy." Adam sounded light, amused, and Bronwyn bit the back of her hand to keep back a sob. "Who knows, Northrup? Perhaps if I seduce her, it will so addle her brains she'll lose that distressing tendency we discussed."

"What tendency?"

If Northrup sounded suspicious, it was nothing compared to the foreboding Bronwyn experienced, and she put her hand to her mouth.

"The tendency to sound learned."

Bronwyn groped behind her, found the riser, scooted her bottom up one step. With that supercilious voice, he'd sliced her to ribbons. She didn't want to hear any more, but when he spoke she couldn't help but hear.

"It's well known if a woman is kept busy in the bedroom and in the nursery, she'll have no time to make a fool of herself."

A fool of herself? She went up another step. How could she make a bigger fool of herself than she'd made tonight? In the woods, in the parlor, she'd been embarrassed by Adam, by her response, but only because she wasn't used to such intimacy. Now she was ashamed, and she could kill him for destroying even the memory of physical enjoyment for her.

She knew he wanted her to be someone she wasn't. She'd always known it, but she thought they were reaching some kind of accord. He seemed so interested tonight when she'd told him about the Gaelic manuscripts.

It struck her like a blow, and she leaned her head onto her knees. Oh, God, had she truly told him about the manuscripts? Wasn't it a figment of her imagination, created by a combination of her longing for empathy and the abundance of church ale? She hadn't told anyone about those manuscripts for years. When she'd left Ireland, the nuns had let her take them, wrapped in brown paper and tied with a prayer. They'd let her take them in the hopes she'd translate and return them. Every spare moment she'd worked on those translations, telling no one for fear they'd object because the manuscripts were Irish, or because they were Catholic, or because she was a woman and she might "sound learned."

She whispered the words, "Sound learned." It tasted bitter in her mouth, as bitter as the tears that trickled down. In a flurry, she stood and scrambled up the stairs.

If only she could hate Adam. She *should* hate Adam, but one night had proved the truth of Olivia's accusation. She loved him, and she didn't think she'd ever be able to rip that awful emotion from her soul.

Like an avenging angel, Bronwyn stalked into the breakfast room.

"You look refreshed." Adam stood and smiled, all his charm directed at her. "Did you dream about your future husband?"

She shriveled him with a glare. At least she tried to shrivel him, but he seemed unaffected. As she went to examine the sideboard where the food rested, he strode to her side. Taking her chin in his hand, he dropped a kiss on her lips. She didn't respond, didn't swoon, didn't even close her eyes, and he frowned. "Too much ale? Still half glazed? I've got something to make you feel better."

"I feel fine." She spoke without unclenching her teeth, a clear signal, she thought, that she wished him in hell.

He didn't pick up on the signal. Instead, he turned her toward the table and gave her a little shove. "Go sit. I'll fix you a plate."

In lieu of Adam, she glared at the other occupants of the table. "Olivia, we missed you last night."

"So I told her." Adam placed a heaping plate in front of his betrothed and slipped onto the chair beside her. "I suspect the festivities would have cured her headache."

"And your mother," Bronwyn said. "Where was she?"

"She made no excuses, sent no regrets." His warm chuckle sent an unwanted thrill along her nerves. "I believe she hoped the evening would fall out much as it did, but without the roadblock Northrup represented."

"She would." That sounded like Mab, and Bronwyn knew she wouldn't scold the lady. Friends they might be, but Bronwyn never made the mistake of presuming on Mab's good nature. If a situation would further her son's happiness, Mab did what she perceived necessary, and damn the consequences. As Adam poured her milk, Bronwyn looked at the food before her. "I can't eat all this."

"It's a seaman's breakfast. No one knows more about curing a hangover than a seaman." Adam picked up her fork and inserted it into her hand. "Now eat."

"I'm not ill."

He put a piece of bread into her open mouth. "Chew."

She could do no less, and Olivia giggled behind her hand. Adam winked at Olivia, saying, "Your sister's not a person who rises with a smile, I see."

"No," Olivia admitted. She squirmed, swallowed, as if the effort of conversation with Lord Rawson intimidated her. But the sight of Bronwyn's misery must have moved her to pity, for with a visible effort she added, "She likes to work late, and that affects her disposition."

"On the manuscripts?" Adam asked.

As Olivia gaped at them both, he cut a bit of beef and fed it, rather forcibly, to Bronwyn. "Oh, yes, she's told me about them. Do you share her interest?"

Mute with surprise, Olivia shook her head.

"A pity. It sounds fascinating."

"She says it is." Something about Adam's interest must have convinced Olivia to speak, for she added, "When she tells me tales of early Ireland, I'm engrossed. But the work seems tedious and difficult to me."

"I can't imagine the patience such work requires," Adam said.

"I'm glad you support her." Like a swimmer preparing to submerge, Olivia took a breath, then another, and appealed to him with enormous eyes. "I believe Bronwyn would run away rather than give up her precious studies."

Bronwyn moved aside from the threatening fork. "Perhaps after the wedding I'll be so witless with love I'll no longer entertain notions above my womanly station."

Adam's gaze sharpened on her rebellious face. "More bread," he decided, and barely avoided losing a finger as he fed it to her. "With a tutor such as I, you'll be proficient in both love and learning." He grinned, inviting her humor, but she scowled. Puzzled but determined, he said, "In fact, I have a present for your feminine side, something I ordered just for you." From beside the jug of milk, he lifted an ivory fan. As he spread it wide, the lace scrolls and carvings gleamed with gold leaf trim.

Admiration overwhelmed Olivia's reserve. "It's a work of art."

"It's from China," he told them. "It has no edges to fray, no silk to destroy. You can pick at it all day, Bronwyn, and you'll not hurt it."

Fury, instant and blinding, roiled through her veins. How dare he? How dare he spell out his preference for a different woman so blatantly? He didn't want *her*, he wanted an elegant caricature of her. Never in her life had she spit food into someone's face, but she was tempted now.

He knew it. Wary as an unarmed man facing a bear, he asked, "Bronwyn? What have I said?"

From her other side, Olivia murmured, "Bronwyn? He's being nice to you. Really, he's being quite pleasant."

Her sister's frightened voice shattered Bronwyn's mad impulse. "Thank you, my lord." Careful not to touch his hand, she took the fan. "I'll never forget this moment." She paused. "Will you be working with Mr. Northrup this day?"

Adam straightened, his mouth a grim line. "Not today. Northrup has quit me, I'm afraid, and I'll have to find another secretary."

"He's quit?" Olivia asked, startled. "But I understood his employment was necessary. That is . . ."

"Quite so. But his newfound wealth from his dabblings in the stocks will provide for him. The only thing between him and the top of the ladder . . . is the ladder. Northrup is not important." He dismissed Northrup without a qualm. "Secretaries are easily replaced."

"So are fiancées," Bronwyn said.

"Bronwyn!" Olivia gasped.

Adam ignored her rudeness. Keeping his gaze fixed

on Bronwyn, he suggested, "I had hoped I could give you a personal tour of the house today. Explore the gardens. I'm anxious to show my bride the wonders Campbell designed for our home."

Olivia clapped her hands with pleasure and said, "A novel idea."

"Then you'll accompany us?" Adam asked.

"I'd love to." Olivia touched her sister's cheek. "If you don't mind, Bronwyn?"

"Not at all." Olivia remembered her duties as chaperone late, Bronwyn thought, but she stretched her lips into a smile. "Perhaps, for the sake of efficiency, it would be better if you left me to finish my breakfast alone."

"Of course." He stood and extended a hand to Olivia. "We'll meet in the drawing room when you've finished."

Bronwyn nodded and watched as they left, arm in arm. They made an attractive couple, she thought, lifting her hand to her mouth and biting her thumbnail. The gift of the fan had softened Olivia's prejudice against Adam. The fact that Bronwyn had told Adam about the manuscripts, and that he had approved, seemed to weigh heavily in his favor. Even now, Olivia was losing her fear of Adam, and she was the wife he described to Northrup. Beautiful and kind.

And he—he was gentle with Olivia. He'd never subject her to his scorn, or his passion.

Leaving the fan, she went upstairs to pack.

Adam lifted his sherry to the setting sun and stared through the window, open now to the cooling breezes. He was thinking of Bronwyn's eyes, thinking of the scorn he'd seen reflected there so often today.

What was the matter with the woman? If she disliked him, she'd certainly concealed it well last night. In fact—his hand tightened on the cut glass until tiny points bit into his palm—she'd been all he'd ever dreamed of, all he'd ever wanted. True, he shouldn't have urged her to join him in his bed. And that business last night with Northrup had been embarrassing. Only too well he knew the need for privacy when passion held sway. Only too well he knew how ale loosened inhibitions.

Today he'd tried to tell her, explain to her, that passion was nothing to be ashamed of. But she was having none of him.

He rubbed his aching leg. He'd walked too far, danced too much, while trying to make the lady happy.

Clearly Olivia had been puzzled by Bronwyn's behavior, also. During the tour of the house and garden, Bronwyn had spoken of the property in ringing tones, calling its fine points to Olivia's attention. If he didn't know better, he would have thought she was selling the property to her sister.

The only explanation he could conceive, the only explanation that made any sense at all, was that she'd heard Northrup's reproaches last night. If that were the case, he'd have the devil's own time convincing her of his blamelessness. He should have defended her, he supposed. He should have said that conventional scorn for educated women was so much nonsense, that he'd rather have Bronwyn than those silly twits who cared only for their gloves and fans.

But in truth, he felt like a man who'd been served oatmeal mush and discovered a diamond at the bottom. He couldn't decide which actions would be correct. Most especially, he couldn't quite decide if he liked being so surprised. For years he'd survived, *prospered,* by anticipating life, by planning every maneuver, by logically seeking an opponent's weakness and exploiting it. Yet he'd never imagined a woman like Bronwyn. From the first moment they'd met, she'd upended his expectations. She'd broadsided him with surprises, and he feared he wasn't the ice man he had previously believed. His mother claimed he wasn't cold, that he wore a mask, and he'd denied it vigorously.

Masks could be stripped away, destroyed.

So last night, he should have defended her against Northrup's poisoned kindness, yet the shaft contained within his breeches had left him feeling perverse. Adam had bought this wife to protect him from the contempt of society, and instead he found himself having to defend her. And not just having to defend her— wanting to defend her. He wanted to build a wall around her, protect her from the arrows of contempt shot at learned women. Emotions he'd believed to be atrophied were laid bare, and he didn't know how to conceal them—or even if he should.

He heard the crunch of carriage wheels on the gravel drive, and he relaxed. Bronwyn's parents were back from their revels in London. They would advise him on how to handle their prickly daughter, he was sure. He waited, listening for Lord Gaynor's hearty call, for Lady Nora's tinkling voice.

He heard nothing. The carriage waited at the front door, an unusual stillness about it. The door opened and shut, ever so quietly, and the coachman spoke to one who failed to answer.

Assailed by a dreadful suspicion, Adam stood and leaned out the window. He couldn't quite see the carriage, only the horses as they stirred restively. The springs creaked as someone entered the carriage. They creaked again as the coachman mounted to his box. Someone was leaving. Someone who didn't wish it known.

With a crack of the whip, the carriage sprang forward, and there she was. Eyes forward, chin thrust out, Bronwyn rode away in *his* rig. Propelling himself through the casement, he howled like a madman. He tumbled onto the porch, raced down the steps. "Bronwyn!" he roared. "Damn you, come back!" The carriage never paused, gaining speed as it bowled along *his* driveway, the driveway he'd taken care to make smooth.

Impetuous as a boy, he ran, and his leg gave way. He sprawled facefirst on the gravel. He tried to stand, but the pain of his old wound knocked him down again. Spitting rock, he watched the carriage as it rolled out of sight.

With the dawn, Bronwyn's eyes opened on a new room. A small room, elegantly furnished, it manifested a taste for light furniture, light colors. Through the open window on the third story, she heard the first calls of the vendors, the rattle of a wagon, the cook's voice scolding as she left for the market in the heart of London. She smelled smoke and the stink of the river, ever-present as the weather warmed. This was the start of a new life, yet her thoughts leaped back to yesterday, and she said aloud, "I'm not going to compromise myself for him."

Rachelle's voice agreed, "Nor should you."

Startled, Bronwyn stared at the lady in the doorway. Rachelle hadn't changed since their encounter last month. Still thin, still kind, she radiated a strength, an anger, that overrode the sorrow in her eyes.

"As I told you last night, you are welcome to stay with me as long as you wish." Entering the room with a maid on her heels, she indicated a small table. "Place *le petit déjeuner* there." Rachelle remained silent as the maid set out the tray and left. "Is your mind still made up?"

"I said it was."

"Only a fool never has second thoughts." After arranging a comfortable chair beside the bed, Rachelle sank down with a sigh.

"It's no shame to be without a husband," Bronwyn said.

"It is no great honor, either." Dry humor lined Rachelle's face. "It is a man's world, and a man can smooth the way. Believe me." She tapped her chest. "I know."

"Why do you seek to dissuade me?"

"I would be remiss if I did not warn you of the thorny road you tread. Adam Keane will not take his dismissal lightly."

"Then he shouldn't have insulted me so." Bronwyn flounced up on the bed, plumping the pillows behind her. "I expected better of him."

"As women have been doing of their men for centuries." Rachelle poured the tea. "And almost always have been sorely disappointed, I might add. Do you wish for something to eat?"

"No." Bronwyn slipped from the mattress. With agitated movements she drew the curtains and gazed on Rachelle's tiny yard, at the stables, the fence, the alley. "I couldn't eat. I feel so . . . betrayed."

"Betrayed? By a man?" Years of bitterness ran in Rachelle's tone. "You would be ill advised to expect anything else."

"Then I was ill advised." Hugging herself, Bronwyn turned to Rachelle.

Rachelle stood and advanced, caught her chin. "You are young. It would not be natural if you were not impulsive. Just so my Henriette was, not too long ago, yet she was wiser than you."

"How can you say so?"

"I had taught her the danger of loving too much." Rachelle's eyes filled with tears. "I am afraid I taught her never to love. She was, in her own way, cold and seeking, willing to use a man's foibles for her own advancement."

Bronwyn's anger cooled at the sight of Rachelle's grief. "What do you suspect?"

"Men speak of many things at my salon. I suspect she heard something she should not have and made it known. Anyone who attempts blackmail reaps a bitter harvest, and Henriette was young and untried."

"Have you discovered the identity of the man who hurt her so dreadfully?"

"The man who killed her?" The tears overflowed, dripped off Rachelle's chin, and she made no attempt to wipe them away. "You might as well say it. He killed her. *Non*, I have no suspects. The young lord who pursued her sobbed at her funeral, offered me the services of his men to beat *la canaille* should I ascertain his name. All of London buzzed with excitement, seeking the murderer who could lure my daughter with no struggle into his net, but nothing came of it."

Bronwyn drew a handkerchief from the sleeve of her nightgown and handed it over. "Is it someone she knew?"

"So I believe." Rachelle accepting the offering and dabbed her face.

"Has someone disappeared from your gatherings?"

"Non." Determination transformed Rachelle. "So I will find him, the man with *le visage fardé.*"

"I don't understand."

"Le visage fardé means literally 'the painted face.' " At the table, Rachelle lifted a cover. "I would better say it is one who dissembles."

"I see." The yeasty scent made Bronwyn's mouth water. Rolls of every shape were piled there, recalling her diminished appetite of the day before. She was hungry after all. Taking a roll, still warm and soft, she said, "When I arrived, I didn't tell you my plan."

Rachelle collected herself. "Tell me now."

"I have in my possession Gaelic manuscripts, epics of a time long past. Some I have translated, some I still labor over, but I know they would be of interest to the public. If I could find a sponsor, I would publish them—"

Lifting her hand, Rachelle commanded, "Say no more. I will sponsor you until we can find better."

"There can be no better," Bronwyn said fervently.

"Princess Caroline, wife of the Prince of Wales, would hardly be complimented." Rachelle nodded. "I believe she could be pursuaded to pension you, to support your aspirations."

A little smile crept up on Bronwyn. "That would be flattering."

"You are worthy." Rachelle cocked her head. "In the meantime, I would be complimented if you would join our salon as one of our luminaries. You will join our evenings as a language expert, if you would."

"Oh, yes. It's what I've dreamed of."

Crumbling bread between her fingers, Rachelle said, "When Monsieur le Vicomte arrives, you will be distant and cold."

Bronwyn clutched her throat.

Rachelle watched Bronwyn carefully. "Had you not thought he would visit?"

"No." Bronwyn's heart started a slow, steady thump as she thought of seeing him again. Fingers trembling, she placed the roll on her plate.

"He is a serious man, with serious concerns. In my salon, he finds people who think as he does, speak of matters interesting to him. He comes, perhaps not as often as he would like, but he comes."

"Do you know why . . . ?" Bronwyn shifted, uncomfortable to be prying into his affairs yet unable to resist the temptation. "That is, I can't get anyone to tell me why he's so serious."

"No, your parents would not tell the blushing bride the details of the disgrace, would they?" Rachelle said with a bite in her voice.

"The disgrace?" Bronwyn remembered Lord Gaynor's words and guessed, "It's something to do with his father, isn't it?"

"It is indeed. But you must understand my knowledge is only hearsay. At the time of *le père infamant*, I lived not in England."

"Rumor is better than no information at all."

"This I know for sure. His father was hanged for counterfeiting."

"Nonsense!" Bronwyn reacted with skepticism. "Adam's father was the viscount of Rawson, his mother is the daughter of a duke. There's no way the Crown would have ordered him to be hanged."

"The story says he dangled on Tyburn Hill almost before Adam's ship cleared the harbor. Adam's mother was destitute, starving. When Adam returned, he searched and found her, at last, in a workhouse. They say her bones poked from her skin, that he had to feed her liquids only."

"Oh, come now."

"They say that with Adam's help, the director of the workhouse died in the worst slums of London."

Her hand lifted to admonish, Bronwyn paused. That sounded too true. Adam would wreak vengeance with the rancor of the Furies. "But Mab is immense."

"His mother? So would I be, had I ever starved," Rachelle said with composure.

"Do they gossip about it?"

"They? Do you refer to the cream of English society as 'they'?" Rachelle laughed at Bronwyn's grimace. "Of course they gossip. Adam fans the gossip, with his growing fortune and his scorn for their shallow activities. It all combines to cause a great deal of envy, a great deal of speculation about him."

"I still can't believe . . ." But Bronwyn could almost believe. It explained so much. Adam's fury when he'd met her. His willingness to take her for the prestige of her family. Even his lack of pity for the noble family whose lands he had bought. A man who had nothing, not even a reputation, would hardly pity a nobleman who'd had everything and thrown it away.

Covering her eyes, Bronwyn said, "I can't see him."

Rachelle's mouth twisted in pity, and her brown eyes shone with comprehension. Prying Bronwyn's hands away from her face, she said, "Are you a child who believes such behavior renders you invisible? He will see you." Bronwyn started to protest, but Rachelle lifted one finger. "You cannot hide in this room forever. He will see you. But if you will listen to me, he will never notice who you are."

"What do you mean?"

"Trust me." Rachelle rolled up her sleeves. "We begin at once."

Chapter 8

"Where is she?" Adam tried to get out of bed; he wanted to put his hands around Olivia's white throat and rattle her until she spoke.

"Son, the doctor said you'd be well with a few days bed rest." Mab pressed him back on his pillows. "As long as you stay in bed."

He glared at the assemblage. Still in their travel clothes, Lord Gaynor and Lady Nora paced or fretted as befitting their respective natures. Olivia sat on a chair, twisting her hands. Mab hovered over him as if she'd catch him should he try to escape.

All through the night he'd tossed with pain and fury. He'd been right at the first. Bronwyn was nothing but an unattractive spinster. How could he have thought he wanted to marry her? He'd been seduced by a lively mind, a lovely smile, a pert curiosity. But at the same time, he wanted her back. He wanted to love her, show her what she was giving up, make her beg to wed him. His contrary emotions made his head whirl, and he insisted, "Damn it, I want to know where she is."

Lord Gaynor thrust his hand toward Adam to stop him. Kneeling before Olivia as if she were a child, he coaxed, "Come, tell us. Where do you think Bronwyn is?"

"I don't know for sure," Olivia faltered.

"Yes?" Lord Gaynor encouraged.

Biting her lip, she said, "She said she wanted to live away from society, away from men. I don't know . . . I thought maybe . . ."

"Maybe what?" Adam roared.

She jumped, but his anger seemed to galvanize her, and she said defiantly, "I thought maybe she wanted to go to a convent."

No one spoke. No one moved. Every eye in the room rested on Olivia in frozen horror.

The wind had been knocked from Adam, seizing his reason. Bronwyn? His plain little fiancée, with her hidden repository of passion, of humor, in a convent? It wasn't possible.

"A convent?" Lord Gaynor whispered at last. "No, lass, tell me it's not true."

Olivia stared down at her own hands. "But, Da, you remember how much she enjoyed working at the convent in Ireland. She spent hours with their books, and talking to Brother Brendan when he visited."

Toe tapping, Lady Nora snapped, "That was one of the reasons we moved you girls to England. You were getting too attached to the Papist customs, and that would have been fatal to our aspirations."

The voice of reason, Mab interceded. "Bronwyn and I spoke many times about many things, and I never saw any evidence of such a vocation. What would cause such a change of heart?"

Olivia blushed and hung her head, her color all the more pronounced in her fair skin.

Regaining his voice, Adam asked, "Mab, did you tell Bronwyn about my father?" Mab shook her head. "Did you, Lord Gaynor? Lady Nora?" They denied it, and he fixed Olivia with a look that stripped her to the bone. "Did Bronwyn know about my father?"

Too frightened to speak, Olivia shook her head.

"Then this convent theory is the stupidest I have ever heard," Adam pronounced.

Olivia looked up, eyes flashing with some of the fire he'd come to associate with Bronwyn. "I don't know, with any certainty, why she'd want to join a convent. All I know is—Lord Rawson kissed her."

He bounded up under the sting of insult and betrayal and hardly noticed the pain. "She told you, did she? Well, I tell you this. When I get her in my bed, I'll do a damn sight more than kiss her."

"Wait." Lady Nora held up one long, white hand. "It seems we're making too much of this. Bronwyn is not irreplaceable. We have two daughters of marriageable age."

"What?" The cry broke from every throat.

"Maman, no," Olivia whispered.

Every gaze accused Lady Nora of coldness, and she hastened to smooth the ruffled feathers. "Of course I'm concerned about Bronwyn. She's my beloved daughter. But I'm also concerned that this alliance between our houses not be jeopardized."

"Just what she planned," Adam muttered. Every gaze turned on him, and he realized it was the truth. Bronwyn had planned this. What had she said? That fiancées were easily replaced. Her defection lashed at his pride, at his newly discovered emotions. Emotions he would now relegate to their proper place in his life. Emotions he could starve for lack of nutrition. "Do I understand you correctly? You are suggesting a betrothal between Olivia and me?"

Lady Nora shrank back from the fire of his demand. "Well, I . . . yes."

Seeking to slacken her discomfort, he smiled, but it didn't seem to ease the tension in the room. "An excellent idea. Have my new secretary write up the contract. I will sign it today. I do not understand how I ever imagined an impetuous young woman like Bronwyn would be a suitable mate for a man as cold as I."

"My dear, from the first moment I saw you, my fingers have itched to redesign you." Rachelle stepped from in front of the mirror and pushed Bronwyn forward. "Look."

Bronwyn looked but saw no one she knew.

Then, with a start, she did. It was Bronwyn in the mirror, but no Bronwyn she'd ever seen before. Her hair hung loose, a tangle of unsubdued curls, tied in a ribbon at the back of her head. Its pale blond color accented the tan on her face and made her appear foreign. Rachelle's charcoal wand had darkened her lashes, and they swept around eyes that sparkled with the flavor of the exotic. Her cheeks flushed peach. Her mouth was colored, vivid, showing off the lips her mother complained were too wide. A borrowed emerald-green dress, devoid of decoration, brought length to her body, slimming it until she suspected she would sway like a reed in the wind. In a dream, she reached out a hand to herself. "Rachelle, I'm beautiful."

"So you are."

"I've never seen myself like this." Bronwyn pursed her lips, wiggled her brows. Convinced that woman in the mirror was really Bronwyn Edana, she asked, "Didn't my mother know?"

"How could she?" Rachelle produced a Gallic shrug. "She is English."

"Do you think I'm as pretty as my sisters?"

Perceiving the deep insecurity underlying the question, Rachelle replied patiently, "Your sisters are all women cut from the same stamp. If a man cannot have one of them, he will be satisfied with another. You are unique."

Bronwyn turned with a laughing face. "Is that a tactful way to tell me no?"

Brushing a lock of hair away from Bronwyn's face, Rachelle said, "It is the only way I can think to tell you that there is no comparison."

"My hair." Bronwyn touched it with shy fingers, afraid it would somehow disappear. "Can I wear it loose like this? Won't the matrons whisper I look ready to bed?"

"And the gentlemen, too, I vow." Rachelle pulled one lock over Bronwyn's shoulder. "All will be mad with envy, and you will start a new fashion. We will call you 'Cherie,' and you will be the toast of London."

"I can't wait to be seen." Lifting her arms, Bronwyn twirled in a circle.

"You are in for a shock."

Bronwyn halted. "Why?"

"All your life, you have been recognized as an intelligent woman. Perhaps the men were not enticed by it, but they respected it." Rachelle took her charcoal pencil and touched Bronwyn's brows. "The more attractive a woman is, the less a man thinks of her intellect."

"You mean they'll think I'm stupid?"

"Oui." Rachelle studied the results and turned Bronwyn back to the mirror. As Bronwyn preened, Rachelle said, "When in truth, it is quite the opposite. An attractive woman makes a man stupid."

Bronwyn paid no attention to Rachelle. "When Adam comes, I'll demonstrate my independence to him. I'll make him sorry he thought I was ugly. I'll make him squirm."

Rachelle interrupted her gloating. "Why do you care what he thinks?"

Meeting Rachelle's eyes in the mirror, Bronwyn flushed miserably and looked away.

"My invitation to stay with me remains open," Rachelle said gently, "but it grieves me it is being used as a refuge against love."

"I don't want rest," Adam roared. "I just want my walking stick."

Suffering as only a servant caught between the mill and the stone could suffer, the footman said, "Lady Mab says I must help you to the couch. She says you've been working too much and are in pain. She says—"

"My mother is a—"

From the doorway of his study, Mab said, "Your mother knows where Bronwyn is, and if you'll stop acting like an ass, she'll tell you."

Adam halted in midroar, his hand frozen in an uplifted position, his head thrown back. Slowly he pivoted to face his mother. "Mab?"

She settled onto a chair beside the couch, her needlework in her hands, ignoring his most charming smile.

Waving the servant out of the room, he interrogated, "Where is she? Is she in a convent? Is she taking her vows?" Mab unrolled her canvas and separated her threads, and Adam cursed aloud.

For four weeks he had sought the missing girl. Not because it concerned him, of course, but because her parents were worried. Now, he would indulge his mother by resting this wretched leg that so persistently pained him. Leaving his desk, he limped over to ease himself onto the couch.

She observed him as he placed his foot up. "If you hadn't tried to chase after her the day you fell, you wouldn't still be suffering."

"To say 'I told you so' is most unattractive." Her gentle smile graced him, and he whispered, "Where is she?"

"Why should I tell you? So you can go shout at her until she knows she did the right thing by fleeing this accursed prearranged marriage?" He opened his mouth to object, but she waggled that motherly finger, and he subsided. "You never wanted to hear what I thought of your grand plan to return respectability to our family, but you'll hear it now."

Subsiding onto the pillows, he rested on his spine, tucked his chin down on his chest, and thrust his hands into his pockets.

"How sulky you look," she observed. "Like a child about to be scolded."

He wiggled his shiny boots and stared at them. "Aren't I?"

She ignored his pique as she ignored his impatience. "Adam, this honor you hold so dear is of a lesser importance. It's the family that matters. You are my son, the only person in this world who has ever loved me.

Like any mother, I cherish a dream for your future. I want you to be happy. For you, I dream of a wife who treasures you for yourself, not for your money. I dream of a wife picked not for her breeding ability or her fine lineage."

He'd been too impatient to allow his valet to shave him this last week, and he rubbed his fingers across his chin. "What are you saying? You want me to marry her, don't you?"

"I want you to marry Bronwyn. I don't want you to marry Olivia."

Under her gaze, so similar to his own, he complained, "Bronwyn left me. Doesn't she realize the favor I'd done by agreeing to marry her?"

Mab rubbed her eyes, looked at her son, rubbed her eyes again. To no one in particular, she said, "It doesn't appear to be the prince of dreams sitting on that bed. It appears to be Adam, but perhaps my vision is at fault."

He sighed.

"You've become conceited," she admonished.

"I have not. It's just Bronwyn is so—" He was going to say homely, but he'd imagined her stripped of her clothing, and he knew she would be fatally alluring.

"Olivia is no woman for you," Mab said. "She'll melt like slush beneath a carriage wheel the first time you scowl at her. Already she scurries into a corner every time you approach."

"I know. Olivia will never do."

"Bronwyn fulfills your requirements, and she fulfills my requirements, also. She's a fine girl, with a swift mind and a generous heart. Even you, for all your smug blindness, have realized that."

Adam rubbed his hand through his hair, torturing the black swirls. "Yes, I've realized it. But my father—"

"Your father has nothing to do with this." Mab leaned toward him in earnest appeal. "He wasted a plentiful fortune, abandoned us to the wolves, brought us from an estate to a cottage, but what difference does that make? You and I were happy in that cottage, boy, and he was never happy for all his spendthrift ways."

"He brought you to the workhouse," he said, savage in his bitterness.

"You found me."

"Barely in time." He swung his legs down and braced himself against the floor. "I have got the money. Now I want the respect."

Placing her veined hand across her forehead, Mab snorted in disbelief. "And you care?"

"Not for myself. But my children will have only the best. The name of Keane will have no blot on it. That's my plan, and it's never wavered."

"Never wavered, but one small woman may destroy it." She smiled slyly. "You *could* marry Olivia."

Coldly, he denied the beautiful Edana daughter. "No, I can see now she will not do. I want Bronwyn back. Will you help me?"

Mab shook her head before he finished speaking. "Absolutely not."

She wouldn't compromise, he knew. Mab sought his cooperation, his sworn word, and he would give it. He would give it because he could never deny his mother and because he had no desire to court Olivia as he had Bronwyn. After all, he reasoned, he'd already made the effort for Bronwyn; why waste his time with Olivia? He sat forward, his elbows on his knees and his hands clasped together. "Where is she, Mab? I'll do as you wish. I'll be a true husband, not treat her as a woman bought with worldly goods. I'll stay in her bed at night and keep her company by day."

"You should be weaving your spells around Bronwyn."

She reproved him, but he knew she'd heard what she wanted. He coaxed, "I will, as soon as you tell me where she is."

"She's living at Madame Rachelle's salon."

He didn't move, didn't blink.

"I was afraid you'd react in such a manner." She lifted her canvas and stabbed her needle into the midst of the flowers, showing too clearly her disgust with her son.

"Madame Rachelle's." He ran his fingers over his lips. "I'm relieved, I suppose. That's better than a convent. How did she find Madame Rachelle's?"

"You'll have to ask her that."

Speaking more to himself than to her, he said, "I should have thought of it myself. Where else would an intelligent, gently bred woman go?"

"Not to you, prince of dreams." She put down her sewing to watch his face. "This is a difficult, awkward situation, but I know you, Adam. You'll treasure Bronwyn all the more for the effort you'll put forth."

He shouldn't ask, but he couldn't contain his curiosity. "Why would you say such a thing to me?"

"The passionate boy you were could not be destroyed. He was only hiding, and I think Bronwyn found him. I think that mask you wear so well crumbles when Bronwyn assaults it, and I think"—she chuckled—"I think Bronwyn doesn't even know what she does."

Adam could no longer refrain from asking the question haunting him. "Has it ever occurred to you, Mab, that perhaps I'm not the man you believe I am?"

"What man is that?"

"You seem to believe that beneath this hard exterior beats a heart filled with compassion. Have you never thought you might be wrong?"

Her lips trembled as if he'd hurt her, and she set a few stitches before she answered. "I only know there's a heart, Adam. I know nothing has killed the passions that drove you as a child. Those passions are redirected, yes, but your eyes still burn with fervor when you discuss a profitable stock transaction, or our family honor"—she looked up and caught him staring—"or Bronwyn. That's why I honor her above all other women. She has shaken you from that arrogance, that coldness you wear so well."

"Mab, if Bronwyn had actually assaulted this mask you say I wear—I'm not saying she did—" His mother appeared unconvinced, and he hastened to finish. "Surely you understand her betrayal has strengthened my determination to be untouched?"

He had admitted to his mother his childish passions still endured. That his soul wasn't frozen. He knew it, she knew it, but she kindly refrained from pointing it out to him. "The question is, will you be able to tamp down these newly discovered affections?" She posed the question, then competently changed the subject. "I'm interested in seeing how you deal with this complication. How will you fetch Bronwyn back?"

"I'll take her from Madame Rachelle's quickly."

She held her needle poised above her canvas. "Is this salon not a respectable place?"

"It is . . . and it isn't. The best minds in Europe can be found there, expounding on science, literature, music. Yet Madame Rachelle herself . . ."

"Is a mystery, I hear." Mab selected another silk and threaded it through her needle. "Is she a courtesan?"

He should never be surprised at his mother's far-reaching connections, he supposed. She knew of the salon, she knew of Bronwyn's lodging there, why wouldn't she know of the mystery surrounding Rachelle? "Not at all. The French nobility seem fond of presenting their daughters to English society through her."

"Their legitimate daughters?"

"No"—a smile hovered—"but they're charming women nevertheless. Several have made brilliant marriages with Madame Rachelle's help."

"Then what is your objection?"

"There are rumors about Madame Rachelle. Unsavory rumors from her past. It is said she's a member of the nobility, was popular at Versailles, yet she left France suddenly. No one knows why." Mab seemed unimpressed, and he continued, "When young women come to her for help, she gives it. She's supported several well-bred English girls who were in desperate straits. Madame Rachelle is kind to a fault. You'd like her, Mab."

"Then why are you worried that Bronwyn is living with her?"

"Because Rachelle is a *salonière,* a free thinker." He turned to look out the window. "If Bronwyn becomes painted with that brush, she loses much of her value to me as an opener of society's doors. Also, Rachelle doesn't live under a man's protection, and regardless of my respect for her, her morals are suspect. So, therefore, would Bronwyn's be."

Mab tucked her lips together in annoyance. "*I* am not a snob, but it would seem my son is."

"A snob?" Adam considered her. "No, I'm not a snob. But I would prefer to know the first child to bear my name is my own."

"Are you questioning. Bronwyn's virtue?" In the

space between each word, Mab inserted disbelief. She tossed down her needlework and rose, fire in her eye. "I tell you, Adam, I have never been ashamed of you before, but I am now. You want this girl. God willing, you will marry her, if you can get Olivia to end this betrothal, and you whine about Bronwyn's virginity! Stop worrying about your precious reputation and start planning how to capture your Bronwyn."

With dignity, she turned, gathered her handiwork, and went to the door. There she fired her final salvo. "I doubt your own virginity bears looking into too closely!"

With that, Mab snapped the door closed, leaving Adam stunned at her vehemence and wondering about the truth.

Was he fooling himself about his feelings toward Bronwyn? It seemed unlikely. On the day his father had taken him, bought him his naval commission, and put him on a ship at the age of twelve, he'd sworn to face life without sentiment or tenderness. Through the years that followed, he'd grown to accept the flawlessness of such a course. True, as the scion of a disgraced English family, he shouldn't marry the black sheep of the Edanas family. But she *was* an Edana, and infinitely better suited to his nature than the fragile Olivia. He believed he could curb Bronwyn's propensity to impetuous action, if in no other manner than with the lessons of the bedchamber.

In fact, Bronwyn Edana stirred him. Even now, he visualized that finely structured face and slender body beneath him in his bed. His fingertips tingled as he recalled the texture of the rosy nipple he had caressed. Suddenly, he came to a decision. Rubbing his chin, he limped to the door and called, "Send my valet up to my room. I need to be shaved."

Chapter 9

 he charming, fascinating, exotic Cherie entered
the large salon. Her silver hair was threaded with
ribbons and tiny flowers, her vivid pink silk dress
hugged her tiny waist and billowed around her feet, she
carried her signature fan—and the men crowded
around her. Cherie was the toast of Madame Rachelle's.
Here she was in her element.

A student of the Royal Academy of Music knew of
her fondness for opera, and the notes of Handel's newest, *Radamisto*, drifted from the harpsichord. Waving
like a princess on parade, she indicated her pleasure,
and he beamed. She smiled an enigmatic smile as she
heard her name called in tones of reverence and desire.

"Mademoiselle Cherie! Please, I have composed an
ode to the goddess of my heart."

She turned to the fledgling poet who thrust his way

forward. "We'll be enchanted to hear it when Madame Rachelle arrives."

The poet stammered under the spell of her sherry-colored eyes, but young Humphrey Webster elbowed him aside. "Mademoiselle Cherie isn't interested in the babblings of a word pusher. Everyone knows she shows a superior interest in scientific experiments. Mademoiselle Cherie, I have brought the one we discussed."

Cherie tapped the pompous youth with her fan. "Mr. Webster, you're being rude. A true scholar is interested in every branch of education."

Webster flushed. "Are you saying you're a scholar?"

"Not at all," she said seriously. "I'm saying you are."

Glancing at the slight poet beside him, Webster chewed his lip. "Of course. But I read only the classics."

"I think Mademoiselle Cherie would tell you that even the classics were new once." With a bow that made his corsets creak, the elderly Lord Sawbridge added, "When I was a boy." He laughed at his own joke, and Cherie joined him. Encouraged, he continued in the ringing tones of the slightly deaf, "Remember Plato, I do. I advised Will Shakespeare on his plays."

"And was the model for Polonius," Webster muttered.

"Heh? What's that?" Lord Sawbridge put his hand to his ear.

"He commented on your wisdom." Cherie stepped away from Sawbridge's wandering fingers with an ease born of weeks of practice.

Sawbridge smirked, presenting a long, thin package. "For you, mademoiselle."

"*Merci, Monsieur le Duc.* You are most kind."

Tearing away the tissue, Cherie spread the ivory fan wide and held it aloft. "*Ah, c'est très beau, non?*"

Blushing like a boy, Sawbridge said, "I saw it and thought of you. . . ."

"A fitting addition to my collection," she assured him. He turned his cheek as if expecting a more concrete form of thanks, but she pretended she hadn't seen. Instead, she smiled on the three young blades who crowded forward. "I don't believe we've been introduced."

"No, mademoiselle," they chorused.

The most extravagantly dressed of the three stepped forward. "We've heard tales of your charm and beauty and came to see if it was the truth." All three bowed. "We are in awe."

"Awe will not earn you a place at Madame Rachelle's salon," she reproved. "You must be ready to learn, and to share your knowledge with others." She linked arms with two of the gentlemen and strolled forward, her admirers following like a train behind her. "Our function here is to encourage the arts and sciences."

She would have continued, but a circle of men and women crowded the center of the large salon, and from the depths of the group she could hear Daphne's voice. She shut her fan with a snap. What was the girl up to now? Daphne had a reputation for saying what she liked.

The evening was young, and Cherie functioned as unofficial hostess until Rachelle arrived. Having excused herself from her devotees, she insinuated herself between two gentlemen, and using her elbows, she edged forward to hear Daphne pronounce, "Male body parts are the converse of female body parts, facilitating the mating procedure."

Before Cherie could stagger under the shock, the man she feared most asked, "Where did you learn that?"

Adam.

In an instant transformation, the scintillating Cherie became plain Bronwyn. She couldn't breathe. Her heart functioned haphazardly, beating in bursts of speed and sudden cessations. She touched her forehead and found it beaded with sweat.

He was here, just as Rachelle had predicted four weeks ago, and she still wasn't ready to face him. She'd never be ready to face him.

Yet when Daphne answered proudly, "Out of a book," Bronwyn knew she must move, but she couldn't seem to tear her feet from the rug.

A murmur rippled through the assembly, and Bronwyn remembered how kind Rachelle had been to her. She couldn't allow this to continue, but before she could act, Adam spoke again. "Did they explain what happens when the male is aroused?"

Propelled by horror, Bronwyn squeezed forward. Catching Daphne's wrist, she squeezed.

"Cherie!" Daphne said. "I've been having a fascinating discussion with *Monsieur le Vicomte*."

Out of patience, out of breath, Bronwyn snapped, "I heard you. So did half of London. The other half will know before the evening grows older."

Glancing around, Daphne saw the censure of the crowd. "But . . . the study of the human body is of interest to everyone."

Praying for patience, Bronwyn answered, "In England, anatomy is discussed discreetly, if at all, and never in public."

Again Daphne looked around her. The offended ladies raised a breeze as they fanned their hot cheeks and waited to hear more. The titillated gentlemen smirked boldly. For the first time, Daphne thought better of her discussion. She glared at Bronwyn as if it were all her fault, and Bronwyn realized how much Daphne resented her. She braced herself, not surprised when Daphne lashed out, "Look, Cherie blushes. She's so embarrassed, her chest is red and mottled."

Bronwyn resisted the temptation to cover her bosom with her hands. Quietly she asked, "Is this how you repay Rachelle's kindness?"

Daphne couldn't back down. To Adam she said, "Cherie is older than I, yet I suppose this *poulette petite* knew not how animals mate."

Bronwyn could taste her dismay, but she retained her composure enough to say, "It's not the subject that embarrasses me as much as your behavior."

From the doorway Rachelle said, "Daphne, if we could speak?"

The girl tossed her head as she curtsied to Adam, nodded at Bronwyn. The gathering broke into gossiping groups as she left, but Bronwyn beheld none of it. She could see only Adam, austerely handsome, dark and haughty. She squeezed her eyes shut, hoping he would disappear.

When she opened them, he still stood before her, but she'd never seen him dressed like this. Gone was the country squire he had been. In his place stood a gentleman dressed in the height of fashion. Gold braid trimmed his dark blue velvet coat. Dark blue breeches and blue stockings hugged nicely formed legs. He posed with one foot extended, his tall walking cane at an angle.

He showed no respect, no interest, only an insulting curiosity in her décolletage. "Charmed," he drawled. "How do you get your hair that color?"

In her mortification, Bronwyn thought about how she had blushed before. Now fury washed over her, and she replied hotly, "I'm sorry you don't like it, but I'll not don that wig again, not even for you." She swiveled on her heel to stalk away, but his walking stick snagged her elbow and turned her back.

"I can't imagine why you would." He only smiled, untouched by anything but a distant amusement. "Are you a new stray Madame Rachelle has picked up?"

Speechless, Bronwyn stared with her lips parted.

"Catching flies, mademoiselle?" he mocked.

Didn't he know her?

Here in the salon, she was Cherie, the intriguing woman with no background. Freed of the burden of her family's expectations, she had discovered in herself a female who could flirt, discourse, tempt.

Noblemen who'd ignored her in previous encounters now stared at her without recognition and complimented her on her exotic appearance. She had learned to smile and lower her lids over the eyes they described as enormous, cinnamon-colored, inscrutable. To move aside when they rubbed her hair between their fingers, trying to make the color come off.

With an irony unappreciated by others, she carried an ivory fan at all times. Almost without volition, she had cultivated a French accent, wondering all the time what she would do if a visitor from France should address her in the language. She played a part, the part of a siren, and discovered her own acting talent. Perhaps, just perhaps . . . Cautiously, testing Adam, using her new accent, she said, "We haven't been introduced."

"Since when do the French rely on the courtesies?" He turned and limped to a settee.

She followed him, consumed with curiosity. He

lowered himself onto the cushion. Appalled, Bronwyn watched as he examined her, every inch from top to bottom, then leaned back, his wrist limp. It shocked her to find his vitality replaced with indifference.

What had changed him so?

She glanced at the mirror over the fireplace. Nothing had changed him, it was she who had changed. Changed out of recognition, it seemed. Groping for a semblance of dignity, doubting his sincerity with every step, she advanced on the lounging Adam. "Should you be here if you think so little of the French? Your hostess is French."

He placed broad hands one atop the other on his malacca cane. "Madame Rachelle has gained my respect."

Delving into the deep pockets of his coat, he removed a carved, painted, ornate box and opened it. With outstretched hand he asked, "Would you care for a mint pastille?"

She shook her head, and he popped one in his mouth. "One of the few useful French inventions," he assured her. He scooted closer to the arm of the narrow settee to make room and then patted the place.

She lowered herself to his side. She laid her hand on his arm, felt the caress of velvet on her fingertips, and swiftly removed it. Regardless of her role, regardless of her confidence, she couldn't touch him without a jolt of memory, a jolt of pleasure. "I am Cherie."

"Which is not your true name." She didn't deny it, and he mocked, "A mystery. How I love them. I must warn you, I will do my best to solve yours."

She had heard that before from the endless, infatuated visitors to the salon and replied smoothly, "You may try."

"I'm not familiar with your accent. Where are you from?"

The falsehood came easily to her. "From the north of France, in Picardy."

"You just arrived from Picardy?"

"Oui."

"Yet you speak English amazingly well."

She looked him right in the eye. "My governess insisted I learn the language of Norman and Anglo-Saxon. Do you speak French?"

"Touché." He touched his forehead in a salute. "My French is inadequate." She relaxed until he added, "When I speak French, I'm fluent in only the language of love."

Thoughtlessly she chewed on her index finger.

He rescued the abused hand, drew it from her mouth to examine the ragged nails. "You mustn't bite yourself so," he chided. "Save that for a lover."

She blushed. Although she'd been fielding such intimacies with ease from other men, when Adam spoke she could think of no riposte. Jerking her hands out of his, she asked, "What brings you to London, monsieur?"

"I allow you to divert me"—he contemplated her hands as they twined together—"for the moment. I've been neglecting Change Alley, and she's a fickle mistress. I'll be there tomorrow, circulating among the coffeehouses."

"You speak of Change Alley as a woman?"

"An exaggeration, of course. A woman is twice as fascinating"—he touched her cheek with one finger—"and twice as fickle."

"What good does it do you to come to the Alley now? The South Sea Company closed their books at the end of June, and Sir John Blunt took his family to Tunbridge Wells for a rest."

"*Sir* John?"

"Haven't you heard? The profit he made so delighted the king, he rewarded his faithful servant with a baron-etcy." She chuckled as she spoke of the head of the South Sea Company, for Adam cradled the sweep of his forehead in his palm in mock despair.

"Fools, all of them. Where stands the South Sea stock now?"

Forgetting her role, she told him, "Over a thousand, and Change Alley still mad with investors."

A small smile molded his lips. "You're knowledge-able."

Slipping back into the persona of Cherie, she said, "La, how could I help it? Madame Rachelle tries to keep the conversation to the arts and sciences, but one and all want to discuss their profits on Change Alley." Daring, she added, "I've discovered an inexplicable distaste for monetary matters."

"Have you?" He sounded dangerously neutral. "As I've always said, a woman should never muck up her pretty head with such matters."

She opened her mouth, then shut it. She'd almost begged him to say that; she couldn't blame him for giv-ing in to such temptation. Seeking a diversion, she cast her gaze around the room and found a remarkable gen-tleman peering at them through silver eyeglasses. He dressed well, his wig designed in the newest style, his cravat tied in a French twist. His face was smooth, the color of his complexion even. Like a portrait, he looked perfect—and contrived.

"Who is that man?" she asked. "The man who stares at us?"

Adam lifted his attention from her with flattering reluctance. "I see no one staring."

Contemptuously she said, "I can best describe him as the marvel of the paint box."

"Ah." He chuckled, and the sound sent thrills up her spine. "You must mean Carroll Judson. He comes to speak to us. Look closely at him, Cherie, and tell me what you see."

Judson minced up on high heels and bowed to the couple on the settee. "What a pleasant surprise, Lord Rawson."

"A surprise, anyway."

Amazed by his rudeness, Bronwyn glanced at Adam and observed the tense muscle of his jaw. It was the return of the old Adam, the man who'd met Bronwyn and found her lacking. He found Carroll Judson lacking, also, and displayed it with no finesse. Did Adam have any measure of tact in his bones?

Judson seemed to take no offense. He smiled, displaying a fine set of Egyptian pebble teeth, and asked gaily, "How do you stand the brute, dear?"

"My visit with *Monsieur le Vicomte* has been a delight." More than anyone could know, indeed.

Judson positioned himself just beyond the illumination of the candles. "He's so like his father, I hear. A veritable ladies' man."

Adam's teeth, fine, white, and his own, snapped together as he replied, "I am nothing like my father, and I'll shoot the man who says I am."

Taken aback, Judson batted his eyelids. "My dear man, I meant no offense. After all, who better to tease you about your pater? We have so much in common, you and I."

With only a small change, Adam repeated the phrase.

"I am nothing like you, and I will shoot the man who says I am."

"There's just no pleasing you." Judson flounced. "Very well, I'll leave you to your conversation, but remember, dear lady"—he turned to Bronwyn—"when you weary of this creature, come to me."

The interlude left Bronwyn with nothing to say, nothing to do, but watch as Adam's fingers strained to shape the round amber knob of his cane. She liked the length of them, the breadth of his palm, the whole of his hand, but disliked the frustration that brought him such anguish. "He has no hair."

"What?" The fingers relaxed a bit, and he asked in tones of simulated amazement, "Do you mean his disguise didn't hoax you?"

"The wig, the penciled brows, the false lashes? No, they were no deception. His skin appears to be putty, with only a coating of paint to give it color." She lowered her own lashes to shield herself from his admiration.

"Smallpox so damaged him, his hair disappeared. His skin, as you observed, is filled with coarse white in the hopes it will fill the pits left by the disease, and that covered with carmine, ceruse, powder, and all the rest." He caressed her cheek with his knuckle. "Its texture is crude enamel, not the fine china of your own skin."

She wanted to turn her lips to his fingers, and her reaction, so contrary to the ill will that she should bear him, brought her a pain in the region of her heart. Faltering, she asked, "Who could be fooled?"

Toying with the top bow of her bodice, he leaned closer, and the scent of mint brushed her face. "I assure you, my dear Cherie, the hope rattles in his vacant breast all will see him as he wishes to be seen." With a little jerk, the bow was untied.

Bronwyn slapped at his hand. "Monsieur, you mustn't play such games with my clothing. No one here wishes to see my corset."

"On the contrary"—he spread aside the material and touched the flesh that swelled above the whalebone— "many may wish to see it. I find, however, I desire to be the only one so privileged."

Bronwyn was shocked at his desire, expressed so boldly. She caught the ends of the bow and retied it in a flurry. "Isn't that what we all seek? To be seen as we wish to be, rather than as we are?"

Adam untied the lopsided bow once more and retied it with an elegance that revealed experience. "Some seek to hide themselves beneath a mask, some seek to hide themselves by revealing."

Rattled by his insight, she flipped open her fan, placed it between them, and peered at him from beneath lowered lashes. Again he appeared faintly bored, as if he'd said nothing of significance. Afraid to make much of it, she asked, "Would you care to join a discussion on Pope's translation of the *Iliad*?"

Adam curled his lip as he considered the possibility. "I'd rather discuss you and me, the maze of our lives, and how we came to this predestined meeting."

That was exactly what she did not want to talk about. "One of our ladies is an astronomer. Perhaps you would like—"

He shook his head.

"Would you like to join the experiment being performed?"

"How have I offended you, Cherie? We speak of the

general, and you're willing to converse. We speak of the intimate, and you wish to fly." Before she could answer, he waved a regal hand. "No matter. You wish to observe this experiment. Let us do so."

"It's not that I don't want to . . . that is, the experiments performed in the salon always interest me, and I wish to observe this one."

Leaning heavily on the arm of the settee, he stood. "What is so special about this one?"

"Young Mr. Webster just returned from his Grand Tour, bringing something from Germany."

"Yes?" he encouraged. He grimaced as he put his weight on his leg.

"He calls it a vacuum pump. Insert a clock within, he says, pump the air out, and the chiming of the clock will be silenced. Light a fire, place it within, pump the air out, and the fire will fail."

Adam sighed. "And you believe him?"

She would have been annoyed with his skepticism, but the obvious discomfort of his leg made her answer gently, "I've seen many strange things demonstrated during my visit here."

"Charlatans."

She longed to put her arm around him as he limped to the table surrounded by chattering people, but the image of his displeasure stopped her. "I confess, I still view it as magic rather than science."

"Perhaps you're not so credulous after all," he grunted, adjusting himself until most of his weight rested against his walking stick.

She didn't reply, standing on tiptoe to watch as Webster displayed the German globe he claimed would miraculously silence a clock and kill a flame.

Judson stepped up beside them and said in a superior

tone, "I saw this demonstrated when I toured the Continent fifteen years ago. It's old science."

"You toured the Continent?" Adam conveyed amusement and scorn. "I believed it wasn't so much a tour as an exile. Your father barely escaped prison, did he not?"

Flaring like the spark that ignited the experimental fire, Judson snapped, "He was clever enough to avoid hanging."

"I'm clever enough to avoid pretensions," Adam shot right back. "Clever enough to take fortune by the neck and twist it until my life is my own, and not dependent on a patron."

Judson stuck out his chin. "Fortune is mine today, Lord Rawson. Remember that when she abandons you tomorrow."

Laughing lightly, Adam said, "Your threat is as impotent as you are. Never think I've not noticed you scurry from coffeehouse to coffeehouse on Change Alley, sticking your long nose into everyone's dealings. No doubt the man who employs you finds you useful, but does he realize your perfidy? Does he realize that should another wave a larger fist of money, you'll leave like a well-fed rat abandoning ship?"

"You've watched me?" Judson's eyes went vacant with dismay, then filled with cunning. "What does that make you? The rat catcher?"

"I have no desire to catch such a vermin," Adam said congenially. "I'll simply step on you." As the little man stormed away, Adam muttered, "But I will discover what you're about."

Beside him, Bronwyn asked, "Should you have antagonized him?"

"He's waving the coin around now, but mark my

words. Soon he'll be starving once more. I'm amazed he has survived on Change Alley for this great time." He glanced toward the corner where Judson sulked. "He takes his luck and squanders it, rather than building to provide for tomorrow."

"You despise him."

He looked down on her and smiled. "An astute observation."

She smiled back, unable to resist the juxtaposition of muscle, bone, and skin that composed his mirth. Then, embarrassed by the reaction she couldn't contain, she looked with simulated excitement on the experiment. The gentleman had placed a small flame inside the glass globe and repeatedly compressed his hand pump. Her observation must have remained fixed on Adam peripherally, for just as the fire began to fade, so did Adam. His leg collapsed at the knee; she caught him with an arm around his waist.

He gained his balance in only a moment, but pain deepened the lines bracketing his mouth. "Come," she decided. "Sit here by the door."

He accepted the chair gratefully, apologizing, "I didn't mean to drop on you like that. Did I hurt you?"

"Not at all," she lied, ignoring the bruise his hand had left on her shoulder.

He massaged his thigh. "Valiant girl, of course I did."

She pushed aside his hand and kneaded the injured leg herself. "Perhaps, but I'm no frail vessel. You'll find I'm quite sturdy, quite—" The muscles tightened beneath her fingers and she lost her train of thought. Her face flamed as she contemplated her misguided massage, begun so innocently. How could she halt it without embarrassment? More important, did she want to halt it? His body was a pleasure to touch, and the stirring within his breeches created a curiosity in her.

Would she surrender to her curiosity? My God, she was considering seduction.

Seduction. Despite Adam's enticement on Midsummer Eve, she had never understood all the mechanics of physical love. Her mother's vague warnings had been explicit as to place—the bedroom—and time—at night.

Perhaps if she provided the place and the time, the wherefores would take care of themselves. And she was not, after all, Bronwyn Edana, but the French girl Cherie. The sophistication, the playfulness, the *joie de vivre* of Cherie could guide her.

She would do it. She nibbled her lower lip. She *would* do it, and she'd do it so cunningly he would never suspect her inexperience.

Invigorated, she rubbed his thigh once more, taking pleasure in the firm contours below the cloth.

Adam groaned quite without pain and commanded hoarsely, "You should call for my carriage before the others are distracted from the experiment."

As if to mark his words, the crowd around the table oohed.

"The flame is extinguished," he said.

"It grows stronger." She looked up at him; he looked down at her. The flame she spoke of glowed about him, transforming his face with the beauty of a dark angel. She rose to her feet and extended her hand to him. He contemplated it with an emotion she couldn't define.

Before she could wonder too much he took it, pulled it to his mouth, kissed the palm with open mouth. A thrill quite different from her former urge made her knees tremble. When massaging his leg, she'd felt quite strong; now she felt weak and very feminine.

"Such a contradiction," she murmured.

Understanding without explanation, he refuted, "Such a promise."

Carroll Judson, Daphne noted, couldn't tear his gaze from the tender scene by the door. The vapid fop might prove to be a good conspirator in her campaign to drive Cherie from Madame Rachelle's. Gliding forward, taking care not to call attention to herself, Daphne stepped close behind him and said, "You don't join in our scientific discussion."

"I don't choose to."

She followed his gaze. "Yes, I agree with you. Human reproductive habits are much more interesting."

"So sarcastic," he rebuked. "Why do you care?"

How much to say? Should she acknowledge her jealousy? Should she speak of her special relationship with Rachelle? Perhaps that wouldn't be wise, for no one understood how much she worshiped Rachelle. She settled for Cherie's lesser transgression, admitting, "*Monsieur le Vicomte* is a prize."

He sneered. "One not for the likes of you, little bastard. You reach too high."

She didn't resent the slur to her birth. Why should she? It was the truth. What she resented, what galled her, was the ease with which this Cherie had stolen Rachelle's attention from her own budding talents. That Cherie had stolen the man she coveted simply added to Daphne's envy. "Too high? Not I. A cloud hangs over the handsome lord's reputation, and as a man he is a decent specimen. He would suit me well."

"He is betrothed."

"His betrothed escaped him."

Judson grabbed her arm and hustled her into a corner. Keeping an eye on Adam and the woman, he said, "Tell me what you know."

"Haven't you heard?" She permitted a small smile to tug at her lips. "They say his betrothed ran from him in fear, cloistering herself in a convent rather than sharing his marriage bed."

"Is that girl, that Bronwyn Edana, really gone? Is this the truth?"

"Part of it is the truth. She's gone from his house." She nodded at the couple at the chair, sure she'd found a pleasant way to make mischief. "Too obviously, the rest is nonsense. What is the identity of the enigmatic Cherie?"

At first he seemed not to understand, then he jerked his head toward Adam and his lady.

"I'm not at liberty to speak," she purred. "Rachelle would kill me."

Before her eyes, the man's demeanor transformed from fop to savage. Swift as a striking snake, his hands found her neck and squeezed. "*I'll* take great pleasure in strangling you if you don't speak."

Panicked, she swatted at his hands, wrestled away from him. He easily loosened his grip but kept her within reach.

Rubbing her throat, Daphne realized that perhaps she had miscalculated. Perhaps this wasn't the way to make mischief after all. Thrilled and appalled by what she was doing, she plucked at her lip. Rachelle claimed Daphne acted with too much impetuosity, and she respected Rachelle's opinion. Rachelle, who had been a mother to her. Rachelle, who would care for her more if Bronwyn were gone. Daphne's resolve firmed. "That's her. The woman with the harlot's hair. That's Bronwyn Edana."

"Impossible." His hands trembled on her shoulders. "Bronwyn Edana is Adam's betrothed. That humorless male busybody would never allow her to escape his clutches."

All was fair in love and war, was it not? "Monsieur, I know only what I've heard between Cherie and Rachelle."

"If this is true . . ." His hand crept toward her throat again.

She shrank from the hairless one. "It is." His expression threatened murder, and the grip of his hands still marked her throat. Fright overwhelmed her, and she tried to edge away. His hands shot out, halting her.

He gripped her chin in both palms, stroked her cheeks with his thumbs. She whimpered as he increased the pressure, but his grip kept her quiet. "You will say nothing of my interest. I have ways to ensure your silence, should you fail me."

She nodded, eyes wide.

As if he were satisfied with her capitulation, he put her away from him. Ignoring her as if she were of no importance, he said, "Nothing could be worse. Nothing could be more disastrous."

She watched as he put the back of his hand to his forehead like a Drury Lane actress.

"Bronwyn Edana. Here in Madame Rachelle's, with Adam Keane. I will have to see what can be done about this."

Chilled and thinking second thoughts, Daphne left him.

He never saw her go.

Chapter 10

Adam leaned against Bronwyn's shoulder as they climbed the stairs, but she noticed a new agility in his movement. She wondered if he had been exaggerating his pain to elicit an invitation to her room and wondered more that she liked the notion.

She flung the door wide. She'd forgotten the petticoat she'd dropped to the floor, the collection of slippers tossed by a whirlwind around the rug. The branch of candles he held revealed it all. She blushed and apologized, "You'll excuse the mess."

"But of course." He placed the candelabra on her dressing table before the mirror and tucked his walking stick under his arm. Hand under her chin, he lifted her face. "Housekeeping is the province of a wife, and a siren such as you could never fit that dry description of a woman."

A pang that he so easily dismissed his betrothed

zipped through her, but he gave her no time to think.

"'Tis hot in here, for all that the windows are open to catch the breeze. Will you be valet as well as siren?" He stepped back, extending his arm. *"Déshabilles-moi."*

He wanted her to undress him.

She stared at his outstretched hand. So at odds with the elegance of velvet and lace, its broad, hardened palm and long fingers betrayed a seaman's labor, the labor that had made him who he was. It recalled the formidable man she knew him to be and, for some inexplicable reason, thrilled her into obedience. Catching the cuff, she tugged off his coat. He took it from her and tossed it atop her petticoat and indicated the buttons of his embroidered waistcoat. In the carefree fashion of a rake, he'd buttoned it only at his waist. As he leaned against his walking stick, she freed him. His stillness was a hoax, she knew, for he gave the impression of a great cat, reserving its strength as its prey wandered closer.

She wondered at her willingness to put her head in the lion's mouth, but when he slipped out of the waistcoat, she knew why. His shoulders, clad only in white muslin, recalled Midsummer Eve and the passion in the wood. He promised, implicit in his knowledge, an excitement such as she'd only suspected.

Stepping close, she untied the white lace cravat and spread the neck of the shirt. As her fingers touched the hollow above his collarbone, his palm slid behind her neck. He threaded his fingers through her hair.

For a man who'd only moments before been on the verge of collapse, he gave a gratifying imitation of vigor. He kissed her with a flattering appetite that never diminished even as she yielded. He took her tongue, pushed his way into her, and filled her mouth with the taste of mint. When she was gasping, out of breath, he released her and went to her chin, her cheeks, all over her face. It wasn't affection so much as a suggestion of ravishment, and the hint of his impatience brought her surging to meet him. As wild as he, she kissed every bit of skin she could reach, amazed at her own exuberance. The experience in the woods had whetted her appetite, she knew. Fulfillment had been promised, but long denied.

Not true, her reason chanted. Not true. Not even her inexperience could disclaim it. When Adam reached for her, they ignited as surely as phosphorus exposed to air.

She thrilled at his fascination with her hair. He kissed every inch of her hairline, murmuring, *"Clair de lune."* He ran his fingers through it, groaning at its length, its silky texture. He bunched it in his hand. He lifted it to his nose. *"Les fleurs."* He groaned. *"Votre chevelure sent merveilleusement."*

"Oui," she murmered with barely a clue to his meaning.

He chuckled deep in his throat and tried to wrap her closer. "Your hair smells wonderful." The whalebone cage of her panniers fought him, and he set her away. "Let me remove that contraption," he ordered. "Nothing must come between us."

He reached for her skirt, and she stepped back in a rush of doubt. Stupid to balk at the idea of him undressing her, yet Bronwyn did. *Bronwyn* did. I am Cherie, she reminded herself. Continental, experienced. What would Cherie do in this situation?

He encouraged, "Remove it yourself," and it seemed the answer she sought.

With a faint smile, she lifted her silk skirt and petticoat. He watched avidly as her slippers, her hose,

appeared. Before she revealed more, she tucked her
hands beneath and fumbled for the tie at her waist.
The panniers dropped to her feet, then she stepped
out.

His gaze never left the now revealed shape of her
hips as he kicked the cage into a corner. "Your petticoat," he commanded. "Your stockings."

"Monsieur, you go too quickly," she remonstrated.

"Not as quickly as I would like, *ma cherie*."

He glanced at her face, then hastily turned his head
away. Even that brief contact heated her. He created an
itch she couldn't scratch, an urge she longed to comprehend. "Dear God," she whispered. Suddenly aware of
her strength, suddenly a tease, she pretended she was
alone. Turning her profile to him, she lifted one foot to
the seat of the chair beside her and removed her leather
slipper. With both hands, she clasped her ankle and began a long, slow trek up her leg. Inch by painful inch,
the skirt rose. At her garter she hesitated, fingering the
rosette decorating it.

"Do it," he whispered, his voice husky with strain.

Using the greatest of care, she pulled the bow loose
and rolled the stocking all the way down her leg once
more. Arching her foot, she whisked the hose away. It
fluttered to the floor as she put her foot down, lifted her
other leg onto the seat. After removing her shoe, she
bypassed the garter on the way to her waist. Taking
care that the drape of her skirt revealed only hints of
thigh and hip, she loosened her petticoat, loosened her
garter, glanced at Adam.

His nostrils flared; his face was stiff with control;
his hands caressed the knob of his cane. The predatory
lion watched her.

That brief glance stripped away the guise of Cherie.

Again she became Bronwyn, pinned by the gaze of a starving man.

He sensed her trepidation. His cane clattered to the floor as he sprang forward to catch her before she could withdraw. He replaced her soft hands with his rough ones and rolled the other stocking down.

Now it was he who teased. His hands moved as slowly as hers, but they tickled the inside of her knee. They massaged her calf muscle. They spanned her ankle. And all the while, he flicked her sensitized skin with torrid glances.

What had been hidden from him was revealed. Not well, for flickering candles couldn't completely conquer the night, but well enough to make her tense with embarrassment and pride.

The stocking ripped as it left her foot, and he stared, amazed, at the silken disaster clutched in his fingers. Taking advantage of his distraction, she tried to push her skirt down, but his hand clamped onto her lifted thigh.

"*Non, allumeuse*, you have teased me, now take your punishment."

She flinched back, but he stepped between her legs and pulled her close. The warmth of his body replaced the warmth of his gaze—worse by far, for all he was fully clothed. He wrapped both arms around her, placed both hands upon her buttocks and moved them in circles. The thin silk of her skirt offered no protection. "You see, *ma cherie*, in this way I can acquaint myself with every delectable curve. I can acquaint you, too, with the sensation of silk against your skin." The circles became smaller, more specific. "Indeed, the silk lends a whisper of decadence, does it not?"

Beyond speech, she nodded.

He bent her back over his arm, leaning to kiss the expanse of her chest. His free hand rotated a path around her hip, up to the bows that both decorated and closed her bodice. One by one, from her waist to her neckline, he loosened the ties. With his fingers, he spread the silk to reveal the front of her corset. He touched each embroidered flower, smiled at the dainty stitchery. Her chemise still covered her bosom, a thin cotton against her skin.

She could scarcely breathe as she awaited his touch. She dug her fingers into his arm, tugging at him.

"A woman who knows what she wants, I see." He nipped her ear. "A woman who demands her due. A woman most rare." Boldly he sculpted her flesh. "Is that what you want, *ma toute belle*?"

Speech was beyond her, but he seemed to expect no less. His eyes drooped with pleasure, his mouth half smiled. "A rare thing, to find a woman who doesn't pad her natural riches with wads of cotton."

Forming the words with difficulty, she said, "I don't need it."

"Too true," he crooned. "Nor do you need this corset which binds you so tightly." With nimble fingers, he loosened the string.

Although she wasn't cold, goose bumps chilled her from toes to hairline.

The agony of it, the pleasure of it, showed in his face. *"Je suis fou."*

"Oui," she breathed, although she didn't know to what she agreed.

A small push of his hand had her falling onto the chair. The cushions received her kindly. Her eyes stretched wide as he stood above her. His shirt came off over his head, revealing toasted skin thatched with black curls.

Leaning over her, one hand on the padded chair arm, he took her wrist and placed it on his breastbone. The hair crinkled beneath her fingertips.

He guided her along the line that led down and disappeared into his breeches. There she stopped, uncertain, but he urged, "Go on, little *allumeuse*. Show me the skills of a Frenchwoman."

The breeches had to come off, she supposed, and she supposed he expected her to remove them. Very well, so she would. But if she was Cherie, with the skills of a Frenchwoman, then she should pay special attention to the bulge that resided therein. Seduction, she remembered, was her game.

In a rush, she pressed her hands to his groin. He jerked. She explored with her fingertips. He groaned, a harsh sound torn from him. His pleasure brought a rush of pleasure to her, and when he stood she whimpered an objection.

"You push me too far." He jerked his open breeches, removed his garters and stockings and everything in one furious sweep. "You deserve—"

He stopped, arrested by her gaze. She hadn't known a man would be so large, so swollen with impatience. For the first time she knew this wouldn't work, and she shook her head silently.

"You deserve . . . damn, I'll give you what you deserve." The wrath disappeared from his tone, but not the threat. He tossed a fringed pillow on the floor and lowered himself before her where she rested on the chair. Some reflex made her press her knees together tightly, but he made no objection. He only stroked her belly with his hands until suspense made her quiver. He touched the corner of her mouth with his fingers, separating her lips, and leaned into her. Now he kissed her as she remembered, and she couldn't speak.

Then she didn't want to speak.

He tasted her, moved his lips on hers, sipped at her mouth. Their breath dueled, their tongues stroked sweetly. Bronwyn was swept away for hours, for years, lost in the darkness and reveling in it. What he had taught her before was nothing compared with this, and when his mouth retreated, she followed, murmuring complaints.

He sat back on his heels and found her ankle beneath the hem. Stroking the bone, he asked, *"Tu veux que je mets ma langue dans la chatte?"*

Rich with promise, his voice persuaded her. *"Monsieur? Ah, oui."*

Lifting an eyebrow, he smiled and pointed to his tongue. *"Vraiment! Ma langue?"*

Anything involving his tongue would be heaven, she was sure. *"Oui, oui."*

"Vous êtes ma chouchoute."

Trepidation touched her. *"Oui?"*

"Very much *oui*. You make me a beast with your daring." He fondled the back of her knee, then placed it on his shoulder. "Most women wouldn't agree to such a thing, not even with a lover of long standing."

Before she could ponder such an enigmatic observation, he lifted her skirt and slid under it.

In the mirror the reflection of the candles flickered and glowed.

Like that flame, his tongue singed her flesh as he neared it.

It burned. She burned.

His mouth touched her, kissed her in a way she'd never imagined. She closed her eyes.

She wanted to push him away; she wanted to hold him close. She flexed her hands, curled her toes. She opened her eyes, and he rose above her, so close his shoulders blocked the light.

"Tu as le sang chaud," he said.

She made no mistakes this time. She didn't agree, only reached out and wrapped her trembling arms around his waist.

"Tu veux coucher avec moi, oui?"

She stared, uncomprehending.

"You must agree to make love with me, *ma vie.*" He laid his cheek against hers. "I'll not have you denying your consent later."

"I would not." Her indignation was weak, but only because her body waited and trembled. Still he stroked her, waiting, and she croaked, "I will make love with you." She pushed his head back and glared at him, even though he lowered his gaze. She insisted, "Now."

"A demanding woman," he marveled.

Shaking his shoulders, she insisted, "A frantic woman."

He refused to move with the speed she instructed. Almost as if he wanted to punish her for some trespass, he slid slowly to his knees on his pillow, pulled her to him, and positioned her. With all the time in the world, he fit them together as she watched anxiously.

He pushed inside her.

Her flesh burned. He hurt her. He was too large, just as she'd thought. "Please," she faltered. "Don't."

He lifted his gaze and looked at her. Really looked at her for the first time that evening.

Reality struck her like a blow. He was Adam, the Adam as she'd known at Boudesea Manor.

And she was Bronwyn.

She'd never deceived him. He'd always known who she was, and he possessed her like a man intent on establishing a claim. No wonder he'd avoided looking at her—the truth was written in his eyes. "No," she whispered.

"Yes." Smiling with all his white teeth, he never slowed.

"No!" She pushed at him, but he adjusted his grip on her legs, widening them.

Her maidenhead yielded, unmatched by his relentless advance. He pressed on until he rested against her. He stopped, breathing as hard as if he'd run a great race. "You gave your consent. You swore you'd not abjure."

Untouched by the resentment clouding her mind, her body adjusted to his invasion, easing about him. A residue of the need she'd experienced still rushed in her blood, augmented, perhaps, by her anger. "Finish, then. Finish, but I hate you. I hate you forever."

"Forever is a very long time." His eyes burned her as he moved once more. "And you have a great reserve of passion . . . Bronwyn."

"Did you think I would not seek such meager revenge as I could manage?" Adam rubbed his aching leg and glared at Bronwyn's back. "You humiliated me."

"Taking my virginity is not a meager revenge." Enveloped in a satin wrap and lying stomach down on the fainting couch, she twisted his lace cravat as if his neck were inside it. "At least, I don't consider it so."

He pressed the heels of his hands against his eyes.

He was usually not so clumsy, but her unforgiving fury had taken him by surprise. She acted as if she were the offended party, not he, refusing to admit her culpability. "We must come to an understanding in this matter before we return to Boudesea Manor."

"I'm not returning," she said in a monotone. "I told you before."

"Of course you are. You can't stay here. It's not proper. Should word of your identity escape, your reputation—"

"As the ugly Edana sister," she interrupted, "will be ruined. So you've said. And I say—"

"I don't like it when you use language so vigorously." He sounded like a prude, but he couldn't seem to stop himself. Having Bronwyn treat him as if he were a cad grated. He'd sworn that when he caught up with her, he'd make his opinions known. She'd experienced the sting of his anger, the fury of his possession— so why did he feel guilty? With a patience he didn't know he retained, he said, "You expected I would be incensed at your defection."

"I didn't know that you would sneak around like Molière performing in that"—she searched for the title and finished petulantly—"that play."

He hid a smile, although she still declined to look at him. Probably because he refused to don more than his shirt. "Are you speaking of *The Doctor in Spite of Himself?* The play in which the woodcutter masquerades as a doctor by speaking Latin gibberish?"

"That's it." She hunched her shoulder expressively.

"I spoke French, not Latin, and it was not gibberish." He stepped close behind her and stroked the fall of her hair, amazed anew at its color and flyaway texture. "I once said I could make love in four languages, and it's

true, although the idioms are not the kind a gently
bred woman would know—even if she actually spoke
French."

Springing away from his hand, she raged, "You
laughed at me."

He was silent. Better than most, he realized how
love shriveled when exposed to mockery. Speaking
French to her had been an irresistible impulse, one
born of her sham accent and his temper. Trying to
make her understand, he said, "When first I met you at
Boudasea, I didn't know you. I saw only that dreadful
wig, the cosmetics which hid, I thought, greater horrors. Then as I became acquainted with you, I realized
you concealed your soul."

"I don't know what you're talking about. I don't conceal myself."

"Don't you? Don't you play games with us lesser
mortals?" He caught her hair again and pulled, demanding an answer. She shrugged, and he chuckled. "See?
You can't deny it. I was discovering you, stripping away
your disguise, anxious for the final unveiling."

"You're talking nonsense," she said coldly.

"Tonight in Madame Rachelle's salon, I could only
stare. All your masks were gone, you were as magnificent as the moon on a cloudless night, and I had not
been there." He experienced a sincere stab of grief, of
jealousy. "Other men had seen you, spoken with you,
fallen in love with you, and I had not been there. I felt
like a mother would feel, forced to leave her baby, only
to return and find the child walking. So you see, you're
not the only one with a complaint."

She whipped her head around and glared. "A complaint? Is that what you think I have? A complaint?"

Her gaze flamed with contempt before she turned

her back once more. His sincerity hadn't touched her. She still thought him a whoreson. This came of trying to explain his emotions to a woman. He snapped, "Marriage is a bargain, and someone must get the worst of any bargain."

"I don't want to get the worst of this bargain," she answered sullenly.

He clenched his fists and hoped he could keep from strangling her. "You're not getting the worst of the bargain. I'm the one who's providing the money, the home, the stability."

"I'm the one who'll live under your thumb. I'm the one who'll suffer when my enemies taunt me with your mistresses." She stared into the fireplace, seemingly fascinated by the cold ashes. "I'm the one whom you'll have the right to beat if you so choose."

Stung, he snapped, "As if I would."

"Few men go into a relationship expecting to hate their wives, but it's more common than everyday affection." Pulling the wrap close around her as if she were cold, she said, "You say I'm not a gambler, yet you wish me to marry and gamble on your continued interest."

The cobalt-blue satin molded her, and his gaze lingered on the tensile strength of her spine, expressed so plainly in her posture. "I do not see how I could fail to remain interested in a woman who leads me on such a chase."

She ignored him as she cradled her chin in her hand. "What greater gamble is there? For if a man is unhappy with a relationship, he can leave, find another woman, beat his wife. A man has all the rights. If a woman is unhappy with the marriage, she can do nothing."

"Except make his life miserable, as you're doing with me." Exasperated, he watched as she swung her bare feet restlessly in the air. The wrap slipped away, leaving her ankles and calves bare, but he acquitted her of deliberate incitement. Indeed, he even acquitted her of teasing. She was so bound up in her mortification, she didn't care that he was there.

"You ghastly creature." She drew out the insult as lovingly as a caress. "At least I haven't been chatting with my secretary about the disadvantages of marrying a learned woman."

Ah, so there it was. "I was afraid you heard. Freely I admit my guilt, and can offer no reasonable defense. I'm a clumsy man, rough and uncultured as any common seaman." Only a lecher would desire a virgin so recently deflowered, he mused.

"Teaching me to kiss and then complaining because I was too good a student." With a sharp tearing sound, the lace of the cravat ripped in her hands. "Making me want to visit your bed, then heaping scorn on me."

Still, he couldn't forget the recent sounds of her pleasure and the movement of her body against his. She'd tried to dismiss him when she realized his perfidy, but she hadn't been able to maintain her scorn. He couldn't forget the sweetness of her surprise, her amazement, as she discovered passion. He felt ten feet tall when he remembered how she'd dismissed his expertise at first; then feared it; then sought it.

Tossing the shreds of lace into the fireplace, she said, "You were surprised to discover I was a virgin, weren't you?"

"No, not surprised." Relieved, but not surprised. Overjoyed, but not surprised. Surprise was too small a word, and that in itself shocked him. He'd told his mother her virginity interested him only in as much as he wished to prove his paternity. Was this possessiveness he experienced?

"Why would you be surprised? After all, I am the ugly sister."

Traps lay buried in this conversation, traps to catch any man preoccupied with the shape of the woman rather than the verbal sparring. "You are so beautiful you make my heart stop."

Clearly disbelieving, she pulled a long face and issued an ultimatum. "I'm staying at Rachelle's."

Cautiously he perched at the foot of the couch. "Madame Rachelle is a kind woman, but you'd be embarrassed to have her paying your support."

She glanced over her shoulder at him, distrusting his every movement. "The Princess of Wales is interested in my work on the manuscripts, and has agreed to my petition for pension."

"Ah." He caught her ankle and smoothed one finger along her arch. Her toes curled; she jumped and tried to wrestle away. Casual as the lecher he now knew himself to be, he kneaded the muscles of her foot. "I suppose you have more time to work on the manuscripts here than at Boudasea Manor, also."

To resist such a massage proved beyond her powers of resistance. As he'd known she would, she relaxed in slow degrees. "Yes, my time is my own here. There are no social engagements unless I wish them, no . . ."

He moved to her other foot. Her head sank down onto the couch and she seemed to forget what she was saying. "No . . . ?" he encouraged.

"No . . . um." She'd lost her train of thought, and she frowned. "I like meeting important men."

Forcing himself to continue his massage, he asked, "Has anyone recognized you?"

She moaned when he found a particularly tender place between her toes. "It always hurts there when I walk in slippers with those high Louis heels."

Her moan distracted him, but only for a moment. "Recognize?" he prompted.

"No, no one knows who I am."

Cheered, he asked, "Do you want me to rub your calves?"

Lifting her head, she snapped, "Absolutely not."

The rhythm of his fingers never broke. "Of course those fools who call themselves gentlemen wouldn't identify you. The change is remarkable. I always knew you were attractive, but somehow it all seemed skewed. Now it's as if a butterfly has struggled from her cocoon. How did you do it?"

"You thought I was attractive before?"

It was the only thing she'd heard, he noted with satisfaction. In tiny increments he moved up to her ankle, her calf. "You don't think I tried to seduce you just because of your mind? I'm not so altruistic."

"I never thought . . ."

Such craftiness was unworthy of him, he castigated himself. But it was nothing less than the truth, and she was such an easy mark. Almost as if she'd never heard a sincere compliment before. "I can't imagine why you covered your hair with that dreadful brown wig. Even if you put this glorious mane up and covered it with one of those lacy caps, you'd still be one of the most striking women I've ever seen." He tickled the sensitive skin behind her knee.

Her muscles twitched beneath his ministrations. "Honestly?"

"Don't you remember how frantic I was for you in the woods?"

In the voice of sweet sarcasm, she said, "It was dark in the woods. You couldn't see me."

"I'd been looking at you all evening long. I knew what I was getting." Leaning down, he blew in short puffs, lifting the light silk over her thighs.

"Don't think I don't know what you're doing." She shivered. "It's no use. I'm furious with you."

"But how else can I apologize?" he protested.

"You're going to apologize by doing the same thing that made me angry?" She sounded incredulous, but her voice caught.

He laughed low in his throat and feathered touches up the inside of her thighs. "Was that really what made you angry?"

"We shouldn't—"

Sinking one finger inside her, he marveled at her body's compliance. "Oh, shouldn't we?"

Chapter 11

$\mathcal{A}$dam wiped the sweat from his brow. He'd never seen so much prime society in London in August. For the noble and wealthy, the Season was over. Normally they escaped the heat by retiring to their country estates. But not this year. This year ladies and their maids jostled with tradesmen and the scum of the city to cling close to Change Alley, where fortunes changed hands daily and the porters now rode in carriages.

He didn't want to be here, shouldn't even be walking on his aching leg, but where else had he to go? Bronwyn wouldn't budge from that salon, and he wouldn't return to Boudasea Manor without her.

"Lord Rawson! Good to see you back on your feet." Northrup slapped his back like a cohort of long standing. "Heard you were ill."

Adam staggered a bit under the unnecessary force. "Not at all. As you see, I'm healthy as ever."

"I would have bet on it." Tucking his thumbs into the pockets of his velvet waistcoat, Northrup nodded sagely. "Yes, my lord, I would have bet on it."

Adam eyed the younger man. "The Change has been treating you well, I see."

Northrup grinned, a bit deflated, a lot proud. "Very well, sir. Your teachings have sustained me." Like a boy with new toy, he promenaded away, then back, flaunting his expensive new outfit.

"I'm glad to hear it." A Playhouse actress pushed Adam sideways, and, disgusted, he swung his walking stick sharply at her rump. She shrieked in protest and turned to scold.

Taking Adam's arm, Northrup asked, "Would you like to visit Garraway's? Possibly I could catch you up on the gossip which thrives so in this hothouse atmosphere."

"You'll not have to talk long to persuade me." Adam glared at the saucy actress. "This financial district has become a madhouse equal to Bedlam."

"That it has, sir." Northrup swung wide the door to the famous coffeehouse where the practice of exchanging stock centered.

Acquaintances hailed Adam, and he returned their greetings. "Various rumors have come to your ears, I suppose."

Northrup ushered Adam to a corner table where both could sit with their backs to the wall. He lowered his voice. "Rumors, but no facts."

"Tell me all," Adam commanded.

With a lopsided grin at Adam's tone of authority Northrup lifted his hand to the owner and called, "Coffee." He turned back to Adam. "Many companies petitioning for charters to operate have been refused."

"That's surely not a surprise. Parliament's Bubble Act classed any company operating without a charter as a public nuisance."

"Yes, the proclamation is working well for the South Sea Company. The flow of money that was siphoned away from them and to the other companies has been halted before it begins. But—"

Northrup stopped as the hefty man they called Garraway brought over the fragrant blend.

"Good t' see ye, Lord Rawson." Garraway pocketed the coin Adam laid on the table. "Been missin' ye."

"Not too much." Adam nodded to the crowd milling about the tables. "Business is booming."

Garraway snorted. "I'd take th' business an' toss out th' stock jobbers, if ye catch me meanin'."

"Are they thick on the ground?" Adam asked with interest.

"Can't spit without 'itting one." He spat for emphasis and grinned when a gentleman yelped. "Ye licensed brokers are a rarity now."

"But dull," Adam suggested. "Very dull."

"I'd not say that." Garraway grinned, revealing two missing front teeth. "Leastways, not t' yer face."

Adam laughed. "I could always trust you, Garraway, to set me down when I grew top-lofty. Is it as busy as it was?"

"Not a'tall, a'tall." He lowered his voice. "Not since th' really wild bubble companies decided t' pack up shop an' leave."

"The Bubble Act—"

"Ain't worth th' paper it's printed on without someone t' come in an' kick those companies out, ye know that."

"Are you saying someone is persuading the owners it's time to quit?"

"All I'm sayin' is that there's been a bit of violence done t 'th' owners o' these companies."

Adam whistled and sat back.

"Mind you," Garraway continued, "not that it couldn't be a disgruntled stock buyer who discovered 'e'd been bilked."

"What do you suspect?"

"Damn it," Northrup exploded, "I was going to tell him."

"'A course." Garraway stepped back. "Don't want t' steal yer thunder."

Northrup had the grace to look embarrassed but told Adam, "I believe there is an enforcer from the South Sea Company who encourages"—Northrup lifted a significant brow—"the companies to collapse."

"A cutthroat who works for John Blunt," Adam mused.

"A very clever cutthroat," Northrup answered.

Garraway wiped his fingers on his apron. "Aye, too clever fer th' likes of me. I'd 'ate to run into 'im in a dark alley, if ye take me meanin'." Glancing around, he said, "Better scoot. Asking fer trouble talking t' ye like this."

"Then go at once. But first . . ." Adam reached for his purse.

"Some other time." The big man rubbed his nose in a parody of sentiment. "Been good talkin' t' someone who's not 'alf mad fer money."

As Garraway stomped toward the bar, Northrup moved his chair closer to Adam's. "You got more information in ten minutes than I've been able to pry out of anyone in a month. I tell you, sir, everyone knows I'm not working for you anymore, but they're still tight as a clam with me."

"Old contacts," Adam soothed. "You'll cultivate them eventually."

"But I wanted to pay you back." Northrup looked wretched. "I've felt, well, guilty, leaving as I did, and I wanted—"

"There's no debt." Amazed and a little disgruntled at this display of commitment from one he wanted to cut from his life, Adam said, "You performed a service for me, and I paid you."

"I know you hired me from kindness."

"Kindness?" Almost alarmed at the accusation of humanity, Adam glared at Northrup. "Not at all. I needed a secretary. You were trained."

"Yes, but—"

"It was business."

Northrup ducked his head. "But you taught me so much. That wasn't just business."

"What I taught you made you valuable to me." His brutality was akin to kicking a stray dog, but Adam meant to discourage this sentimental drivel. "It was coincidence that it also made you capable of earning a goodly fortune."

Earnest as only the young can be, Northrup said, "Sir, whether you meant to be or not, you have been kind to me. You treated me with dignity when others scorned me."

"A seaman performs his duties better when he's assured of his pride." With the scorn of a ship's officer for a landlubber, Adam declared, "I have never seen any reason to believe different of those who work on shore."

Northrup bit his lip. "I do not believe, sir, that you are as heartless as you profess to be."

"I am. Believe me, I am." His hand placed over Northrup's wrist, Adam squeezed hard enough to grind bones. "But say no more." Northrup tried to protest, and he said again with great meaning, "Say no more."

Northrup jerked his hand back and stared, amazed, at the creation of paint and ribbon and wig that stood beside their table.

Carroll Judson's Egyptian pebble teeth gleamed in a smile. "Such a pleasure, Lord Rawson." Without taking his gaze from Adam, he ordered, "Cease your whining, Northrup, my boy, and fetch me a glass of wine. French, the best Garraway has to offer."

"Humpty Dumpty commands me?" Northrup asked incredulously.

Judson's smirk disappeared, and he sputtered, "You are insolent."

Adam gained control of his amusement and snapped his fingers. Northrup and Judson interrupted their mutual glare to inspect him, and he jerked his thumb at Northrup, just as if the young man were some lesser creature in his employ. Offended, Northrup stood and bowed, doing Judson's bidding with ill grace while Adam reflected grimly that Northrup would no longer whine about too much kindness.

But that was no concern of his. Judson hadn't sought him out to exchange pleasantries. Perhaps he had information to be sold or bartered, and Northrup's ego couldn't stand in the way.

"Not that Garraway's best will be drinkable," Judson said. "I have such a superior palate, you realize." He smiled as he slid onto the chair opposite Adam. "May I sit down?"

"Be my guest."

Fluttering like a moth exposed to daylight, Judson fussed over his cuffs, his cravat, the elegant frogging of his coat. "So amazing to run into you last night, and again this morning." He peered at Adam over his silver spectacles. "You look tired. Did you sleep well?"

Adam examined his nails.

"Quite right. Quite right. I'm too nosy by half. But that's how I've come to make so much money these past few months. Drop a hint here, listen to a suggestion there. Soon it's possible to gather every bit of loose stock to my bosom, as it were"—Judson pressed one hand to his chest—"and save it to sell at the proper moment."

"When is that?" Adam asked coldly.

"Why, before the crash." Judson shook his finger at Adam. "Come, come, you're too astute not to realize the South Sea stock will tumble."

"I am too astute, but I didn't realize you were."

Judson sniggered. "You're so boorish, Lord Rawson. I don't know why I even speak to you." Adam opened his mouth, but before he could answer, Judson continued, "Of course the stock will go down, but when? That's the question. I suppose that's why you're here in London rather than home with your lovely bride. What's her name again?"

"Is it any concern of yours?"

"Bronwyn . . ." He tapped his fingers on the table. "Bronwyn Edana, was it not? Has the wedding taken place?"

"Not yet," Adam snapped.

"Ah, that would explain your sour disposition. She's one of those Edana beauties, and you're not in her bed," Judson cooed. "Will the happy event take place soon?"

"If you have anything to say, say it. Else I put this to better use." Adam placed his cane on the table in hard evidence of his displeasure.

Smug at having pushed Adam to violence, Judson

whispered, "This stock situation is so distressing. You're scouting out the evidence, eh?"

Adam sat back slowly. "Indeed, and it would seem I've found the right man. You can tell me what's happening."

As Northrup set the glass of wine on the table, Judson snipped, "Certainly better than your young friend."

Adam pointed at the empty chair, and still resentful, Northrup sat. Too bad Northrup's bit of money had gone to his head, Adam noted, for the young man comprehended Adam's wishes with an acumen that bordered on genius.

Judson cleared his throat noisily. Adam had been staring at Judson, he found, from sheer lack of attention. It had shaken Judson's composure, for Judson fussed with the velvet patches on his face and complained, "That gaze of yours would pierce steel. I wish you'd turn it elsewhere."

Lifting a lazy brow, Adam complied, but not before commanding, "Don't pick at those. Your valet would scold you."

Judson snatched his hand away from his face. "My valet does take my grooming to heart. Rather more than I do, if I may say."

Northrup made a sound of disbelief that rapidly changed to a cough when Judson turned to him. "Have you the consumption? It's so common among the lesser folk."

Northrup didn't flick an eyelash, but nothing could halt the red tide of blood that flushed his cheeks.

With a phony smile Judson said, "You'll have to train your servants better, Adam."

Nostrils flared, Adam said, "Northrup is not now, and never has been, my servant. He was my secretary and, but for a bad stroke of fate, would even now be the marquess of Tyne-Kelmport. He'd be looking down his nose at the likes of you, Judson, so I'd temper my disposition."

"That's right," Judson simpered at Northrup. "Your bachelor uncle married and fathered an heir before he had the good taste to die, didn't he? Don't worry. Children are notoriously unhealthy. I mean, look at old Queen Anne's brood. Nineteen children, and not a one of them lived. Perhaps this brat will perish, too."

"You really are mouse meat," Northrup said with a notable lack of emotion.

Now it was Judson's turn to flush. "Well! And I was just wishing you good luck."

With a secret grin at Judson's discomfort, Adam sipped at his coffee. "When is Sir John Blunt returning from Tunbridge Wells?"

"Soon," Judson said. "That is, I imagine he'll be returning soon to check on his company."

Adam's eyes narrowed as he considered Judson. He'd sounded so sure, then feigned to cover his knowledge. Interesting. "He'll be selling another subscription of stock soon."

"I'm sure he will, and it will be a grand time to invest." Judson twisted toward Adam to whisper, "I've heard Sir John has plans to quell these companies that infringe on his grand plan."

"What companies are those?"

"Royal Lustring, Yorks Buildings—"

Adam set down his cup with a distinct clink.

"—the English Copper Company, and the Welsh Copper Company."

"How does Sir John think he can pull such nonsense off? Those companies have had their charters for years."

"He'll prove nonuse of the charters. They've already spoken with the chancellor of the Exchequer and Lord Townshend, and Lord Townshend is acting regent while the king is gone, you know." Judson crooked one elbow around the back of his chair.

"But those companies are stable ones with a good record."

Judson lifted his painted eyebrows. "So?"

"Quite right," Adam said dryly. "Logic has no place in this mad world of finance. Yet if this is true . . ."

"Who are you going to believe?" Judson tapped his wineglass with his fingernail, and the arrhythmic tinging grated on Adam's nerves. "Me, or your sickly little secretary?"

"Neither. I'll believe no one until I consult all my sources."

"You'll see." Judson stood and adjusted his clothing. "I'm right."

As he strolled away, Adam turned to Northrup. "Is he right?"

"There are rumors, and that's one of them," Northrup agreed.

"That's the one rumor that foretells the end. Sell your stock, my boy. Sell your stock." Adam stood, noting the denial that stained Northrup's countenance. Shrugging, he said, "You can be a fool if you like, of course. You're no responsibility of mine."

"Wait!" Northrup stood also. "Where are you staying?"

"Why do you ask?"

Taken aback, Northrup stammered, "In case I hear news I would like to pass on to you."

"Of course." Adam relaxed. He should be staying at a friend's, or at his club, or even at an inn. No gentleman would go back and visit his betrothed as if she were his mistress. He really shouldn't even see Bronwyn again. He should let her fret about him—it was a strategy he'd used on other women, with great success. Unable to follow his own advice, he said, "If you need me, send a message to Madame Rachelle's in West London. They will know how to contact me there." He walked away, stopped. "Humpty Dumpty, eh? A pithy description indeed, Northrup, Humpty Dumpty."

Bronwyn's beautiful sister dabbed frantically at the corners of her eyes, trying to hide her distress from the finest of society as they milled about Rachelle's drawing room, "Look what you've done." Lady Holly, viscountess of Sidkirk, showed her snowy handkerchief dotted with black smudges.

Shifting from one foot to the other, Bronwyn denied, "I didn't do that."

"You made me cry with your willfulness and your unreasoning stubbornness, and just because of you my cosmetics are running." Seated on a low ottoman, Holly raised her face to Bronwyn. "Have I ruined my powder?"

When Holly had discovered her in the salon, Bronwyn had cringed, but now her panic slowly dissipated, and she prepared to wheedle her way around Holly's sense of duty. Eyeing the parched surface of her sister's skin, she said, "No. But, Holly, why are you using all that stuff on your face? You're so beautiful."

Looking away, Holly muttered, "I'm not as young as you are."

"But it will make your hair fall out," Bronwyn protested.

Patient with her sister, Holly sighed. "I wear a wig."

"How could you be so resigned? You don't need it! You're one of the Sirens of Ireland," Bronwyn insisted.

"So?" Holly shrugged petulantly. "That hasn't stopped the onslaught of nature."

"Better to look like you at thirty-one than like me at twenty-two," Bronwyn answered with a fair amount of bitterness.

Holly flashed a glance over her sister. "You dare to complain, when your appearance is so cosmopolitan, so piquant, so *magnifique,* so *chic?*"

With faint humor Bronwyn protested, "Please, no French. It gets me in terrible trouble." She debated but couldn't resist asking, "Do you really believe I'm attractive?"

Holly reached up and pulled her down on the chair beside her. Bronwyn winced as her bottom made contact with the hard cushion, but Holly never noticed. "You look wild, like a lioness. You almost frighten me, for you draw every eye, and that's dangerous. You're attracting almost too much attention, and that will bring the envy. Trust me, it's not a comfortable feeling to know that other people will do you a wrong just because they're jealous. Be careful, little sister."

Feeling giddy and a little embarrassed, Bronwyn realized for the first time in her life that her looks were valued above her sisters'—by one of her sisters.

Studying Bronwyn, Holly decided, "I have something you need. I purchased it in Nice this spring." She rummaged in her fringed purse. "Parfum d'Orange, made by a little old man in this cunning shop who warned me it wasn't my scent at all, but I wouldn't listen and bought it anyway." Holly took Bronwyn's lacy handkerchief from her lax hand and drenched it with perfume, then dabbed it around Bronwyn's ears, along her arms, and on the part of her chest revealed by her décolletage. "There, isn't that devastating?"

Bronwyn breathed deep the fragrance of oranges. "It's wonderful."

"It's you." Holly slipped the glass bottle into one of Bronwyn's deep pockets. "Take it as a gift."

"Thank—"

"And go at once to Maman and Da and beg their pardon for worrying them."

Bronwyn laughed at her scheming sister. "I can't imagine they're worried. When has anything other than the next party ever worried them?"

"You're being terribly cold." Again Holly's big eyes filled with tears.

"I'm being terribly practical. Who's going to recognize me? Even your own husband hasn't figured out who I am, and he's ignored me for years."

"Of course he knows who you are." Holly refused to look toward the viscount of Sidkirk. "He's dissimulating."

"Holly," Bronwyn said in exasperation, "he's flirting with me."

Lines deepened around Holly's mouth, and two crevices creased the skin between her brows. "How could he? My own sister!"

"I never thought he could walk past a knothole in a tree." Bronwyn watched as Holly's chin quivered and asked hopefully, "You don't still love him, do you?"

Holly pulled out a handkerchief. "You know I do."

"Why?" Bronwyn pleaded for assurance. "You married him because Maman and Da told you to. He's ghastly rich, but he treats you with contempt. He's getting stout, I bet he has gout, and he's only interested in women much younger than himself."

"If you ever fell in love, you wouldn't ask that." Holly nodded. "That kind of love twines itself around your heart until you can never root it out."

"Sounds like a noxious weed to me."

"Sometimes I think so, too." Biting the perfect, well-rouged lips, Holly laid a hand on Bronwyn's arm. "But when it's wonderful, it's so wonderful. I wouldn't dream of living without it. When Sidkirk comes to me, I thrill with happiness. If we could just find you a man you could love . . ." Her eyes narrowed. "How is your fiancé?"

Bronwyn jumped. "What do you mean, how is he?"

"Ah," Holly breathed. "I begin to understand."

"Understand what?"

"Lord Rawson is a formidable man."

"Is he?"

"You answer everything with a question," Holly accused.

Bronwyn picked at her handkerchief. "Do I?"

"He's in the City, you know."

"I know." Desperate, Bronwyn smiled at the approaching Sidkirk. "Brother, how good to see you."

"Brother?" His corset creaked as he bent over Bronwyn's hand. "I wish to form a relationship with you, m'dear, but brother it isn't."

As his wet lips came in contact with her flesh, Bronwyn cracked her fan across the side of his face. "We already have a relationship, you dolt. I'm Holly's sister."

Holding his cheek, he squinted at her nearsightedly. "Impossible. All the Edana gels look just alike."

Holly laid a consoling hand on his other cheek. "La, Sidkirk, it's little Bronwyn."

He stared, goggle-eyed. "Little Bronwyn?"

"Your astonishment is flattering," Bronwyn noted sarcastically.

"Little Bronwyn!" With hearty goodwill, Sidkirk flung his arm around her waist.

The smell of lavender perfume, body odor, and bad teeth struck her at once. His pudgy fingers pinched her, then began a slow crawl up toward her breast. She brought up her elbow and struck his chest, while at the same time he fell back. She swung about to see Adam, holding Sidkirk by the muscle near his neck.

"Sidkirk!" Adam said cordially. "Keep your stinking hands off my wife."

At the sight of the dark lord, Bronwyn's heart slammed into her chest. She wanted to sink through the floor when she thought of what they'd done the night before. She wanted to stand tall with the pride of how he'd reacted to her. Her skin felt like fire, whether from embarrassment or desire, she didn't know. She held her hands together to avoid reaching for him and stepped back to avoid him. Dear God, she could hardly remember her name.

The beleaguered Sidkirk shrugged himself out of Adam's grip and took a quick step back. "Your wife? Then why do you care if I avail myself of a few of her charms?"

"I'm not—" Bronwyn began.

Adam's arm snaked around her shoulders, and his hand covered her mouth. She found herself melting like candle wax as he declared, "For all intents and purposes, she's my wife. My dearest wife. My treasure."

"Just as I thought," Holly said triumphantly. "The lion to tame the lioness."

Bronwyn stiffened.

Sidkirk knit his brow as he concentrated. "I hadn't heard you were married, so I s'pose you haven't been under the harness too long." He clapped Adam on the back. "Don't worry, Rawson, I'll take no more interest in her until your heir's safely in the nursery."

Bronwyn sank her teeth lightly into the flesh of Adam's palm and freed herself. Ignoring the man who stood much too close for comfort, she asked Holly, "You won't tell Maman and Da?"

"La, child. Of course not." Holly was the image of her mother as she put her cheek to Bronwyn's in the one gesture of physical affection she allowed herself. "If you're here with Lord Rawson, you couldn't be safer."

"Who's going to protect me from him?" Bronwyn muttered.

Adam pried open her fist. After taking the handkerchief she'd wadded into a ball, he shook it out. "*Merci, Madame la Vicomtesse.*"

Holly cocked an eyebrow at Adam. "You're the reason for her sudden dislike for French?"

Chuckling deep in his chest like someone who knew better, Adam said, "I would have thought I was the reason she adored French."

"I don't like being ignored," Bronwyn warned.

Adam smiled down at her, too many memories in his eyes. "*Ma petite, je ne peux jamais t'ignorer.*"

"What did he say?" Bronwyn demanded at the same moment.

"He could never ignore you," Holly translated.

"Thank you," Bronwyn said crisply, backing away as Adam's hands sought her bosom.

He caught her before she'd taken two steps. Brandishing the lacy handkerchief, he lifted it to his nose. "Parfum d'Orange. Clever girl, the scent fits you." He tucked it into Bronwyn's cleavage, spreading it to cover her chest.

"Really, Rawson, spoil the fun," Sidkirk remonstrated.

Torn between pleasure and annoyance, Bronwyn sniffed at Adam's breath. "He hasn't been drinking," she pronounced. "That's coffee. Where have you been?"

"At Change Alley," he answered, "listening to the gossip."

"Surely you know men don't gossip," Bronwyn said with sweet sarcasm.

Her brother-in-law didn't notice the slur but leaned forward eagerly. "What news?"

Adam smiled at Bronwyn, enjoying the bite of her wit. "A great deal of stock has been sold."

Sidkirk scratched under his wig. "So?"

"The directors are exchanging their stock for cash." Adam glanced at Sidkirk. "Do you comprehend what that means?"

Sidkirk still scratched, although whether from puzzlement or lice, Bronwyn didn't know. "Have you sent word to my father?" she asked.

"Of course." Adam grabbed her hands as they moved to remove the handkerchief. He explained to Holly, "Isn't she charming? She nags just like a wife."

"Amusing," Bronwyn spat.

"When will you come home with me and be my wife?" He still smiled, but his fingers squeezed hers. He used his eyes unfairly, gazing at her soulfully, sweetly, almost as if he loved her, adored her. It was heady stuff, and she was almost swayed. Almost.

Until Holly whimpered, "If she won't go back with you, you'll stay here with her, won't you?"

"I don't understand any of this," Sidkirk complained. "If you want the gel home, pick her up and take her home."

Adam still held her hands, still looked down at her. "I could do that," he conceded.

"Oh, Sidkirk," said his loving wife, "don't you understand anything? If Bronwyn doesn't want to go, she'll just run away and Rawson will never find her. Isn't that so?"

Neither Adam nor Bronwyn answered, their eyes locked in a battle of wills.

"I said, isn't that so?" Holly insisted.

At last Adam answered, "That's so. So I will be here at Madame Rachelle's for as long as it takes to persuade Bronwyn to come home."

Sidkirk rocked back on his heels. "Eh, well, don't let it drag on more than a few days."

Adam's declaration was all the more potent for being simple. "Days, weeks—I will be here for however long it takes."

Chapter 12

Whirling on her heel, Bronwyn began to dodge through the crowd. Anything to get away from Adam. Anything. He only pretended affection for her. A man whose heart was an abacus couldn't truly love. He only pretended he wished to marry her. She knew he worshiped the social esteem she would bring him. He only pretended she was pretty when she knew—

She stopped walking, stopped breathing. She was pretty. She was. Surely these weeks at Rachelle's had taught her the truth of it. Yet . . . when Adam had seen through her disguise, it seemed he had crushed more than her self-deception. He'd crushed her confidence. For if she looked like the Bronwyn of old, then she couldn't be attractive.

She slipped through the door, intent on escape, and fled up the stairs.

Someone followed her.

"Adam!" she exclaimed as he caught her arm. "What are you doing?"

"Why, I'm going to my room." He spread his hands and pulled an innocent face. "Are you retiring, too?"

Her heart thumped at the fire in his eyes, at the dark beauty that tempted her. Too well she recalled the tales of Satan and his seductions. How could she forget when the devil himself stalked her? She backed up the stairs, not certain if she sought to lure him or escape him. "You can't live with me."

"You were willing enough last night." Adam followed her up.

"Last night was different. You weren't living with me. I was seducing you." He smiled as if he had fond memories he'd like to reenact, and she added swiftly, "Last night you didn't know who I was."

"Believe me, I did. I knew immediately. Your appearance has changed, indeed, but not so much that the man who gazed into your eyes and gave you your first kiss wouldn't know you."

"You were guessing," she accused.

"So I *was* the first man to kiss you," Adam crowed.

Too late she perceived his trap. She thought about lying. Saying she'd kissed hundreds of men. But how could she? Plain Bronwyn would never lure a sweetheart, and her falsehood would be exposed for what it was: a desperate attempt to impress a man who happened to be her lover. "Were you guessing?" she asked hopefully.

He crushed her hopes without conscience. "Not at all. And for confirmation, there was the occasional lapse in French accent."

Bronwyn groped for the post at the top of the stairs.

"What did you think when I invited you up to my room?"

He stopped below her and glared. "I thought you'd be coming home with me today."

She stopped on the landing and glared right back. "A very mannish thing to think."

"I am a man. Do you wish to know what I think right now?"

"What?"

"That we will put teeth into the adage that most babies take nine months, but the first one can come anytime."

At first she didn't understand. Then she did. She lowered her eyes and studied the feathery carving of her fan. "I doubt I am with child."

"Yet," he said pleasantly.

Trying to sound stern and imposing, she answered, "There will be no repeats of last night."

He said nothing, and she looked up. A glow surrounded him; he burned so hot that she could have warmed her hands. But she didn't want to put out her hands; she was afraid to move. Yesterday he had been a lion in search of his prey. Today he was a lion whose prey had escaped him, and he was meaner and hungrier.

She heard the small snap of ivory as she squeezed her fan, and as if it were a signal, she whirled and ran.

He didn't catch her until she reached her door, until she had her hand on the knob. Then he turned her into his arms. "Cherie, there's no need to run to the bedroom. We should save our energy and walk."

Suspecting he'd caught her at his convenience, she pushed at his chest. "We can't do this."

"On the contrary. We are very good at 'this' "—his

teeth flashed in the dark—"and we'll do it until I've convinced you."

"Convinced me of what?"

"Convinced you that we—"

Stricken by the thought, she said, "I've injured your pride."

He blinked. "What?"

"I've injured your pride." Amazed, she gripped his shoulders. "You thought I'd be so unnerved by love for you, I'd give up all my ambitions, all my dreams and hopes. I heard what you said to Northrup. You said if you seduced me, I'd stop sounding like a learned woman."

He reared back, offended. "I didn't mean it."

Convinced, she tapped the cleft of his chin. "Maybe you didn't think you meant it, but that was what you hoped."

"I never—" He tried again. "I'm sure it was not my intention—"

She stared at him.

He softened. His mouth curled with chagrin; he put his forehead against hers. "Perhaps that was my intention, I don't know. Perhaps I still believe if I bed you enough, you'll be what I wish you to be. I do know I don't wish you to change—so much for a man's logic." His smile teased her. "I do know that, one way or the other, we'll have a good time proving the truth." Flattening himself against her, he bent to press his lips to hers.

She knew how to kiss now; he'd taught her. She opened her mouth to him, greeted him with the touch of her tongue, dug her fingers into his shirt to pull him closer. Sandwiched between him and the door, she knew the fluctuations of his temperature and respiration, and they seemed to keep step with her own.

When he pulled back she was panting and afraid her

eyes glowed like his. Too plainly she could see he wouldn't be swayed—and plainly she didn't want to sway him. Yet when he pushed against her, she remembered she really couldn't repeat the previous night's activities.

"Adam," she stammered.

"My love?"

"Adam, you must understand. It's not that I'm a tease."

He rubbed her shoulders. "I know that better than you know yourself, I think."

"Yes, well . . ." She lost her concentration when he rubbed his cheek against her hair.

He murmured, "Such a crime to hide this glorious sight beneath that ghastly wig. A crime for which I'll have to discipline you."

He made it sound good. Her eyes widened. "How?"

"I'll show you."

He reached for the doorknob, but she caught his wrist. "Adam, I can't. I just . . . can't."

Catching a bit of her mood, he sobered and stroked her cheek with his knuckles. "Tell me. I'll understand."

Staring at her hands as they twisted in his cravat, she stalled until she could stall no more. "I'm sore," she whispered.

"What?" He sounded a little hoarse, and she twisted a little harder.

Taking a breath, she wailed more loudly than she meant, "I'm sore." Mortified, she hid her head in his shirt.

One by one he pulled her fingers out of his cravat and kissed them. He drew in a deep breath, then kissed her ear until she squirmed and raised her head. In fervent apology he said, "I'm sorry. It's my fault. I knew better, but what can a woman like you expect? You sow temptation, you must expect to reap desire."

Flattered and flustered, she stammered, "But—"

"But that doesn't cure your problem. Too true." He turned the doorknob behind her back and spun her into the bedroom. He shut the door with his back and leaned against it. "I know other ways to make love. Let me teach you."

Adam slowed his horse to a walk and looked at his riding companion. "Madame Rachelle, I cannot approve of Bronwyn living in your home."

Rachelle smiled pleasantly. "I am sure you cannot."

"You're going to be obstructive about this, aren't you?" Adam asked.

She nodded to an acquaintance. "About what, *mon ami*?"

"I want you to toss Bronwyn out onto the streets so she's forced to return to my home."

"But that is no way to treat a friend," she said. "And Bronwyn is my friend."

"I know." He had to proceed with care, he realized. Rachelle wasn't Bronwyn, clever but unworldly. Cynical and protective, Rachelle was well aware of her worth to society. "You've made her more than she was before."

She seemed less than pleased with his tribute. "Not at all. She was always the wonderful, witty, lovely woman she now professes to be. No one has ever before encouraged her to blossom."

"I suppose that's an assault on me."

She widened her eyes in obvious guile. "If you believe it is, perhaps there is some justification, hm?"

"You are an exasperating woman."

Stiffening, she said, "So my husband used to tell me." She touched her horse with her whip, and the gallant animal responded with the burst of speed she seemed to desire.

Hostility rode in the saddle with her, and he marveled how his attempt to appease had so quickly turned to battle. He galloped behind her, wondering what to say. With any other woman, he would compliment her dress, her hair, instigate a bit of gossip. With Rachelle, such maneuvering would only annoy her more.

She slowed, dropped back. Her hand on his made him turn to her. "Come. You must forgive me. You did nothing but say the words that carried me back to another, less inviting time." Her rueful smile apologized.

"Of course, madame. It's forgotten." He inclined his head, wondering at this sign of moodiness in the normally self-possessed woman. "But you could grant me a boon."

"I will not throw Bronwyn onto the streets," Rachelle answered at once.

"I never thought you would." He grinned at her wordless skepticism. "I had to try. All you could say is no, as you did. No, my true desire is for something quite different."

All gracious noblewoman, she nodded cordially. "I'll grant it if I can, then."

"I want you to hire a footman."

Taken aback, she exclaimed, "A footman!"

"Or a butler." He pulled his mount beneath a tree and waited until she brought her mount around to join him. "Or any man who would provide a household of women with some protection."

"We do not need protection."

Serious and persuasive, he said, "I think you do. Violence stalks London streets. Only a fool never fears."

Her mouth tightened as she remembered her daughter's death. "That does not mean we should corrupt our salon with the presence of a man."

"I'm a man," he pointed out. "Fully functioning, not too obnoxious, and living in your house."

"So we do not need a footman," she answered triumphantly.

"I spend only the nights there. My days are spent at Change Alley, and I find myself distracted by fears for Bronwyn's life." Hand outstretched in appeal, he said, "I can't concentrate, madame."

"And I did promise to grant a boon." She mulled it over. "But there are few men who wish to work for a single woman."

"Ah." He fished a letter out of his pocket. "I have here a letter from an excellent young man, an immigrant like yourself, who seeks employment. Amazingly enough, he worked in a salon in Italy, performing just the functions I require."

Madame laughed aloud. "You amaze me. First you want me to have a footman, then you conjure one out of thin air."

"Actually, it was this letter, listing his qualifications and experiences, that made me consider the dangers of London for my Bronwyn." Adam opened the letter and scanned it. "He sends references from the *salonière*, as well as references from several titled employers. I'm unable to verify immediately, of course, but I interviewed the young man, and he would blend into any circumstances with impunity."

"A chameleon?"

"Surely that is an asset to a salon." She lifted a brow

of inquiry, and he shrugged. "Also, the young man is in need at the moment. English noble houses hesitate to employ foreigners, and the man has to eat. I thought that if you hired him, it would solve two problems, both mine and his."

"You are a hard man, Adam Keane."

"A hard man?" Startled, then disgusted, he protested, "I think I'm becoming positively philanthropic."

"Yes, and there is the other. *Fidélité est de Dieu.*"

"Fidelity is of God," Adam translated. "Why do you say that?"

"I admire your fidelity. For the last week, you have been the sweetest of suitors for the hand of your lady, and I admire you for your restraint. Most men would have performed less nobly than you. Very well," she decided. "I will do as you ask. I will hire this man. Did you say his name?"

"Gianni," Adam answered. "His name is Gianni."

The tap came on the door early in the morning, but Adam was awake. How could he help it? This bed was of generous size for one, most unsuited for two. The week he'd spent sleeping in it hadn't hardened him to the discomforts, or the joys, of sharing it with Bronwyn.

"Lord Rawson?" Rachelle spoke quietly through the panel. "There is a man here who is most insistent he see you."

Ever wary, Adam asked, "Who?"

"He says his name is Northrup."

Adam rolled out of bed. "Thank you. I'll be down at once."

Pushing her hair out of her eyes, Bronwyn struggled up onto her elbow. "What is it?"

Adam grinned at his darling, yawning and rosy from the night's lovemaking. "Nothing. Go back to sleep. Bronwyn Edana has translations to do today, and Cherie has a salon to entertain tonight."

"I leave the entertaining to Daphne." Bronwyn sank back on the pillow. "Will you go right to Change Alley?"

"Always." He dressed rapidly, now used to doing without a valet.

"You spend too much time down there," Bronwyn complained. "Every day."

"Not every day, although I should be there every day. You must remember, my dear, I have no ancestral lands to wring money from. My father sold all those. I have no court appointments to collect bribes from. I'm not corrupt. I must make my money in Change Alley." He leaned close to her. "You're marrying a man with an unstable income."

She lifted her head and put her nose against his. "I'm not marrying anyone, but if I were marrying you, I'd never worry about money."

Half-pleased with her answer, he said, "Besides, you've managed to lure me from my duty more than once."

She smiled at the reminder. "It's dreadfully early for anyone to be astir at the Alley."

He paused, his hand thrust halfway into his shirt. "Is there a reason for me to return here?"

She stretched, and a nipple peeked from beneath the sheet. "Perhaps."

"Then perhaps I will return." He chuckled at her pout and knew the perhaps would be a certainty. He descended the stairs, entered Rachelle's study, and caught Northrup pacing back and forth in agitated, jerky movements. Seeing Adam, Northrup flew to him and grasped his coat panels. Adam gently put Northrup's hands aside as he said, "Calm yourself. Nothing is so bad one may lose his composure over it."

"I've done it." Pale beneath the carmine he used to highlight his cheeks, Northrup gasped as if he'd run for miles. "I've found a way to pay you back."

Adam studied the young man. "Pay me back for what?"

"For your help, for the training, for—"

"I told you there was no debt."

"To me there was, and I've got information you will kill for."

"Tell me, then."

"After your first visit to Change Alley, and every other time you've come, there has been a problem."

Northrup was serious, deadly serious. Adam sobered and leaned closer. "What kind of problem?"

"Stock." Northrup jerked off his wig and threw it to the floor. "Counterfeit stock is released every time you're in Change Alley, and everyone says Adam Keane, Lord Rawson, is selling it."

Chapter 13

Dressed in her black silk, Rachelle waited in the doorway of her study. "Cherie, it is evening. Will you be dressing soon? Just because Adam did not send word all day, you should not bury yourself in your manuscript."

Bronwyn erased the hopeful expression Rachelle's arrival had brought to her face. "Of course, I'll come." The lettering of a long dead monk blurred before her eyes. She was tired, true, but more than that she was disturbed.

Adam hadn't returned that morning. Confident he would, she'd risen to wash and prepare herself, but he hadn't come. She'd dropped into a doze, and when she woke the sun shone with the fervor of midmorning.

After dressing, she'd sought breakfast and information. He was gone, she was told. Had left early with Northrup.

Bronwyn rubbed the hollow place in her stomach. How odd it felt to be abandoned by Adam.

Not abandoned, she assured herself swiftly. But left behind. Left out.

Rachelle came to her side and touched her shoulder. "You worry too much. *Monsieur le Vicomte* demonstrates *empressement* about your every movement. He will be here tonight."

"Empressement?" Bronwyn asked, stacking up her papers.

"It is hard to translate. It means ardor. Eagerness."

"He has the right to leave me for the day. I'm not offended," Bronwyn assured her. "I'm just spoiled. I've grown used to having him confide his destination and his intentions, as if I have the right to know."

She laughed a little, but the laugh stuck in her throat when Rachelle said, "As if you were his wife."

All Bronwyn's sophistication collapsed with Rachelle's observation. Elbows on the table, she dropped her head onto her palms. "I'm so dreadfully confused."

Rachelle sounded amused as she agreed, "I had suspected that."

"First I was resigned to marrying Adam, then I cared about him and wanted to marry him. Then I found him to be a traitor to me, and running away seemed a reasonable idea. I did, he arrived here, he was still attractive, I thought, Why not seduce him? He'll never know who I am. That seemed a reasonable idea. Now, I'm back to thinking marriage is a reasonable idea."

"Perhaps reason is not the building block on which to build your life."

Rachelle's irony struck an answering chord in Bronwyn, and she gave Rachelle a speaking look as she corked the ink bottle. She stood, stretching. "Suffice it to say I can't concentrate. My confidence is still too new to withstand a whole, long day of being ignored by my lover."

"Bronwyn."

Rachelle so seldom called her by her real name, and her tone was so intense, Bronwyn stopped and stared. "Rachelle?"

For the first time since Bronwyn had known her, Rachelle looked drained of energy. "I just want you to know how much I have enjoyed having you with me."

"As I have enjoyed being here." Troubled, Bronwyn observed Rachelle as she moved away from her. "Am I leaving?"

"All things come to an end. I think perhaps this episode of your life is fading."

"You mean because of Adam?"

"For that reason, also." Rachelle folded her hands before her. By her very stillness, she gave evidence of an inner turmoil. "I am not a woman of intuition, but I predict tonight will be difficult."

Bronwyn grasped Rachelle's wrist. "Adam has returned to Boudasea, hasn't he? He's left me."

"Not at all. I think I can safely reassure you." Rachelle's cool lips brushed Bronwyn's forehead. "He would never abandon you."

Brow furrowed, Bronwyn watched as Rachelle left her. How cryptic she had been! She hurried above to her room, where her maid waited. As a present to her, Adam had rented two rooms in an inn nearby and sent for his valet and the maid. Now she no longer struggled with buttons and corsets or begged for assistance from the other women.

The transformation from Bronwyn to Cherie took

only a little color on the lips, a thorough brushing of the hair, and an elaborate gown. Since Adam's advent into her bed, she'd grown so beautiful that she scarcely needed the paint pot and powder puff.

When the preparations were complete, the charming, fascinating, exotic Cherie entered the salon. Ribbons and tiny flowers threaded her silver hair, her vivid turquoise taffeta dress hugged her tiny waist and billowed around her feet, she carried her signature ivory fan—and no one even noticed her! She was the toast of Madame Rachelle's, and no one even noticed her.

Bronwyn swept a puzzled glance around. What was wrong? No music, no polite laughter, no intellectual arguments hummed in the air. Rachelle stood alone, her hands clasped in front of her like a diva about to render an aria. Her dignity was palpable, her demeanor sorrowful.

Stationed about the large room, little clusters of people buzzed like swarming bees. Like bees, also, they displayed their stingers in their hostile posture. They glanced over their shoulders, they whispered and hummed behind cupped hands.

And there stood Adam, leaning negligently against the fireplace. An inner leap of joy brought her stepping toward him. Then caution slowed her. Why hadn't he come upstairs? Since he'd moved into her room, they'd come down together every evening. They'd made it clear they were devoted, and none had dared comment.

So she slowed, and he watched her with a cynical smile.

She felt almost timid when she said, *"Monsieur le Vicomte,* how good to see you."

"Is it?" He lifted his chin from his palm. "I would have never suspected."

His gray eyes no longer adored her, they skimmed her. He mocked her with indifference, but something about him suggested pain. Compassion drove her to put her hand on his shoulder. "What is it? Have you hurt your leg?"

Adam shook her off. "I have not."

"You walked for too long."

He sighed. "I warned you that Change Alley made a fickle mistress."

She considered him. Financial reverses would explain his preoccupation. He'd already expressed anxiety that he had no ancestral lands on which to fall back; perhaps he believed she'd be fickle if not well supported. She seized that rationalization with the eagerness of the insecure. "Are the South Sea stocks falling?"

In a lightning move, he snagged a handful of her hair. "Have you been listening to the gossip?"

He tightened his grip as she tried to step back, and she complained, "Ouch! That hurts."

His teeth gleamed in his savage smile. "Perhaps you should return to wearing a wig. Accidents such as this would not happen."

He opened his hand, and she whirled away. At a loss to justify his odd behavior, angry at his ruthless dismissal, she stalked to Mr. Webster's side. "Sir!"

Her young admirer tugged at his cravat as if it were tied too securely. "Mademoiselle?"

"You come here with your scientific experiments, your vacuum balls, and your flameless candles." She glared in Adam's direction. "Have you given any credence to the theory of moon madness?"

"Why, I . . . I've never considered such a thing." He coughed.

Bronwyn tapped his chest with her fan. "Perhaps you should. I believe there's a return of the midsummer madness right now." She smiled at him brilliantly, determined to demonstrate her carefree attitude to anyone who might care. To Adam, who might be watching.

But her young admirer seemed horrified at being singled out. He sidled away, and she realized belatedly that all gossip had died on her approach. She had become not the center of attention, but the center of condemnation. But why?

What had Rachelle been trying to tell her earlier? That her time here dwindled, that . . . her true identity had been discovered? She glanced at Adam, at Webster, at the whole buzzing salon. Now she recognized the stares, the false sympathy, the drawing away.

So they knew. She nodded. It distressed her less than she'd thought. Had she been impatient to be revealed?

Her initial dismay baffled her, followed as it was by her determination to brazen it out. With a breezy smile she called, "Mr. Webster, have you brought me another experiment to view?"

He gulped. "Not tonight."

"Then tomorrow night." She turned to the others. "Lady Mary Montagu has sent word she will visit. Have you come to listen to our brightest wit?"

No one answered. They shuffled their feet and poked each other with their elbows, then looked beyond her. She turned to see Carroll Judson, dapper, well made-up, with sparkling eyes that boded ill for someone.

She almost welcomed the challenge. "Have you come to listen to our brightest wit, Mr. Judson?"

"Not at all. I came to view the wreckage." He bowed, his hand on his snowy, showy cravat.

She didn't want him to be the one to tell the world.

She didn't want him here at all. But if this devious little man had unmasked her, she couldn't deny him the pleasure of her public revelation. "Wreckage?" she asked.

"The wreckage of Madame Rachelle's facade." Gesturing about him, he asked, "Can't you see it?"

Confused, she snapped, "I see nothing."

"But it's all around you. Her friends have disappeared. Her salon has dissolved. Her masquerade is over." He lifted a pomander to his nose and sniffed in delicate appreciation. "Her crime is revealed."

His delighted horror scarcely fit her opinion of her own escapade. "I would hardly call this a crime."

He drew himself up, gathering dignity like a cloak. "Perhaps, as her disciple, you approve of parricide."

A tendril of ice touched the back of her neck, trickled down her spine. She didn't answer him, just stared and waited, held in terrorized suspense.

"Haven't you heard, or are you still in ignorance?"

She shut her fan with verve. "What are you suggesting?"

"Rachelle had no reason to seek her daughter's murderer." He raised his voice so all could hear. He leaned toward her to drive the shock deep. "She *is* her daughter's murderer."

A red mist covered her vision. Her nails, newly grown, cut into her palms. From the depths of her memory, she heard her father warning her not to give in to her temper. She recalled how her governess had punished her childish tantrums. She knew she had mastered her wrath on every occasion, but—this seemed to justify an exception.

She drew back and slapped his face. The sound echoed like a gunshot through the salon. All eyes turned their way. In the throes of an Irish rage, she gritted, "You spiteful little worm. How dare you come here, partake of Madame's food, of her wine, of her hospitality, and spread such rumors?"

He stepped back, pushed by the gust of her fury.

"You worthless toad. Get out, and don't ever come back." Her voice lifted like a singer's in an operatic frenzy. She pointed to the door. "Get out."

Bits of his powder flaked off in the imprint of her hand, and the skin beneath was choleric. His face distorted, he leapt at her.

He found his way blocked by Adam, his lifted arm caught in a steel grasp. Soft and low, Adam warned, "You don't want to hit her. I'd take it ill."

Held in Adam's grip, Judson gained control of himself with frightening alacrity. He squealed, "I'll go."

Bronwyn stepped close. "An excellent plan."

Adam gave him a push, and he stumbled backward. He looked at the two of them, one so furious, one so adamant, and clearly he wanted to speak. He shook his finger at Adam; he opened his mouth more than once. At last he snarled, "I'll go, but Cherie—perhaps you should ask your beloved Madame why she left France. Ask her why she left, ask her how she acquired so much money, and be sure you ask her why she can never go back to France. Ask her, if you dare." With that, he stomped away, leaving behind a widening pool of silence.

Feeling like one of the Greek Furies, Bronwyn flexed her stinging palm. She cast her gaze upon the avid faces gathered close to observe the scene, but only Adam dared meet her eye. He moved to her side: amused, pleased, the same man she'd loved this past week.

Bronwyn looked to Rachelle, and Rachelle smiled at

her. Like the sun, her smile warmed Bronwyn, yet at the same time she felt as if Rachelle were as distant as Helios himself.

Determined to bring a semblance of normalcy to the salon, Bronwyn suggested, "Shall we have some music? Perhaps one of Handel's harpsichord fantasies."

"You're a ferocious little thing in defense of your friends. I believe you've cowed these mere mortals," Adam murmured in her ear.

She didn't know what she'd done to bring him back, but she answered, "Your humor is ill timed." Pointing at one of Handel's disciples, she pressed the young man into service, knowing full well the harpsichord would muffle the disdain hanging heavy in the air.

Taking advantage of the civilized atmosphere the music created, she circulated about the room. Adam followed her to comment, "Efficient and ferocious. A good friend of Madame Rachelle's."

She'd had time to reflect, and she spread her fingers. "I probably did more harm than good. Such anger only feeds the speculation. Look at them. They're still not leaving. It *is* the midsummer madness."

"Madness of some kind. They wander about, restless as beasts, waiting for the final act in this farce."

Distracted by her desire to protect Rachelle, she almost failed to notice his self-mockery. "I dare not even visit with her, reassure her. To do so would center all eyes on her." As his words penetrated, she snapped her head around. "What do you mean, they're waiting for the final act?"

"The final act." He bowed to her. "It begins now. Your elderly beau approaches."

Lord Sawbridge bore down on them with Daphne on his arm.

"My elderly beau?" Bronwyn chuckled, wavering with the shocks of the evening. "You jest."

"He would have gladly warmed your bed," Adam told her. "He's been most distressed that I took what he was too impotent to achieve. Now he'll have his revenge."

"Rawson?" Lord Sawbridge peered at him myopically. "It *is* you. Can't believe you're here tonight."

Adam raised a haughty brow. "Where should I be?"

"You have the nerve to put in an appearance." Lord Sawbridge harrumphed. "After what you've done."

Adam drew out his carved box and flipped it open with an elegant movement of his hand. "Mint pastille?"

"No, damn it." Sawbridge mopped his brow. "Wouldn't take anything from you. God knows how you got it."

Dizzy with the malice that filled the air, Bronwyn asked, "Why wouldn't you take anything from Lord Rawson?"

"Like father, like son," Sawbridge quoted. "As the sapling is bent, so grows the tree. The sins of the father and all that."

"Polonius indeed," Bronwyn observed. "Pray continue."

Lord Sawbridge smirked in self-righteous indignation. "If you wished to take a lover, m'dear, you should have taken me."

Cold as the north wind, Bronwyn retorted, "I didn't want you."

"Your mistake. Your mistake." His pudgy fingers pinched at her side before she could step away. "I'm as rich as Rawson, and my father never taught me the trade his father did."

Blank as a schoolboy's slate, Bronwyn stammered,

"Taught a trade? What do you mean? Lord Rawson was never taught a trade by his father."

"He can tell you, m'dear." Lord Sawbridge rubbed his belly in solemn emphasis. "He can tell you."

Bronwyn looked to Adam.

A bored smile stretched Adam's lips. "He means I am a counterfeiter."

"A counterfeiter?" Bronwyn suspected she'd stumbled into a nest of Bedlamites. "Of what?"

Daphne clarified it for her. "Your lover has been counterfeiting South Sea stock."

The two bearers of bad tidings, Lord Sawbridge and Daphne, awaited Bronwyn's reaction. She stared at them, noting their pleasure. She wondered what they expected from her—another explosion of wrath? A scene of denunciation?

She stared at Adam, noting his studied indifference. She thought she knew what he expected of her. A modicum of dignity, a dismissal of few words. "What rot," she said crisply.

Lord Sawbridge and Daphne still waited with avid anticipation. Adam still smiled his chilly smile. Pinching the skin between her eyes, Bronwyn pronounced, "This is a most unusual evening."

"Is that all you have to say?" Lord Sawbridge asked.

She took her hand away. "What do you want me to say?"

Swelling with triumph, Daphne suggested, "Perhaps her callous attitude betrays her knowledge of the crime."

"Madness." Bronwyn turned away from all of them. She wanted to be with someone sane, someone who understood the people and events surrounding them. She started across the room, no longer caring if she brought attention to Rachelle. At Madame's side, she repeated, "Pure madness."

"You're in the midst of a whirlwind, aren't you?" Rachelle took Bronwyn's hand.

"I'm in the midst of a whirlwind?" Bronwyn gave a half-hysterical laugh. "You heard what Judson said about you?"

"How could I fail to hear?"

"Now Daphne and ol' Sawbones are accusing Adam of counterfeiting."

"I know." Leading her past the new footman, Rachelle asked, "Do you believe it?"

Rolling her eyes, Bronwyn protested, "No one who is acquainted with Adam would believe it. Only a fool would fail to see his integrity. But why are they saying such a thing? Don't they understand how he can hurt them?"

Rachelle stopped on the sill of her study. "Hurt them?"

"A rich man has his ways," Bronwyn said sagely, "and Adam is a very rich man."

Rachelle suggested, "Perhaps they believe they can hurt him more."

"How?" Bronwyn demanded.

"By striking at his reputation and his family honor." Rachelle put her cool hand to Bronwyn's cheek, as if she wanted to emphasize her words with her touch. "It is well known Lord Rawson is tender about his honor."

Repulsed, Bronwyn pushed her way into the study. "I wish to scream at them."

Shutting the door behind her, Rachelle followed in a graceful glide. "Why didn't you?"

Flopping back in a delicate chair, Bronwyn grimaced. "A childish tantrum will impress those idiots in quite the wrong manner. I apologize for my earlier outburst."

Rachelle hesitated as if torn. Bronwyn lifted her brows in inquiry, but Rachelle shook her head in some inner denial and said only, "I thank you for your spirited defense."

"If I had been free to speak, I would have told them how Henriette died. How did such an ugly rumor get started?"

"Once someone discovered the old tale of why I left France, I suppose it was inevitable they would accuse me of Henriette's death."

"It's an indication of the small minds that litter our society. . . ." Bronwyn tilted her head. "What old tale?"

Moving cautiously, as if she didn't want to alarm Bronwyn, Rachelle perched atop the desk. "They say I left France because I killed my husband."

Her legs stretched out before her, Bronwyn wiggled her feet and watched them with a detached fascination. "Outrageous."

"Not at all. It's the truth."

All Bronwyn's joints locked. All her mental functions ceased. She couldn't speak.

"I did kill him. He was a nobleman, I was his wife, and I stabbed him to death."

Forsaken in the salon, Adam ignored the whispers, the stares. Bronwyn had abandoned him. Abandoned him like a newly diagnosed leper. Sawbridge and Daphne had brought their accusations, Bronwyn had made a weak comment, and she'd left. Gone to Rachelle and left.

The blow staggered him. He'd expected, he'd hoped for, loyalty from Bronwyn, and she'd deserted him.

Sickened, bumping into furniture and people, he walked out. He would go now. Go back to Boudasea Manor, go back and try to rescue his ailing business. He would just walk out—

But he found himself climbing the stairs to the room under the eaves, going like some wounded animal in need of succor to the den he shared with Bronwyn.

Maybe she'd made a mistake, he thought as he climbed. Maybe she'd been so stunned by the counterfeiting charge, she'd been unable to deal with it in public. Opening the door, he heard movement within, and his heart leaped when he saw Bronwyn's beloved face, streaked with tears. He opened his arms, and she rushed to him. She crushed his waist with her hug, and he hugged her back. His jubilation couldn't be contained.

Bronwyn supported him. She believed in him.

Without care for his still formal toilette, she clutched his waistcoat. "Do you know what Rachelle just told me?"

His leg collapsed under the impact of his surprise. "Rachelle?"

"Are you well?" She led him to the chair, settled him on the cushion, perched on the arm, and wrapped her arm around his shoulders. "This night has been a shock, I know, but Rachelle gave me permission to confide her secret in you." Anguished, she dug her face into his cravat. "Dear God, Adam, she killed her husband." He stiffened, and she hastened to add, "For good reason."

"I see." He didn't see. He didn't see anything. Why was she talking about Rachelle?

"He beat her. He beat her so badly she still bears the scars. She showed me. . . ." She shuddered.

Unable to help himself, he offered comfort in the squeeze of his hand.

"Her family wouldn't help her. They blamed her. No one would help her, although everyone at Versailles knew what he was. She could do nothing, nothing." Her voice broke, and his other arm hugged her waist. "Then she became pregnant."

"Was it his child?"

She glared through threatening tears. "Of course it was his."

"It's a reasonable question," he pointed out. "If he beat her so unmercifully, perhaps she found solace elsewhere."

"It's a stupid question!" she ripped at him. "Why would a woman who'd been raped in every way by her husband, who'd had bones broken by her husband— why would she ever want another man? She has no use for men."

He paid her vehemence the compliment of gravity. "Why did she kill him?"

"Because he beat the baby! Henriette was a child of five, and he broke her ribs." Tears trickled down her face, but she seemed unaware.

Without hesitation he declared, "He deserved killing."

"God, yes. Her family was too powerful for her to be tried. His family didn't want a scandal attached to his name, so they gave her money enough to live the rest of her life. Old King Louis ordered her into exile, and she came here to raise her daughter in safety."

Her nose was rosy, her eyes were puffy, and yet the sight of her tugged at him. Perhaps her compassion to Rachelle had blinded her to his plight. He pushed his handkerchief into her hand. "Wipe your face," he commanded.

A spot spread on the embroidered silk of his waistcoat, and she dabbed at the damage.

"Never mind that. Blow." He directed the handkerchief to her nose and she blew.

Twisting the handkerchief, she said, "Her daughter died of the very fate Rachelle sought to avoid, and the rumors accuse Rachelle of the crime which most fills her with dread."

"Most unfair, but I have reason to know how unfair rumors can be." He was testing her, he knew, and he rejoiced when her hand pressed the place over his heart. Now she would be indignant on his behalf. Now she would be compassionate. Now his faith in her would be rewarded.

Solemn and sweet, she replied, "And I, but I don't believe our troubles are as weighty as Rachelle's."

Incredulous, he searched her every feature. Her tender mouth trembled, her sherry-colored eyes clung to his. The blotchiness of weeping was already passing.

Where was her righteous indignation for *him*?

Her calm passed, changed to bewilderment. "Adam? Why do you look at me like that?"

"Is this all you have to say to me?" he demanded.

"Well, I—no." She fumbled for words, her face suffused with guilt. "I suppose you're talking about Henriette."

His calm exploded. "Henriette?" he shouted.

She flinched. "I know I should have told you before, but Olivia and I rescued Henriette before she died."

Her audacity confounded him. How dare she discuss a dead woman whom he'd never met, when he'd been stripped of trustworthiness? "You're talking to me about Rachelle's daughter *now*?"

"I should have trusted you, but I was afraid you'd be angry." She took a breath. "As you are. I didn't even tell my father, but she said something I think you'll understand."

"Henriette said something you think I'll understand?"

"And if you'll stop yelling at me, I'll tell you what it is."

Rage, thick and blinding as a sea fog, overwhelmed him.

"She said that the bastard who abducted her had threatened to kill a man by dropping a stock on him. Now I have deduced—"

He didn't shout this time. He whispered, "Don't say another word."

She opened her mouth.

"Nothing." The ice of his soul chilled each word, and her eyes widened as the cold struck her. "I don't want to talk to you, and I don't want to hear you."

Her mouth worked, tears welled up once more, and she asked, "Are you going to leave me?"

Bitter laughter rocked him. "You'd like that, wouldn't you? It would make it so easy for you." Some monster reached up from inside him and made him say the one thing he shouldn't. "No, I won't leave you. I'm going to stay here and make your life hell, my dear. Living hell." His walking stick in hand, he opened the door, then turned back. "Be here when I get back."

Her cry didn't bring him back, but he was tempted. Damn her, he was tempted. That made him angrier than ever, for he knew his father had destroyed him once more, but this time he had an ally. Bronwyn, his beautiful Bronwyn, had stabbed him through the heart.

Chapter 14

Change Alley had a frantic look about it. Noblemen and chimney sweeps scurried like ants, as if by their activity they could create prosperity where there was none. A September heat wave never checked their enterprise, for ruin stalked them. Adam sat at his table in Garraway's, watched with grim amusement, and wondered how he would ever find a conspiracy in a place where no one would speak to him.

Whoever had created the rumor of counterfeiting had chosen his target well. Adam had never been popular in himself. As Walpole told him, he was too serious, too menacing. But people used to deal with him because he was a respected, licensed broker.

Now he was only licensed.

All believed he'd cheated them. They wanted to believe it—they liked to believe it. Why not? It provided them with a focus, a person on whom to blame their troubles.

He lifted his finger for a refill of coffee. Garraway glanced his way and sent the barmaid.

He wouldn't have minded the snubs, the jeers, the overloud comments, but did Bronwyn have to pretend she thought nothing of his disgrace? She never questioned him about his father, so he knew she'd been gossiping behind his back. It grated at him when he thought of how she'd shrugged or, worse, laughed. Like a fool, he stayed at Madame Rachelle's, waiting for the moment Bronwyn would declare her faith in him. The moment never came, and the tension between them mounted.

Oh, she felt it. But she considered any agony of his to be unimportant. Why? Too easily he knew the answer. She only toyed with him. His grand design to seduce her, trap her by affection, and then marry her had fallen to dust. Seduced, trapped, he cared for a woman who believed every lie spread about him. Believed them and didn't care enough about him to clear his honor.

He wouldn't even make love to her, although she pleaded for reasons. He slept on a chair, ignoring her temptations. Something in him rebelled at being used like a fancy man, to assuage the desire he'd taught her. But he wanted to. Oh, God, he wanted to. Misery moved through him slowly, like the darkest sludge of the river Thames.

A harsh, feminine voice interrupted his melancholy. "Ye Lord Rawson?"

The woman, painted, thin, obviously a prostitute, stood with one hip thrust to the side, her arms crossed over her chest. The odor of the docks clung to her. Warily Adam answered, "I am Lord Rawson."

She threw a clump of paper on the table before him. " 'Ere's some of yer stock."

After picking one certificate loose from the damp wad, Adam held it up. Ink ran from it, blurring the picture on the stock certificate. "If I had printed this, I would have done a better job."

"They tell me this ain't South Sea stocks. They tell me t' find ye an' get me money."

"Who told you?" Adam asked.

"That snip o' a clerk at th' South Sea Company." Hands on hips, the woman sneered, "Ye're a fine gennaman, ain't ye? Got so much money, ye got t' rob us that ain't got so much. I know men like ye. I've 'ad customers like ye. Cheat an 'onest woman out o' an 'onest wage."

Adam held up his hand. "Madam, cease your harangue."

"Who's goina make me?"

Although her tone was belligerent, her expression belied her resentment. Tears hovered in her eyes. She wiped her nose on the fringe of her shawl. With a calm born of seaboard command, Adam ordered, "Straighten that back! Pull back those shoulders!"

Instinctively she did.

"First of all, I would know who sold you those stocks."

She slumped again. "Some flunky o' yers, no doubt."

"Describe him, please," Adam said crisply. "If you can describe him so I can discover his identity, I'll pay your debt."

"M'Gawd!" The woman sprang erect. As respectfully as any of his seamen, she asked, "Are ye ajokin' me, m'lord?"

He reached into his pocket, pulled out a handful of

gold coins, and tossed them on the table. She edged
closer, gaze bound to the money. "Go on, take it," he
invited. In the blink of an eye, she snatched at it. He
caught her wrist before she could bury the money in
her pocket. "Tell me."

"'Twas another 'ore, just like me." She glanced
around. "I know 'er. I'll ast 'er who sold t' 'er."

"You know where to find me." He released her and
sat back.

She bounded away as if she expected him to change
his mind, but when he didn't move she whispered,
"Ain't ye th' one?"

"No." His lips formed the word, and he burned with
renewed fury.

"Then I'll find th' bumhole bastard." She grinned a
gap-toothed smile. "Me loyalty can be bought, an' ye
jus' found th' way t' do it." Her hips rotated in wide circles as she left.

"At least the whores will talk to me," he remarked to
no one in particular.

"I'll talk to you, too."

Adam looked up at the young man who hovered before him. "Northrup. Good to see you. If you have information to impart, you'll stay close enough for me
to hear, yet far enough to avoid any watching eyes. Sit
down"—he pointed toward a table nearby—"over
there."

Northrup wavered, stricken with the conscience of
the young. Obviously he wanted to thumb his nose at
public opinion, yet at the same time dreaded the treatment meted out to Adam.

Adam insisted, "I will not sit at the same table with
you."

Relieved of the choice, Northrup stumbled in his

haste to sink out of sight on a chair against the wall.

"Have a drink," Adam instructed. "Say what you wish, but don't look at me."

"This is wretched," Northrup said.

"I'll not argue with you." Adam risked a glance at Northrup. The young man's new boots were scuffed, his new clothes were wrinkled. The powder clung in patches to his wig, and he sat in round-shouldered misery. Adam inquired, "About what do you speak?"

"Everything. Everyone sneers about you, the directors of the South Sea Company are promising a dividend they can't pay, the stock is plunging—"

"Didn't you sell when I told you to?" Adam asked.

He received no answer.

The barmaid sauntered over to take Northrup's order, saying, "Garraway tol' me t' tell ye I 'ave t' see yer coin before I can serve ye."

Adam's lips tightened at this reply to his question, and he smacked the impudent girl with his walking stick. "I'll stand the bill for Mr. Northrup. Bring him what he wants."

She shrieked and swung on him, angry until she saw who had treated her so. Then she smiled in malicious amusement and assured him, "Garraway's none too 'appy t' 'ave th' likes o' ye clutterin' up his coffeehouse, either."

Poking at her with the tip of his stick, Adam said, "I'll take no messages sent through his trollop. If Garraway wishes me to leave, let him come and tell me."

Stomping her foot, she said, "I'm no trollop."

Adam said nothing, only looked at her.

She bore it for a moment, then made a sign to ward off the devil and whispered, "I'll do as ye say, only stop lookin' at me wi' those eyes." She stepped back. "Stop it, do."

Adam continued to stare until she broke and ran back to the bar. "Silly twat," he commented. Northrup laughed weakly, wiping a trickle of sweat from his brow with a lacy handkerchief, and Adam returned to his attack. "You bought the third subscription released by the South Sea Company, did you not?"

"Yes." Northrup raised his head. "And before you ask—yes, I bought it on credit. As did everyone."

"Well, if everyone pledged to pay nine hundred pounds for a stock now worth four hundred pounds, you should rush to do so, too." Adam couldn't restrain his sarcasm, but he was sorry even as he spoke. Northrup leaped to his feet, and Adam ordered, "Sit down, boy."

"I will not. I am not a boy," Northrup said with a fierceness a that belied his calm.

"Please sit down, Northrup," Adam amended. Northrup wavered visibly, and Adam said again, "Please."

Northrup sat.

"You'll have to pardon my lack of courtesy. No one has spoken to me for so long, I've lost the accomplishments required by polite society," Adam said, half in jest.

"You never had them," Northrup grumbled.

"Too true." Adam plucked his handkerchief from his pocket and held it to his nose as a particularly malodorous member of the underworld passed. "Did you buy stock in the now outlawed companies?"

"Yes, I thought it wise to diversify. I thought it would protect me if the drop in the price of the South Sea stock came rapidly." Earnest as a minister on collection day, Northrup explained, "You see, I did believe you when you said it would drop."

Adam rubbed the tightness in his temples. "Didn't you realize that when the outlawed companies dropped, all the buyers, not just you, would have to sell South Sea stock to meet their obligations?"

"If that's so obvious, why did Sir John Blunt have those companies outlawed?" Northrup demanded.

"He doesn't understand how this credit works. Buying on margin is a new concept, one we must handle with caution. Damn, Northrup"—Adam rapped the table with his knuckles—"why didn't you sell when I told you?"

Northrup's resentment bubbled over. "Because you *told* me. You didn't tell me *why*, and I thought I was smarter than you."

Adam leaned back in his chair and thrust his feet out before him. "Well, we have both learned something, haven't we? Northrup, if you're going to stay in the money market, you have to remember a few truths. Hunger and greed are similar, but hunger can be satisfied. Be one of the hungry ones, not the greedy ones."

From the room behind the bar, the sound of a scuffle ensued. A few sharp slaps, the barmaid squalled loudly, and Garraway came puffing out, marching up to Adam's table. Drawing himself up, he announced, "I never tol' that idiot what used t' work fer me t' say any o' that, m'lord."

Adam lifted a brow. "No?"

"No, an' ye might as well get that lofty look off yer face. I ain't denyin' sayin' it, I'm just denyin' tellin' her t' tell ye." Using a grubby handkerchief pulled from his apron, Garraway wiped his face. "Ye're bad fer business right now. But Garraway's 'as been 'ere seventy years an' it'll be 'ere another 'undred, so I guess I can lose a few customers because o' ye. Weren't any too good o' customers, anyway."

For the first time in days, Adam smiled. "Thank you, Garraway. You're a gentleman unlike any other."

One pair of feet tramped up the stairs with an exultant beat; one pair of hands shoved open the door at the top of the stairs. In a blaze of victory, Daphne called, "Your parents are below."

Bronwyn lifted her head from contemplation of the Gaelic manuscript that had once meant so much and now merited only a dull inspection. Her bright new world was disintegrating, and she didn't understand why.

"Listen to me," Daphne insisted. "Your parents are here."

"My parents?" Daphne's satisfaction caught Bronwyn's attention, and she focused. "My parents?" Her breath gripped her throat, her hand clenched over her stomach. They didn't know where she was. They couldn't know where she was. Cautiously she asked, "What parents?"

"Rafferty Edana, earl of Gaynor, and his wife, Lady Nora." Daphne smirked. "Sulking up here will not make them disappear, I tell you. Your father is threatening to take you away and beat you."

"Is he? Da always blusters and roars. I'm sorry to disappoint you, but his threats will come to nothing." Bronwyn rose and with desperate calm stacked together her sheets of translation. "Is Rachelle with them?" She worried about Rachelle. The Frenchwoman had grown distant, thoughtful. The crowd at the salon had thinned.

Daphne's voice rose a notch at the mention of Rachelle. "Yes, she is with them, listening as your mother laments the loss of your reputation."

"That sounds like Maman."

"You are not the only one who is worried about Rachelle, you know," Daphne burst out defiantly.

Not understanding, not really hearing, Bronwyn murmured, "Of course not." She straightened the striped silk blouse, then tucked her scarf into her bosom. As Adam preferred, she used it to shield herself from masculine eyes.

Adam. God, Adam was worst of all. That one dreadful night, the mere mention of Henriette had driven him into a frenzy. She'd told him about the dying girl's words, and he'd shouted at her. Since then, he listened and never heard her. He looked and never saw her. He slept in her room and never touched her.

At the mirror, she dabbed perspiration from her upper lip and her forehead. She picked up the pot of color to apply it to her face. Before she touched her skin, she paused. Putting down the carmine, she nodded at her reflection with determination. "They'll take me as I am."

"They will lock you in your room with bread and water," Daphne taunted, gathering fury as her gibes failed to prick Bronwyn's composure.

"You're such a spiteful little thing, Daphne." Bronwyn smoothed the light, plain skirt. "Someday you'll do someone real harm with your nosiness."

Daphne paled, too young to disguise her dismay, and Bronwyn pounced. "Are you the one who informed my parents of my whereabouts?"

Hands clenched, elbows straight, Daphne answered, "Not I."

"Oh, come now. You look so guilty."

"I am sorry I did not think of it, but no." Daphne smiled tightly. "I did not."

Bronwyn didn't know whether to believe the girl or not. Most likely she would have admitted it gladly had she done it, and what did it matter? The damage was done. After gathering her ivory fan, her patch box, and her purse, she walked to the door. Daphne began to descend, and Bronwyn snapped her fingers. "Go on down. I forgot my handkerchief." She smiled pleasantly at Daphne's impatience. "So I can cry my tears of repentance." She waited as Daphne proceeded down a safe length of steps, then dashed back into her room. Leaning close to the mirror, she pinched her cheeks until they glowed.

Running down the stairs would improve her color, too, but she refused to exhibit such anxiety. Instead she walked, sedate and serene, remembering all the time that she was the flawless Cherie and not the plain Bronwyn. At the door of the salon she paused, as she had seen her mother do countless times. Her mother did it because it allowed the room to savor her beauty. Bronwyn did it because she needed the moment to gather her courage—but no one would ever know that, she vowed.

Inside the room, Lord Gaynor leaned against the wall, his hands in his coat pockets, clearly impatient. Lady Nora and Lady Holly sat on either side of Rachelle, identical bookends around one courageous lady, while Daphne hovered behind. The noblewomen sipped tea, creating civilized chatter as they waited.

Her father spotted her first. "Bronwyn?" Lord Gaynor straightened up. He gaped. With love and pride in his eyes, he cried, "Ah, Bronwyn, how beautiful ye are!"

"Da." Bronwyn opened her arms, and they rushed together in a mighty hug. "Da! I didn't realize how much I missed you."

"Me lass. Me Bronwyn." He held her face up so he could examine it. "What happened to ye here? The London air must agree with ye."

Bronwyn laughed and gulped. "So it does."

"Let her go, Rafferty, and let me look at her," Lady Nora's soft voice commanded.

Lord Gaynor held Bronwyn at arm's length, twirled her around in one light dance step. "Can you see what someone has done to our brown little elf? She's become a fairy."

Lady Nora trained her educated eye on Bronwyn. Setting down her tea cup, she rose to circle her daughter while Bronwyn held her breath. Her finger on her lips, Lady Nora examined Bronwyn's gown, her hair, her new-grown fingernails . . . and broke into a smile. "Quite marvelous. What a transformation." She enfolded Bronwyn carefully into her arms and pressed a kiss on her forehead.

"I told you, Maman." Holly leaned forward, eyes sparkling. "I barely recognized her myself."

Lady Nora laughed indulgently. "I am her mother. I would recognize her regardless of her circumstances, but this is a splendid surprise." To Bronwyn she said, "And you wondered if you were our daughter. Surely your visage proves it now."

Blushing, Bronwyn glanced at Rachelle. "I couldn't have done it without Rachelle."

"A Frenchwoman's touch," Lady Nora agreed without a trace of malice. "I should have sent you to France years ago. No one knows more about accenting a wom-

an's beauty." She shook her head. "When I think of all
the years wasted . . ."

"Not wasted," Rachelle said. "Our Cherie is intelligent enough to have done this for herself. She did not
care enough."

"Not care enough?" Lady Nora laughed a chiming
laugh. "Of course she cared. Many a time I remember
her unhappiness when the Sirens of Ireland lined up
and she was so different."

Rachelle corrected firmly, "She cared because you
cared. She did not care for herself—at least, not enough.
Not until she had a reason to care."

Lady Nora whisked that away with a flutter of her
well-manicured fingers. "Whatever the reason, it's a
pleasure to welcome Bronwyn into the fold. And a relief, a real relief——she dabbed at an imminent tear—
"to know she is safe."

Bronwyn's tears refused to be restricted as her mother's were. She loved her parents, for all they were shallow and selfish. They were hers, and she adored them
for their gaiety, their pleasure in living. "I'm so glad to
see you again," she sobbed.

Lord Gaynor replied promptly, "And glad I will be
to take ye with us."

Bronwyn jerked her head out of her handkerchief,
tears drying on her hot cheeks. "No, Da, I won't go."

Looks were exchanged over her head; strategies were
implemented on the moment. "How did you meet Madame Rachelle?" Lord Gaynor asked, suspicion tense in
his every word.

Innocent as the dew on the rose, Bronwyn tapped his
chest with her finger. "Remember, Da, when we were
on our way to Lord Rawson's and Olivia and I left the

inn? We told you we came to Rachelle's salon, and you didn't believe us."

Dumbfounded, Lord Gaynor rocked back on his heels. He checked with Rachelle, and Rachelle nodded without words. "Saints preserve us, ye really meant it!" He stared at Bronwyn, then burst into laughter. "Fooling me with the truth. Well, aren't ye the sly one?"

Bronwyn grinned at him, and while she was unwary, he asked, "And just what kind of place is this salon? I can scarcely believe it's respectable."

"It is respectable, Da," Bronwyn burst out. "Rachelle allows no hint of notoriety to taint her salon."

"Not even these rumors of murder?" he insisted.

Her da had come better prepared than she suspected, Bronwyn thought glumly. "The rumors are a lie. I know that better than anyone."

Something about her, or about Rachelle, or a simple disbelief that anyone could kill her own child, convinced Lord and Lady Gaynor.

Attacking from a different angle, Lady Nora said, "Your reputation will be in ruins."

"How? Holly hardly recognized me when she first entered the salon. My dear sister Holly"—Bronwyn glared—"who vowed not to tell Maman and Da where I was."

The front door slammed, and footsteps echoed in the entry. The new footman spoke. A deep, resonant voice replied, and Bronwyn cringed as she recognized it.

Holly leaned forward and grasped the arms of her chair in earnest goodwill. "I wasn't going to, but when Da told me—"

Lord Gaynor waved her to silence as he stared toward the entrance, and Bronwyn was very much afraid he, too, recognized the masculine voice. The footsteps moved toward the study. Bronwyn tensed.

Trying to divert the pending explosion, Rachelle said, "Lord and Lady Gaynor, my home is most respectable. No one has ever taken advantage of one of the girls while they lived under my room. All are chaste."

With an eerie sense of doom, Bronwyn saw Adam framed in the door. His brooding eyes took in the whole seen, and her heart plunged when Daphne pronounced trumphantly, "Lord Rawson is living here."

Rachelle turned on her young boarder. "Betrayal is ugly, Daphne, and unforgivable."

The color washed from Daphne's cheeks, and she shrank back. Extending her hands, she pleaded silently for understanding, but Rachelle turned from her.

"He's living here?" Lord Gaynor asked with a dangerous calm.

No one spoke.

It was up to her, Bronwyn realized. Adam wouldn't disgrace her by declaring she was his paramour, and she dared not tell her da. He looked dangerous, with narrowed eyes that examined Adam and found him wanting. Bronwyn cleared her throat and lied, "It's not what you think."

Lord Gaynor turned his head and looked at her. "What do I think?"

He sounded genial, but she wasn't fooled. He was as furious as only a father could be—a father whose favorite daughter had come to disgrace. She lifted her hand. "He lives in this house, but—"

With a roar like a cannon, Lord Gaynor turned on Adam. "I hold ye responsible. Ye have ruined me daughter, me babe. To think I admired ye, thought ye the best of my sons-in-law, and ye've brought the Edana family low."

Adam held up his hands. "I'll make amends as you require."

"Ye'll marry her!" Lord Gaynor bellowed. "Never think ye'll get off without giving her reputation back on one of those golden platters your servants wave about."

"Lord Gaynor, I'd be glad to marry—"

"Da, you can't make me marry—"

Lady Nora's chiming voice ordered, "Quiet!" She spoke so emphatically, all obeyed. All eyes turned to her as she sat straight on her chair. "Lord Rawson can't marry Bronwyn."

Lord Gaynor turned a distinct shade of mauve. "What?"

"What do you mean?" Bronwyn asked.

"Oh, hush, Maman," Holly begged.

"Lord Rawson can't marry Bronwyn," Lady Nora insisted. "He's betrothed to marry Olivia."

Bronwyn hadn't heard correctly. She knew she hadn't heard correctly. Adam would never do such a thing. With her gaze, she sought her mother's face. This must be humor from a singularly humorless lady.

Yet Lady Nora was gazing earnestly at Lord Gaynor and saying, "We can't have this kind of scandal. First we announce Lord Rawson is marrying our daughter Bronwyn, then that there's been a mistake and he's marrying our daughter Olivia. He's been betrothed to Olivia ever since Bronwyn ran away. Can you imagine the talk if we said we were wrong once more?"

Adam would never become betrothed to Olivia. Bronwyn knew it. Her da avenged himself on her for her defection, nothing more. She turned to Da, expecting him to be watching her with a sly twinkle in his eye.

He was not. He answered, "Don't ye think our con-sequence is large enough that we could pretend we'd never made the second announcement?"

"La, there's a fond father." Lady Nora shook her fin-ger at Lord Gaynor and called to Bronwyn, "Did you hear what your father wants to do? Isn't it absurd?"

Bronwyn nodded numbly. Her parents spoke, to Rachelle, to her, but she couldn't understand the lan-guage. They stood. They kissed her cheeks, preparing to take their leave, so she supposed an arrangement for her care had been worked out. Still, she didn't under-stand anything. With Holly, her parents walked to the door.

Bronwyn looked to Holly. She moved her lips: "Please."

Holly's big blue eyes teared in sympathy, and she shook her head sadly.

It was true.

Bronwyn caught a chair and held it, fighting to main-tain her balance against the wave of pain sweeping over her. When she opened her eyes, she found intense gray eyes anchored on her. Adam still stood in the doorway, still armored in his indifference.

Her heart had been torn out, and *he* was indifferent.

Eyes locked with his, she pulled out the scarf that, at his request, shielded her bosom, and ripped it across with the hiss of tearing silk. She threw the shredded cloth to the floor. She wasn't restrained. She wasn't adult. She lifted her foot and stomped on it. She ground it into the floor. She jumped on it, and then she stalked to the stairs, where she looked Adam up and down. She sniffed in contempt. She snapped her fingers under his nose, then with one hand on his chest she shoved him aside. She would go to her room and pack. No, she would go to her room and never leave. She'd lock herself in and they could pass food under the door.

No, she'd go to her room and dress for the salon, and come down and charm everyone and Adam would be sorry—

Adam let her set her foot to the first step before he called, "Please remember, you don't want to marry me."

Bronwyn didn't throw her patch box on purpose; it simply flew out of her hand at high speed. Adam dodged, and she shouted, "Damn you!"

Skirts gathered well above her knees, she raced up the stairs. She didn't know if he followed her, but she hoped he did. She hoped he did, for when next an item flew out of her hand, it would hit him. She swore it would hit him.

Bursting into her room, she found the maid picking up her clothes. "Get out!" she yelled, holding the door open. The stunned girl ran past her, and Bronwyn shoved the door just as Adam's palm slammed against it. She put her shoulder against it. He pushed it open without effort.

Her fan burst from her grip and made contact with his forehead.

A spot of blood appeared, and he touched it with his finger. He stared at it in amazement, then slammed the door shut behind him. "You little termagant."

Awash in grief and fury, she shouted, "How could you do this to me?"

"Be logical, Bronwyn." He grinned, baring his teeth. "You don't want to marry me."

"I don't have to be logical." Arms crossed over her chest, she turned her back on him. "You came to

Rachelle's knowing who I was, knowing you were betrothed to my sister—my sister!—and you still seduced me—"

"*You* seduced *me*," he corrected, infuriatingly calm.

"And I liked it."

"Of course."

His acknowledgment did nothing to restore her temper. She swung around to face him again. "Do you feel no shame?"

"None." He twisted the key in the lock and lifted it to show her.

She sucked in the stifling air. "If you believe you can debauch me any time you wish, you're due for a sad awakening."

His tones were heavy with surprise. "Debauch? That's not what you called it before."

She tossed her head.

Weighing the key in his hand, he came to a decision. With a flick of his wrist, he tossed the key onto the chest of drawers. "I *can* debauch you any time I wish. It's what you've been wanting these last three weeks, is it not?"

"You!" Taking deep breaths did nothing to alleviate her fury. Indeed, it only made her sorry for tearing the scarf, for her breasts strained against her low neckline, and he didn't fail to notice. Nor did he try to hide his appreciation. "Two and a half weeks! And I only wanted you when I believed you free of entanglements."

With his gaze still on her bosom, he removed his waistcoat. "I told you I would do anything to get you to marry me, and a lively night life seemed an ostensible persuasion."

"You'd do anything but end your betrothal to my beautiful sister."

"Did you want me to cry off?" He moved toward her, stalking her, discarding his cravat as he came. "Such conduct is impossible for a gentleman."

She wanted to scorch him with her disdain. "When did you ever worry about your reputation as a gentleman?"

Grinning offensively, he said, "I doubt your sister will appreciate being the center of such a tidbit of gossip."

"Oh, I see." Too angry to be cautious, she stood her ground until he stood so close, she had to tilt her head to look into his face. "You were being considerate of Olivia. It couldn't have been that you hoped to land in her bed, too?"

His hands, reaching out for her, stopped, dropped to his side. "I have no interest in Olivia. You of all people should know that."

"Olivia is one of the Sirens of Ireland. Olivia is as lovely as the rising sun. I've seen men fall and worship at her feet with their first glance." Her lip curled. "Do you expect me to believe you don't want her?"

"Foolish woman, I fell and worshiped at her feet with my first glance, and stood up on my second." He laughed, brief and bitter. "Don't think you can fool me. You use this betrothal as a way to tell me you want me to leave you alone."

"Leave me alone?"

"Believe me, I understand."

"Understand what?"

"I always knew you would be horrified when you discovered my family history. I tried to keep the stain of it away from you. I failed. Why would any woman stay with the son of a criminal?"

"Your father?" She began to understand his babblings. "Are you talking about the story ol' Sawbones and Daphne told me? That you're counterfeiting South Sea stock?"

"That's the story all London believes."

Incredulous, she held up her palm as if to halt his flow of words. "That's the reason you give for no longer wanting me?"

"No longer want you?" He grabbed her outthrust hand and pressed it to the front of his breeches. "I want you so much I ache with it."

She snatched her hand away from the heat, the hardness, and bunched it into a fist. "If you think I'm going to fall for a lame tale like this one, you're mad. You may want me this minute, but by tonight you'll be satiated and on your way. This is just an excuse to discard me."

His eyebrows shot up. "An excuse? To discard you? Why would I want to do that?"

"Because I'm not beautiful like my sisters," she answered, exasperated by his deliberate obtuseness.

"What nonsense. That's an excuse to discard *me*."

"Very funny," she fumed. "Why would I want to discard you?"

"Because I'm the son of a counterfeiter and a possible counterfeiter myself," he roared. "Haven't you been listening?"

"I've been listening." She lifted the weight of her hair from her shoulders, fanned the back of her neck with her hand. "Listening to a lot of drivel."

"If my background doesn't mean anything to you,

why did you pay so little attention when the rumor of my counterfeiting came to your ears?"

She spread her arms wide. "What did you expect me to do?"

"When Judson told the tale of Madame Rachelle's husband, you slapped him. You screamed at him. You threw him out." Staring down the end of his nose, he said, "None of that righteous indignation spilled over for me."

"Judson sought to do real harm to Rachelle. She operates a salon. She's a foreigner. She could be harmed by these rumors—and has been. No such harm could come to you." Prodding him, wanting to make him ashamed, she mocked, "If I'd known you were going to be such a baby about it, I would have kicked ol' Sawbones and pulled Daphne's hair. Would that have made you happy?"

Insufferably superior, he said, "At least when I went to Change Alley and the lowest scum shunned me, I would know I had the support of my mistress behind me."

"Your mistress?" Wanting to get back at him, she leaned forward until her gown revealed her and enunciated, "I'm not your mistress anymore."

His hands shot out and grasped the neckline of her gown. In a kind of triumph, he tore it from top to waist. "We'll see about that."

She looked down at herself, at her unadorned linen corset revealed by the shredded edges of her fragile blouse. She couldn't believe this. She couldn't believe his nerve. "Do you think you're the only one who—" Grabbing the lapels of his shirt, she jerked down and out. Buttons flew in every direction, and she smiled tightly.

Her smile faded as he dipped into a pocket in his breeches, pulling out a long, thin leather case. It produced an efficient-looking knife, and he flipped it as he said, "A seaman goes nowhere without his blade."

His narrowed gaze produced no alarm, only a pronounced thump of her heart. He wouldn't hurt her. She knew that. Knew, too, that her dignity would suffer should she fight.

At least—that was what she told herself.

She stood motionless as he pulled out her waistband, panniers, and petticoats, and cut them. They dropped around her ankles, and in outrage she asked, "I suppose you're happy now?"

"Not quite." With a steady hand, he slit her corset along one whalebone until it gaped wide. He nicked her chemise close against her bosom, and then, inserting his finger into the hole, he tugged until the material tore.

The only garments on her body unaffected by his barrage were her stockings. Ignoring the relief the air provided, she stood in the ruin of her best working dress and sneered, "You've proved yourself to be a real man. Now let's see if you'll stand still for my retaliation."

He grinned offensively and offered his knife, handle first. With the air of a queen receiving a tribute, she accepted it.

"Trust a woman to hold a knife incorrectly," he sneered.

She looked down at the hand grasping the hilt, saw the fingers tighten. "Trust a man," she sneered back, "to fear to teach a woman how to hold a knife."

He jerked her around so her back met his chest and wrapped his arms around her. "Give it to me."

Heat flowed from him like a white-hot fire as she slapped the knife into his palm.

He flipped the knife, caught it. "Like this. See how my fingers are positioned?"

"I see, I see," she replied in irritation. She wiped perspiration from her forehead with her shoulder, then wiped her palm on her shredded chemise. Grasping the knife, she imitated him exactly.

He said not a word of praise; he only grunted.

Irked by his nonchalance, she taunted, "Is there anything else you want to show me?"

He tried to take the knife, and for one insane moment she wrestled for possession. "Do you want to know how to throw?" he snarled. "Or not?"

She released it.

"Hold the blade with your fingertips. Balance it. Aim. And when you throw, don't throw like a woman." Disdain for feminine ability coated his tone. "Pull back your arm and make sure it sticks in your target. Here, you try it."

Holding the blade with her fingertips proved more of a challenge than simply grasping the handle. Razor sharp, the point sank into her index finger as if it were butter. She tucked her lips tight against the pain and adjusted her grip until she duplicated his grip. She thought.

"Not like that." He adjusted her fingers forcibly. "See? Like that. You know you're doing it right when it feels like an extension of your arm."

She doubted that.

"Let's see how you prime yourself." He stepped away. "And remember, don't throw like a woman."

If he'd stood in front of her, she could have done a smashing job. As it was, she pulled back her arm and threw as hard as she could. To her surprise, the blade sailed across the room, end over end, struck the chest of drawers, and stuck there, quivering with the shock of impact.

She, too, quivered with the shock. Pleasure and a sense of accomplishment brought her pirouetting to face him.

With an inscrutable expression on his face, he looked at the knife. "You forgot to aim."

Screaming at him would accomplish nothing. But she knew how to make him cower. She stalked to the drawers, jerked the knife out of the wood, and stalked back to him. "My turn to undress you."

Her skill could not match his, and the side fly of his breeches lost its buttons helter-skelter. To his credit, he didn't flinch as she slit the seam down to his crotch—but perhaps he feared to move, she thought with glee. Kneeling before him, she sawed through the buttons at his knee and jerked down the breeches. She looked up at him, up past the confirmation of his passion and to his stomach, his chest displayed through the white rags of his shirt. From this angle he looked like a god, fearless, imperious, demanding. Her gaze skimmed the muscles that rippled like ocean swells beneath his skin, lifted to the column of his neck, stared into his eyes.

The barbaric fury transformed itself in an instant.

Chapter 15

L ike a flash of lightning on this sunny afternoon, Adam remembered. Remembered what attracted him to her. Remembered how long it had been since they'd embraced. Remembered how good love had been.

Her lips opened; her tongue slipped out to lick her lips as though she were a child who had been offered a sugarplum. The lightning had struck her, too.

Her hands crept up, skimming his calves, his thighs. The pleasure, too intense, too sudden, singed him. He caught her wrists and plucked her hands away. Her soft protest was lost as he dragged her to her feet.

Her shift was white, in shreds, and in the way. Desperately in the way. His need flamed beyond control. He yanked the shift from her so quickly that he heard a tearing sound, and the sound reminded him of the scene in the salon.

She'd ripped the scarf, the symbol of their accord, and her aspersion added strength to his recklessness. He twirled her toward the bed; somehow she served as a pivot, and he landed on his back on the mattress. Squares of sunshine lifted and fell on the white coverlet, writhing with their skirmish. The warmth from that bright orb seeped into his buttocks as he struggled up on his elbow, but Bronwyn leaped atop him before he could maneuver.

He forgot why he should be in command. Scooting to sit with his shoulders propped against the wall, he found that the sight of her appeased one longing, activated another. The scent, the savor of her orange perfume, wafted in with his every breath. She whispered his name, just "Adam," but in tones of such desire that he shivered with elation.

She swarmed over him, took him inside her. And all along his length her body touched his, melded with his, until he was a part of her, yet whole in himself. Without understanding him, without reassuring him, she mended his tears, healed his hurts.

No finesse sweetened their loving. He grasped her hips, lifting her in a wild rhythm she already knew. They were close, so close her panting exhalations touched his cheek. Her eyes closed, opened, closed, as if the pleasure of all her senses overwhelmed her.

"Hurry, hurry," she urged, and his elation rose with her snarl of impatience.

Her slight round bottom filled his hands. Sunshine lit her curves, turned the droplets of perspiration between her breasts to diamonds. Her garters scraped the side of his hips, yet it wasn't discomfort but only another part of the friction that bit at him.

Exertion stung his biceps as he lifted her, rocked her.

She fought to move quickly; he struggled to slow her, and laughed aloud as she clenched her teeth, flung back her head, scraped his shoulders with her fingernails.

Briefly her eyes opened, and she glared. "Too much," she muttered. "Too hot."

She sought restraint, but he would incite a frenzy. His head bent, he caught her nipple in his mouth, suckled until she cried out. When he felt the surge within her, the renewed dampness, the coming storm, he bit down lightly.

She screamed, spasmed, collapsed for a brief moment.

"More," he commanded.

"I can't." Her teeth almost chattered with her tension. "I can't," she insisted as he rolled his hips beneath her.

His own needs drove him now, blocking thought and releasing an instinct that toppled her from one orgasm to another. Water splashed on his chest: perspiration, tears, he didn't know. He knew only that when his own release seized him, he could scarcely restrain his shout of gratification.

Bronwyn withered down onto him. Clasping her, he reveled in the accord carried on the wave of physical pleasure. It was a false accord, he knew, for they had settled nothing in their fiery quarrel. Nothing, except that in the crucible of their passion they were melted into one entity.

For now that was enough.

He fanned her with a pillow he pulled from behind him, but she whispered, "Don't."

"What?"

"Don't." She sighed and rubbed her face into his chest like a kitten seeking comfort. "It's cooler."

He looked out the window. The sunshine had vanished, blotted from the sky by an onslaught of clouds. The heat had broken at last. He could hear the city below them as it hurried to escape the first raindrops. He could hear, also, the distant shouts of an angry man, and he urged Bronwyn to look at him. "Your father?"

"Yes."

"Will he come up?"

"If he hasn't yet, then he will not. My mother, and Rachelle, I suspect, have restrained him."

Her lips stretched in a smile he'd missed these weeks. "I never kissed you," he mused.

"You didn't," she agreed.

"A grievous oversight."

"Easily rectified."

She incited him: with her teasing, with her warmth so close against him, with the shy gleam of her eyes.

Shy? After such a romp? He peered closer. Every inch of her blushed, every inch he could see . . . and he could see quite a bit. Chuckling, he caught her neck in the crook of his arm, brought her lips to his, and as the first raindrops splashed to the thirsty earth, he began the long, slow seduction of a woman already seduced.

The evening crept in, gray, damp, sweet with the relief of autumn's first chill. He lit the candles while she watched, her hand tucked under her cheek. "You have goose bumps. Odd to think that only a few hours ago, it was hot."

"Very hot," he agreed.

She turned her head into the pillow just enough to cover one eye. With that minor adjustment, it seemed she could block out the pieces of life that distressed her. Her focus changed. The room looked different.

Adam looked different as he paced about. She didn't want to think tonight, but she had to comment. "You're restless."

"I'm thinking."

Thinking about their impossible situation. Thinking about the things she feared to think of. Thinking about Olivia. She covered her other eye.

"Yesterday," he continued, "I discovered a lead, a possible break in this conspiracy."

Conspiracy? His betrothal was a conspiracy?

"Robert Walpole believes there's something odd occurring in the financial world."

She suffered about their personal situation, and he thought about Robert Walpole and his stupid financial world. "How can he tell?" she said. "It's all odd."

"Something odder," he clarified. "He heard rumors that puzzled him and asked me to use my connections to find the source."

A giggle escaped her. What ghastly timing the man had!

"Is there something wrong?" he asked.

"No." She struggled to contain herself. "No. What . . . what have you discovered?"

"That he was both right and wrong. There's more to this than simple financial manipulation. Someone is seeking power."

That brought her to a sitting position, away from the safety of her pillow. Power created greed, created danger, and Adam strolled right through the midst of it. "What kind of power?"

"Power over the king, I think. Power in Parliament. There's a void within the government, and Robert wants to fill it. He's capable of filling it, is the best man to fill it." He splashed water on his face and groped for the towel. "If I can find the source of this conspiracy, it would help him immeasurably."

Timidly she suggested, "You don't suppose this is related to Henriette's murder?"

He paused as he wiped his face, half turned to her. "Henriette?"

"Rachelle's daughter." She hugged her knees. "If you will recall, I told you she was murdered by someone who said he would kill a man by dropping a stock on him."

"No, I don't recall."

Before he could remember the night when she'd told him, she said, "Yes, well, could this be part of your conspiracy?"

"Kill a man by dropping a stock on him," he repeated thoughtfully. "Interesting phrasing."

"Henriette was French." She watched him, yet she wouldn't let her fondness for his long limbs and lean muscles distract her. "I thought Walpole was at his home in the country. When did he ask you to help him?"

"Months ago. The end of April."

"April? April, and you have discovered nothing?"

A passing glance from his eyes scorched her. "Robert wanted me to deal with it personally, and my private life intruded for too long."

She remembered how she'd distracted him, was flattered she'd distracted him.

Watching her in the mirror, he dabbed at his chin. "Well might you smile. I've danced to your tune and neglected my duty to my country."

Ignoring the conscience that spoke sharply, she lifted her hair and arranged it artfully over her chest. "I would never ask you to neglect your duty to England."

He lifted a light, shone it on her silver tresses. "Of course not."

A delicious thrill ran up her spine as he started toward her, candle in hand.

Placing the light on the nightstand, he accused, "You're to blame. To blame that I neglect my duty, and to blame that I remember it." He stretched, tensing the muscles of his arms, his chest, his stomach. Groaning, he flexed his thighs, his calves, cupping the old injury as if to protect it. "With quite irrational confidence, I know I will solve this mystery. You make me strong."

The ardent tribute left her without a reply.

He seemed to expect none. The supple line of her back attracted him, and he stroked up its length with the care of a man caressing a kitten.

Purring, she savored the ripple of vitality that stole through her veins. "Come to bed, I'll warm you." She brushed her palm up the side of his body, delighted as more goose bumps blossomed.

He shifted, pressing one knee into the mattress to ease the weight on his leg. "I suspect you of ulterior motives."

Dropping her gaze to his thigh, she leaned toward him and pressed her lips to his old scar. "Did it hurt?"

"Like fire." Running his finger along the curve of her shoulder, he said, "That wormhole of a surgeon wanted to amputate."

Wincing, she shook her head.

"No, I wouldn't let him, but there is still a bit of the ship's deck inside. It troubles me occasionally."

"Not that I've noticed," she retorted. "Would you like me to kiss it better?"

"I'd like to rest." At his emphatic statement, her lower lip drooped and she peered at him with the soulful reproach of a street singer who'd been cheated. He lifted his knee atop the bed. "What the hell. I can rest afterward." He sank onto the bed and let her pull the sheet over him, adding, "After you've killed me. That is your plan, isn't it?"

She didn't deny it. In a husky voice she promised, "Slowly. Very slowly."

"My sister!" She rolled over and grasped a handful of chest hair, pulling him to wakefulness by the ungentle tug on his roots. "Why are you betrothed to my sister?"

He shoved her hand away. "Ouch, damn it."

"That's no answer." She reached for him again, and he fended her off.

"Do we have to do this first thing in the morning?" Shielding his eyes against the sun which peeked through a brief break in the clouds, he peered around the room.

"Yes." She flounced into a sitting position and crossed her arms across her chest. "We do."

"All right." Wearily he pulled himself up. "We do." Rubbing his head with his hands, he said, "Perhaps you should ask yourself why you're upset."

"I would never knowingly sleep with my sister's betrothed," she answered, flaunting the lofty ideals that had started this attack.

His gray eyes mocked her fury. "You just did."

"It was a mistake," she protested.

"Not just one mistake. Several mistakes. Over long hours." She turned her head away, and he brought it back with his palm on her chin. His words and gaze pierced her soul. "Perhaps you should ask yourself why you abandon your principles so readily when you're hungry and remember them so indignantly when you're satiated." Lip stuck out, she refused to answer, and he dropped his hand. "My betrothal to Olivia stands until the day you demand I be released."

"How can *I* demand you be released?" She waved her arms in a windmill. "I'm Olivia's sister."

His glare seared her before he rolled off the mattress. His feet hit the floor with a thump.

He was displeased with her. All the satisfaction of the night had dissipated. He acted as though the injustice were hers, and somewhere in the back of her mind a disturbing thought niggled at her. Was she wrong? True, she'd left him, she'd wanted him to take Olivia in her place, yet somehow, deep inside, she'd never believed he really would. The Adam she'd first met had worn a mask, hard, brittle, cold. But on Midsummer Night, under the moon, he'd convinced her of his sincere passion—for her, for Bronwyn. Had she thrown away a love to last a lifetime, all for foolish pride?

At the mirror, he lifted his brush and stroked it through his hair, easing the wildness into some semblance of decorum and tying it back. "Does that look civilized?" he asked, making conversation, saying nothing.

She tugged the sheet up over her shoulders. The chill in the room was not solely from the air. "Not in the least. You look like a seaman with a thin facade of polish."

He attempted a simper, but his reflection didn't lie. He couldn't accomplish it, and he scowled instead.

"Where are you going?" she asked, *Are you coming back?* she meant, but she didn't dare ask.

"To Change Alley."

With the greatest delicacy she inquired, "To find out the truth about this conspiracy?"

"Yes."

"You say Walpole spoke to you about this in April? Well, this is September twentieth. Perhaps there's nothing to discover."

He turned from stranger to enemy as she blinked. His sharp white teeth snapped as he snarled, "If there were nothing to discover, why would fake stock be circulating, passed by one who styles himself as Adam Keane, viscount of Rawson?" He stalked toward her. "Has it occurred to you that the board of directors of the South Sea Company perpetrated one of the biggest frauds ever to take place in the history of mankind? They have stolen millions of pounds from unsuspecting, foolish people, ruined good lives and bad, and are taking the English government to the brink of chaos."

She considered. "But I don't believe in conspiracy by committee."

If he hadn't been so angry with her, he might have smiled. "You are a very intelligent woman about finance. In matters of the heart, you're incredibly stupid." As she gaped, he adjusted the large rings that adorned his fingers. "I do not believe in conspiracy by committee, either. If I were to point at one man, I would say John Blunt, newly created baron, is the culprit."

"But what is the conspiracy?"

Rubbing his forehead, he said, "I don't know. Everything so stinks of dishonesty in Change Alley, it's hard to distinguish a conspiracy from a plot."

"Then maybe it's nothing serious, not worth your attention."

He dropped his hand. "Haven't you been listening? If all the rest is not enough for you, then think on this. The South Sea Company has hired cutthroats to 'encourage' other companies to leave the market."

She flinched. Here was the core of her worry, tossed

at her like a scrap to a beggar. She couldn't restrain the anxious query that rose to her lips. "Are you endangering your life?"

Belligerence, confidence, and his mad male relish for a fight merged on his face. "I doubt it."

Furious with him for his lack of caution, furious with Walpole for asking for such a sacrifice, she snapped, "How dare Robert Walpole ask you to spy for him out of mere friendship?"

"For what other reason would I do it?" he asked, a dangerous edge to his voice.

Bouncing up, she said, "I don't know, but I want you to stop."

"To stop? Stop, when I am so close? Stop, and break my word to my friend?" His hands closed over her shoulders, and he dragged her close. "Why should I stop? Is it because you think the counterfeit stock will disappear from Change Alley if I do?"

She fastened her hands on his wrists. "Don't be an ass."

His fingers dug into her skin as he asked, "Are you worried your relationship to a counterfeiter will ruin your reputation?"

Tugging as his grip tightened, she said, "You're being stupid. My reputation is already ruined."

He dropped her like a stinging nettle.

One look at his frozen face assured her she'd said it poorly. "I didn't mean it like that."

He picked up his waistcoat and overcoat.

She flew off the bed and grabbed his arm. "You can't walk out like this."

Paying her no attention, he opened the door. She dug in her heels, but her puny weight impressed him not at all. She couldn't follow him down the stairs, not naked, and she shouted after him, "I meant my moral reputation." He didn't turn. "Coward!" was her parting shot.

He flinched, and she gained comfort from that as she dressed for the day. Adam was a reasonable man. Surely he'd think about her words and realize why she sought to dissuade him from pursuing this quest. He'd know she worried about his safety. He couldn't believe she was so shallow as to care how his reputation affected hers. And, oh God, he wouldn't take her taunt of "coward" as a challenge to put himself in danger.

Awake before the rest of the household, she crept to her desk. She laid out her manuscript, her sheets of paper. She sharpened her quills, uncorked the bottle of ink—and stared out the window at the mist of rain. Translation held no interest for her today. Instead the quill in her hand scribbled everything Adam had confessed, everything she knew about the South Sea stock. Henriette's words, too, came to haunt her, and she wrote them at the top of the page. Idly she underscored them. <u>He's going to kill a man by dropping a stock on him.</u>

What did it mean? She had already concluded the stock could be—must be—the South Sea stock. Adam said he thought the conspiracy revolved around the hunt for power. Someone lusted after power, and they would stop at nothing.

She blinked. Greed, money, an English politician who spoke out against the men who promoted the nefarious South Sea bubble . . .

Her throat closed, and she lifted her hand to ease the constriction.

Robert Walpole.

Nonsense. She shook her head to clear it. If someone wanted to kill Robert Walpole, why hadn't they done it sooner? But wait. Walpole was out of town. Wasn't he? *Wasn't* he?

She rushed out of the room, slumped against the wall. Pressing her cold hands on her hot face, she groaned. Another attack of nausea? Another dizzy spell? The sleepless night, the early rising, the tension of the weeks: they all contributed to her state, but, oh God, she had no time for this now. After groping up the stairs, she rapped at Rachelle's door. Rachelle's grouchy voice did not dissuade her; she only rapped harder. "Rachelle, it's Bronwyn." She listened, but heard nothing. "Rachelle, I need to know something."

She knocked again, and finally the door opened. Rachelle's sleepy glare gave her pause. She took a few deep breaths, but nothing could quench her now. "Forgive me for waking you, but I have to know something."

Rachelle adjusted her nightcap with a yawn. "Such a rush, child," she rebuked. "I thought I had cured you of that."

"Is Robert Walpole out of London?"

"Cherie . . ." Rachelle groaned.

"It's important." Fervor returned a bit of her good health, and Bronwyn insisted, "The gossip in the salon last night . . . did anyone mention Walpole's return?"

Plainly irked, Rachelle snapped, "You expect me to pay heed to the comings and goings of one insignificant man?"

"Please?" Bronwyn pleaded. "You remember everything, and Adam says Walpole is going to be prominent."

"So Walpole says, also. He has convinced quite a few people, it seems." Rachelle closed her eyes and thought. "Walpole came back to the City yesterday and was visited by his financial advisers."

"Why?" Bronwyn's peace of mind hung in the balance.

"They say he has lost money in the South Sea scheme."

"The devil take the man! How dare he fall into their hands so neatly?" Her indignation left Rachelle with open mouth. Making her decision, she said, "I have to find Adam. I'll go to Change Alley, find Adam, tell him . . . I'll make him listen to me. Will you order a sedan chair?"

"Of course, *ma cherie*." Rachelle eyed her skeptically. "I trust you know what you are doing?"

"I haven't got much choice," Bronwyn said. "If I don't tell Adam, Walpole's life could be in danger."

Rachelle never doubted her. "Send a note to Walpole," she urged.

The fever of alarm touched Bronwyn's face. "Adam's life could be in danger."

"Then you must go. I will get you a sedan chair and rouse Gianni to run beside." Rachelle gave her a push. "Get your cloak."

Bronwyn hurried to the entry and with dismay realized her illness had not yet completely fled. The excitement that drove it from her returned it twofold when she hurried or even moved with too much vigor. Cautiously Bronwyn lifted the maroon velvet from its hook and slipped it on. Her purse contained enough to pay the sedan chair and to bribe those with information of Adam's whereabouts. There were no other preparations she need make—except to banish this creeping affliction and steel herself for the confrontation with the man she loved.

She peered out of the front door and waited. The rain fell with a dreary rhythm. Vapors wafted on dismal breezes. She concentrated on what she would say. "Adam," she'd say, "I know you think I'm a treacherous hussy."

No. Perhaps she shouldn't remind him that he thought her treacherous. How about "Adam, I've discovered the key to your mystery."

In her mind she fantasized the meeting between her and Adam. They would embrace. They would explain, all would be well. . . .

Not even her fertile imagination could see it. More likely Adam would be cold. No one could be colder than he. Even now she could feel the imagined chill of his displeasure.

A large covered carriage rolled up and stopped. Painted shiny white, it sported a gilt trim that made it appear big and embarrassingly gaudy. Fashioned of stained glass, each window pictured classical Italian architecture. In size and shape, the coach resembled a traveling Gypsy lodge, yet this type cruised London streets more and more. The South Sea boom had brought such wealth to the common folk that they bought madly, greedily, looking not to practicality, but to ostentation.

Eagerly she waited for a glimpse of the guest who rode in such a monstrosity and who visited so early in the morning.

No one descended. The coachman leaped down, opened the door, bowed to her without a word.

Of course. Rather than a sedan chair, Rachelle had ordered a carriage and had secured one whose owner had already slipped back into the ranks of the impoverished. How kind of Rachelle to consider the effect of the rain. How extravagant.

Locking the town house, Bronwyn gave the coachman her hand, ascended the step, and stopped. Dizziness halted her, and she put her hand to her head. " 'Ey, move in," the coachman advised without respect, and thrust her inside. Unsettled by her ailment and his rudeness, she blinked as the door slammed. The windows made it dark inside, and when she glanced out, the colors of the ancient world stained the landscape. The carriage jerked into motion, and she sat down hard.

Oh God, she'd forgotten to give the coachman her direction. She reached up to rap on the roof, then faded back onto the seat as a wave of nausea rocked her.

The footman. She remembered now. Gianni had told the coachman where she wished to go.

Closing her eyes, she noted gratefully that the dim interior smelled of something besides body odor and dung. Such odors made her queasy, and the mingled scents of powder, perfume, and tobacco were almost pleasing. For a hired coach, it was unusually well sprung. Yet . . .

Above the clatter of the hooves and the splash as the wheels emptied the puddles, she thought she could hear breathing.

Was someone in the carriage with her? No, for anyone else would have spoken up when she entered.

Silliness. She would open her eyes, see that she rode alone. It took a greater effort than she'd realized, but her courage could not fail so early. She pried her lids up, turned to look—and saw the gleam of two eyes in the dusk.

Heart pounding, she muffled her shriek with her hands.

A skinny, feminine hand clamped onto Adam's wrist and twisted him behind a barrel.

"Yer Ludship, ye amember me?" The prostitute from

the day before gawked at him. Her hair dripped little rivulets onto her face, and trickles of dirty water ran off her chin.

Squinting through the gloom of the day, Adam said, "Indeed I do. Have you information?"

"Indeed I dew."

Her imitation of his accent made him grin. Was *that* what he sounded like?

"I got th' 'ore what sold me th' stock, an' she showed me th' man what sold it t' 'er."

That wiped his grin away. "Have you told him about me?"

"Nary a word." Pointing her grimy thumb at her chest, she boasted, "A woman doesn't get t' me place in th' world without some smarts, ye know. I knew ye'd want t' talk t' 'im all unawares. Now come on."

Gripping his walking stick firmly in his hand, he followed her. He stepped around barrels and over garbage but couldn't resist asking, "What is your place in the world?"

With fierce satisfaction she said, "I ain't dead yet, am I?"

A grim reflection on society, he supposed. "And I'm grateful you're not."

Taking him to the edge of a long dock where a merchant ship bobbed at rest, she pointed her finger. "See that line o' men, all gruntin' an' strainin'? See th' big lout with th' red kerchief 'round 'is neck?"

"I see him."

"'E's th' one. 'E's Jims. 'E sold th' stock t' me friend."

"Thank you." He expected her to fade away, but she hung close as he strode across the slimy boards. "Do you plan to introduce us?"

"I want t' see."

"To see what?"

"If 'e knows ye or not."

Lifting his head to the rain, he laughed aloud. He'd left Bronwyn in anger, but his anger hadn't lasted. The night before had been long and fulfilling and too sweet for resentment. His confidence had returned, shiny bright and beneficial. Today he would get to the bottom of this madness.

At the sight of a gentleman on the dock, the workers faltered to a stop. Boxes dropped to the ground. The stevedores stared as Adam removed his wide-brimmed hat, tossed back his cape, placed his fists on his hips. A living challenge, he stepped up to Jims and waited. The big man glanced from side to side. "M'lord? Did ye want somethin'?"

"Don't you know me?" Adam demanded.

Bewildered, uneasy, Jims shrugged his massive shoulders. "I . . . m'lord, should I?"

"So I hear." From the corners of his eyes, Adam saw a battalion of prostitutes move close. He heard the whispers as his harlot acquainted them with the story; he noted how the stevedores strained to hear.

"Are ye some kind o' reformer?" Jims asked. "Because I ain't done nothin' t' be ashamed of."

Adam chuckled, amused by the mound of gnawing discomfort before him, sure of his imminent victory. "I am not a reformer, not interested in your morals or lack of them. I am simply trying to settle the issue of my identity. Look well on me. Are you sure you don't know me? Don't recognize me? Have never seen me before?"

Still uneasy, Jims said, "Naw."

"Yet my name is known to you."

"Naw."

"I am told it is." Taking a breath, he announced, "I am Adam Keane, viscount of Rawson."

A smile broke across the stevedore's broad face. "Ye're not."

Realizing what his denial meant, the assembled whores gasped. Adam bared his teeth in a savage grin and insisted, "I am."

Jims snorted vigorously, wiping his dripping face on his sleeve. "Naw, ye're not. Lord Rawson is a shorter genna-man, with a wig"—he indicated massive hair— "an' th' dammest face I ever seen."

Adam dropped his guise of cocky self-confidence and gripped his walking stick with a kind of knowing disgust. "What kind of face?"

"All plastered with powder an' drawn with colors."

With his hand, Adam indicated a height. "About so high in his heels, elegant and—"

"Bald," Jims finished. "Bald as a' egg. When th' wind kicked up off th' river, 'is wig lifted an' I could see 'is bare 'ead—"

"Judson," Adam groaned. "That bastard Carroll Judson is saying he's me."

Chapter 16

From the corner opposite her, Carroll Judson said,
"A fortunate coincidence, that you and I should
be going the same way."

Bronwyn pressed her hand to her heart to still the
frantic thumping. "Mr. Judson, you frightened me."

"Not I," Carroll Judson denied. His voice sounded
deep, significantly masculine, suave.

What are you doing here? The demand hovered on
her tongue, but some wisdom stopped her. He'd been
watching her since she'd entered the carriage, and he'd
said nothing. She didn't like it, or him, but for the moment she was trapped. "I didn't realize you were here.
Foolish, I know, but the day has been quite insane, and
I snatched a moment of rest. . . ." She bit her lip to still
her nervous chatter. "I've been warned so often of the
dangers of traveling the London streets alone, our

meeting is a fortunate coincidence. How did you come to be in my carriage?"

"'Tis my carriage."

He was so emphatic, she found herself babbling again. "Did you know I needed a ride? Did the footman tell you?"

"Gianni did indeed tell me." In the dim light she could see Judson's teeth gleam in a smile. "Madame Rachelle's footman and I are in close communication."

Bronwyn didn't want to understand his intent, didn't like the sound of any of it. "You're on your way to Change Alley, also?" she asked tentatively.

"Why should you think that?"

"That's where I wish to go. If you're in such close communication with the footman, surely he told you—"

"I don't care where you wish to go," he answered.

She wished she could see him, see more than the glint of eyes and teeth. She wished she hadn't chosen this moment to remember her last encounter with him, the way she'd slapped his face. She'd not put it past this man to take her to the seamiest part of town and push her out to fend for herself among the cutthroats and drunkards. "Then could you stop and I'll seek other conveyance?"

"That's quite impossible." He moved closer; she moved back, her skin crawling in an instinctive reaction. "I said I was in close communication with Madame Rachelle's footman. Wouldn't you like to know why?"

"I doubt it."

"But I want to tell you." He laughed, again with that deep, impassioned tone. "He's in my pay."

Nausea began to inch up her throat. "For what reason?"

"His instructions were to send word to my rooms— my rooms located so close to Madame Rachelle's—when you decided to go out." His breath fanned her face as he leaned toward her. "I wanted to make sure you accepted my hospitality."

She turned her head away. "A slap on the face is hardly worth a kidnapping."

"A slap in the face?" He smirked. "A slap in the face? My dear, you underestimate me. I do not kidnap you for that puny defense of your friend. No, no, not at all."

He hadn't denied it. He'd repeated the word she'd flung at him. Kidnapping. This man was kidnapping her. Oh God, why?

His soft leather glove caressed her cheek. She wanted to spit at him, but her queasiness pressed her too hard. She clamped her mouth shut, tried to relax the knots of her muscles, took deep breaths untainted by his air. She soon realized he played a waiting game. He wanted her to ask, to draw him out, to inquire about his plans. And what choice had she? She must distract him as she reached for the door. Jumping out onto the cobblestones frightened her, but Carroll Judson frightened her even more.

"Then why do you kidnap me?" Deliberately she used the word again. Easing around, she used her skirt to hide her fingers as they crept toward the handle.

"Well, not for your fortune." Throwing back his head, he cackled as if at a great witticism.

She laughed, too, an unconvincing chuckle. "No, no one wants me for my fortune. Is it, perhaps, to settle a grudge with Lord Rawson?"

"Ah, yes, Lord Rawson. My dear old friend Adam." He lifted his handkerchief and sniffed. "He does seem to be fond of you—such a dividend. At first, you realize, I feared I'd be doing him a favor by disposing of you."

Disposing of? Her hand halted its journey. Shocked, she heard the thumping of her heart in her ears, felt it in the pulse at her throat.

He seemed not to notice. "My valet called you quite plain. Then Madame Rachelle worked her magic, Adam was entrapped, and I knew that this time, I would—"

She hit the door with her shoulder, the weight of her body behind her. It yielded—to a point. Then bounced her back inside. She ricocheted against the seat, sprawled on the floor.

"—win." He finished his sentence with appalling confidence.

Pushing her hair out of her eyes, she glared up at him. He hadn't moved, hadn't flinched during her rush for freedom. Fussing with the fingers on his gloves, he said, "I had the coachman tie the door closed. You'd better come up here, or you'll miss my surprise."

Marshaling what dignity she could, she crawled back on the seat. She peered out the tiny bit of clear window beside her, trying to ascertain her route, but the houses and shops slid past too quickly for her eyes to follow. Her forehead slipped forward to rest on the cool glass; she noted, in some corner of her mind, that it was clean. Not encrusted with a hired coach's smoke and spittle. "But you still haven't told me why." Even as her lips formed the words, alarm stiffened her spine.

She recognized the street outside, recognized it even as she denied it. Surely she was mistaken. Surely this was some trick of the light. She would not see, at the corner, an inn called the Brimming Cup.

Yet there it was. A plain, common place, where she

should never have stayed. There she'd broken into a room, saved a woman from a lonely death, and started a chain of events that had brought her to this.

By slow degrees, she turned to look at Carroll Judson. He held a silver mirror up to his window and swept powder over his face with a pad of sheepskin. The feeble light reflected onto his features, lightening them to an abnormal whiteness.

Yet he didn't look like a monster. He looked like a dandy, a gossip, a fool. What had Adam said of him? A well-fed rat? The son of a corrupt father?

Not even Adam suspected what hid in the scurrilous corners of Judson's soul. Remembering Henriette's battered face, her twisted body, Bronwyn covered her mouth to contain her nausea.

Judson lowered the mirror. "So. Now you know."

"Are we stopping there?" Her hand muffled her words, and she lowered it cautiously.

"When the landlord saw the blood in the room, he proved to have some rather inconvenient scruples." He pursed his full red lips in a pout. "And an eye for blackmail. I'm afraid he doesn't know my true name, nor where I live. Despite my own nostalgic leanings, I'm afraid we'll have to go to my flat."

"I still don't understand."

"Nonsense, of course you do. Everyone says you're intelligent."

She found herself unable to restrain her sarcasm. "If I were intelligent, I wouldn't be here now."

He sighed with exaggerated patience. "What don't you understand?"

"Why did you take me? I didn't know who had killed Henriette."

Even now she hoped he would deny knowing Henriette. Her heart sank when he said, "She may have told you."

Seeking the cool air, she loosened the clasp of her cloak. "If she had told me, you would be imprisoned even now."

"True." He pouted sympathetically. "I am afraid you're going to have to put the blame for your demise on Adam's broad back."

"On Adam's back?"

"Do you know, when I heard you were betrothed to him, I laughed, my dear, just laughed." Giving an airy chuckle to illustrate, he continued, "Adam is such a churl. I knew he'd ignore you, perhaps even send you away. I knew he'd never lower himself to speak to you, and certainly never pay attention to your prattling of murder."

"You admit it was murder?"

"Of course it was murder. What else would I call it?" She had no answer, and he brushed it aside. "Murder is of no consequence. I've seen worse."

She only stared, sickened by his breezy dismissal of Henriette's bloody death.

"I'll never understand what you did to Adam. At Madame Rachelle's he danced attendance to you, he courted you and showed all the signs of a man infatuated. My dear, I found myself feeling betrayed." At her instinctive objection he insisted, "Yes, betrayed! I had depended on Adam's personality to keep me safe, and somehow you'd made a gentleman out of him."

"I'm sorry," she said faintly.

"So you should be." He fanned himself with his handkerchief. "Adam, with his license to sell stock, knows too much about the South Sea Company. You knew too much about Henriette. That combination was volatile. I had a decision to make."

Made shrewd by necessity, she asked, "Was it not your own jealousy that decided the matter?"

"Jealous? Of you?"

"Of Adam."

"Of Adam?" His mouth drew into a thin line. "Why should I be jealous of Adam?"

"At Madame Rachelle's you compared yourself to him, and he seemed not at all flattered."

He sat straight, lifted his chin. "He should have been. I move in society's highest circles. I no longer need to deal with merchants and street scum to obtain the finer things in life."

"Adam doesn't have to hide his face for shame behind a mask."

He lifted the mirror to his face and squinted at it anxiously.

"A mask?"

"A mask of powder, of paint, of wigs and silks and satins, to hide his degeneracy." She touched his cheek. His cosmetics flaked off onto her finger, and she displayed the results to him.

With that one gesture she broke his facade of superiority. He threw the mirror to the floor, where the glass shattered, grabbed for her wrists, and missed, leaving long scratches on her hands. She stared at the blood welling up, looked at him. He'd given her a warning, one she must heed.

"You're very pale," he pronounced.

In a frightened, little-girl voice, she said, "You hurt me."

He preened. He actually preened, like a boy who'd just discovered his manhood. Or like a man who could realize his manhood only by inflicting pain. She had to get away, but how?

"If you had to"—she hesitated, then used his term—"dispose of Henriette, why did you do it so gruesomely?" She knew she shouldn't speak of Henriette, yet she found the French girl's fate filled her mind to the exclusion of all else. "Why not shoot her and get it over with?"

"Dear lady! That wouldn't have been at all interesting. You see that, don't you?" Sweat sprang out on her brow, and he waved his handkerchief before her face. With what seemed to be genuine concern, he asked, "You're not going to faint, are you?"

"No," she denied automatically. Realizing weakness could be an advantage, she said, "Perhaps. I don't know." Closing her eyes, she slumped against the seat.

With a rustle of silks, he moved close and patted her cheek. "Oh, dear, she is going to faint. She'll be no fun at all."

At his touch, her nausea rose. "I'm not going to faint. I'm going to be sick."

He leaped back. "Be sick?"

"Vomit," she said succinctly.

As she'd hoped, he gasped, "In my carriage?"

"Have I a choice?"

He didn't answer, and she wanted to peek and see his reaction. Did he suspect her ruse? Of course he did. He was too clever not to. But she was pale, she knew. Her fear made her perspire, and that, too, was a symptom. And if he would not let her out, by God, she felt ill enough to actually—

He rapped on the top of the carriage. "Stop!" he bellowed. "Stop the carriage and let us out."

* * *

"The stock has dropped more than two hundred points in five days." Like a boy walking with his father, Northrup skipped along beside Adam, splattering the puddles without conscience. "Look at all these people. London is in a panic. Countless families are faced with bankruptcy and ruin. Rumors of suicide already are making the rounds."

Adam grunted, peering into a dark, noisy coffeehouse.

"Don't you want to know?" Northrup cried.

"It's no more than I expected. Has anyone seen Carroll Judson?" Adam's annoyance bubbled over. "Damn the man! When I don't want him, I can't avoid him." Gripping Northrup's arm, he dragged him along until they reached the street where the crowds were thinner and less wild-eyed. "Now, Northrup—"

"Someone's calling your name, sir. Can't you hear them?"

"Of course someone's calling my name. They're like hounds with a fox at bay, thinking they can blame me for counterfeiting stock and bringing disaster on them all." Wiping the grime of the wharf from his cuffs, Adam tried again. "Northrup, I want you to—"

A girl tugged at his sleeve. "Lord Rawson?"

"Good woman," Adam said impatiently, "I had nothing to do with your stocks. Now be so kind—"

"No, my lord, you don't understand." She smiled with bold admiration. "I come from Madame Rachelle's salon."

Adam pushed back her cloak to reveal her face. The rain had slackened, leaving a murky day draped in clouds, but by degrees he recognized her. "Daphne, isn't it?"

The girl's eyes flashed with a disappointment he didn't understand. "Don't you even remember me?"

"Of course I do. I just called you by your name," he said impatiently. "Why are you here?"

Her fists clenched.

"Who sent you? Was it Madame Rachelle? Or was it Cherie?" With his very tone, Adam caressed the name.

Daphne's chin dropped, she fumbled with her purse. "Here." She thrust a piece of paper at him and swung away, disappearing into the mob.

Adam stared after her. "An odd girl." He ripped open the message and read the contents. Vaguely he heard Northrup call his name and knew he'd betrayed his emotions. Right now he didn't care. Right now he didn't even know what they were.

"Sir?" Northrup grasped Adam's shoulder. "Sir, are you well?"

"Madame Rachelle's footman was caught packing his bag and preparing to leave after putting Bronwyn into a covered carriage."

Northrup looked blank. "Bronwyn? Bronwyn Edana, your betrothed?"

Unaware of Northrup's blossoming wariness, Adam agreed.

"What was Bronwyn Edana doing at a place like Madame Rachelle's?"

"She lives there, you know that," Adam said impatiently,

"I most certainly did not," Northrup huffed. "I knew you could be found there, but I never imagined a lady of Bronwyn's station would ever be found in such a place."

"It's not a whorehouse, man, it's a salon. And what difference does it make what she was doing there? The important thing is, she left amid suspicious circumstances." A tingling at his fingertips and toes signified the return of his feelings. A return carried on the flush of anger; a return he didn't desire. "Bronwyn is supposed to be here with me."

Northrup glanced about as if he expected her to pop up at any moment. "Good God. Do you suppose she's in one of those coffeehouses?" He made it sound more alarming than the prospect of a whorehouse.

"No." Adam crumpled the paper. His hand, he noted, gripped the little wad as if it contained the secret to transmuting metal to gold. "Rachelle's suspicions were roused, for the footman was supposed to accompany Bronwyn on her journey. Madame managed to convince him"—Adam smoothed out the precious note, read it again—"she didn't say how, to confess the truth."

"Sir, you're frightening me."

"Bronwyn has been kidnapped by Carroll Judson, and Madame insists I come at once to the salon, for she believes she knows where they are." Glancing about him, Adam sought a friendly face, a ray of sunshine, a bit of hope. Northrup remained with him. Despite his own rudeness and impatience, Northrup's loyalty had never wavered, and for the first time Adam was grateful. He grasped Northrup's elbow. "You'll come with me?"

Northrup gaped. "But—"

"I may have need of you," Adam said simply, and Northrup responded as Adam knew he would.

"Of course, Lord Rawson. If you need me, I'll be there."

Bronwyn staggered along the dim alley, one hand on the filthy wall of the building beside her, the other unfastening her cape. Judson watched from his carriage. She kept her shoulders hunched, her head down; occasionally she moaned with enough heartfelt intensity to keep her guard-coachman well behind her. As she walked, she searched the ground. She knew what she wanted; she knew she could find it, given enough time. She only hoped it would be sufficient to distract the guard while she escaped.

"Don't let her wander too far," Judson called. "Keep close."

The burly coachman stepped closer, but she'd seen what she sought. She'd seen her salvation, and she refused to be thwarted now. Using acting talents she'd never realized she had, she retched. The coachman stepped back.

"She's going too far." Uninterested in her distress except as it disturbed the interior of his coach, Judson said with a snap of decision, "Come back. Come back right now."

Bronwyn walked faster. The guard grunted as he speeded up. Her goal filled her vision, if she could just get close enough . . . The guard breathed close against her back, but she stopped, slumped. He caught her arm. She reached down, dug her fingers into the pile on the street, turned, and flung a handful of horse dung in his face. Fresh, odorous, steamy, it plastered his beard.

In that instant she slipped out of her cloak and left it in his grasp as she ran. Her panniers, unwieldy, heavy, tried with some malevolent intent to trip her. Her corsets constrained her breathing; she wanted to scream, call for help, but had to reserve her air for the effort of escape. The broad-shouldered coachman panted in great gulps behind her. She concentrated on keeping her ankles straight as the rounded cobblestones beat bruises into the soles of her feet. Her leather slippers splashed mud up her calves; she slipped as she rounded the corner onto the street.

Empty. In a nightmare personified, she'd found the one deserted London street. Like faces that lacked all expression, the barren warehouses stared but offered no assistance. In the gloom of the day, she couldn't see the brown doors in the brown walls, and she inadvertently passed more than one before veering to press on the wooden panels.

It yielded; she flung herself into a giant room stacked with crates. "Help," she shouted, fleeing into the darkness. "Help me!"

No one answered, but the door behind her banged back as the coachman charged in. She dodged around a column; she screamed as the column—a large man, the largest man she'd ever seen—moved to intercept her. The sound echoed eerily, and the coachman raced toward her.

To the column she cried, "Help me." The column didn't respond, and she said, "Please. Adam Keane, viscount of Rawson, would pay you to—"

The coachman tackled her around the waist, lifted her off her feet. She kicked at him, shouting, "Let me go."

Slow as an elephant trained to entertain, the warehouse occupant blocked them. "What are ye doin' wi' th' gel, Fred?"

His speech proved as sluggish as his movements, but the coachman paused. "Eh, Oakes, that ye?"

The massive man thought about it. After a painful pause he agreed, "Aye, it's Oakes."

The coachman tilted her panniers away from him, using her own clothing to shield him from her blows, and started away. "Oakes, if ye know what's good fer ye, ye'll mind yer concerns an' let me mind mine."

"No, no, no." Bronwyn flailed wildly.

Oakes's lumbering stride brought him between them and the door. "The lass don't seem t' want t' go wi' ye."

"I'm bein' paid t' take her," Fred answered sharply. Oakes didn't move, and with forced camaraderie, Fred said, "'Ey, we're mates, ain't we? I'm a dock walloper, ye're a dock walloper. Ye know I wouldn't do somethin' not ethical-like."

"Liar," she cried.

Fred squeezed her ribs, digging the boning of her corset into her skin, forcing the air from her lungs. "I'm as 'onorable as th' day is long. This 'ere lady is . . . mad. Aye, she's mad as a rabbit under th' full moon. I'm assistin' th' genna-man what's takin' 'er back t' Bedlam."

Bronwyn could only choke, then to her distress the big man moved aside. "Please," she gasped with her last bit of breath, but Fred moved inexorably to the door.

A few people traveled the street now, but, pleased with his story, Fred shouted, "Make way fer th' madwoman." Her heated protests availed her nothing, only brought the curious as Fred alternately tugged and carried her back to the carriage. Hearing the hue and cry, Judson waited with a smug smile and a strong rope, and Bronwyn found herself bundled into the carriage and carried away.

Adam's anguish wrote itself in grim lines around his mouth as he read the sheaf of papers Madame Rachelle had discovered littering Bronwyn's desk. "That pissabed Judson is responsible for . . . all this?"

Grave and straight, Madame Rachelle nodded.

"What is Judson responsible for?" Northrup asked eagerly.

Adam never moved his gaze from Rachelle. "He's the one who enforces the arbitrary laws for the South Sea Company? He's plotting the assassination of Walpole?" Every muscle of his body tightened as he tried to deny, to wish away, the truth. "How could I have missed it?"

"Perhaps you saw only what you expected," Madame Rachelle said.

Savage in his unhappiness, Adam snapped, "And you were more clear-sighted?"

Her voice sounded wispy, embarrassed. "This has been a humbling experience. I suspected others of Henriette's murder, yet even when Judson accused me, I thought he repeated the current gossip."

"Judson has no character?" Northrup asked.

Still ignoring him, Adam said, "Judson was nasty even as a boy."

Rachelle now slapped her fists against the desk. "Then why did you not suspect him before he killed my daughter?"

The heat of her anger reached Adam, made him respond with perverse calm. "I wanted to be fair. So many people judged me by my father's actions, I refused to do the same to Judson."

"Fair!" She tossed her hands in the air in an excess of Gallic exasperation. "If he was vicious as a boy—"

"He wasn't vicious. Cruel, as boys are, and rude. But if you'd met me when I was a boy, you'd have thought the same."

"I can't imagine such a thing," Northrup interposed.

For the first time, Adam acknowledged his assistant.

"I'm good with my fists, but a misplaced sense of justice is no excuse for my current stupidity."

Desperate and eager, Northrup asked, "What will you do now?"

"There should be no doubt, should there? This is England. It's green, beautiful. It holds my heart like no woman ever could." Rachelle laughed rudely, and Adam thought he hated her. He hated anyone who could see him as clearly as this woman could. "If Walpole is killed, the country I love, the country I longed for on the long voyages, will suffer. My fortune could well suffer. Yet if Bronwyn is killed . . ." The papers fluttered to the floor. "How could I miss this?"

"You've been distracted," Rachelle said.

"You make excuses for me?" Adam swung his tortured gaze on her.

"A man in love is the most vulnerable of all."

"In love?" Northrup's voice squeaked with his indignation. "A man in love could never do what Lord Rawson had done to Bronwyn Edana. He's ruined her reputation, put her in the path of danger. Even now, when she could be murdered, or worse, he's talking about his fortune." Stepping closer Northrup shook his fists in Adam's face. "She doesn't have to marry you. I'll marry her, if need be."

Adam considered the pale and frightened Northrup, standing up for the woman he called his friend. "She can't marry you," he answered mildly.

"And why not?"

"Because I'd kill you both before I'd allow that to happen."

"Maybe you won't have to kill her," Northrup huffed. "Maybe Carroll Judson will do the deed for you."

The blood drained from Adam's face, and when

Northrup caught at his elbow, he knew it showed. For all Northrup's pugnacious threats, he watched Adam with the kind of fondness a hound feels for his master. "I didn't mean it, sir. I'm sure Bronwyn will be fine." Adam just stared, and Northrup stammered, "If you recall, you defended her right to be a learned woman. Even if you feel you must attend to Walpole first, I'm sure she'll outsmart Judson."

Rachelle moved to Adam's other side and said, "A man has to decide. Will he love and open himself? Or will he deny that part of him and be so strong no one can ever touch him?"

"She didn't let me decide. I'm bound so tightly—" He strangled on his dilemma. What should he do? Should he look for Bronwyn, who was in danger of her life? Or should he seek out Walpole and warn him of the danger that stalked him closer all the time?

A choice, Adam reflected grimly, he had never wanted to make. The fate of his love rested in his hands. The fate of England rested in his hands. He had no option, he supposed, but—oh God, how would he face the consequences of his neglect?

$\mathcal{A}$dam took Madame Rachelle's hands. "Will you go to Walpole and alert him to the danger?" Rachelle didn't seem surprised at his decision. Indeed, she took it so calmly that he wondered how well he knew himself.

She pressed his fingers, lending him her strength. "Of course, but what makes you think he will listen to me? His contempt for foreigners, especially the French, is well known, and I am not only French, but a woman."

"He doesn't despise women," Adam assured her.

"Nor does he treat them seriously."

Northrup stepped up, twisting his cravat as if he would strangle himself from nervousness. "Let me go, sir. I'll convince him."

"It's not possible." Adam grimaced. "I need you to search for Bronwyn."

"Me? But what will you do?"

Adam's patience stretched as thin as a razor, but he explained, "If I search and you search, we can cover twice this city."

Ever pleased to be included in Adam's plans, Northrup beamed.

From amid the mess on Bronwyn's desk, Rachelle plucked a quill, found the unstoppered bottle of ink, and pushed a precious scrap of paper toward him. "Write your friend Walpole."

"I have no time," Adam said.

"Write him briefly, and I will fill in the details."

Adam's brief glare met with solid feminine composure. Snatching the quill, he muttered a curse, then scribbled a pithy warning and thrust it at her. She left with the words, "*L'amour et la fumée ne peuvent se cachet.*"

Adam rubbed his forehead fretfully. "I'm in no mood for a French riddle."

"She said, 'Love and smoke cannot be hidden.'" Northrup stood at attention before Adam. "Where would you like me to start searching?"

"*We'll* start." Face set in lines of grim satisfaction, Adam rolled up his sleeves. "With the footman."

At least the carriage door wasn't tied shut anymore, Bronwyn thought miserably. But why should it be, when her hands were bound so the bones ground against each other? Her shoulders still ached from Fred's rough handling as he knotted the rope behind her back. Even now she couldn't stand to look at Judson's smirking face. "I still don't understand why you kidnapped me. What did I know?"

Judson seemed astonished at her stupidity, but how

much was true amazement and how much mockery, she didn't care to guess. "I don't know what you knew. Don't you see? I couldn't take the chance Henriette had told you anything. Your continued intimacy with Adam simply sealed your fate. For all I knew, you sent him to Change Alley to sniff about and ask questions."

"Not I," she denied. She kept her gaze steady on his face. "It was Robert Walpole who sent him."

A variety of expressions chased across Judson's face. Loathing, amusement, concern for his own skin. He pronounced, "Walpole is too clever by half."

"And you're not clever enough."

Losing interest in her, he mused, "Robert Walpole, eh? What did Adam discover for Robert Walpole?"

Should she tell him what she suspected and let him think Adam knew, too? Or would it push him into action before she could get word to Adam? She had no time to decide, for he crowed, "Look, there's my flat."

Outside the windows were the homes of the fashionable, and she asked, "You have a flat in this part of town?"

"I leased it when I showed the amount of South Sea stock I possessed. Of course, the lady who owns it is fussing a bit now, thinking the stock is worthless." He sighed with satisfaction and leaned against the seat, waiting for Fred to open the door.

"The stock is dropping."

"The stock will rise again." He laughed with excessive carelessness. "I have connections. I know."

"Such a blessing," she drawled, and he sprang at her. At first she thought he sought to hurt her, and forgetting her shackles, she struggled. But he only thrust his clean handkerchief in her mouth, and in comparison with her imaginings, this seemed so innocuous that she let him do what he would. A mistake, she found, when she was carried, unable to speak and hardly to breathe, past a doorman and into the well-equipped apartment.

Judson dismissed the coachman before removing the gag and smiled at her in the most gracious way. With all she knew of him, she still had trouble comprehending his villainy. "Adam Keane's father was hung with the silk rope reserved for aristocrats, did you know that?" he said. He patted his chest. "*My* father escaped that fate. *My* father left England while he could."

"Wouldn't the magistrates have hung him with a silk rope?"

"Insightful girl," he said, but he didn't mean it. "No, he would have had no silk rope. But we were rich. There were tables loaded with food, servants who jumped to do my bidding. The Keanes weren't rich. I remember seeing Adam Keane dressed in rags, living in a hut. I laughed at him."

She could imagine Adam's reaction—being taunted by a jackstraw like Judson. "What happened to bring you down from your mighty perch?"

"A trumped-up charge of counterfeiting."

Shocked, she asked, "Isn't that the same charge that brought Adam's father to the gallows?"

"The late Lord Rawson implicated my father. He couldn't keep his mouth shut, couldn't go down without pointing his finger in random, widening circles."

Deliberately obtuse, she asked, "But if your father was innocent, wouldn't the court have dismissed the charges?"

"My father invested a bit of money in the business to help Rawson along, and that ensnared him. How was my father to know Rawson was so clumsy he would be caught?"

Too shrewd to accuse the elder Judson of misconduct, she asked, "What did your father do to create the wealth you speak of?"

"He held the position of trading justice in the worst part of London."

"Ah." She understood immediately, but because she wanted to be released, she kept her tone bland and unaccusing. "Could you untie me?"

Cocking his head, he thought about it.

She shrank down to make herself look smaller than she was and pasted a simper on her face. "A trading justice is a very important person."

"People don't realize how important. Do you know how many of the aristocracy complain the trading justices are unfair to the peasants?" He opened a drawer in the end table and rustled through the contents, tossing aside complexion creams, powder boxes, papers.

The handle of the knife he found was decorated with ornate carving, but the blade glinted with utilitarian strength. It attracted her eye like a magnet attracted iron. Only last night, Adam had held a knife, brought it close against her skin, and she'd reveled in it. She'd never once considered he could hurt her, for her faith in him transcended the bounds of good sense. The contrast of her plain, strong man and this stylish, murderous fop brought a heated sweat to her palms. Oh God, where was Adam? She wanted him so badly she fantasized about the taste of him, the scent of him, the touch of him.

"Are you sick?" Judson demanded.

She lifted her dry, burning eyes. "What?"

"You look sick." He flicked his thumb against the true edge of the blade. "Lovesick."

His considering gaze brought a fantasy to mind.

How easily the knife would sink between her shoulder blades under the guidance of Carroll Judson. How happy he would be to so direct it. Yet she didn't want to give him ideas; she turned her back to him without obvious inhibition and said, "I can't imagine anyone complaining about the justices. Who else could keep the London underworld in order? And so cheaply, too."

"Quite right, quite right." He grabbed the rope that bound her hands and jerked her hands up. Her shoulder blades strained together. The sinews of her back complained. She grunted, found the moment too brief to prepare for her death.

Then her hands were free.

Moving slowly and painfully, she brought them to rest in her lap. As the blood flooded back, they pricked with a thousand needles just below the skin. She inched off her gloves and tucked them into the chair beside her hip. For some reason she wanted to look at her hands, bare and unornamented. They were nice hands, long and narrow with a few tiny freckles that floated atop the golden skin. She wiggled her fingers. She rotated her wrists in gentle circles, then massaged the reddened skin where the ropes had burned her. Funny, to be so absorbed in the sight of her own hands, almost as if she were looking at them for the first time—or the last.

Yet Judson seemed oblivious of her, still bragging about his wicked father and how well he did his wretched job. "All the fines he assessed for criminal activities went into his pocket. All the monies collected when a criminal was committed to prison, all the bail-out monies also. That's how my father met Rawson, and out of the kindness of his heart he allowed the man to move his family into a hut at the edge of our property. Little did he know the perfidy that ungrateful wretch embodied."

"I see." She did, more than he could imagine, and she wondered at his audacity. Did he hope she would tamely submit to his tyranny? He was not a large man; did he hope she would not fight him? She turned to face him and found the blade held close to her cheek, right against the bone. Cautiously she turned to face forward, keeping the point within her peripheral vision. "So when your father was exiled to the Continent, he dragged you along?"

"I went along gladly." He shrugged. "Better that than a seaman's fate."

"Better murder than work?" She gazed at him. He held the knife in a fighter's grip, blade tilted up, point extended. It seemed only to emphasize the contrast between Adam and the beast before her. "You have an odd sense of morals."

"Morals are for wealthy men, my dear, not for those who are left to fend for themselves at the age of fourteen."

Forever secure in the bosom of her family, she was shocked. "Your father died when you were fourteen?"

"He married a woman with money, and she found me repulsive." He touched his penciled brow with his little finger. "I had to grow up then, you see. I lived on the streets of Rome. I learned Italian, especially the word for 'freak.' I worked in a kitchen. I worked in the fields. I worked like a slave. I survived, survived by my wits. Through the years, I've brought myself up in the world, and I swore I would never have to work with my hands again."

"Work with your hands?" She spread her fingers,

looked at them incredulously. "You've been killing people."

He looked down at the knife as if he'd forgotten he grasped it in his hand. "So I have. And I'm very, very good at it."

"He's no footman," Northrup said with scorn. "He's Carroll Judson's valet. Don't you recognize him? He followed Judson about Change Alley, adjusting Judson's clothing and chirping about his makeup. You're Gianni, aren't you?"

The footman made a gurgling noise, and Adam unwrapped his fingers from around his throat. It took effort, for Adam wanted, so badly, to strangle him, but Northrup's composure acted as the perfect foil for his own savage inclinations.

Indeed, as Gianni stumbled backward, Adam realized how well he and Northrup acted as a team. Inclined to exploit their unity, he watched Gianni bump against the kitchen table and come to rest against the closed pantry door. "Speak, scoundrel," he snarled, but Gianni massaged the marks Adam's fingers had left, stalling until Adam propelled himself forward.

Hastily he agreed, "I am Gianni."

"You are dead," Adam said. "If anything has happened to Bronwyn, I'll dismember you with my own hands."

"Lord Rawson," Northrup reproved. "Intimidation will avail us nothing. There's a proper way to do these things. First we offer a bribe. Then we threaten him."

Adam glowered at his proper young secretary and the suave valet. "I stand corrected."

Gianni sniffed. "The English are so barbaric."

Adam's resolve died a swift death under Gianni's

disparagement, and Northrup halted Adam's forward rush with a stiff arm across the chest. "Gianni, I won't be able to control Lord Rawson if you don't keep a civil tongue in your head."

Subdued, Gianni nodded.

"Now, about the money—" Northrup began.

"You cannot offer me enough to betray my master." Dramatic as an opera singer, Gianni pulled himself up. "His wealth is beyond measure."

Northrup and Adam chuckled in unison.

"It is!" Thumping his chest, Gianni bragged, "My master has the inside line to information about the South Sea stock. He has assurances. . . ."

In a carefully measured tone, Adam asked, "From whom?"

The Italian wilted under Adam's frosty gaze as he hadn't beneath the threat of violence. "From someone high in the South Sea Company."

"And what does this mysterious person say?" Adam demanded.

"That as a reward for his services"—Gianni inhaled but seemed to find no sustenance in the air—"Mr. Judson will be informed when it is time to sell his stock."

"The time has passed to sell his stock." Northrup sounded shocked at such ignorance.

Rolling his eyes in alarm, Gianni said, "No, no, he has assurances."

Northrup asked, "Does Judson truly believe the stock will rise again?" Gianni nodded, and Northrup *tsk*ed as if he were saddened.

Adam laughed briefly. "Poor imbecile."

More than Adam's sarcasm, Northrup's pity convinced Gianni, and his conviction showed on his handsome face. "So. We are devastated once more."

"He is devastated," Adam corrected. "You need not be."

"I will not betray him." Gianni's brown eyes flashed with indignation. "You are the imbecile if you think I will. We have been devoted for years. He is all I have in the world."

"You don't have to betray him," Northrup soothed. "Miss Edana is our only interest. All you have to do is tell us where he has taken her."

"And ruin the one true pleasure he takes in life?" Gianni sighed in exasperation. "I cannot do that."

Adam's patience broke like a log licked by fire. He sprang at Gianni. Northrup made no move to stop him, but when a woman screamed, he swung on her like the angel of vengeance.

A large man, the largest man Adam had ever seen, stood at Daphne's elbow, and she pushed him forward as she shrank under the flame of Adam's gaze. "I'm sorry," she babbled. "I'm sorry. I'd do anything to take it back. Promise you won't tell Rachelle."

"What are you blathering about?" Adam roared.

Her chin trembled, her eyes teared. "Nothing. Nothing, but I brought this man to help you. Talk to him."

Skirts gathered, she fled, leaving behind a perplexed Adam. He looked to the giant for explanation. The dockworker shrugged, moving his shoulders like mountains during an earthquake. In a slow rumble he said, "I don't understand th' gel, neither."

The fellow said no more, and in exasperation Adam asked, "What do you want?"

"A lady o' quality tol' me t' find Adam Keane, viscount of Rawson."

"And you are?" Northrup prompted.

Determined to tell the story his way, the man said, "Is one o' ye gennamen Lord Rawson?"

"I am," Adam answered. "What young lady are you speaking of?"

The big man shuffled his feet and fingered his hat.

Adam waited, then prompted, "A blond lady?"

A single nod answered him. Adam shot a triumphant glance at Northrup and saw, from the corner of his eye, Gianni sliding out of the room. "Catch him!" Adam yelled.

Northrup started forward. The giant man started forward. They met, tangled, fell in a heap with the giant on top. Ignoring Northrup's heartfelt groan, Adam raced after the wily Italian. But Gianni was younger, faster, unmarked by cannon fire, and before Adam reached the top of the stair, Gianni was gone.

Adam limped back down to the kitchen, gathered the giant's shirt in his fists. "What do you know about the young lady?"

Unworried by the implied threat, the fellow answered, "I didn't trust th' man what 'ad 'er, ye see."

Keeping tight hold of his patience, Adam nodded.

"I followed 'er t' see she took no 'arm." The big man looked up through greasy hair. "Me name is Oakes."

"No one's here, sir."

Adam massaged the shoulder he'd just used as a battering ram and agreed. "No, Northrup, no one's here." From the corner of a chair, he plucked a crumpled glove. "But she's been here, just as Oakes said."

The door of Judson's Curzon Street flat gaped, the lock broken by the two men who stood, desolate, in the middle of the room. Adam was surprised by the blight battering his soul. He had expected to find Bronwyn here. He'd come ready to save her, to break Judson if he'd hurt her, to end this nightmare. He'd been charging in one direction, blind to the alleys that opened to the side, and now he didn't know what to do.

"Do you think it was wise, sir, putting Oakes on the alert for Judson?" Northrup worried.

"It's a big city." Adam tapped his fingers on the end table, awash with the clutter Judson had left. "I doubt Oakes will find Judson."

"But if he did, and did what he threatened, things would go ill for a man as simpleminded as Oakes."

"If he finds Judson and does as he threatened, I'll personally guarantee his safety. Do you think Judson left a clue to his destination here?" Adam pawed through the collection of powder boxes and papers.

With brisk sarcasm Northrup said, "Of course, sir. No doubt Judson left a map for us to follow."

Adam lifted one paper and stared at it. "Perhaps he did."

"You didn't find a map?"

Northrup wasn't as credulous as he used to be, Adam noted. "Not a map. The floor plan of Walpole's town house."

"Good God." Northrup stood perfectly still. "I didn't believe Judson would really dare to kill Robert Walpole."

"For what other reason would he have made such a drawing?" Northrup had no answer, and Adam asked, "How long ago do you think Judson left with Bronwyn?"

"I don't know, sir." Northrup stooped, touched the arm of the chair where Bronwyn's gloves had rested. "Not long ago, I surmise."

"Why do you say that?"

Northrup shook his head, and Adam's wit returned.

"What's there?" Leaning over the place where Northrup had stood, Adam saw the spot. Brown against the green brocade fabric, it still glistened with the damp. When Adam touched it, a red smear shone on his flesh. Blood. The hair on the back of his neck stood up, and an awful calm seized him. "Where could they have gone?" He didn't recognize his own voice, it sounded so guttural, like an animal afflicted by the summer madness.

Adam thought he heard Northrup speaking at a great distance: down a tube, in a tunnel, in the dark. Yet Northrup stood not two feet from him. "The doorman will know, Lord Rawson, and doormen aren't as loyal as that fiend Gianni."

"Heaven help the doorman if he is." The calm still permeated Adam's soul, putting his emotions on ice as he strode to the outside.

Whether the elegant doorman responded to the coin Northrup offered, or to the waiting menace of Adam, Adam did not know or care. All that mattered was the ease with which the man gave up his information. With a curl of his narrow lips, the doorman said, "I ordered Mr. Judson's carriage half an hour ago."

"Did he have anyone with him?" Northrup asked.

"A woman accompanied him."

"What did she look like?"

Rubbing his forehead, the doorman mourned, "My memory is so faulty at times."

Northrup slipped him another coin.

The doorman pocketed the silver without a glance at its denomination. "She was heavily veiled."

"Good God," Adam ejected. He had seen Bronwyn

covered with cosmetics, hidden by a wig, strangled by corsets, but never had she concealed herself with a veil. Had Judson so injured her that he dared not allow her face to show? "Was she well?"

The doorman recognized the cut of Adam's clothing, and his respect seemed genuine. "I would suppose, sir. She had to be rather forcibly thrust in the carriage by Mr. Judson. Mr. Judson tied the door shut, and she thumped at it most energetically."

"You stood and watched it happen?" Adam barked.

"'Tis not my place to interfere with the gentry," the doorman answered without emotion.

Before Adam could blast him, Northrup snapped, "Where were they going?"

"I can't imagine, sir." Gold glinted as Northrup held it aloft, but the doorman refused. "There are some pieces of information which can't be bought."

Northrup still hugged the coin between two fingers, keeping it within easy reach of the doorman's greedy fingers. "Then you know Judson's destination?"

"It would reflect poorly on my reputation if I were to tell the destination of the flats' inhabitants."

Adam tucked his walking stick beneath his arm and flexed his hands. "It will reflect poorly on your health if you don't provide the information we request."

The doorman eyed the money, tempting and within easy reach. He eyed Adam's fists, held at the ready and closer still. And he told them what they wanted to know.

The barren road stretched from London to nowhere, bizarre when seen through stained-glass windows. The rain settled in the ruts, making it difficult for Judson to maneuver the carriage in a circle so it faced the city once more. The box quivered as he dismounted; Bronwyn shivered as she awaited his arrival.

He hadn't called his henchman again, not trusting Fred, so he told her, as he trusted Gianni. Nor had he tied her hands again. Instead he had proved his wiry strength wrestling her into the carriage, and proved it so successfully that hopelessness almost overwhelmed her now. He would kill her, toss her body out for some poor shepherd to discover, and she couldn't stop him. Oh, she'd struggle, of course. She had too much pride, too much Irish in her, to give up without a struggle. She only knew it would take a miracle to save her now.

The door rattled as he untied the handle, and she prepared herself. As he opened the door, she flung her whole weight at him. Braced for her assault, he knocked her back inside. He grabbed for her flailing hands and missed. She grabbed for his eyes and missed, catching only the edge of his face and drilling long scratches along his cheek. She followed it up with a blow to his nose. He retaliated with a blow to her chin that slammed her head against the wall. She slumped. Her ears buzzed. The pain crushed her.

In some wonderment, he reached up and touched his cheek. Staring at his hand as if he couldn't believe the blood smeared there, he hissed, "Shrew. Unworthy twat." He sat up and tore at his breeches. "I'm going to give you more than you deserve."

"No." Even that single word hurt her, but she had to speak. "You're not worthy to be a man."

"What?" Dropping his breeches, he revealed himself. "Look!"

"No!" Rejecting him, rejecting everything, she closed her eyes, kicked out with her feet, flailed her hands. "No, no! You're nothing. You can hit me, but you can't rape me." She drummed her heels on the seat until his silence eased into her consciousness.

Then only the patter of rain and the breeze through the door broke the eerie quiet until he whispered, "How can you say that?"

She pressed her palm against her eyes until gunpowder exploded behind her lids. "You poor man. You pitiful excuse for a man."

Her pity seemed to convince him, for he tugged up his breeches and buttoned them.

When she was sure he was covered, she eased herself upright. She rubbed her jaw, checked her teeth, and wished he would say something.

His gaze fixed on the floor, Judson appeared to be thinking. "You said you knew I couldn't rape you. How did you know?"

She blushed, in embarrassment for him and for herself. Shrugging helplessly, she said, "I just knew."

"Women's intuition?" he suggested.

"I suppose you could call it that."

"Then everyone knows."

"Well, I—"

"There's no place for me here in England. Even if my every plan succeeds, there's no place for me on this island." He lifted his gaze and stared at her with such malevolence that she forgot pain, abandoned hope. "Do you know why I murdered Henriette?"

"Because she overheard your plans to—"

"Because she said what you said. Not so politely— the French are so crude—but because she said what you said."

Chapter 18

I don't like this," Northrup whispered. Shoulders hunched against the rain, he stood on the street before Robert Walpole's town house. He held the reins of both their horses in his hands and glanced about in distress.

"Why not?" Adam rapped on the door with his walking stick. "It seems quite serene."

"That means Judson's not here."

Adam stared at the door panels, memorizing the wood grain as hopelessness beat through his veins. "I know that. But we really have no place else to look, and there's a chance—just a chance—he will arrive. Would you take the horses back to the stables, so if he does arrive, he's not frightened off?"

Subdued, Northrup said, "Of course, sir."

The butler, when he answered the door, seemed openly delighted to see Adam. As Adam shed his soggy overcoat, the butler confided, "It's been quite a day, Lord Rawson, with the oddest folk arriving and departing."

"Madame Rachelle arrived, then?"

Drawing himself up, the butler sniffed. "She is one of the odd folk, my lord."

It should be funny, but Adam's face felt carved in stone. "Is she still here?"

"Indeed." The butler opened the door to the drawing room. "Everyone is still here."

Adam stepped across the threshold and into the midst of buzzing conversations barren of listeners. "So they are."

Mr. Jacombe sat beside the big desk, papers in hand, addressing the matter of Walpole's investments. An attractive young woman, dressed in nothing but her stays, snored on the couch. A tailor leaned over his drawing board, scribbling furiously. Only Rachelle stood silent at the window, looking out on the rain.

"Where's Robert?" Adam asked. "Where's Robert?"

Rachelle swung around at his exclamation. "Lord Rawson, thank God you have arrived." She hurried to his side. "That idiotic man you call your friend has retired to his den to work alone."

Adam turned to the butler. "Take me to Robert at once."

"I'm afraid I can't do that, Lord Rawson. Mr. Robert gave instructions he was not to be disturbed. But if you'd wait here—"

He spoke to Adam's back as Adam stalked toward Walpole's den. Rachelle smirked. "Lord Rawson is not one to let courtesy stand in his way."

The butler sniffed. "Obviously not."

Adam's first impulse was to slam back the door, but

he contained himself. Judson might, even now, be holding Robert at gunpoint. He put his head to the solid wood and listened, but he heard nothing. Kneeling, he peered into the keyhole, but the room looked dark. Dark?

Too late, he realized he gazed on the fabric of Walpole's coat and failed to scramble back fast enough. As Walpole jerked open the door, Adam fell forward into an ignominious heap.

Walpole stared at his friend, huddled at his feet. "Good of you to drop in."

Furious, Adam stood up and dusted himself off. "What the hell are you doing?"

"Working. In privacy, I thought." To the butler Walpole called, "Are my pens sharpened?"

"Indeed, sir, and waiting in the right-hand drawer of your desk," the butler answered.

Walpole nodded and asked Adam, "Did you want to come in?"

"Damn it, Robert." Adam stomped into the den. "Can't you even be assassinated correctly?"

"Good to see you, too." Walpole slammed the door. "What's the meaning of this ridiculous message given me by the salon keeper?"

A great swell of exasperation caught Adam, and he retorted, "It means, you idiot, that Carroll Judson's going to try and kill you."

"That worm?" Walpole strolled to his desk and rummaged in his right-hand drawer. "Here they are." He laid a pen on his paper and asked, "Should I be concerned?"

"The bullet from the gun of a worm is just as deadly as the bullet from the gun of the bird that eats the worm—" Adam rubbed his forehead. "Good God, Robert, do you hear the ludicrous things you're having me say?"

"I?" Walpole asked blandly. "I have no control over your speech."

Adam covered his face with his hand and fell back against the wall with a thump.

Chuckling, Walpole insisted, "Whoa! Rein in that somber attitude. I've warned you about it before. So you believe this nonsense about assassination?"

"I not only believe it, I wrote you a note about it."

"*You* wrote that note?"

Exasperation welled in Adam at this Englishman, so smug in his home and his country. "I signed it."

"It had no seal," Walpole said.

Incredulous, Adam said, "No seal? Robert, I wrote the message at Madame Rachelle's, and in a tearing hurry." He glanced around the large room. "Where do those doors lead?"

"The one you're standing next to leads to the hall," Walpole offered.

"Thank you, Robert, but I know where I've been. I want to know where Judson is coming in."

Walpole pointed at the portals one by one. "That one leads into the library. That leads to the kitchen passage. That one goes to one of my private chambers, where a lovely young whore was entertaining me when your Frenchie insisted on interrupting me on this matter of life and death."

Walpole glared, but Adam ignored him as he tested each door to see if it was unlocked. "So Judson will probably come from the kitchen."

"Or a window." Hunched over, Walpole tiptoed to

Adam in his imitation of an assassin bent on murder. "Or maybe he'll slip some poison under the door, with a polite request I ingest it?"

"Sarcasm is unattractive in a man of your girth." Adam peered out the window into the garden. "Try to take this seriously."

Walpole straightened up. "It's stupid. Why would anyone murder me?"

"Because of your charm," Adam snarled, turning on him.

"Buck up!" Walpole ordered. "I'm a nobody."

"Who, with a little luck, is going to be somebody. You've already proved your worth with the government once. No one doubts you'll do it again."

"Nothing's as boring as yesterday's villain." Walpole clapped his friend on the back. "Unless it's yesterday's hero."

"If that hero has been boasting to all of his plans to direct England's destiny, someone might find it of interest," Adam said pointedly.

Quick with guilt, Walpole protested, "I didn't do that."

In no mood to humor his friend, Adam said, "Robert, you did. You confessed to it once, and no doubt that confession covered a multitude of sins."

Walpole had the grace to look sheepish. "Oh, I don't believe this!" He lifted his hand to still Adam's protest. "But if it's true, couldn't you have sent someone besides a frog eater to warn me about Judson? I would have believed a solid Englishman."

Adam rapped the floor with his walking stick. "Robert, you'd only believe the Second Coming if it put money in your hands. Now pay attention. We need to make arrangements for Judson's capture."

"Capture?" Walpole harrumphed and started for the door. "I'll tell my servants to shoot on sight."

"No!" Adam leaped forward. "Please, Robert, Judson still has Bronwyn, and I must know where he's stowed her."

Puffed and indignant as a ruffled grouse, Walpole said, "That's the real reason I didn't believe that frog woman! She told me your betrothed had been living at a salon. Are you saying it's true?"

Supremely uninterested in Walpole's skepticism, Adam answered, "Oh, that. Yes, Bronwyn's been living at Madame Rachelle's. You owe Bronwyn a rather large debt, Robert. She's the one who discovered Judson's plan."

Groping for his chair, Walpole began to speak, then thought better of it and sank silently down behind his desk. At last he began again. "Adam, what have you been doing these past hours? I thought you would have rescued the gel by now."

"Judson has been two steps ahead of us the whole time. But now—" Adam shook his head.

"Now, what?" Walpole asked.

"Judson's doorman said he was coming here. Why hasn't he arrived? Did he stop somewhere with Bronwyn and . . ." Adam couldn't finish. He'd almost admitted his fears, and speaking them aloud made them too real. "I have to know what has happened. Whatever you do, don't shoot him."

"At least"—Walpole opened the left-hand drawer and lifted a gun from his desk—"not to kill. Do you need a pistol?"

"A pistol is not my weapon, you know that." Adam loosened his seaman's knife from its case.

"What if he doesn't arrive?" Walpole asked shrewdly.

"What will you do then?" Adam just looked at his friend, and something of his bleak depression must have impressed Walpole, for he protested, "Damn, Adam, you can't be attached to this woman. Not you!"

Adam was spared a reply by a creaking noise at the kitchen door. He tensed, laid his hand on the hilt of his knife. The image of relaxation, Walpole leaned back in his chair, but his hand rested on the drawer with the gun. They waited, silent, watchful, as the doorknob turned with excruciating slowness. The brass decorations on the escutcheon around the twisting knob branded themselves on Adam's brain.

Inside him, the desire to kill Judson warred with his need to know—know where Bronwyn was, know how she was, know he could hold her once more.

Squealing on its hinges, the door swung open. Damp with face powder glued to his frock coat, Judson gazed at Walpole, gazed at Adam, smiled with crooked cordiality. "I never expected to see you here, Lord Rawson." He laid heavy emphasis on Adam's title. "Have I interrupted a party?"

Behind him the smells of the kitchen wafted up the passage. A dim light shone through the open window where he'd entered. But no one moved behind him.

Disappointment clawed at Adam. Judson was alone. Madness to hope Bronwyn would be with him, of course, but a madness he had indulged in.

As the seconds ticked by, Judson mocked, "Ineloquence has never been the bane of the honorable Robert Walpole before."

"Nor is it now." As the reality of the threat struck him, Walpole marveled, "I thought Adam had run mad. I never thought you would really come."

Judson's gaze slid to Adam. "Just a friendly call."

"Friendly callers come through the front door," Adam admonished. "But then, friendly callers don't sketch a plan of the room arrangement and study it until the ink smudges."

"You've been spying on me." Judson's hand clenched at his side, and he jeered, "You're just like your father."

Adam took a step forward. "My father? My father never stooped to murder."

"Murder?" Judson repeated in arch amazement. "I don't know what you're talking about."

Voice rising, Adam threatened, "I warned you I would stomp you into the dirt, and now—" Walpole snapped his name, and he subsided, but he discovered his knife now rested in his palm. Forcing himself to relax his grip, he took several long breaths. He couldn't throw accurately under such tension, and he owed it to himself, to Walpole, to Bronwyn, to pin Judson against the wall.

"You really came," Walpole said again. "What do you expect to accomplish with this lunacy?"

"Lunacy?" Judson inquired, his painted eyebrows tilted in reproach.

"Did you think no one would notice you killed me?" Walpole slammed his fist on the desk, and Judson jumped.

"Nervous, Judson?" Adam mocked. "You work better alone, in the dark, with no one to watch and expose you. How will you kill us both?"

Walpole glared at Adam. "Damn it, shut up. He wants to kill me, so stop interrupting." Transferring his attention to Judson, he challenged, "So kill me, but I must warn you—I am prepared for your scurrilous attack."

"It seems everyone here knows my agenda." Judson's

hand slipped into his pocket, but he maintained a guileless facade. "I'm curious, though. Why should I attack you?"

"A good question, when your true enemies have led you to financial disaster," Adam said.

Soft and sweet, Judson asked, "What enemies are those?"

"The directors of the South Sea Company. The company's stock is plunging. Your stock is plunging with it," Adam told him brutally.

At the mention of finance, Judson sacrificed his pretense. "This is a false drop in price, much like the drop experienced in June when the king left the country."

Adam shook his head. "The directors lied to you. The bubble has burst."

"No."

Impatient, Walpole interrupted, "Look at the facts, man! The stock has dropped more than two hundred points in five days!"

"They've manipulated the market so the stock appears to be a failure," Judson replied.

"Why would they do that?" Walpole asked.

Judson smiled, almost cocky. "You're ruined, aren't you?"

Taken aback, Walpole sputtered, "Why . . . no. What makes you think so?"

Judson's smile slipped. "You bought the stock. For all your high principles, you invested heavily."

"Yes, and I sold it." Walpole stared grimly, challenging Judson. "I sold it on the recommendation of my friend, Adam Keane. Almost I bought again, not trusting his advice, but luck and poor communication with Mr. Jacombe saved me."

Breathing heavily, Judson said, "That's not true. They would have told me."

"Why?" asked Adam, knowing the answer. "Why did the state of Robert Walpole's finances matter?"

As Judson's control broke, he screamed, "He's a menace! He's always sticking his nose in the Treasury, telling the king what to do, knowing the best way to handle the fortune of the kingdom. Sir John Blunt is the one who knows what's best. Sir John Blunt should direct the course of the country."

"So you're going to kill Robert for dear ol' England?" Adam laughed, brief and bitter. "Come now, tell me another tale."

Judson stuck out his tongue at Adam, for all the world like the child he'd once been. "You think you're so clever. Sir John Blunt is paying me well, and will continue to pay me well when he is appointed to his rightful post in the government. First lord of the Treasury and chancellor of the Exchequer." Judson rolled the title off his tongue. "Sir John has assured me I'll remain behind the scenes to instruct the unwilling in his methods."

"Blunt is not stupid. After you've performed your duties here, he'll have you put down. He can't afford to have a rabid dog like you roaming about." Before Judson could protest, Adam added, "Blunt has already sold his stock, stripping the South Sea Company's coffers early and often."

"It's not true," Judson said, but it sounded as if he begged to be told a lie.

"What difference would it make if I had lost everything?" Walpole asked. "Why would that help your plans?"

"I thought . . ." Defiant, Judson said, "*We* thought if you were ruined, I could kill you and all would believe it was suicide."

Hearty, bluff Walpole burst into laughter at the ludicrous plot.

From the copious pocket of his coat, Judson pulled a pistol and pointed it right at the convulsed Walpole.

Adam balanced his knife on his fingertips, aimed, yet as he threw Judson shouted, "Die slowly, like Bronwyn."

The knife buried itself in the wall beside Judson, and Adam leaped after it.

Judson's arm, extended out straight, swerved toward Adam, and Adam skidded to a halt. "If Bronwyn is alive," he whispered, his preposterous promise balancing his despair, "I'll smuggle you out of the country with enough money to set yourself up nicely."

Indignant, Walpole snapped, "You'd reward him for trying to assassinate me?"

Ignoring Walpole, Adam kept all his attention on Judson and that pistol. The pistol never dipped, but, like a snake prepared to strike, it wavered between its targets. Adam coaxed, "You know you can trust me. It's the only way you'll get out of this alive."

"And if she's dead?" Judson asked.

Adam laughed, but it wasn't a pleasant laugh. "You'd better kill me now."

Walpole insisted, "The worst crime you could commit is to kill an aristocrat."

The black eye of the pistol pivoted toward him once more, and Judson stepped farther into the room. The light fell on his face, and what Adam saw there put a shaft through his heart. "Your face is marked."

Judson jerked his shoulder up to cover the telltale scratches.

"Your cheek is marked by a woman's fingernails." Tempted beyond logic, Adam prepared to spring. The air trembled with the intensity of his impatience.

"I'll shoot you," Judson threatened.

Judson would put down the gun, Adam determined, or Judson would use it. "You can't shoot us both."

Eyes locked, Judson and Adam stared, weighing one another in wordless communication.

Until the hall door burst open and Northrup called, "Sir!"

Chapter 19

As Northrup realized the situation, his face paled, his mouth created an O. Judson swung on him, the gun blasted, Northrup flew back under the impact of the bullet. Too late, Adam sprang for Judson's throat, but the door stood empty. The sound of Judson's heels striking the hardwood floor echoed loudly.

Adam raced to Northrup's side and reached for the pulse at his neck, but Northrup's fingers caught his wrist. Hoarse with pain, Northrup said, "Carriage." He shook Adam's wrist. "Carriage . . . in the alley." Blood spurted from a wound at his side; Walpole knelt beside him and smothered the stream with a pillow.

"Go," Northrup murmured.

"We'll take care of him." Walpole shoved Adam's walking stick into his hand, and Adam needed no more encouragement.

He ran down the hall past the milling servants, out

the kitchen door, through the garden. Sprinting down
the alley, Adam saw a broad carriage, splattered deep
with mud. It swayed as Judson clambered up onto the
driver's box. Adam leaped as it lurched away. He
missed, yet with a burst of triumph he knew he'd catch
it. Judson couldn't drive that unwieldy carriage with
any finesse.

Adam ran, but Judson whipped the horses. Mud
splattered Adam in the face. The carriage rounded the
corner onto the street, leaning so far to the right that
Adam expected it to topple. It did not. It righted itself,
and Adam heard the whip crack. He ran for it, but Judson careened down the street without regard to pedes-
trians or other vehicles. Adam skidded to a stop, his
hand on his throbbing thigh.

In a kind of despair, he murmured, "Judson, you
bastard." He limped toward the stable, cursing his
luck, the weather, and most of all, Judson. Too aware
of his injured leg now that the burst of energy had
failed him, he glared fiercely as a frightened-looking
boy accosted him.

"M'lord? We're 'olding yer horse at th' front door."

From black fury, Adam's emotions swung back to
exultation. He clapped the boy on the back. "Good
man. Bring him around!"

The stable boy took off, echoing the cry, "Bring 'im
around!"

Adam climbed the mounting block and as his stallion arrived, slid into the saddle, crying, "My thanks."

Rounding the corner out of the alley, he searched
anxiously for a glimpse of the carriage. No luck. Judson had gone too far, too fast. But Adam had only to
follow the trail of indignant folks, toppled in Judson's
reckless dash. Not blessed with the indifference that

enabled Judson to drive over beggar children and vendor wagons, he dodged and weaved through the streets, on his way to Change Alley.

What madness had induced Judson to go to Change Alley, Adam didn't understand, but without a doubt they were headed for the narrow, cobbled lane that lay between Lombard and Cornhill streets. As he neared the Alley, a taste of hysteria filled the air. The dropping stock had taken its toll, and—if anything—carriages, berlins, landaus, and chariots clogged more of the area than in the summer days of success. Adam struggled along on his horse, looking over the top of heads and around the bulky vehicles, seeking Judson's four-wheeled carriage. At last his horse balked at the crush, refusing to squeeze through a narrow opening between two coaches.

He could hear the distant roar of the seething crowd, smell the wet, evil scent of bodies crammed together. He could see the preacher who shrieked at sinners from atop his box, see Judson—

Relief and apprehension roiled in Adam. The towering wig looked much the worse for the rain, the face no longer wore its disguise with suave urbanity, but it was Judson. He flew from seller to seller, seeking reassurance, and seller after seller shook his head.

Hating to abandon his fine beast, Adam cast about for a solution and found one in the sly-faced boy creeping his way. Pretending ignorance, he waited until the lad reached up to cut his purse strings, then snatched him up by the nape of the neck and boomed, "That's a hanging offense."

The boy struggled, kicking his skinny legs, cursing with gutter efficiency, until he realized the futility. "Eh, gov'nor, didn't mean no 'arm."

"Of course you did." Only a bit of his attention on the thief, Adam watched Judson flounder through the milling crowd.

"But ye'll forgive me, gov'nor? If I promise never t' do it again . . ." The boy's speech trailed off when Adam turned his gaze on him.

"Don't gammon me, you little brigand. But to show you how lenient I am, I'll not turn you over to the magistrate." A quick glance at Judson showed a desperation Adam hadn't seen since the pitched battles aboard his ship. Judson's violent gestures, his indifference to the jabs of the crowd, spelled a reckless abandon that boded ill for Bronwyn. Only men who believed their death was upon them comported themselves in such a manner. With a surge of ferocity, Adam shook the miniature thief. "I'll give you tuppence now to watch my horse, and tuppence when I return—if the horse is where I left it."

The boy stopped squirming and stared, charmed. "Aye, gov'nor, I'll do it wi' pleasure."

"Right." Adam set the lad down, dismounted, and dispensed the promised recompense. "Remember, another tuppence when I return." Without waiting for reassurance, taking only his walking stick, he dashed away. If he returned and had no horse to claim, he decided, he'd take it out of Judson's hide.

On foot, down among the tangle of duchesses and yeomen, he couldn't see his prey, but far ahead he heard someone call, "Adam Keane." He ignored it. Squeezing through the warm, sweating bodies, he made his way toward the place where he'd last seen Judson, following the track he believed he would go. The crowd did not easily yield to Adam's agitation. In their own frenzy, they had no tolerance for his. A full-bottomed wig hustled through the rabble; Adam grabbed the man, swung him around—but it wasn't Judson. "Damn you," Adam cursed him most unfairly.

The nobleman's eyes lit with recognition. "And be damned to you, too, Lord Rawson." Wild-eyed, he snatched Adam's lapel. "You ruined me, with your false stocks and your false advice."

Adam jerked out of the man's grasp and shoved the evangelist off his box, interrupting the shouted sermon. After leaping up, he scanned above the tangle of heads. In none too gentle a tone, someone called his name, but he was too intent, too terrified for Bronwyn, to pay attention.

And there he was! The familiar big-boxed carriage was shackled by other vehicles, and Judson wiggled toward it. Hands pushed Adam from behind, and gladly he jumped down. Behind him, the preacher shouted, "Wretched sinner! You'll burn in hell!"

With an irony none could appreciate, Adam muttered, "Too late, I'm already there."

Again he heard his name called. "Adam Keane, Lord Rawson." A fist smacked his chest. He smacked back blindly, instinctively, respecting no one in his surge to catch Judson.

"Damn you, Adam Keane." A hand clutched his hair, and his walking stick dealt roughly with the culprit. Building like a rumble of thunder, he heard his name repeated, in a variety of voices—but only one tone. He heard the call in front of him, he heard the call behind him. He realized trouble stalked him even as he stalked Judson.

Adam broke through the seething mass of people, caught Judson's coattails as the blackguard tried to mount the box of the carriage. With a jerk, he knocked Judson to the ground, then dragged him up by his cravat. "Where's Bronwyn? Where's Bronwyn?"

Judson's face screwed up into a little knot of features, then he spit at Adam.

"That's it!" a woman's voice said shrilly. "Spit in his eye!"

Paying the heckler no heed, Adam roared, "Where's Bronwyn?"

"What do you care?" Judson asked shrilly, delving into his pocket and pointing his pistol right at Adam's nose. "You'll never see her again."

Adam remembered the missile had struck Northrup down and didn't hesitate. "It's not loaded," he bellowed, and reached for Judson's throat.

As if in response to Adam's fury, the door of the carriage rammed into Judson's back, pitching him forward. Gagged, bound hand and foot, Bronwyn tumbled out.

Dropping his walking stick, Adam lunged for her, caught her before she struck the cobblestones.

She was warm, struggling, fierce.

And safe. Pure as the spring wind, joy overwhelmed him. He hugged her for a brief, ecstatic moment, then hard on the trail of the joy came the cold whistle of terror.

Judson still had a gun—and perhaps, perhaps it *was* loaded.

Adam had to leave, lead the bullet meant for him away from her.

But he had misread his enemy. The sight of Bronwyn galvanized Judson. He aimed the pistol at Bronwyn, at the helpless woman who, even now, radiated defiance.

Without a sound Adam launched himself, catching Judson's wrist and shoving it above his head.

Clutched tight in Judson's fist, the pistol was the wild card. Its single shot could turn the tide in either direction. The men and women of Change Alley crowded around the fighting pair.

Bronwyn struggled to stand, bumping a gentleman who watched with his spectacles held to his nose. "Watch yourself," he ordered. She bumped him harder, and his belly quivered with indignation. "I said—" His eyes widened at the gag that held her silent. "Did he do this to you?" he demanded.

She nodded, and he cried, "Look! Here's another one of his victims."

A lady in dove gray, by dress a seamstress or governess, clucked in dismay. "You poor child." She raised her voice. "Another one of that perfidious man's prey. Help me take this cloth from her mouth."

They freed her from her bonds, then Bronwyn plunged to the front of the crowd. Locked together, Judson and Adam strained mightily. She couldn't see all four of their hands—most important, she couldn't see the pistol. She cast about her for something to smack Judson with, but there was nothing, only a circle of faces mirroring a savage appreciation.

Muffled yet penetrating, the crack of the gun struck her as the bullet struck flesh. But whose flesh? Both Adam and Judson tumbled to the street. First Adam, then Judson, then Adam reached the top, pounding each other with their fists, kicking, kneeing, brawling with dedication. Blood smeared their skin—or was it mud? The gun skidded across the slime and wedged between two cobblestones. The crowd bellowed, "Kill the bastard! Break him!"

The pain of Adam's leg drained him. Judson's shot had probably lamed him, possibly killed him. With angry despair, Adam pummeled Judson. Judson struggled spasmodically until Adam stung him with an open-handed slap, then Adam forced the words between swollen lips. "If you've sent me to hell, rest assured you'll accompany me."

Judson's eye developed a tic, and he squalled. "Sounds like a babe," Adam heard from the crowd, and if he could, he would have smiled.

Instead he pushed Judson's wig aside. It disappeared beneath the trampling feet of the onlookers, and shock brought silence. "Why, that Adam Keane's naked an' shiny as a baby's behind," a woman marveled.

Startled into inaction, Adam glanced up at the gawking housewife.

Unveiled, Judson tore himself away from Adam, and screeched, "You stupid tart!"

Adam grabbed, not Judson, but his long forgotten walking stick. Like a good friend, the rod fit in his hand, the amber globe weighed heavy on the end. He twirled the knob around, cracked Judson beneath the jaw. Judson's head jerked back, crashing against the cobblestones. Drowning in victory and in pain, Adam throttled him.

The crowd howled. Bronwyn howled with them, thundering her approval. Judson struggled, and the noise of the crowd shifted from the appreciation for a good fight to the sound of a vendetta.

"Adam Keane is killing that poor man," the governess complained.

"'E's not Lord Rawson," argued a tired-faced whore. "'Tis th' other one what ruined us. He sol' me stocks on th' street."

"You idiots! The bald one's not Lord Rawson," an aristocratic voice said. "Lord Rawson is the other one."

"Lord Rawson is the man on top." Bronwyn smiled savagely. "He's the one who's winning!" All faces turned to her, ignoring the struggle on the ground for the even more interesting quarrel above.

" 'E's not," the whore insisted. "Th' other one's been sellin' th' stock."

Silence chilled the air, and the aristocrat insisted, "I've met him at court."

"Who cares?" a hoarse voice from the back sang out. "Let's string 'em both up. That way we'll be sure to get the right man."

"String 'em up."

Maddened by bloodlust, cheated of their livelihood, the crowd pressed in, closing on both men.

"Leave him alone," Bronwyn yelled, but they caught Adam by the arms and jerked him off Judson. He collapsed where he stood. Bronwyn tried to run to him, but the crowd pressed together.

The same hoarse voice screamed, "Hang the rich one first!" and the impassioned street minister stepped into the center of the mob. "Hang them from my preacher's stand."

"Hang 'em," the call rang out again.

Bronwyn fought to gain ground, clawed at the faceless people, yet Adam moved away from her. They propped him up on the stand. He slid back down out of sight, and someone snickered. "He fainted."

Fainted? Panic pounded through her veins as Bronwyn strained to see. Adam fainted? She didn't believe it. "It's a trick."

Beside her, a dockworker heard and laughed coarsely. "Nah, 'e fainted all right."

Even faced with his own hanging, Adam would command with impatience, not wither like a flower in the heat. "What's wrong with him?" she cried.

"Ye're not much bigger than me daughter," said a big-armed, big-bellied man, swinging her up like a sack of potatoes and placing her on his shoulder.

She grabbed at his throat; he grunted and tore her hands away. "I'll not drop ye. Can ye see?"

She could. Packed together like a coven of witches, the mob surged ahead of her. She could see the rope the young, hoarse-voiced ringleader had flung over a protruding roof beam. She could see Adam shrouded with blood. "What happened to him?"

The shoulder beneath her shook with laughter. "Th' bloody bastard took that gunshot in th' leg. Serve 'im right fer causin' all this trouble."

Fists doubled, she smacked him on the side of the head. "You fool, he didn't cause this trouble, the South Sea Company did."

He shook off her blows as if they were the bites of a mosquito. "Everyone knows—"

She dug her fingers into his hair and jerked his head back until he looked into her face. "Everyone's wrong. Now you take me to him."

"Now, ye listen 'ere, little lady—"

"That's right, I am a lady." She kicked him in the ribs. "I can pay you for your assistance."

"I don't 'ave t' put up wi' this." He tried to dislodge her from his shoulder, but she pulled his hair until his eyes slanted.

"I can pay you, and Lord Rawson can pay you."

Shoving people aside, he moved purposefully toward a wall, intent on scraping her off.

Adam now stood on the box, knees locked, eyes

fixed grimly ahead. He ignored the noose. He ignored the men who shook their fists, the women who demanded their money or his life. He ignored Judson, muddy and sniveling. He could see only Bronwyn, held aloft on someone's shoulder.

How bitter this tasted. She'd given him the illusion of normality. He'd become one of those individuals he despised, a dreamer. He'd believed for a few short, sweet weeks that his family history could be dismissed. Yet Judson had so easily convinced London of his guilt because of that same family history, and that was something he should have never overlooked.

What had he brought Bronwyn to? He'd destroyed her virtue, ruined her so thoroughly that she could never be married. If she were with child, she'd be shunted aside to raise his babe alone. Because of him, she'd been kidnapped and brutalized. And now she was in the midst of a London mob, watching as they hanged him.

Bronwyn's gaze cruised the crowd and bumped against a large man, the largest man she'd ever seen. She tensed, strained to see, took a gamble. "Do you know a man named Oakes?"

Her bearer froze. "Oakes?"

"Oakes."

"Must be a lotta Oakes in Lunnon."

"Only one could be this big, and work in a warehouse near the docks. See him plowing his way through the crowd toward Lord Rawson?" She pointed at the man—could it really be Oakes?

"Oakes?" her bearer repeated. "Does Oakes know Lord Rawson?"

"He's our friend," she confided, promoting her acquaintance into a relationship. In Oakes's wake she could see a series of gray-cloaked figures moving with him, and she wondered—

A harangue from the impromptu hanging tree brought her gaze back to the front—back to her love. She wasn't so far from Adam. In fact, she was close enough to see him, blotched with bruising. Close enough to have him staring at her as they looped the noose around his neck. His eyes, so gray, so intense, spoke to her, but in her privation she couldn't comprehend. Her chest clutched in a great pain. Her heart should be located within, but her whole system shook with such anguish that she knew no such organ could reside there. There was only thorns, and needles, and a great gaping horror that festered.

The minister bellowed, "This is Adam Keane, viscount of Rawson. He brought this disaster on us all. I say hang him!"

A roar of assent answered him.

Beside Bronwyn's bearer, the whore shook her head. "'E's not th' man what sold me th' fake stock. 'Tis th' other."

"What?" Bronwyn's bearer turned so quickly, he almost dislodged her.

The whore repeated, "'E's not th' one—"

"Damn it." The bearer inspected Oakes and his progress. Looked up at Bronwyn's still, set face. Remembered the kind impulse that made him pick her up. And separated the people in front of him with the swath of his beefy arms. "Get outta th' way, we're hangin' th' wrong man."

The mob rumbled as they turned on the man beneath her, prepared to kill him for interfering. From the other direction, a now menacing Oakes waded toward the ringleader. The gray-cloaked shadows fanned out around the box, closing in a tight-knit snare.

The helpful assistants of the mob tightened the noose around Adam's neck. The minister called, "So must all swindlers perish!" He failed to notice the danger until Oakes stepped up on the box in one oversize step. As Oakes straightened, the ringleader craned his neck back, and back, and back. He retreated several steps and in a painfully comedic move fell backward off the box.

The fickle crowd guffawed.

Oakes turned on the other men who had so eagerly volunteered for the hanging, and they abandoned the box like fleas off a drowning dog.

"It's Oakes!" someone called. "'Ey, Oakes, *you* wanna 'ang 'im?"

Oakes faced the crowd and seemed to swell. His face contorted, his arms swung back and forth, back and forth, and that same someone asked, "'Ey, Oakes, don't you want us t' 'ang 'im?"

Oakes glared.

Willing to abandon one victim for another, the someone yelled, "Then we'll 'ang th' other one."

But the other one had disappeared, mysteriously whisked away by gray-cloaked figures.

"Oakes!" Bronwyn shrieked. "Catch me."

The man beneath her helped her launch herself into Oakes's arms, and from Oakes she flung herself toward Adam. With one bleak glance he collapsed into her arms. "Help me get this noose off him," she commanded.

They laid the unconscious Adam down. His leg now gaped where the bullet had entered, and Bronwyn tugged her scarf tight to slow the bleeding. She looked up; the crowd had melted away, except for a few who remained in ghoulish curiosity. Coldly Bronwyn made use of them, ordering them to lift her love and carry him to Judson's carriage. This she would commandeer. Wherever he was now, he owed her that much.

Oakes loped along beside them, keeping the bearers in line by his mere presence. "Where will we go, m'lady?"

"To Madame Rachelle's."

"Good." Oakes nodded. "That's one cunnin' woman, even fer a frog."

Gaping at the massive fellow, she asked, "You know her? Be careful with him." She caught Adam's lax hand before it bumped the frame of the carriage door and frowned at the men. "He's not a sack of potatoes. Let me get in first, and I'll hold his head in my lap."

They smoothly maneuvered him onto the seat. Bronwyn flinched as they tucked his legs up, but she demanded, "Can any of you drive?"

They backed away, but Oakes plucked one of them up by the neck. "He can drive us."

"Us?" Bronwyn asked.

"I'll go wi' you t' see you get there wi' no trouble." Oakes glared at the designated coachman, and the driver scrambled onto the seat as if his breeches were on fire. Oakes gave him directions, then entered and sat opposite Bronwyn. As if she'd just asked, he answered her previous question.

"Madame Rachelle brought me 'ere. She 'as Judson in 'er 'ands, an' that froggie will know just 'ow t' treat a scum like 'im."

Bronwyn bit her fingernails as Oakes laid the unconscious Adam across Rachelle's bed.

"Do ye want me t' call a doctor?" Oakes asked.

"Do you wish to kill him?" Daphne snapped. "He has lost enough blood, and all your English physicians would do is bleed him again." She rolled up her sleeves. "Leave him to me. I will pull him through."

In a pig's eye, Bronwyn wanted to snap back. But here in the sickroom, the reckless French girl demanded respect.

It seemed Oakes thought so, too, for he said, "I'll just be goin', then."

"Where?" Bronwyn demanded.

"Home."

Bronwyn prodded, "Where's home? I wish to reward you for your help."

"Naw." He shook his head and kept on shaking it. "I 'elp folks so's they'll treat me good."

"And do they?" Daphne asked.

"Aye." He shambled toward the door. "No one ever tries t' beat me or nothin'. Take care of 'is Ludship." His last words echoed down the hall, and the women turned back to their gruesome task.

Bronwyn glanced around. "Should I light the candles?"

"As many as you can find, *s'il vous plaît*. I need the light."

Bronwyn watched as Daphne brought shiny instruments out of a black bag and laid them on the table beside the bed. She trembled as Daphne inserted the scissors to cut away Adam's breeches and she saw the shredded skin and muscle.

"Oh, stop whimpering." Daphne rinsed her hands in the basin by the bed. "This is what I trained for, practiced for. If you cannot help me without fainting, I will ask one of the others."

"No!" Bronwyn leaped forward. "I'll assist you."

Daphne smiled with grim appreciation. "I rather thought you would. The bullet struck only the fleshy part of his leg, and left the necessary parts intact." She glared at Bronwyn. "You must be happy to hear that, mademoiselle."

Without a blush, Bronwyn glared back.

Satisfied with her composure, Daphne pointed at the wound. "The bullet entered the leg in the front, exited through the back. That's good."

"It went out the back?" Bronwyn asked, dumbfounded. "He has a wound at the back, too?"

"You had not noticed?" Daphne snorted. "Have you no practical function in this world?" Without waiting for an answer to that hypothetical query, she continued, "I could sew him up immediately—"

"You're going to sew him?"

"How else would I put this together?" Daphne waved an encompassing hand.

Bronwyn cleared her throat. "I don't know."

"I could sew him up immediately, but he has bits of cloth from his breeches contained in the wound. They must be removed, or they will fester. *Monsieur le Vicomte* may struggle when I probe and clean."

"He's unconscious," Bronwyn objected.

With brisk efficiency, Daphne wrung out a cloth and laid it on Adam's forehead. "Pain has a way of bringing the patient to life, and I want to do a good job on him."

"Because he's your first gunshot patient?"

"Because he is going to take you away from here and you will never come back," Daphne declared with a fervency that almost frightened Bronwyn. "You think you can sweep in here and capture my mother's heart, but I tell you, when you are gone Rachelle will remember me once more."

"Rachelle isn't your mother," Bronwyn retorted.

"No, but she cares for me as if she were." She lifted her head and glared. "She's all I have in the world."

Silence reigned, then Bronwyn asked, "Where is Rachelle?"

"She and the others are stowing your Carroll Judson in the pantry below."

"Bless them." Bronwyn imitated a smile through lips so tight they were bloodless and grasped Adam's wrists firmly.

Mixing water with brandy, Daphne bathed the wound and picked away bits of thread and cloth. With her forceps she began to probe into the muscle. Adam twitched and moaned, and Bronwyn leaned her weight against him.

Daphne took his leg between hers to keep it still. Her fingers flew, her brow puckered. Her breath sounded loud in the room, and she muttered as if she were puzzled.

"What's wrong?"

"There is something in here."

Dreading the reply, Bronwyn asked, "Did the bullet hit the bone?"

"*Non*. It is not a bone fragment, but it is loose."

"There are chips of a ship deck in there."

That caught Daphne's attention.

"That's why he limps. A cannonball struck near him, and— "

"I see." Daphne slipped a finger in beside the forceps. "When *Monsieur le Vicomte* recovers, he will thank me for this."

Her glib guarantee reassured Bronwyn even as the slow torture dragged Adam back to consciousness.

"There." Daphne held up a red fragment. "I will go back for more."

Sickened, Bronwyn looked away, but she saw the leg that looked so like a display in a butcher's window. She took a breath, but the odors of blood and muck fogged her mind. Light-headed, she wavered, but a mutter from the bed made her look down.

Adam was awake.

Delight filled her with a manic energy, sweeping her faint away. She wanted to hug him, kiss him, assure herself—and him—of his health. Instead she whispered, "Adam, you're going to be well soon."

He didn't answer, only stared. Stared so fixedly that alarm touched her. He looked at her as if she were a stranger. His complexion was bloodless. Beneath his shirt his chest rose and fell, endlessly seeking oxygen.

"Adam?"

"Is he awake?" Daphne asked.

"He is, but he doesn't speak."

Daphne abandoned the leg that so fascinated her and came to his head. She groped through his thick hair. "There isn't a bump." With her thumbs she lifted his lids and peered into his eyes. "Do you know who you are?"

"Yes, and what's worse, I know who you are. Can't I afford a real doctor?"

Bronwyn's relief found voice in laughter, and it escaped in a *whoosh*.

Unamused, Daphne stepped away. "You are ungrateful, monsieur."

Reminded of Daphne's dedication, Bronwyn sobered. "Yes, you are, Adam. Daphne has done all a doctor could do, and more, I suspect."

"She's hurting me at least as badly as any damned doctor who's worked on me before," Adam allowed. He hesitated for the beat of a heart, then asked, "Will I lose my leg this time?"

"No," Bronwyn cried, but he paid her no attention.

"No," Daphne answered firmly. "I don't even believe there will be infection. The powder ignited so close to your leg, it purified the wound as it inflicted it."

He searched her face, then nodded, satisfied with her competence and her truthfulness. "You may continue."

Daphne returned to the leg while Bronwyn poured a large glass of brandy. Sliding her arm under his shoulders, she supported him while he drank; then he sank back.

Doggedly Bronwyn ignored Daphne's work, but she couldn't ignore Adam's groans as Daphne delved deeper and deeper, or the way he jerked and clenched the sheets.

At last he burst out, "Woman, must you maul me?"

Daphne lifted her face in triumph. "I got it!"

"Got what?"

Bronwyn wiped his forehead with a wet rag as Daphne exulted, "I found the splinter that caused you such pain. Look!" She thrust the forceps before his face, and clamped between their steel jaws was a dripping piece of wood, encased in slime. "You will have no limp now!"

Gripping Daphne's wrist, Adam brought it closer to inspect the chip. "You've done something no other doctor could do. I thank you. Bronwyn, look—"

With one sigh as she passed into unconsciousness, Bronwyn slid off the bed and onto the floor. Daphne made a disgusted noise and prepared to help her, but Adam stopped her. "No. She doesn't want to be here with a man all London despises, and I don't want her here. Leave her. Just . . . leave her."

Chapter 20

Adam was sitting up for the first time in days. His color was good, he moved with an ease that amazed Bronwyn.

And he had become a stranger.

Not a stranger, really. She recognized this Adam, remembered him from the first time she'd met him. His lips curved in an insincere smile. He radiated hostility. Somehow, some way, he'd become the Adam of long ago. He'd retreated behind a mask as stiff and as cold as any worn by Carroll Judson, and she didn't understand why.

She only knew he wore it well. He wore it with the ease brought from years of practice.

She brushed the velvet material on the arm of the chair with the edge of her hand. The light fell on it, sparking it to beauty. Trying to maintain her composure, she admired it while avoiding his gaze. "We have arranged for you to be transported back to Boudasea Manor tomorrow."

"Fine."

Hardly encouragement, but she had to try. She wanted to speak with him, be with him, as she had been with him before. "Madame Rachelle has Judson locked in her pantry."

One elegant brow lifted as he drawled, "In her pantry?"

"It has the best lock in the house." She smiled slightly. "She visits with him every evening, making sure he's comfortable and well fed."

"I would think she'd be anxious to place him in the prison, where he'd be uncomfortable and ill fed."

"Not at all." She smoothed the green velvet the other way until it displayed its dark side. "The jailers can be bribed, she says, to provide pleasant surroundings and decent food, and if enough money is produced, to provide escape."

"I see." His hands, which had been resting on the covers, rose and templed at his chin. "Why not keep him here, then, and torment him as he tormented . . . others?"

Unable to help herself, she asked, "Like me?" His mouth tightened, and she lost her nerve. "She wants to keep him healthy, the better to have him survive the travail she plans for him."

"What travail is that?"

"I don't know. She says he will decide."

"Interesting." His eyes narrowed.

"Your mother wanted to come into London, but she found the excitement too much for her."

"Lord, yes." The mention of his mother brought a

spark to his eye. "Don't let her risk her health. She's all I have."

She recognized a cutting blade when exposed to one. She'd seen too much of the knife, and his words stabbed at her deliberately. "You have more than that."

"You mean my betrothal?"

A step in the right direction, she determined. "Exactly."

A smile played about his mouth. "Olivia should not be exposed to the evil London vapors."

Her fingernails lurched through the nap of the velvet, destroying the pattern she'd so carefully created. "Oh, Olivia didn't even want to come. Not even when she was told you were sick, and she adores nursing. I don't, you see. It makes me ill. Invalids are quite beyond my ken."

"Are they? Yet you revived from your ordeal with scarcely a whimper. You were kidnapped, bound, gagged, used as a pawn in a dreadful maneuver."

It sounded as if he accused her, but she refused to experience guilt for recovering from her bruises without scars. "Yes."

"You were there when Judson and I were trying to kill each other."

"Yes." She had to try and explain, make him see she would have given her life for him. "I was there when the mob took you, too. I forced this big man to carry me forward. I kicked him, trying to make him intervene. I did what I could to rescue you"—she faltered at his forbidding frown—"but the mob proved too much for me."

He dismissed her earnest plea with barely a shrug. "I wouldn't expect one small woman to stop so determined a lynching. It's you I am concerned about." So serious he seemed almost caring, he asked, "Are you well?"

Unsure of the dependability of her voice, she nodded.

"Did he hurt you?"

"Judson?" Her voice rasped in her throat. "He tried."

"Did he rape you?"

As plain as that. The seaman had overtaken the gentleman, and Adam didn't wrap his query in any pretty camouflage. She could be plain, too. "No. He tried. . . ." She wasn't as tough as she wanted to be. The memory of her wrestling match on the seat of the carriage made her choke. She wanted comfort. She wanted to throw herself on Adam's chest and weep, but no sympathy swayed that cold man seated on the bed. A wave of nausea struck her, and she put her chin down, breathing deeply until she could finish. "He tried, but was incapable."

He never flinched, never moved. Her emotion meant nothing to him. "Is that why he was late coming to kill Walpole?"

"I suppose." Was that all he had to say? Was he repulsed that Judson had tried to assault her? Did that make her dirty in his eyes? She rose, clung to the back of the chair as dizziness swept her. "I must go. There are things I need to attend to."

Adam watched as she walked to the dresser, found it with her hand, moved to the door casing, caught it, held it, then groped out of the room. Remorse gripped him, but he held tight to his resolve. He must not involve Bronwyn in his exile from society, but how difficult it was to deceive her. She knew him better than anyone alive. She knew him too well. She had become everything his mother wished for him.

This mask he wore, so familiar, once a part of him, no longer fit. Under the reproach of Bronwyn's gaze, cracks developed. Chips threatened to break off and reveal his true countenance, but he could hardly let that happen.

What kind of man would subject the woman he loved to the censure of society? Not he. He had always known innocence was no defense, but a London mob had had to beat it into him before he had truly understood. Even now he cringed as he remembered standing on the platform on Change Alley, a noose around his neck, and seeing Bronwyn on the shoulder of some dock walloper. She hadn't been cheering his demise, he knew, but she had been about to witness it nevertheless. She had seen the scorn of the crowd, of the gentlemen and the streetwalkers.

She thought she wanted him, and without conceit he knew she did. Physically they were a match. He'd told his mother he wanted to be the father of his first child. He'd told Bronwyn he'd use any method, including passion, to keep her close. He'd told himself he'd seduced her just to bend her to his will. He didn't mind hiding the truth from his mother, from Bronwyn, but he knew now he'd been hiding it from himself.

He wanted her. He wanted her above him, below him, in daylight, in candlelight. He wanted her head on his shoulder, her breath in his ear.

But in that place where his demons lurked, he knew he would rather hurt her now than have her turn away from him when she realized how thoroughly society despised him. He felt better every day, and when he was capable he would flee Bronwyn's vicinity like the coward he was and never see her again.

His life had been arduous, and it had made him

strong. He would do what was right—but oh, how hard it was, to place the brightest star of his sky beyond his own reach.

The scene in the entrance hall at Boudasea Manor rivaled the most dreadful amateur dramatics Adam had ever seen. His mother wept in his embrace while Lady Nora wiped invisible tears from her artfully rouged cheeks. Lord Gaynor slapped Adam on the back and roared, "Good to see you, me boy," while a sobbing Olivia gripped Bronwyn in what looked like white-knuckled desperation.

Bronwyn patted her sister on the back while supervising the transportation of their luggage up the stairs.

"Come into the parlor at once and put your feet up. Got some of your finest brandy waiting for you there." Lord Gaynor winked. "Gave m'wife and I quite a scare with your little illness."

"I'm sure." Adam watched with a sardonic gaze as Lord Gaynor led the way, ordered the seating, poured the drinks, made it clear how well he played host in Adam's own house. Mab, he noted, let Gaynor do as he would, and he wondered at it. What game was his mother playing?

"But relieved we are to have you here at last." Lord Gaynor smiled fondly at his wife. "Lady Nora and I feared the first of the wedding guests would arrive before you."

As Adam watched, little waves rippled in his brandy glass, and he noted the tremble in his hand. After placing his drink on the table, he twisted to face Lord Gaynor as his mother's hand tightened around his fingers. "Wedding guests?"

"You could have at least let him rest before you told him our surprise," Lady Nora reproved. Abandoning her own advice, she said, "We've planned the entire wedding, Rafferty and I, set the date and ordered the dress. You will marry our very own Olivia a week from tomorrow. Isn't that breathtaking?"

"Exactly the word I would have chosen." This was a joke. A joke of phenomenal bad taste, but a joke nevertheless. "Mab?"

Mab answered his reproach with a reproach of her own. "When I heard of your injury, my health failed me for a short time. When I recovered, I found the Edanas had taken care of the wedding, right down to the details."

Horrified at his mother's defection, he gasped, "But Mab—"

"And as they pointed out, the reasons for this marriage still exist, just as they did when Bronwyn first came to the house to be your bride." Mab smiled at him like a woman who understood fate and had at last become resigned to its workings. "You want an impeccable bride who will advance your standing in society. The Edanas want money."

"Mab, you and I discussed this, and we decided that—" That Bronwyn was the woman for him. What malevolent demon had changed his mother's mind? Seeking support, he looked about for Bronwyn, but he saw only Olivia. Never before had the beautiful Edana sister looked gawky in his eyes, but she did now. She stood awkwardly, like a bird undecided about flight. She flapped her arms, bit her lips, shredded her handkerchief as her sister used to do.

"Olivia!" Lady Nora's sharp tone brought her to

attention. "Tell your bridegroom how happy you are to share the marriage rites with him."

Olivia tried to speak, but though her lips moved, no sound came out.

Lady Nora provided the dialogue. "She's thrilled."

Awash with pity, Adam protested, "I doubt I'll be a worthy bridegroom in only a week's time. Perhaps—"

"You'll have your whole life ahead of you to perform a bridegroom's duties," Lady Nora told him coyly.

"Besides, the autumn has far advanced," Lord Gaynor added. "'Tis October, and Lady Nora and I have a desire to see our Olivia settled before we go into London for the Season. So when Lady Nora suggested we use this as the Season's first party, I agreed. Of course."

"Of course. But I think you underestimate the depth of society's abhorrence for me." Adam's smile stretched his mouth, but his lips felt tight with tension, and he abandoned his attempt to be tactful. "No one will come to this wedding."

Lady Nora sucked in her cheeks in a practiced expression of superiority. "Of course they will. You underestimate the influence my husband, my daughters, and I have on society. And"—she held up her hand to stop his protest—"should society really be so disapproving of you, there is still the curiosity factor. Oh, they'll come, for one reason or the other." She looked about her. "Where's Bronwyn? I haven't got to greet my own dear child."

Bronwyn was nowhere to be seen, and Olivia stammered, "She went upstairs. Perhaps she is exhausted from the journey."

"More likely she is exhausted from her family," Mab said. "Poor girl, what a thing to come home to."

* * *

"You can't hide from me forever." Olivia stood before Bronwyn, twisting her handkerchief. "I'm your sister. I love you."

Bronwyn settled her back firmly against the stone bench artistically placed beneath a spreading yew. The fall colors of the garden comforted her, turning as it was from living bits of creation to the dead dull of winter. As the cold of the seat seeped through to her spine, she replied, "I know you do."

Shuffling the gravel of the garden path beneath her shoe, Olivia said, "I can't stand this estrangement between us. You're my best friend. You're the only person who understands me."

Brief and bitter, Bronwyn laughed. "I don't understand you. I thought I did, but I don't."

Olivia dropped her outstretched hand. "What do you mean?"

As it filtered through the leaves, sunshine speckled Olivia's lovely face as if nature herself were complimenting the girl. That infuriated Bronwyn. Since she'd returned from London and discovered the wedding date set, everything had infuriated Bronwyn. "You said you didn't want to get married yet," she accused. "You said you didn't want to marry Adam. Yet tomorrow you're going to."

"You're just angry because you love him and you can't have him," Olivia cried.

"A silly little reason, I know."

"Then you admit it?" Olivia pounced like a cat on a juicy mouse. "You love Lord Rawson?"

Sulky at being cornered, Bronwyn drawled, "Yes. I suppose."

"I told you so! I told you you loved him." Olivia

ground her fist into her palm. "Well, it's your fault I'm marrying him."

"My fault?" Bronwyn put incredulity into her tone, but not much conviction. She knew what Olivia would say.

"Yes, your fault. You ran away and stuck me in that situation. You even knew Maman and Da would suggest I take your place."

"I didn't know it." At Olivia's skeptical sniff, Bronwyn admitted, "I suspected."

"So it's up to you to avert this disaster and stop the wedding." Olivia tried to sound authoritative and succeeded in sounding doubtful.

"How do you propose I do that?"

"Just tell Lord Rawson you want him." Olivia's authority strengthened. "He'll take the appropriate steps."

Brushing a leaf from her lap in elaborate carelessness, Bronwyn asked, "What makes you think he cares?"

Olivia laughed, a merry, tinkling laugh that ran like the bells of the chapel. "I think he would not only do anything not to marry me, I think he would do everything to marry you."

Mulling that over, Bronwyn said, "Think of the scandal. First me, then you, then me again."

"That's Maman talking." Olivia sat beside Bronwyn and caught her hands. "You've always been the brave one. In Ireland you used to jump off the cliffs onto the sand, remember?"

Bronwyn smiled. "You used to stand on the beach with bandages."

"You snuck into that dark old tomb."

"You ran and got help when I got stuck."

"You're the one who insisted on rescuing Henriette."

Bronwyn sobered. "You made her last moments comfortable."

"You wanted to live like a scholar, and ran away to that salon." Olivia glowed with excitement. "If you want Lord Rawson, you could stop the marriage."

"Olivia, the wedding's tomorrow."

"All the more reason to do it now."

"Why are you begging me to make a scandal? Is Adam cruel to you?"

"Oh, no." Olivia's hands jerked as she twined them together. "If I had to marry someone, he would do better than most. He doesn't want me."

"Then why—"

"I don't ever want to get married."

"Don't be silly," Bronwyn said. "Every woman has to get married."

Straight and stubborn, Olivia retorted, "No, they don't."

"You want to be a spinster?"

"No." Olivia took a big breath, then another. "I want to be a nun."

"A nun?" Bronwyn screamed, but it came out in a tortured whisper. "A *Catholic* nun?"

Olivia nodded, her enormous eyes pleading for understanding.

"Olivia." Bronwyn gulped. "Olivia. Olivia, listen to me . . ."

"I know what you're going to say."

"I'm glad someone does," Bronwyn muttered.

"You're going to say we're not Catholic."

Bronwyn tried to keep the sarcasm out of her tone, she really tried. "That's a point."

"But I remember the convent so well," Olivia explained patiently. "I remember all their teachings. I loved the chapel, and the singing, and the nursing. I loved Ireland, and the feeling that God dwelt so close among the crags and the mists."

Hoarse with distress, Bronwyn offered, "We'll take you back to visit Ireland."

"But it's not just Ireland. No matter where the Church is, I feel at home. I've thought about it all my life, but these last few months . . ." Olivia leaned her head against Bronwyn's shoulder and smiled. "This is all your fault, you know."

Bronwyn jumped. "Oh, no. You're not blaming this on me. I'm not jumping onto the sands with the tide coming in. *You* are."

"When you left, I thought you had run away to a convent."

Bronwyn swung on her sister. "To a convent? What made you think that?"

"You talked about how you wanted to go someplace where you could do as you wish, speak as you wished, not have to marry." Olivia faltered under Bronwyn's incredulous gaze.

Comprehension burst on Bronwyn. "You thought I was in a convent, because that's where you wanted to be."

"Oh, yes." Olivia sighed in relief. "I knew you'd understand."

"Understand? I don't understand. Not at all," Bronwyn said in horror. "And even if I did, do you understand what you would do to us all if you became a Papist? You don't even have to become a nun, just a Catholic. The whole family will be disgraced. The ministers will roar at us from the pulpit. Da would be justified if he locked you up with bread and water."

"You could intercede for me," Olivia said eagerly.

"Intercede for you? You're marrying Adam tomorrow!"

"But if you took him for yourself, then I wouldn't have to marry him, and we could gently break it to Maman and Da about me later."

"Just a minute." Bronwyn turned to her sister. "You want *me* to create the greatest scandal to rock England as a distraction for you? You won't stop the wedding yourself? You won't make the decision to tell Maman and Da? I'll help you?"

"You'll do it, won't you, Bronwyn?"

Olivia had never looked so beautiful. The sun shone on her porcelain skin, her red lips rounded in a pleading bow, her blue eyes sparkled with tears. "If I don't stop the wedding tomorrow," Bronwyn elucidated, "you won't become a nun, because you'll be married to Adam."

Olivia nodded.

"Which would save the family two scandals, me untold humiliation, and you the mistake of your life."

"No!"

Bronwyn stood. "Thank you, Olivia. You've helped me make the right decision."

Olivia dropped to her knees before Bronwyn and grabbed her hand. "Please, Bronwyn. Please help me."

"I am helping you." Bronwyn wrestled her hand away and started down the path toward the house. "If you're too frightened to refuse to go through with the wedding ceremony, then you don't want to be a nun very badly."

"I do."

The sound of Olivia's sobbing followed Bronwyn, and she pivoted. "You're an Edana, just like I am. If you want something, you have to reach out and take it. Just"—she waved her arms—"take it."

Chapter 21

"What difference will it make?" Adam wiped his sweaty palms on the needlepoint cover of his desk chair. "Once the wedding is over, Olivia will never be subjected to the scorn of society. I'll receive whatever benefits of the Edana persona that are possible for me to receive, and Olivia will be everything I ever wanted."

Northrup said nothing. He simply stared at Adam, his mouth puckered, his eyes accusing.

Adam snapped, "Mab looks at me in that manner, Northrup, but I'd like to remind you, she is my mother. I'll accept her evaluation, but not yours."

"Of course, sir." Northrup transferred his gaze to the figures he was adding. "However, I'm not the one who brought up the matter of your nuptials."

It was true. Adam couldn't keep quiet about this marriage. He returned to the subject, prodding it, justifying it, assuring himself he was doing the right thing when he knew damn good and well he wasn't. "Gorgeous, none too bright, a good breeder, a good manager, comfortable on the pedestal I place her on. That's all I ask. That's all I ever asked."

"Is it, sir?" Northrup scribbled something on the paper.

That *was* all Adam had asked from a wife. Too bad it wasn't what he wanted anymore. Now he wanted conversation, love, laughter with a good woman. With Bronwyn. Bronwyn, who whisked around corners and faked headaches to avoid him.

She wasn't pregnant, then. He'd been hoping, praying she would come to him, hand on her expanding belly, and screech, "I'm anticipating. What are you going to do about it?"

In his lonely bed he'd spend long hours comforting Bronwyn, placating the Edanas, rearranging the wedding. He'd imagined Bronwyn at his side as they took the marriage vows and he bounced an infant boy on his knee. Of course, Bronwyn was so obstinate, it would probably be a girl.

God, his own head ached when he thought of Bronwyn. "It's too bad no one will come to the wedding."

Northrup had not followed the switch of subject, for he said, "Beg pardon, sir?"

Restless, Adam stood and limped across the study to the window. "What with the way everyone feels about me."

"I think you're refining a bit much on this, sir. I'd like to point out that this evening the house is filled with guests awaiting your nuptials tomorrow."

"Waiting for me to make a fool of myself."

"I'd say you're already doing that, sir."

Adam swung on Northrup, but Northrup bent to his work. Adam sighed. Reinstating Northrup had proved to be a problem. The young man no longer respected him. Actually, Northrup respected him, but he no longer feared him. He seemed to think that the gunshot wound he'd suffered freed him to make comments about the wedding, about Adam's cowardice, about Bronwyn's sorrow. All in a deferential tone that made it difficult to upbraid him.

"Does your wound ache, sir?"

Unconsciously Adam had been rubbing his recent wound, and he snatched his hand away. "Better call for candles. You'll hurt your eyes working in this dim light."

Again Northrup said nothing with great eloquence.

Adam rubbed his leg again and admitted, "Itches like the devil. Looks like hell. Yours?"

"I'm going to burn these bandages when they're removed," Northrup groused.

From the door Bronwyn asked, "Yet Daphne did do a marvelous job, did she not?"

Adam spun around. In a simple dress of sapphire, Bronwyn looked wonderful. Her silver hair trailed over her shoulders and caressed her breast, exposed by the bodice and not shrouded by a handkerchief. Her eyes reflected the blue velvet. Her skin appeared to be golden, and a delicate blush tinted her cheeks. Her lips were red, and he found both her lip and cheek color to be suspect. She'd been biting her lips, probably unconsciously, and pinching her cheeks, quite intentionally, he was sure. He'd seen her do that when she wanted to make an impression.

She had succeeded. He was impressed.

He wanted to run to her, take her hands, hug her to him, lead her to his room . . .

Northrup stood up, straightening slowly, favoring his hurt side like some war hero who wanted to impress a maiden with his courage. "Lady Bronwyn, how beautiful you look, like a rose in spring."

Perversely, Northrup's admiration made Adam angry. Perhaps, too, his own unrestrained emotion irked him. Whatever the reason, he decided he would regain control of himself. He wouldn't let her know how he felt. "Northrup, don't you have something to do somewhere else?"

He spoke to the empty place where his secretary had been. Northrup had already slipped away, had shut the door behind him.

At the cabinet that held the drinks, Adam poured a shallow draft of brandy. Glass in hand, he saluted her with it. "Daphne did a marvelous job—for a woman."

Bronwyn's maidenly blush faded. Her eyes sparkled, her bosom heaved. Fists clenched at her sides, she stepped into the room. "No man could have done any better. No man ever searched for the slivers of wood that caused you so much discomfort."

He lifted the glass and swallowed. The brandy stung his throat, enlivened him in a way no spirits had ever done before. Surely it was the spirits. Surely it wasn't the proximity of one indignant woman.

"Do you know what your problem is?" she asked.

"No," he drawled, "but I'm sure you're going to tell me."

She stalked to the liquor cabinet, pulled a clean goblet from the tray, placed it with a crash that almost broke the delicate stem. "You're ungracious and ungrateful."

The scent of oranges tickled his nose, titillated his taste buds, made him hungry—for her. She stood too close. How was he supposed to remain distant when she came so close? "It's a family failing," he said.

She poured herself a brandy.

"Rather strong for a lady, isn't it?"

After checking the level in his goblet, she lifted and poured again.

"How childish."

The golden liquid swirled as she lifted it. "You think that excuses everything, don't you?"

Startled, he demanded, "What?"

"Your father was hung as a counterfeiter, so you think it doesn't matter what you do—society will never approve of you anyway. You think you can buy a bride, and when she proves to be too ugly for your taste, you can trade her in for one of her sisters."

He meant to sound patient, dignified. Instead his reply came out in a yell. "Now wait a moment. I didn't just trade you. You ran away."

Jutting out her chin, widening her eyes, she said, "Humph."

She made him so angry. Grabbing her bare shoulder to shake her, he found his palm filled with the heat of her. He'd grabbed a hot poker, and he let her go, knowing he'd been burned.

She knew it, too, and juggled the goblet carelessly in her fingers. "Why shouldn't I run away from a man who's so intent on correcting the past that he's incapable of recognizing the quality of the present, the potential of the future?"

"A pretty way of telling me you've at last realized the repercussions of my father's crime will echo forever."

She finished her brandy in one irritable gulp. "Why should I care what your father was?"

He grabbed her hand and held it still to refill her glass, then filled his own. "You were supposed to marry me. Do you want to take the chance our children will be tainted with such dishonesty?"

"I have an Irish great-grandfather who was hung as a murderer. My mother's family can be traced back to William the Conqueror, and a right bunch of knightly thieves they were. Do you want to take the chance our children will be tainted with such dishonesty?"

Was she making a joke? Why did she refuse to see how his paternity had stigmatized him? "That's different," he shouted.

"How?" she shouted back.

Clenching his jaw so hard he could scarcely speak, he said, "We have talked about this before. I have been marked by my father's crimes."

She choked on the rich brandy and in meaningful tones said, "I find that hard to swallow."

"You can joke about this?" he asked incredulously.

Waving her hands, glass still clenched tight, she ignored the liquor that slopped onto the rug. "Joke about what?"

"I was almost killed for counterfeiting South Sea stock."

"Judson very skillfully set you up to take the blame."

Like a mouse on a treadmill, he explained the same thing over and over, changing the words, hoping this time she would understand. "Judson chose to set me up because my father counterfeited good English money. If anyone, *anyone* else needs a dupe, where will he look? Why, to me."

"That's true," she agreed, "and there's nothing you can do about it. But why spend your whole life trying to convince the world you're honest?"

A bitter note tinged his voice. "A situation such as Judson set up must always cast doubt on my character."

Patiently she asked, "Did you counterfeit South Sea stock?"

"No."

"Would you ever do anything so deceitful?"

"No."

Lifting her glass in a toast, she said, "Very well, I support you. Your word is good enough for me."

In a rage, he threw his glass at the fireplace. It shattered into a thousand shards, brandy spraying the marble. The strong scent of it struck him, pleased him with its statement. "You're a stupid woman. You shouldn't trust someone just because he tells you something."

She threw her glass after his. Its splatter was equally satisfying. "I don't trust everybody, but I do trust you. Don't you know why you're not a popular man? It's because of your total honesty, your rigid refusal to take bribes or play social games. Oh, when you make the effort, you can be polite, make small talk, pretend to be like the other dilettantes. But you can't sustain the effort. It becomes too much for you. You revert to being Adam Keane, former seaman, merchant, broker. You're as steady as a rock, and when you say you haven't been counterfeiting, I believe you. If you had never spoken of it, I would still believe *in* you. You have never told me a lie."

The violence of her action shocked him. The vigor of her words convinced him. His gaze bored into her with all the intensity of the temperament she described. "You don't believe I'm a counterfeiter?"

"How silly do you think I am?"

"If I told you everyone else in London believes it, what would you say?"

"That they're fools." She sighed. "Like someone else I could name. But not everyone in London believes you're a counterfeiter. If they don't know you, they may believe it. If they are acquaintances of yours, they may pretend to believe it, to further their own ends. But your friends don't believe it. Robert Walpole doesn't believe it. Neither does Northrup, nor Rachelle."

"You don't know that," he said automatically.

"Of course I do. Ask any of them."

He staggered under the impact of these new ideas. He'd lived his whole life proving his worth, proving his reliability, and knowing all the time it counted for nothing because of his father's corruption. Now this bit of a woman before him insisted . . . "Northrup believes in me, of course."

"Of course."

"And if you say Madame Rachelle does . . . well, I'm flattered."

"Good."

"Robert is here." He rubbed his chin with his fingers. "I could ask him."

"You do that."

"You believe me?"

"I believe *in* you," she answered steadily.

"You never doubted me?" he probed.

"No."

He pressed his fingers to his face. Inside, he experienced a subtle shift. If Robert believed in him, and Rachelle, and Northrup, why hadn't he been able to accept it? Not even his mother's support had convinced him of his worth in others' eyes. What was the difference? Cautiously he lowered his hands and looked at Bronwyn. Bronwyn, impatient, quick-tempered, impetuous with her affections, yet intelligent enough to attract the admiration of some of London's best minds. It was Bronwyn's assurances he'd needed, Bronwyn's logic that convinced him. "Then what my father did doesn't matter."

Briskly she agreed, "That's correct."

He reached out his hands, took hers, squeezed them. "No, I mean—I can give him up. All the hurts, all the abandonments, all the careless affections he lavished on us even as he destroyed us."

Something in his countenance must have alerted her to the changes sweeping over him. Never releasing his hand, she led him to the chairs beside the desk and pressed him down there. Seating herself, she asked, "Did you love him?"

Instinctively he said, "No!"

"Oh. I thought perhaps you did. I know I love my father, despite his failings." Amusement curved her lips. "Because of his failings."

Relaxing back on the chair, he thought about his father for the first time in years. "Did I love him? I don't know. Maybe. Yes, I suppose. Sometimes I wonder if he knew it was too late for him. He bought my naval commission with counterfeit money and put me on my ship before I could even say good-bye to my mother. Years later I found out he was arrested within the week, hung within the month."

"Did they let you keep your commission?"

"By the time word reached my captain, we'd been around the world twice and I was his right-hand man." He smiled harshly. "British ships avoid home port when possible. The conscripts leap from the rails."

She pressed him for revelations. "Did your father know it would be years before his crimes caught up with you?"

"No doubt."

With delicate good sense she pointed out, "Then perhaps he loved you."

Why not admit it? The healing Bronwyn had imparted to him provided sanctuary even for his father. "As much as was possible for that shallow man to love, I suppose he did." Cupping her face, he confessed, "I've searched the world over for someone like you."

Bright and jagged as a bolt of lightning, she said, "Don't worry. You're not stuck with me. I may howl a bit, but you can marry Olivia. I'll even be her bridesmaid. Why not? I've been bridesmaid to every one of my sisters."

Olivia. "My God, I'd forgotten about Olivia."

"Everyone has," she said, jerking her hand from his and ducking away from his caress. "That's why I came in to see you. She's miserable. Can't you take the time to reassure her about this marriage?"

"Olivia," he repeated.

"Yes, Olivia. You know, the beautiful sister? The one you're going to marry?"

She sounded so flippant. She thought he didn't want her—because she wasn't as glamorous as her sisters. How dare she mock him, when she was so pigheaded? With all the cunning of a hunter, he said, "You say I've never lied to you."

"Never."

"You're beautiful."

She made a soft sound of disgust. "I also said you could play the social game if you chose."

He ignored her. "You're the only woman I want. All of London knows it."

Head turned away, she riffled through a pile of papers. She didn't speak out loud, only mumbled, "Then why have you abandoned me?"

Savoring his incipient victory, he said, "You've been behaving oddly."

"Oddly?" Her voice rose. "You're a fine one to talk. You're going to marry my *sister*."

"I didn't think I could have you. Olivia hasn't your intelligence, and I believed she would never trouble herself about my honesty." With his index finger, he pressed on her cheek until she faced him. "I told you, I thought you were measuring me against my father."

"That's ridiculous."

He leaned back, crossed his ankles, and smiled. "Almost as ridiculous as measuring yourself against your sisters."

She lifted his paperweight, hefted it as if she would throw it, too. "That's different."

"How?"

"Your father is dead. Cruel people keep the myth alive, and only because they know it hurts you," she insisted. "My sisters are alive, alluring—"

"Vain, simple-minded, and dull," he finished for her. "However, they are accomplished social butterflies, and what does that win them? They'll never grow. They have no ambition to be more than they are"—he pulled her into his arms—"and they'll always be less than you are."

He sounded so genuine, so honest. He knocked the support of her indignation from beneath her, and without her anger the misery crept in. Feeling bruised, she whispered, "Why are you being so nice to me?"

Knocking his knuckles lightly against her forehead as if he could pound the truth into her, he said with slow, plain emphasis, "Because I love you."

Adam's declaration echoed in the night air, but Bronwyn said nothing. Impatient with her reticence, he prodded, "I said I love you. Have you nothing to say in return?"

She started to speak, did not. Said his name, but no more. His darling, the lady who lived to translate documents, to use language with precision, appeared to be inarticulate. He smiled, more charmed by her speechlessness than by any other's eloquent declaration, and he leaned close to encourage her words with his kisses.

The sharp rap of knuckles on the door had them springing up and apart.

"Come in," Adam called gruffly.

The door swung wide, and a maid bustled in carrying two candelabras alight with flame. "Got candles fer ye, master."

"So I see."

The perky maid stood, awaiting instruction.

"Oh, put one on my desk and another over there somewhere." He waved vaguely.

"Aye, master. Gettin' dark earlier an' earlier, ain't it?"

"That it is." With the newfound illumination, he could see the flush bathing Bronwyn. It scarcely seemed possible, but that warm color made her more attractive than ever. Never taking his gaze from Bronwyn, he fished in his desk drawer until he found a coin. He tossed it to the maid. "Close the door behind you."

The girl observed them, standing so stiff, and she stifled a giggle. "Aye, sir." She curtsied as she pocketed the coin. "Thank ye, sir."

As the door clicked shut, Adam and Bronwyn rushed together. As she clutched him around the neck and lifted her face to his kiss, he knew he'd come home.

Their lips melded like iron in a forge. Nothing could ever separate them.

"Bronwyn?"

From outside the study door he heard a woman's voice, but nothing could break through the sensual fire that enveloped him.

"Bronwyn?"

In his arms, Bronwyn began to struggle.

"No," he moaned.

"It's my mother." At the knock, she jerked him back by his hair. "Let go. It's my *mother*."

Her frantic demand penetrated. Reluctantly he loosened his grip and slithered onto a chair. Bronwyn started for the door, and he woke to his situation. He was alone with Bronwyn, he was aroused, and he most definitely didn't want her mother to see. Scooting the chair beneath the desk, he folded his hands before him and tried to look businesslike and calm.

Bronwyn flung wide the door. "Maman! What a surprise to see you."

Lady Nora frowned.

"I mean, to see you here." Bronwyn smiled brightly. "In Adam's study."

"Yes, I can see it would be." Lady Nora watched as Bronwyn licked her lips. "I thought we should have the final fitting on your dress for tomorrow. We have to make sure you're displayed to your best advantage. There are many eligible men here for the wedding."

Adam's knuckles cracked as he tightened his grip.

"The dressmaker did the final fitting today," Bronwyn said.

"I want to assure myself of her reliability. You know she measured the waist wrong the first time she—"

"Ooh, Maman, you're absolutely correct," Bronwyn

interrupted. "I'll be up to my room as soon as Adam and I finish our discussion of the stock situation and its effect on the English treasury."

Snatching at the bait, Adam invited, "Would you like to stay and debate it with us?"

"No." Lady Nora took an involuntary step backward. "Bronwyn, I'll expect to see you in your bedroom on the hour."

"Yes, Maman."

Bronwyn waited until Lady Nora was well away, then shut the door once more.

"Come here." Adam pushed away from the desk and pointed to his lap.

With a light step, she moved to him and pressed her hand to his breeches. "What's this?" she teased. "A dreaded swelling? Perhaps I can heal it for you."

The warmth of her seeped through the material and heated him once more. "I suspect you can, and I'd love to suggest—"

One huge thump on the door made them jump. Another followed, then another.

"Damn it!" Adam said.

Walpole yelled, "Adam, I know you're in there. Come on, man, I've prepared a pleasant send-off."

"A send-off?" Bronwyn murmured, puzzled.

"He wants to—"

"Come on, Adam! Before you join the ranks of leg-shackled men, you must have a proper send-off. All your friends are gathered in the blue room with refreshments." Walpole's voice lowered to a confidential roar. "And there are women with the most novel entertainments in mind."

Adam's gaze met Bronwyn's, and without words

they understood each other. Silently he rose and tossed his cloak over his shoulders. He offered his hand, she took it, and they tiptoed toward the windows.

"Adam, if you don't come out peaceably, I'll bring every man here to get you."

Adam untied Bronwyn's panniers, then helped her through the window and lowered her to the ground. He followed as quickly as his leg would allow. He pointed at the stable; Bronwyn nodded. Together they hurried across the grounds and slipped inside the dusky barn.

From the window of Adam's study, Walpole watched them, looked at the discarded panniers and whispered, "I'll be damned."

Rachelle smiled as she descended the stairs to the kitchen, jingling the keys.

Such an annoying sound, and so sweet to her ears.

She had never experienced such satisfaction in her life. Judson remained in her hands, and he was miserable. She'd learned a lot about him since she'd imprisoned him in her pantry. She knew his fears, his hates, his history. He'd told her everything, hoping to sway her to mercy. He had not. He had only planned his own future.

Physical labor made him ill? Wherever she sent him, he would work. He feared to expose himself without makeup, without his wig? He'd show all London his deformities before he left. He despised Adam Keane and the man that he was? Judson would soon discover the realities of Adam's life.

Through the louvers that fed air into the pantry, she heard the chain move. Good. He was restless, waiting for her evening visit. The key clanged in the lock.

Slowly, so slowly, she opened the door, giving him light and a release from the closeness. "Monsieur Judson, I have come to take your dinner dishes away."

There was no answer from the dark.

"Did you not enjoy the dinner?"

Still no answer, and she stepped through the door. "I have plans for you. Tomorrow morning, a gentleman is coming for you. Do you know who he is?" For the first time, the silence unnerved her. Judson sat so still, so quiet, she leaned closer to see if he still tarried in her prison.

He did. His eyes shone in the dark, fixed on her with malevolent interest. A shiver ran up her spine as she thought about the brutality of her daughter's murder, and she grasped the chain that bound his foot. She held it aloft, and his foot rose. He was fettered, as he should be, and her pleasure returned. "You must not sulk," she said. "Your long confinement is almost over. The gentleman is a sea captain. He'll bring a few men, and they will take you with them. They will teach you honest employment. Isn't that a delightful thought?"

The chain rattled in the dark, and she dropped it with a thunk.

Guttural with horror, Judson asked, "A press-gang?"

"Ah, you understand." She smiled, caressing the keys. "The image of the elegant Carroll Judson aboard one of Brittania's finest ships, serving as the lowest seaman, fills me with the sense of achievement I have not felt since the death of my daughter."

"You bitch." His voice shook with intensity. "After all I've told you—"

"Superb conversation," she agreed.

He sprang at her, but she was prepared. She stepped

back, and the chain caught him. He sprawled at her feet, close, but not close enough. "You must not fret so. It will be only for the rest of your life." Behind her she heard a shuffle, but as she turned to see, a club descended on her head.

"There! Take that, Madame Know-so-much." Gianni gloated over her still body.

"Get the keys, get the keys," Judson chanted. "Free me."

Gianni groped at Madame's waist and jerked the keys loose with a flourish. "Now, my master, I will save you." Kneeling at Judson's feet, he unlocked the manacle and tumbled aside when Judson kicked at him.

Rising, Judson shook out his legs. "At last. It took you long enough, stupid."

"I had to wait until most of the other ladies were gone," Gianni answered, staggering to his feet. "They wish to dispose of me, too."

"Yes," Judson drawled. "So they do. Do you have the money I saved from this debacle?"

Gianni patted his stomach, and coins jingled. "Hidden on me. It will be enough to keep us for a few months, yes?"

"Yes." Judson aimed his boot at Rachelle. As it connected with her ribs she groaned, and he sniggered. "You didn't kill her."

"You know I have no stomach for that." Gianni lifted a bag and dangled it before his master's eyes. "But look what I brought you." Affectionate and eager, he dug into the sack and brought up the contents one by one. "Cosmetics. Powder. And most important, a wig." He gloated as Judson exclaimed in ecstasy. "Let me work my magic."

Subsiding onto the cot, Judson said, "Gianni, you are a marvel."

"I will be quick," Gianni promised. "Just enough to make the ladies turn and admire when they see you on the street."

"Yes," Judson hissed. "Make the ladies sorry they never begged me to pleasure them on the seat of my carriage."

"That will be no problem, my master." Gianni dabbed the cosmetics over Judson's face, filling the pockmarks, etching quick eyebrows. After settling the wig on the shiny pate, he stepped back and squinted through the dusk. "All women must envy you your beauty."

Judson's hand flashed out and slapped Gianni across the face. "You fool."

"Master?" Gianni watched anxiously as Judson leaped up and paced across the pantry in quick, jerky strides.

He stumbled on Rachelle's arm and cursed. Then he smiled, the kind of smile that boded ill for his jailer. "I had forgotten she lay there." He lifted his foot and he brought his heel down, hard, in the lower left of her back. Even though she was unconscious, her breath left her in a gasp of pain.

Gianni averted his eyes. "We will go to the Continent now? We will go back to Italy?"

"Perhaps." Studying Rachelle, Judson nodded as he made a decision. "Give me a knife."

"Oh, master." From his belt, Gianni pulled the long blade that had so terrified Bronwyn. "We have no time."

Judson took the knife. "Time for just a taste of fun."

"You said it was no fun if they weren't awake." Gianni tugged at Judson's arm. "I don't know when those other women will be back. We must go."

"You go to Dover. Take the money. Get us room on a ship leaving for France. Wait for me there." Judson swooped down, and in the dim light blood sprang from Rachelle's cheek like water from a spring.

Gianni gasped in exaggerated upset. "I will not go without you."

Judson studied Rachelle's face and neck. "Yes, you will. Don't stay on England's shore, no matter what. The money must be safe. I have one thing to do before I leave."

"So kill her, but do it quickly." Gianni wrung his hands.

"Kill her? How did you know"—Judson glanced down at Rachelle. "Oh, *her.* Yes, of course I'll kill her, but she is not the one of whom I speak. There is another, and the taste of her blood will be sweet as nectar."

Grabbing his master's arm, Gianni argued, "We must go. I didn't wish to tell you, but Robert Walpole has put the blame for the counterfeit stocks on you. The mob of London is baying for your carcass, and if it were known you were here—"

"Yes, yes, Rachelle told me. She used it as an excuse to keep me. Protecting me from certain death, she said." With a delicate touch, Judson traced the length of Rachelle's forehead with the tip of his blade. "That will gush. Whoever finds her will be repulsed."

Gianni put his hand on his stomach and staggered as the red fluid wet his shoes. "Please, my master," he whispered. "Let us go."

With a glance at Gianni's white face, Judson shrugged. "Oh, very well." Like a great bat, he hovered over Rachelle.

"Master," Gianni whispered.

"Shut up," Judson commanded. The knife lifted

once, plunged. Metal scraped against bone. He lifted it again, but Gianni caught his wrist.

"Master, I hear something."

Judson stopped, listened.

"Come, master, the women have arrived." Gianni tugged at Judson. "We must go. Now."

With one longing, lingering glance at Rachelle, Judson followed his valet out the door of his prison toward another, more satisfying revenge.

Chapter 22

The barn smelled of horses and hay, wax and leather. A lantern lit the far end where an elderly stable hand groomed a stallion.

Facing Bronwyn, Adam put his finger to his lips and urged her to the ladder leading to the loft. At the bottom, she kicked off her shoes. Pleased that her panniers had been dispensed with, she gathered her skirts in her arms and put her foot on the first step. Adam steadied her with his hand on her elbow, helping her up the first steps, then he followed. Glowing with desire, with relief and a newfound confidence, she lifted her skirts higher. With each step they rose until Adam groaned quietly, "Have pity, Bronwyn."

She tossed a saucy glance over her shoulder but sobered immediately. His expressive eyes told the tale of passion repressed and clamoring for release. She missed the step; he caught her thigh and steadied her.

His touch was a balm, a healing agent for her lonely soul, and she wanted more. With care she climbed to the top, reached into the loft to pull herself up, and found his hand placed helpfully on her bare bottom. She squeaked as he boosted her up, and the stable hand called, "Is anyone there?"

She tumbled into the straw and huddled in place. Adam remained on the ladder, silent and still.

The stable hand said nothing else. A pitchfork began its rhythmic sound, and Adam slipped up to sit beside her in the dark. Bronwyn sighed in relief. His hand groped for hers and squeezed it. She came close, laid her head on his shoulder, wondering whether this idea had been so marvelous. True, they had escaped the constant buzz of wedding guests, but what satisfaction could they find with an aging retainer ensconced below?

Her answer came quickly. The stable hand spoke, to the horses, she supposed. "Well, ol' boy, 'tis time fer me t' seek me bed. I'll be seein' ye in th' mornin'." The door creaked open. "G'night, now."

Bronwyn waited until the door closed behind him, then in a fit of quiet laughter crawled on top of Adam. "He's an eccentric," she said.

In praise only a man could appreciate, Adam said, "Kenneth has more horse sense than twenty men put together."

"Horse sense?" Bronwyn giggled again. "Is that why you let him take care of your horse?"

"Not my horse." Adam sounded puckishly resigned. "My horse was stolen in London by a small but accomplished thief."

"Stolen?" she asked, incredulous.

He didn't explain, and she didn't ask. Through their silence, the laughter and music from the house party drifted on the breeze. Autumn's first bite chilled the air, but Adam's heat warmed her. She edged up to his chin and she covered it with kisses. "Speak to your valet. You need a shave."

"I'll shave tomorrow, before—"

He cut it off. *Before the wedding.* That was what he meant.

The last time. This was the last time. The thought drifted through her mind, but she put it away from her. The world might end tonight. Tomorrow might never come. Ignore everything, and distract Adam before he remembered it was the last time.

"Mm." She sighed, rubbing her cheek against his. "You're just lazy. You never wear a wig. You never go anywhere without your walking stick. You never smile." She arranged his lips with her fingers in a phony grin. "There. You need to practice."

"I agree I need to practice." His grin became genuine beneath her hand. "Take off your clothes and I'll practice."

"Take off my clothes? Why?" she asked in mock innocence. "It's dark in here."

"I have good night vision."

She jumped when he proved it with one accurately placed hand on her breast. "I have good night vision, too," she bragged, although she couldn't see in the thick black of night. She reached for him, fondled him, frowned.

"That's my knife," he told her. "Sharp as a razor and made of tempered steel. I doubt if it will harden even in your fire." Unwillingly she laughed, and he wrestled with her. "Take care," he warned as she struggled free. "This is a hayloft. No doubt there are mice in here."

Mice. Mice didn't scare her, but if he wanted to play, she knew the rules. "Mice?"

Like any naughty boy, he warmed to his subject at the sound of the shiver in her voice. "And rats."

"Ooh. And cats?"

"Maybe." He thought. "Yes, if there are mice and rats, there must be cats."

"And kitties?"

Clearly he didn't like diluting the menace. Reluctantly he agreed, "And kittens."

"Maybe some puppies?"

He bounded upright. "And snakes."

"That's it." She leaped toward him, knocked him over, wrestled with him, tried to contain his wandering hands. "You're in trouble now."

"Well, there might be snakes." His elusive fingers crept up under her petticoats and tickled behind her knee. "Creepy, crawly snakes that slither along your leg."

"And what will you do if we find snakes?"

He didn't even take the time to think. "What any normal man would do. I'll run."

She shook his neck between her hands, but she seemed unable to vibrate the solidly muscled man who lay beneath her. "Coward."

"Sagacious," he corrected.

Unconvinced, she chuckled.

As if he'd just discovered it, he pronounced, "We're acting like children."

"We are children." She rolled him over. "We are, we are, we are." With each repetition she rolled him again, and he let her, until they bumped against a stack of straw. "We are children," she repeated, but her voice caught.

Children believe ignoring a dilemma will make it disappear. Children dismiss tomorrow. Children frolic when disaster stares them in the face. Oh, yes, they were children.

Adam caught her around the waist and tossed her. She sank, and he followed her, pressing her down. Above her, his rib cage pressed against hers with each of his breaths. Below her, the straw crackled, releasing the stored smell of long summer days. It jabbed at her wherever the material of her dress proved inadequate, but that was part and parcel of the contentment she experienced here, in the dark, with Adam.

He muttered, "This is the best moment of my life."

His tribute sounded so grudging, almost shy, that she couldn't resist prodding him. "What did you say?"

"I said—"

Laughter shook her. Above her, he felt it and lifted himself on his elbows. "You little witch. You're teasing me."

"No, I'm not. I just didn't—"

He stroked the area above her ribs.

"Really, I didn't hear you." She squealed as he found the ticklish places, the places he'd found in the nights at Rachelle's. Struggling with careful uselessness, she gasped, "I have great respect for you. I would never tease you."

"You're the only one who dares." His breath warmed her neck, his lips suckled her earlobe.

"I'm not afraid of you," she said.

"You should be. I'll hold you down, ravish you until you cry for mercy."

She froze as she remembered Judson, promising a similar fate in such different tones.

"Love?" Adam's voice, warm, deep, called her away from the memories. "Bronwyn? What's wrong?"

"Nothing." She snuggled close. "Just a ghost."

"Damn Judson." With one phrase he revealed how empathetic he had become.

"Don't damn him." She drew a deep breath. "He's in hell already."

"I sincerely hope so. I only wish I had been the one to put him there."

"Rachelle believed she had the prior claim," she said softly.

"He tried to murder you."

"He would have, too, but pride was his downfall. He wanted to wait until he'd killed not only Walpole, but you, so he could describe it to me." Adam tugged her head against his chest. Listening to his heartbeat, so reassuring in its steady tempo, she said, "So my claim is greater than yours or Rachelle's."

"We'll let Rachelle take care of it."

His voice echoed in her ear, and she agreed. "Yes. Rachelle will take care of it."

How well they understood each other. And with the years that understanding would grow, until like the old folks she'd seen, they would speak without words.

But that couldn't happen, because this was the last time.

Above her head she saw a square of night through a window. Stars, bits of light, poked through a billowed canopy, commiserated with her until Adam's shoulders blocked them out.

With tender hands he loosened her clothes. Perhaps, he thought, she still feared him, although she clutched him with a strength akin to desperation. Perhaps he felt responsibility for her fear. Or perhaps he wanted to communicate something. But he wanted his loving to cherish her, invite her, warm her. More than an invitation, it was a stroll down a lane of memories not yet created. Memories they had the potential to create, if not the time.

He wanted to be careful with her, yet how difficult a task he had set himself. As he discarded her clothing to reveal her body, her passion unfolded like a well-rooted flower given all it needed to blossom. His own clothes followed hers randomly. They fell away under the urgings of his hands or hers, depending on whose need proved greatest. His shirt, his breeches, his stockings and shoes, knife and handkerchief, found their way to the pile beneath them. The lovers rested on the great jumble of brocades and linens with no regard to the morrow, using them as a protection against the distracting jabs of straw.

She found the bandage on his leg, explored it. "Are you still in pain?"

Her tender murmur soothed the ache of his wound. "Not really."

He found her breasts, explored them. "Does that frighten you?"

"No. But they're very sensitive."

Her breathlessness worried him. He was only a man; how could he know the scarring produced when a woman survived both physical violence and a mental attack? He touched her lightly, stroked her, skimming the hairs on her belly and lower. "Tell me what you like," he coaxed.

"I like that."

Her trembling worried him. Her sighs worried him. In the faint glow of starlight, her eyes glistened with a sheen as she watched him; that worried him. He wrapped himself around her, cradled her with his whole body, touched her with every inch of his skin. He gave comfort when what he wanted, what he longed for, was her passion.

She rubbed against him like an affectionate cat and purred his name.

He kissed her, gracing every bit of her face, neck, collarbones with the ministrations of his mouth.

Her fingernails bit into his shoulder, then scratched a light line down his back. Nerve endings screamed, and he gasped, "Perhaps you *could* harden steel."

Chuckling, she extended her ministrations in a long, continuous torture that reached from bow to stern, from port to starboard. Shuddering beneath the erotic sting, he chided himself. She couldn't know how she incited his senses to chaos.

"I'll always think of you—" She interrupted herself, then tried again. "I think of you when I hear French spoken. Speak French to me."

Her throaty demand saddened him, maddened him, sent him over the edge. Almost over the edge. So close . . . He fit them together. "*Tu es magnifique.*"

"So are you."

He entered her. "This loving is like a first kiss." He didn't know if he could find the words in English, much less French. "*Un baiser.* A kiss."

"This?" With her tongue she traced the outline of his lips.

"*Mon Dieu.*" Without volition he inched deeper. He sucked in air and whispered, "Like the mating of tongues, *les langues*, this loving is tentative."

"Too tentative." With little movements of her hips, she urged him.

Restraining himself forcibly, he dug his elbows into

the hay beside her. "It tastes sweet, like candy. Ah . . . *bonbons*."

Her hands smoothed his hips, and he lost coherence. Her tongue licked his ear, and he lost control. He sank into her, abandoning himself to the pleasure of her body, abandoning his mind to the madness of her whimpers and sighs. Her hips met his in rapture. Her legs clutched at him. Her calls, incoherent, extolling, told him of her pleasure.

His chest heaved with exertion. The friction of their bodies melted his ice, as surely as the warm ocean current melted an iceberg. It stroked his fire to new heights, brought him sweaty and triumphant to a climax that broke over him like a hurricane over a ship.

She wasn't done, and he fed her paroxysms with his mouth, with his hands, with his body. Still he continued, accepting her cries as homage, feeling her arms clutch at him and slip on the perspiration that bathed him. Feeling the muscles within her clutch at him and slip on the reality of her delight.

At last he slowed, unwilling to liberate her from heaven but motivated by exhaustion—both hers and his. Balanced on top of her, he listened as she drew one quivering sigh after another, trembled, murmured, "Oh, Adam."

Now this was a satisfied woman. He recognized the traits. She could scarcely speak, breathe, move. He congratulated himself with rampant arrogance. He had vanquished the specter of fear that haunted her.

Rubbing his cheek against hers, he stiffened. Tears trickled into her hair. "Did I frighten you?" he demanded. She didn't answer immediately, and he lifted his head in alarm.

"No," she sighed at last. "I just remembered—"

The last time. The phrase passed from her head to his. This was the last time.

"I just remembered how wonderful a lover you are," she finished in a rush, and he knew she lied. That wasn't the thought making her grasp him with renewed agitation.

Delicately he inquired, "Did I exorcise the memory of Judson from your mind?"

"Who? Judson?" She rubbed his back in ever-widening circles. "You don't need to worry about Judson. The thought of you and Judson could never exist as one in my mind."

Hand on pounding heart, he assimilated that. His concern had been for nothing. His control had been for nothing. He needed reassurance now, not Bronwyn, for this was the last time. Settling against her once more, he whispered close against her ear, "Prove it to me."

"When I was a young girl, I used to dream of the woman I would be. I would be poised and lovely. My tan would fade and my hair would change color and I would say the right thing at the right time to the right people. Men would worship at my feet. Then one day— I must have been about thirteen—I realized there were no fairy-tale changes in store for me. There would be only me, endlessly stuck in a body too short, with hair too white and tan too dark. The only improvements that could be made had to be made by me in the slow, painful process called maturing, and I didn't see that those improvements could amount to much. So I gave up that childish dream of poise and beauty and became what I knew I could become—a thoroughly improved sort of brain stored in a body best ignored."

Bronwyn and Adam lay in the comforting aftermath of passion, flat on their backs with only their fingertips touching. The moon, almost full, lit the loft and left only a residue of darkness. Bronwyn was surprised to hear herself define half-formed thoughts so eloquently, but she made no effort to stop.

"One day I woke up and there I was, poised, mature, dynamic, beautiful—all because I saw myself through your eyes. Your vision may be faulty, but I am through trying to correct it. If you see a beautiful, gracious lady when you see me, I'll see the same mirage you do when I look in the mirror."

Adam's hand crept over Bronwyn's and squeezed it. He brought it to his lips, and with a laugh in his voice he asked, "What makes you think it is my vision that is at fault, my dear?"

The jingle of a horse's riding tack outside the window woke Bronwyn. "An early wedding guest?" she suggested.

Adam grunted. The sun had barely risen, but already night's magic had fled. Tomorrow had come, and he would marry another woman. He would marry Bronwyn's sister. The last time had come to an end. They were children no more. "I can't break it off," he said abruptly. "Not without gross disgrace to Olivia."

On the defensive almost before he spoke, she snapped, "I didn't ask you to."

"No." Carefully he removed her from his shoulder and flung back the cloak that covered them. "You didn't, did you?"

Harsh reality struck her, as did the chill of the air. "Well, to ask you to disgrace my sister for my own selfish reasons would be . . . selfish."

Rising from the nest in the straw as if he were impervious to the cold, he stretched and dusted the bits of hay from his chest. As the sun lifted above the trees, the straw, piled high behind him, glinted golden. She trembled to see him framed so splendidly, exhibited to his advantage by color and texture. The long line of his spine flexed as he brushed his legs; everywhere he flaunted well-developed muscle and sinew.

Only the white bandage marred his perfection. Yet how should she ask about it? What tactful method could she use to inquire about his pain? Obviously the last time's passion had waned and was best forgotten. "Did we hurt your leg last night?" she blurted.

His sardonic glance answered her even as he said, "I didn't notice."

He jerked the clothes out from beneath her, leaving her lying on the crushed straw. It scratched her, and he irritated her.

He shook his clothes, then hers, and laid them out. "What does Olivia say about me?"

A deliberate reminder, she supposed. Well, if he could be stolid, so could she. Sitting up, she fingercombed the straw from her hair. "She's being brave and silent."

Shoving his arms into his shirt, he said, "That sounds ominous."

She reached for her chemise, pulled it over her head, and heard something, just a whisper of sound from outside. "What's that?"

Cocking his head, he listened, too. "I don't know."

"Do you hear it? Little crackling noises?"

"I suppose a stable boy is performing some chore downstairs." He pulled on his breeches and shoved his bare feet into his shoes. "So speak quietly."

"It's so early."

"We have many guests, with many horses." Shrugging into his waistcoat, he urged, "I suggest you hurry before any of those guests rouse themselves and see us returning to the house."

She leaped up, snatching her petticoats and pulling them on in a flurry of lace. "I know the need for silence, for secrecy, better than you, I expect. *You're* going to be married. *I'm* going to be ruined."

Cold as the winter wind, he said, "That's your choice."

Her mouth dropped. What a thing to say. What a thing to think! As if she could stop this wedding. What did he want her to do? Knock Olivia over the head, steal her wedding dress, and take her place in the church? As she loosely laced her gown and fumed, she wanted nothing more than revenge on this superior, stupid male. "Olivia spends a lot of time praying."

"Praying?" he asked, outraged. "Am I so dreadful?"

She bit back a smile. "She's very religious."

"A clever evasion. You ran away. Olivia is praying. The most dreaded bridegroom waits to consume his—" He stopped, sniffed. "The smoke from the fireplaces must be blowing this way."

She smelled it, too. A hint of smoke in the cool air. "Or the farmers are burning their trash."

"No doubt you're right." He searched the hay. "Have you seen the ribbon to tie back my hair? My handkerchief?"

"Can't go anywhere without your hair ribbon, hmm?"

He glared. "My knife is with it, and no, I can't go anywhere without it."

"I'll help you find it." She thrashed through the

straw, muttering, "Men can't find anything. Helpless as babes. Perfectly willing to let me search—" Annoyed, she glared at the still and silent Adam. "You could at least pretend to look."

"Sh."

She straightened, hands on hips. "What?"

"Listen."

She listened. The crackling sounded louder, closer. Smoke bit at her nose, and she glanced around at the hayloft, stuffed full for the winter. "Fire," she whispered. Then louder, "Fire!"

As if in answer to her alarm, one horse belowstairs whinnied. Then they all whinnied. Hooves crashed against the stalls.

"Stay here," Adam instructed, and when she would have objected, he insisted, "Stay here. I have to get the doors open. Some of the horses are only tethered. You may be trampled." He pointed at the window. "See if you can get that door open and get out that way."

He disappeared down the ladder before she could stammer, "What?"

Get that door open? It was a window. But Adam had never shown previous signs of stupidity, so she went to examine the window. It was, indeed, part of a door. A bolted double door undoubtedly used to load the loft with hay. It looked like part of the wall, except for the slab of wood hanging across the iron hooks to hold it closed. Sucking in her breath, she lifted the beam up and away and dropped it. Pushing the doors, she leaped back from the fresh breeze that whirled the straw into a frenzy. The scent of it mixed with the smoke to set off a strident alarm in her. Fire. Oh, God, fire in the stables. The straw, the parched wood, the living horses: what could be worse?

Leaning out, she searched for a way of escape but saw only torched piles of hay placed against the wall. As the fire consumed its fuel with audible relish, the horses screamed. Someone rattled up the ladder. She turned, expecting to see a servant, but saw only Adam.

"The stable is locked," he said tersely. "The fire started outside." He came to the doors and looked out.

She grabbed his arm and shook it. "You're saying someone set this fire? But why?"

Grimly Adam pointed across the lawn where his splendid house rested. No light, no motion, enlivened it. "To wake us? To take revenge for the devastation of the South Sea bubble? Or—"

Sparks fluttered up, snapped at the breeze, extinguished themselves. They would not do so for long, Bronwyn knew. Soon one would escape its fellows and, like some carrier of the plague, live to transmit fire to the loft.

"Useless speculation," Adam muttered, then said, "There's no ladder. No way down. I'll jump to the haystack. If I make it—"

"*If* you make it?"

"If I make it, I'll find a ladder." He set his legs and eyed the distance. "If I don't, you'll have to jump yourself."

"If you don't make it, how can I?"

He smiled slightly. "Both your legs are healthy."

"Then why don't I—"

She spoke to the wind. He leaped and landed safely, slipping, clawing at the haystack as it slithered from beneath him. The whole stack shivered, gave way, and he landed on the ground atop a golden pile. Adding her voice to the overwhelming tumult, she shouted in triumph.

Then, like some small ferocious dog, a man hurled himself at Adam, knife held high. Unprepared, Adam rolled toward him; the man overshot his mark and tumbled in the dirt. His wig came off, his head gleamed in the sunshine.

Judson. Bronwyn shook in a paroxysm of hate, a hate as hot as the fire around them. This time she would not watch as Judson tried to kill Adam. This time she'd destroy the dirty little cutthroat herself. She whirled and bounded back inside the loft. The boards below her scorched her feet. Little fires had escaped the main one and licked the straw. Somewhere under the piles a knife lay hidden, and Bronwyn Edana was going to use it.

Chapter 23

It had to be here. It had to be. Bronwyn scrambled through the pile of straw where they had slept. Her fingers shoved at the yellow lengths, her eyes darted from side to side, she even used her feet to find the thin dark case that would furnish Adam's salvation.

It wasn't there.

It had to be.

She stopped, took a breath, coughed. Smoke burned her throat and punished her efforts, but she calmed herself. That knife was here. She would find it before the fire consumed the stable. She would find it before Judson—

With grim determination she lifted an armful of straw, shook it, discarded it. She lifted another armload, shook it, discarded it. Another.

A white handkerchief, embroidered with the initials

"A. K." fluttered to her feet, and she sputtered with hysterical laughter. Success was close.

She lifted another armful, and before she even shook it, the knife smacked the wooden floor. Snatching it, she sang, "Thank you—oh, thank you," unhooked the leather cover that held the blade secure, and hustled to the door. She saw Adam and Judson at once. Close below her in the muck of the stable yard, they were locked together. Long and shiny, the blade of Judson's knife dipped and swayed in his grasp. Both of Adam's hands restrained Judson and his murderous intention.

Bronwyn's gaze never left them. She pulled the knife from its case, and for the first time doubts struck her. Adam had showed her how to throw the knife, yet she knew it required practice to hit a target. She balanced the tip in her fingers. How could she hit Judson, when Adam stood so close? Her hand shook. But what choice had she? For all Adam's bravado, she knew he'd not fully recovered from his shooting. She knew he'd strained himself last night, and God only knew what damage he'd done with his leap to the haystack.

Panicked horses shrieked and plunged within their stalls, and she saw servants running toward the stable, yelling, waving their hands. Not one of them even noticed their master. The fire consumed their thoughts as it consumed the building.

The responsibility rested on her.

Judson's eyes gleamed, mad with the need for vengeance.

"This time I'll finish it. This time I'll finish you."

Adam heard Judson's vow, but he spent none of his air to answer. It required all his concentration to scuffle when his leg felt as if it were attached backward. Occasionally his foot flopped out of control, and occasionally Judson's vicious kicks found their mark. But he dared not let go of Judson's wrist.

Someone had to help him, and that someone had to be Bronwyn. Blind faith kept his grip strong when he should have given up. Somehow Bronwyn would help him.

A flash of light above brought his gaze up. There she stood, framed in the doorway. Fire glowed behind her, feeding eagerly on the straw, yet she seemed unconscious of her peril. She held his blade in her fingers. One brief glance, and he knew all her uncertainty. She feared to throw the knife and feared not to. He cursed himself for her lack of experience and praised himself for teaching her a throwing grip.

And with a surge of desperation he communicated his demand to Bronwyn.

Throw it. Just throw it well, and he would take care of the rest.

She firmed her mouth, steadied her hand, flung the knife with the strength of her arm behind it.

Right at Adam.

She wanted to cover her eyes, could not. He saw it, saw disaster aimed right at him, and swung his body around, nudging Judson into the path of the blade. It sank between Judson's shoulders, and Adam didn't wait to see its success. He dropped Judson and surged toward her, terrified by the conflagration that destroyed the stable she stood in.

"Jump!" he shouted. "Jump!"

She jumped. Adam caught her, and they tumbled to the ground.

Babbling, "Is he dead?" she circled his neck with her arms.

"Who cares?" He jerked her to her feet and dragged

her toward the house at a run. At a safe distance he stopped and shoved her down, rolling her on the ground while she hollered.

When he let her up, she said, "What was that for?"

Not interested in her indignation, he examined her, all of her. Her hair and clothes came under particular scrutiny, and he sighed, "We put it out."

"Put what out?"

He brought a lock of her hair around before her eyes. "You were smoldering."

The sight of the frizzled ends of her hair subdued her. "Oh."

"It's a miracle you weren't aflame." He pointed at the burning building.

It seemed to be sucking up the air, exhaling the smoke. Kenneth directed a bucket line from the well to the building, but it held little chance of success. The servants' only desire seemed to be the rescue of the frantic animals within. Wet cloths covered the horses' eyes as they were led out; buckets of water doused them and their smoking coats. The walls puffed bellows of smoke. The roof thatch exploded in flame. Everywhere people swarmed, shouted, ran.

The uncurbed blaze had attracted the attention of the guests in Adam's house. Women in their wrappers and men in their dressing gowns crowded the balconies and porches of Boudasea. Gentlemen, half-dressed and concerned with their horseflesh, hurried toward the barn. Northrup led them, exhorting the servants who straggled along to lend a hand.

A freed horse galloped past, the beat of its hooves so violent that it rocked the ground. Adam dragged himself to his feet and offered his hand. "Up, before you're run over." When Bronwyn stood beside him, he ordered, "Go back to the house."

Astonished, Bronwyn watched him limp swiftly toward the stable. Running in front of him, she yelled, "That building is going to collapse."

He put her aside and hastened on, calling, "The horses," but she hurled herself at him, striking him behind the knees.

He went down, and she straddled his back. "The horses aren't worth your life."

He remained still, but whether she'd convinced him or simply knocked the air out of him, she didn't know. Or care. Trying to sound brisk and firm, she told him, "There's more help than Kenneth knows what to do with. We'll stay here and let the stable hands do what they're trained to do."

His hands wrestled free of hers, circled her wrists. "No one is trained for this." He turned over, dumping her off.

She stood and leaned over the top of him, shaking a finger in his face. "Adam, I'm warning you, don't try to get up."

A half smile crooked his mouth as he stood. "Or what?"

"Or I'll knock you down again." She put her hands on his arms, gazed earnestly into his eyes. "You're not going in that stable."

Cupping her face in his hands, he looked at her. Screaming assailed her ears, soot clogged her nose, fear tasted leaden on her tongue, yet when Adam smiled and whispered, "God, how I adore you," the love within her ran, warm and sweet, under her skin. Closing her eyes, she lifted her face for his kiss.

It didn't come. His touch left her, and when she opened her eyes he was gone, striding toward the fire. Like a mountain goat, she bounded across the grass, adding her call to the cacophony.

She met the whole mass of creatures—workers, horses, guests, Adam—galloping back toward her.

"Collapse! Fire! Run!" the stable hands screamed.

Skidding to a stop, she sighed with relief.

Adam grabbed her arm and hustled her back, yelling, "You silly woman, all the horses are out. Get back!"

With a roar the stable disintegrated. The walls fell, each board a scarlet banner. Flames swooped high, the heat reached out. Spontaneously every haystack around the stable erupted in flames.

One haystack drew her attention. A glowing torch separated, crawled away, and she remembered.

Horror etched Kenneth's wrinkled face. "What is it?"

Grabbing Adam's face, she shouted, "Judson?"

"Damn him," Adam swore. "Couldn't he just die like anyone else? Does he have to—"

He started down the slope to the stable, and Bronwyn turned to Kenneth in desperation. "It's the man who set fire to the stables."

In a mighty swell, the stable hands overtook Adam, dragged him back. Pulling their forelocks, dipping in little bows, showing their respect in every way, still they subdued him.

One said, "Ye can't go down there, m'lord."

Kenneth added, "'Tis so hot you'll ignite from th' heat. Best leave well enough alone. If that fellow's not dead yet, he soon will be."

Bronwyn heard a voice intone, "Humpty Dumpty sat on a wall, Humpty Dumpty had a great fall—"

Northrup stood beside her, and she gaped at him as he finished, "All the king's horses and all the king's men couldn't put Humpty together again." Northrup rubbed the place where Judson's bullet had struck him. "Judson's egg is fried at last. May he burn in hell as well as on earth."

Gianni leaned on the rail and gazed with tear-filled eyes at the retreating shore of England. Where was his master? Why had he failed to catch the packet to Calais as he promised? Never had his master failed to extricate himself from his escapades, but never had his master allowed vengeance to govern him before. Gianni had a bad feeling, here, in his heart. Pressing the affected member, Gianni drooped.

The old woman his master had stabbed with his knife still lived. The one who considered herself a doctor had saved the woman while he and his master struggled with the others. It depressed him to remember how his master had cursed. Another few moments, and the woman would have been dead. Maybe—he brightened—the woman would die of infection.

In the tiny room below the waterline, Gianni had placed the bags that contained all his worldly goods and his master's, too. But in his belt he kept the purse of coins his master had earned with his hard work and stealthy ways. This bag the master guarded, never before allowing Gianni to view the contents, never before allowing Gianni even to carry the contents. Always the master had given him money for the household expenses, and for the quick departures their lives had sometimes required.

Now—Gianni smiled and patted the heavy purse—now his master had proved his trust in his faithful servant. Gianni would look, only once, not for long, on this treasure. There wouldn't be much, Gianni knew, for reverses of fortune had plagued them. But with these poor bits of silver, he would prepare for his master's arrival in Calais. In Calais, he, Gianni, would order a hot dinner, some old wine, perhaps a woman such as his master preferred. Yes. Gianni nodded. He would use it only for his master's comfort.

With a quick glance over his shoulder, he ascertained that no one stood near. His cloak opened, he lifted his shirt, seeking the belt that retained the bag against his skin. Carefully he pulled the leather strings apart, lifted the purse, looked inside.

Gold coins glittered in the sun. Many gold coins, thick gold coins, gold coins such as Gianni had only dreamed of. Gianni stared, twirled his finger among the golden metal, looked once more at the shore of England.

"Good-bye, my master," he called, lifting his hand to wave. "Good-bye."

"Robert." Adam laid his hand on Walpole's arm. "I need you to do something for me."

Walpole grinned. "Today's your wedding day, m'boy. I have helped you dress." He adjusted the ruffles on Adam's white silk shirt and held his waistcoat as he shrugged into it. "I buoyed your spirits with good jokes and good ale. Too late to get you out of it."

"But that's exactly what I want you to do."

Walpole's grin faded, and he stepped out of Adam's grasp. "Damn it, you're joking."

"No, I'm not. I can't marry Olivia. She's a beautiful girl, but—"

"You can't marry her sister, either."

Adam jumped, glanced around. "My God, does everyone know?"

"Everyone with eyes. I saw you enter the barn last night. Everyone saw the two of you returning to the house this morning." Walpole gestured across the lawn to the still smoldering stable. "A fire has a way of bringing out the curious, and Adam—I heard she was sitting on you."

Adam grunted. "She didn't wanted me to risk my life."

"Very touching, but it didn't take a prodigy to observe the hay in that girl's hair."

"That girl's name is Bronwyn," Adam told him austerely.

"Bronwyn, Olivia, what difference does it make? All cats are gray in the dark. Scratch one in the right spot, and she purrs."

Adam refused to respond to Walpole's cajoling smile. "You may understand finance, but you know nothing about women."

Walpole was struck dumb but sputtered to life as Adam buttoned his white satin waistcoat. "I fancy myself a bit of an expert."

"Now you know better. Should I wear my ivory rings or my amber rings?"

"The ivory," Walpole decided absently. "They accent the white satin breeches. The fire, the daring fight in which you killed the man who had destroyed your reputation! Everyone's gossiping about how dashing you are."

"I didn't kill him."

"But they're all gossiping quietly among—what did you say?"

"I didn't kill him." Adam slid the rings on his fingers and smiled at his dumbfounded friend. "Bronwyn killed him. How did you think I stabbed him in the back when we were wrestling?"

"Are you trying to tell me that dewy-faced little woman threw the knife?"

"Exactly."

"Remind me to be polite to Lady Bronwyn." Walpole bristled as Adam laughed. "Damn it, man, that changes nothing. If you should dump one sister for the other—again!—imagine the scandal!" Touching his brow, Walpole complained, "Look what you've done. I'm sweating like a pig."

"You are a pig, Robert, but you're my friend. I'm telling you, I want you to stop this wedding."

Walpole pulled his handkerchief from the copious pocket of his brocade coat and mopped at his forehead.

"Bronwyn and I saved your life," Adam reminded.

"Beholden to a woman," Walpole moaned.

"I did your dirty work at Change Alley."

"I'll pay you for it," Walpole answered immediately.

"Yes, by bringing this wedding to a halt."

"What has that girl done to you?"

Adam lifted a brow. "I'd be interested in hearing your theory."

"You used to be passionate about nothing but finance, family honor, and England."

Not at all offended, Adam said, "I was a ghastly bore."

"Exactly. Now it's as though you've become a"—Walpole waved his hands, seeking inspiration—"a real person."

"Dreadful!"

"You hold real conversations with men about real things, like horses and mistresses. Young women don't faint when you gaze on them. Of course, they pant a bit when you gaze on Bronwyn." Too late, Walpole realized he'd taken the conversation back to the wedding. "But that doesn't mean I'll help you marry her."

Robert Walpole strode through the halls of Boudasea Manor and muttered. What had that girl done to his friend Adam? The man of fire and ice had changed, mellowed. All his fire was directed, controlled, warming rather than scorching. The ice hadn't melted. It had only become something stronger, less brittle, more enduring.

All cats were gray in the dark, he'd told Adam. Scratch them and they purred. He scrubbed absentmindedly at his stomach. Made a man wonder if he'd missed something.

Adam wanted him to stop the wedding. Risk his reputation as a sane man to stop the wedding. But was it worth his government career to do it? He'd stepped into the devastation left by the South Sea bubble and was even now creating a new government, a stable government, a government in which he assisted the king as his most valued minister. Did Adam think his love was priceless?

No. Walpole shook his head. No, damn it, he wasn't going to make a fool of himself. Let Adam get himself out of this mess.

"Robert."

A soft, female, seductive voice beckoned him. He buttoned his waistcoat, lifted his lace handkerchief to his lips, turned around—and straightened so hastily that his back cracked.

"Robert." Mab, his own personal nemesis, gestured to him through the gap of her workroom door. "Come here."

He sidled toward Mab, expecting to be blasted for some peccadillo of his that had gotten out of hand. Instead she smiled on him with charm and warmth, and he knew he was in trouble.

When she had him inside the room, she shut the door, trapping him with no hope of reprieve. Still smiling, she said, "You will stop this wedding."

Chapter 24

he last time. The last time. The phrase echoed in Bronwyn's mind like the chant of some maddened dissenter.

Last night, with the laughter, the tears, the shared dreams and heady revelations, had been the last time. No more would she seek Adam's arms. No more would she rock with him to celebrate a pleasure so complete, they would never seek it again. No more would she smile when they realized no pleasure was ever complete.

She sat on the bed in Olivia's room and bit her fist as she listened to Lady Nora alternately command and cajole. "Olivia, dear, it's time for the ceremony. Stop trembling and stand so we can put this dress on you."

The next woman to lie in Adam's bed would be Olivia. Olivia—writhing, damp, groaning. Olivia.

Olivia. Bronwyn shook her head. Olivia wouldn't

appreciate Adam's skill. She'd be disgusted, using the time of love to pray as assiduously as she prayed right now. Olivia, beautiful sister extraordinaire, would never adore him, would never long for him, would never give him the love he craved.

The sun smiled on the day. Still damp with dew, chrysanthemums decorated every arch and vase. Shrill with enjoyment, the guests streamed out of the house to the chapel close by. Everything, everything was right for a wedding. But it wasn't *her* wedding. What should she do? She couldn't break up her own sister's wedding. Could she?

The mere thought was ludicrous. Everyone—her mother, her father, Olivia, Adam, herself—everyone would be made a laughingstock. London society would never stop giggling.

But, damn it, Olivia would not move. She kept her eyes fixed on the window, kept her knees planted firmly on the cushion.

"This is not the time to pray," Lady Nora burst out. "Tonight will be the time to pray."

Turning her pure, composed face to her mother, Olivia chided, "Any time is the time to pray."

"Not this time. Not—" Lady Nora caught herself as her voice rose. "Every guest is wearing a rosette, tied in a true love knot and constructed of forest green and silver. Your sisters are dressed and waiting. They look so beautiful, each in a pale green matching gown, beaded with pearls and live roses."

Bronwyn almost bit off her fingernail but jerked her hand away just in time. Adam had accused her of forcing him to marry Olivia, and perhaps he was right. He couldn't call off the wedding. To do so would offer Olivia a boorish insult. Only Olivia could refuse—and that would offer Adam an equally offensive insult. Adam and Olivia were locked into a marriage destined to make them both miserable, and only one woman could save them. Only one woman was good enough for Adam, and her name was Bronwyn Edana, translator, lover, knife thrower.

"Even Bronwyn looks gorgeous," Lady Nora coaxed. "All of society is here. Men of all stations are courting her. Lord Sawbridge—he's a duke!—claims previous acquaintance, and is positively drooling on her."

Olivia screwed up her features in disdain, and her gentle voice snapped, "He's so old, he's just drooling."

Lady Nora wrung her hands. "If not Sawbridge, then some other gentleman. Look at her, Olivia. Can you deprive Bronwyn of the chance to make a decent alliance for herself?"

Bronwyn would be miserable, too. She knew it. Three lives sacrificed on the altar of society's morals? That was too much. She'd advised Olivia that if she wanted something badly enough, she should reach out and take it. Hadn't that been what Adam had been saying? Her decision made, Bronwyn stood and ordered, "Yes, look at me, Olivia."

Olivia looked. What she saw in Bronwyn's eyes brought her to her feet. A communication passed between them, and Olivia's back straightened. Her fingers intertwined, her face glowed with an inner joy.

"That's a girl," Lady Nora crooned, bustling to her side. "Let me call the maids and we'll put you in your gown."

"Olivia will allow only me to dress her," Bronwyn interposed. "Isn't that right, Olivia?"

Olivia hesitated, then agreed. "That's right, Maman." She watched Lady Nora with calm eyes, a serene visage. "Only Bronwyn today."

"But I'm your mother," Lady Nora wailed.

"That's why she wants me." Smiling an enigmatic smile, Bronwyn moved to Lady Nora's side and wrapped an arm around her waist. "You're the mother of the bride, and she knows your presence is required as part of the wedding party." She nudged Lady Nora toward the door. "Won't you take this opportunity to manage this wedding in the intoxicating style only you can create?"

"Well, I suppose I should." Lady Nora fluttered under the influence of such brazen flattery. "That is, I am the only true hostess at this affair. Lady Mab has been positively unhelpful."

"I know, Maman."

"I do give the best parties in the best society."

"That's true, Maman."

"But . . . oh, dear." Lady Nora looked back at Olivia with real affection, and Bronwyn thought she'd lost. "How can I leave my baby at a time like this?"

Softly Olivia said, "Maman, I insist."

"You're sure you don't mind?"

"Not at all."

Hurt sounded in Lady Nora's voice as she repeated, "Not at *all*?"

"She means she would trust herself in no one else's hands but mine." Bronwyn smiled as she held the door wide. "Don't delay."

Something about Bronwyn's smile made Lady Nora look closely, and her eyes narrowed. "Bronwyn . . ."

"I'm going to put Adam's bride in the wedding dress

you approved for her, and get her down to the chapel on time," Bronwyn assured her.

Unconvinced, Lady Nora slapped her hand on the closing door. "You don't have any mischief in mind now, do you?"

"What mischief could I have in mind?" Bronwyn pointed to Olivia, still and peaceful against the frame of the window. "For me to make mischief, I'd have to have the cooperation of my sister, and you know my sister never cooperates with mischief."

Lady Nora's expression lightened, but her suspicions still lingered. "She only cooperates with your mischief."

"I can hardly knock her down and tie her up, can I?" Bronwyn chuckled, indicating the difference in their heights.

Skepticism appeased, Lady Nora nodded. "Very well. I'll see you as you walk down the aisle, in *front* of your sister."

Lifting a hand in farewell, Bronwyn shut the door hastily. "Now," she said, advancing on her sister. "Do I have to knock you down and tie you up?"

Tears rose in Olivia's eyes, and with mute appeal she shook her head.

"Then you'll let me take your place?"

"Yes," Olivia whispered. "It's the answer to my prayer."

Bronwyn turned her back to Olivia and ordered, "Unlace me."

"You are so brave, Bronwyn." Olivia wrapped her arms around her smaller sister in a tender hug. "You make me brave, too. I can't do it without you, you know that. I can't face off Da and Maman and all the ministers they'll call in to talk to me if you don't help me."

Bronwyn returned her hug. "Oh, I'll help you. The trouble is, even I think you're meant to be a nun."

"Yes." Olivia smiled down at her. "I am. Just as you're meant to be Lord Rawson's bride."

Puckered by the weight of the wedding broach, the silver lace bodice drooped. Constructed for Olivia's larger head, the traditional garland of myrtle, olive leaf, rosemary, and white-and-purple blossoms slithered from side to side. The forest green skirt tripped Bronwyn until she gathered the front in her arms and carried it along. Her hurry did much to contribute to her clumsiness, but she dared not stop and gather herself together. She wanted no one to note a delay, no one to wonder.

In this, she was unsuccessful. Her mother stood on the step of the church, scanning the horizon as Bronwyn hove into view, and her double take impressed Bronwyn as no comment could. Bronwyn faltered; Lady Nora straightened, tapped her toe, and pointed to the spot directly in front of her. "My forebodings are fulfilled. Come here, young lady."

Lady Nora seldom spoke in such a manner, and with uncharacteristic meekness Bronwyn complied.

"What do you think you are doing, wearing Olivia's dress on Olivia's wedding day?"

"I'm going to get married"—one look at her mother's uncompromising face, and Bronwyn gulped—"my lady."

"You can't do this," Lady Nora fumed. "What will society think?"

"I don't care," Bronwyn declared truculently. "This is more important."

"More important than our social standing?" Lady Nora sounded and looked exasperated. "You jest, child. What could be more important than our—"

"Maman, I love him." Bronwyn held out one hand, palm up, pleading for understanding, and the vast creation of the skirt escaped her and slithered to the ground.

"You love *him*? *You* love him?" Lady Nora tried different inflections to the sentence, quite as if she'd never heard that arrangement of words in the English language. "You *love* him?"

"Yes."

"Do I understand you? You love the viscount of Rawson?"

Bronwyn nodded, and her mother shook her head dolefully.

"Dear . . ."

"I love him just as you love Da."

Lady Nora froze. Her eyes narrowed, she searched Bronwyn's face. "God help you if that's true."

Bronwyn trusted her expression to tell all. It seemed it did, for Lady Nora pulled out her handkerchief and dabbed the tears pooling in the corners of her glorious orbs. "What a disaster. You know how distressing that condition has been to me and to Holly. Couldn't you learn from our mistakes?"

"I didn't have a choice, and it sometimes seems you and Holly are more fulfilled with your loves than the other sisters are with their dry and dusty emotions."

"Oh, I don't know," Lady Nora fretted.

Catching Lady Nora's hand, Bronwyn beseeched, "Tell me it hasn't all been miserable between you and Da."

"No, not miserable." Lady Nora observed Bronwyn's

pleading face and looked beyond it to her own past. Remembering, she sighed. "Some of it has been quite magnificent."

"If you had it to do over again?" Bronwyn prompted.

"If I had it to do over again, I would do exactly as I have," Lady Nora admitted. With a harrumph designed to cover her embarrassment, she lifted the skirt and squinted at its construction. "I wish you'd told me this before. I could have done something with this dress. As it is, you'll just have to carry it." Tucking the material into Bronwyn's waistband, she fussed, "If I didn't know better, I'd say you were already wearing your apron strings higher."

Bronwyn couldn't mask her flash of pride.

Lady Nora touched a manicured finger to her forehead. "It's the truth, isn't it? You are expecting a child."

"Yes, Maman."

"Oh, stop smirking. You're going to make me a grandmother." Lady Nora moaned delicately. "You're going to top the biggest scandal of the year with a premature child. How premature will it be?"

"I don't know a lot about it, but . . . I believe at least three months."

Looking, for the first time in Bronwyn's memory, all of her fifty-three years, Lady Nora pressed a hand on her future grandchild. Then, giving Bronwyn a shove into the chapel, she commanded, "Hurry up and go in. The way you're loitering out here, I'd think you want to make it four months."

Lord Gaynor stuck his head out the door. "Nora, for God's sake, the Sirens of Ireland are lined up at the back of the chapel, awaiting the bride, and their smiles are starting to look practiced. Is that girl ready yet?"

His eyes lit on Bronwyn. "Greetings, me colleen. Those are fine feathers ye're sporting. Ye'll catch a man for sure in such—" As he realized whose gown she wore, his frown snapped into place. "What are ye doing in your sister's wedding garb?"

Bronwyn smiled tentatively. "Now, Da—"

"Don't ye 'now, Da' me!" His Irish accent grew with every syllable. "You can't fool your ol' papa. What have ye done with Olivia?"

"Oh, Da."

He paced across the chapel steps. "I don't know where you got your fecklessness."

"From you?" Bronwyn suggested.

"You keep saying that!" Lord Gaynor paced back to her. "Why do ye keep saying that? I'm not feckless."

"No, Da."

"Wipe that grin off your face, and tell me"—he braced himself, expecting the worst—"did you knock her down and bind her with a rope?"

"She's fine," Bronwyn assured him.

"Ye'll never convince me Olivia agreed to this!"

She didn't know what to say. Olivia's dilemma must wait for another time. "Actually—"

Perhaps he suspected, for he held up one hand. "Don't tell me. Just answer me question. What are ye doing in your sister's gown?"

Lady Nora adjusted the garland of flowers that had slid over Bronwyn's ear. "She's waiting for her father to give her away."

Lord Gaynor gaped at his wife. "Are ye telling me ye approve of these shenanigans?"

With great significance Lady Nora said, "Yes, Grandfather, I do."

Mouth working, Lord Gaynor assimilated the information and let out a whoop. Holding Bronwyn in his arms, he twirled her around. "A babe?"

She nodded while Lady Nora fretted, "Put her down, Rafferty, do. You're ruining her hair."

"A babe." The twirling slowed. He placed Bronwyn on the ground and stalked toward the door. "I knew I should have killed that bastard."

Lady Nora caught him by the elbow and jerked him around. "If you kill him, he can't marry Bronwyn."

"You're right." He took a breath. "First he'll marry her. Then I'll kill him."

"Da, there's no reason to kill him," Bronwyn pointed out. "He doesn't know about the babe."

Astonished, Lord Gaynor said, "He doesn't know?"

Lady Nora echoed, "He doesn't know?"

Bronwyn chewed her lip. "Do you think he'll be angry?"

Her parents exchanged long, meaningful looks.

"Not about the babe, but certainly that you didn't tell him. I think this day's work has saved us from the much bigger scandal of marriage and immediate annulment. If Adam had married Olivia, then found you were with child . . ." Lord Gaynor sighed dolefully.

"I suppose we could have hidden Bronwyn away?" Lady Nora suggested, arranging Bronwyn's unrestrained locks, tucking the singed ends into her neckline.

They considered it. Lord Gaynor shook his head, followed by Lady Nora. "No," Lord Gaynor decided. "The truth would have come out. I'm no coward, m'dear, but I blench at the thought of facing Adam at that juncture."

Lady Nora shuddered. "Indeed."

"How will I tell him, then?" Bronwyn wondered.

"In bed tonight," Lady Nora instructed. "Men are notoriously indulgent on their wedding night."

"Yes." Bronwyn thought, then asked, "What's the French word for pregnant?"

"Enceinte." Lady Nora stared. "Why?"

From the door of the chapel, Bronwyn heard, "Move!"

"You move!"

"Me first, I'm the oldest."

Turning, she saw Holly and Linnet, identical sisters dressed in identical pale green gowns, struggling to exit the church. Neither would give up first place, and at last they popped out onto the porch, their panniers crushed.

"Da, everyone's getting restless," Linnet began. "Where's— Oh God, it's Bronwyn."

"I told you Bronwyn caused the delay," Holly told her sister smugly. "Adam looks ill, Da. Now that the bride is here, shouldn't we begin the wedding?"

"Yes, begin at once," Lady Nora ordered. "Oh, wait! Wait until I'm seated." She glared at Bronwyn as though her daughter were responsible for her own heedlessness. "Six weddings I've put on, Bronwyn, and I've never had these snags occur before."

With absolute certainty Bronwyn answered, "You won't again, Maman, I promise you."

Lady Nora sniffed as she entered the chapel. Linnet and Holly began their struggle to enter once more, and Bronwyn heard two shrieks as her father pushed them in.

"There." He straightened his collar. "How does your ol' da look?"

Standing on tiptoe, Bronwyn kissed his cheek. "Dashing as ever. No one will even look at Adam when you're there."

"Humph." He offered his arm and led her through the door to the vestibule. "Ye've got the gift of blarney. I suppose ye'll try and blame that on me, too."

"No, Da." Faced with the prospect of hundreds of staring, twittering, gossiping faces just beyond the arches, Bronwyn stiffened with nerves.

Impervious to Bronwyn's stage fright. Lord Gaynor asked, "Why didn't ye tell the man?"

Her sisters started down the aisle. Each trying to outdo the other, they scattered flower petals in great, dramatic sweeps of their lily white hands. "Tell who what?"

"Tell Adam about the babe." He waited until his daughters had cleared the aisle and clustered about the altar. Then, beaming like the proud father he was, he guided Bronwyn into the chapel.

Speculation swept the church at her appearance in the bridal gown, and her fear turned to terror. Repeated in loud whispers, her name assaulted her as she stumbled forward.

Never breaking his stately stride, her father nudged her. "Why didn't you tell him?"

She gathered her composure enough to offer an answer she hoped would satisfy her father. "He thought I was ugly."

Lord Gaynor's practiced smile dipped. "Adam? Adam said you were ugly?"

As she saw the matrons with sharp-toothed grins, her teeth chattered. "No, he never said it. I just thought—"

"Look at him and tell me he thinks ye're ugly."

For the first time, Bronwyn looked to the altar where Adam stood. Smooth white satin couldn't compare to the magnificence of his rugged, tanned face and strong hands. His dark hair, combed and left to wave around his shoulders, couldn't compare to the fire in his eyes when he looked at her. And look at her he did, with such pride and passion that her tension fell from her. His hand pressed to the place above his heart. In his smile mixed equal parts of incredulity, relief, joy.

He thought she was beautiful. How could she have forgotten?

He watched her stumble along in a skirt too long for her, in a bodice so low and large that she was in danger of exposing herself, and he saw only her face. Piquant, expressive, adoring him as if he were someone special. She thought he was wonderful. How could he have doubted her?

"Adam." She formed his name with her lips, and he took a step forward. He heard the sigh as romantic delight caught the congregation, but he couldn't tear his gaze from Bronwyn to look at them. He could only reach out his hand; she laid hers within it.

The Anglican minister, who owed his position to the good grace of Lord Rawson, knew better than to question this unorthodox switch of brides. Gracefully he inserted Bronwyn's name into the ceremony. Bronwyn repeated her vows in a whisper. Adam repeated his too loudly. The minister asked if any had objections and paused with a smile. It faded as someone cleared his throat.

A sinking feeling assailed Adam. Not now. Fate couldn't be so cruel as to stop them now. Slowly he turned to face the congregation and found his friend Robert Walpole standing, finger in the air, wearing a brazen grin. "Oh, no," Adam whispered. Then aloud, "Robert." Adam said no more, but even Walpole's name was a threat.

Robert ignored it, and him. "I have the right to speak, I believe."

The minister nodded sickly.

"It's a shame such a charming lady is marrying such a curmudgeon. Does Lady Bronwyn realize what she's getting in this fellow?" Bronwyn nodded in reply to his question, but Walpole ignored her. "I've known Adam Keane, viscount of Rawson, for years, and I tell you the fellow is a stiff-necked, ethical bore. He refuses every bribe I offer him. He insists on total honesty in his business dealings. I ask you, what kind of man would offer assistance to the people cheated by the sale of false South Sea Company stock?" He pointed an accusing finger at Adam. "Only Lord Rawson."

Not pleased with Robert's revelations, Adam ordered, "Robert, sit down."

Walpole pointed instead at Bronwyn. "Lady Bronwyn is going to have to put up with this kind of relentless do-gooding for all the years of their wedded life. The woman is young, beautiful, and, dare I say it?"

Emboldened by the spirits he'd consumed, one of the gentlemen beside him called, "Say it. Say it!"

"Intelligent," Walpole said with a flourish. "Yes, she's intelligent, and instead of dancing the night away with some light-footed, heavy-handed dandy, she'll be forced to listen to Lord Rawson's plans to make ever more and more money until their family is the wealthiest in England."

Another gentleman gasped in simulated astonishment.

"The wealthiest in England," Walpole repeated. "Imagine, if you will, Lady Bronwyn's life, surrounded by luxury, overwhelmed by riches, worshiped by her husband. Why, she'll be forced to spend her time vetting offers of marriage for their children from the finest families in the British Isles."

"Sit down, Mr. Walpole," Bronwyn said.

"And look at them." Walpole waved a beefy hand toward the almost married couple. "They blatantly adore each other. Can we as English aristocrats allow such a marriage to take place? What would be the results of such fidelity within our class?"

"Sit down, Robert," Mab said.

Robert sat so hard, the pew shook. Hunching his shoulders, he rolled his eyes toward the ceiling and whistled softly.

The minister looked over his glasses at the sniggering congregation. "Does anyone else feel the desire to object to this marriage for any *justifiable* reason?"

A few gentlemen cleared their throats, but none could face Adam's menace, all the more powerful for being unspoken.

Rapidly the minister intoned, "Thus two lives become one. May God's blessing follow you all your years as man and wife." He took a breath. "You, Lord Rawson, may kiss the bride."

Adam pulled Bronwyn toward him until he could see down the gaping neckline. He wanted to look there, and at her legs, at her waist, at her back, but he wanted to touch everywhere. Low and deep, he said, "I'm honored that such an intelligent, charming lady has consented to marry such a curmudgeon. I had moments when I doubted she would."

"You aren't a curmudgeon." She cradled his cheek in her hand as gently as she would cradle a bird's egg. "You're just as kind, and generous, clever and honorable as Walpole said."

Kissing her wrist, he breathed in the scent of oranges

and said, "I don't give a damn what the rest of society thinks. I only care what my bride thinks."

She blushed. "You're lucky she came to her senses, or *she* would have had to object in the midst of the ceremony."

"It would have never come to that." Adam lifted his head and glared briefly at Robert Walpole. "Fool that I am, I instructed Robert to interrupt at that point in the ceremony. I just didn't give him alternate instructions, and there's nothing Robert loves more than a jest."

Her mouth curled in a smile. "It was funny."

"You have an odd sense of humor, Cherie. *Mais je t'adore.*"

"Oh, I adore you, too." The fragrant wreath on her head slipped down until it rested on her ear. "Will you teach me French?"

He gathered her closer. "And Spanish. And Italian. And Arabic."

Impatient at last, Walpole shouted, "Kiss her!"

Wrapping her arms around his neck, she promised, "And I'll teach you Gaelic."

Adam smiled at her. As she smiled back, he saw the reflection of his fire in her.

"Walpole's right. Kiss her!" Mab yelled.

From the far back of the church, Olivia's voice chimed, "Kiss her!"

"Kiss her! Kiss her!" The demand came from all sides.

"You'll be mine?" Adam whispered.

"All my life," she vowed.

"All my love," he answered, lowering his mouth to hers.

As their lips mated in the first kiss of their married life, Walpole had the last word. *"Ah, vive l'amour!"*

Good Girls Do

Just because a woman is brought up
a proper lady, doesn't mean she isn't
harboring some very improper desires.
And just because a lady may have led a
more . . . *colorful* life, doesn't mean she
hasn't got a heart of gold. In fact, we're
willing to bet that within the hearts of
the most well-intentioned beauties beat
the kind of passion that conventional
society cannot contain . . . and only a
rare gentleman can capture.

In the coming months, Avon Books
brings you four captivating romances
featuring heroines who live by their own
rules when it comes to matters of the
heart. Turn the page for a sneak preview
of these spectacular novels from bestselling authors Jacquie D'Alessandro,
Christina Dodd, Victoria Alexander, and
Samantha James!

Coming January 2008

Confessions at Midnight

a brand-new *Mayhem in Mayfair* novel
by *USA Today* bestselling author

Jacquie D'Alessandro

Though Carolyn Turner can't believe the Ladies Literary Society of London would choose an erotic novel as their reading selection, she also can't help but read the tantalizing Memoirs of a Mistress *at least a half dozen times! Suddenly the lovely widow is tempted to surrender to her newly fueled fantasies when in the company of roguishly sexy Lord Surbrooke, a man no proper lady should be seen talking to, much less kissing. . . .*

Are you warm enough?" he asked.

Dear God, ensconced with Lord Surbrooke in the privacy provided by the potted palms, Carolyn felt as if she stood in the midst of a roaring fire. She nodded, then her gaze searched his. "Do . . . do you know who I am?"

His gaze slowly skimmed over her, lingering on the bare expanse of her shoulders and the curves she knew her ivory gown highlighted—skin and curves that her

normal modest mode of dress never would have revealed. That openly admiring look, which still held no
hint of recognition, reignited the heat the breeze had
momentarily cooled. When their eyes once again met,
he murmured, "You are Aphrodite, goddess of desire."

She relaxed a bit. He clearly didn't know who she
was, for the way he'd said "desire," in that husky, gruff
voice, was a tone Lord Surbrooke had never used with
Lady Wingate. Yet her relaxation was short-lived as that
desire-filled timbre pulsed a confusing tension through
her, part of which warned her to leave the terrace at
once. To return to the masquerade party and continue
searching for her sister and friends. But another
part—the part held enthralled by the darkly alluring
highwayman and the protection of her anonymity—
refused to move.

To add to her temptation was the fact that this anon-
ymous interlude might afford her the opportunity to
learn more about him. In spite of their numerous conversations during the course of Matthew's house party,
all she actually knew of Lord Surbrooke was that he
was intelligent and witty, impeccably polite, unfail-
ingly charming, and always perfectly groomed. He'd
never given her the slightest hint as to what caused
the shadows that lurked in his eyes. Yet she knew they
were there, and her curiosity was well and truly piqued.
Now, if she could only recall how to breathe, she could
perhaps discover his secrets.

After clearing her throat to locate her voice, she said,
"Actually, I am Galatea."

He nodded slowly, his gaze trailing over her. "Galatea
. . . the ivory statue of Aphrodite carved by Pygma-

lion because of his desire for her. But why are you not Aphrodite herself?"

"In truth, I thought costuming myself as such a bit too . . . immodest. I'd actually planned to be a shepherdess. My sister somehow managed to convince me to wear this instead." She gave a short laugh. "I believe she coshed me over the head while I slept."

"Whatever she did, she should be roundly applauded for her efforts. You are . . . exquisite. More so than Aphrodite herself."

His low voice spread over her like warm honey. Still, she couldn't help but tease, "Says a thief whose vision is impaired by darkness."

"I'm not really a thief. And my eyesight is perfect. As for Aphrodite, she is a woman to be envied. She had only one divine duty—to make love and inspire others to do so as well."

His words, spoken in that deep, hypnotic timbre, combined with his steady regard, spiraled heat through her and robbed her of speech. And reaffirmed her conclusion that he didn't know who she was. Never once during all the conversations she'd shared with Lord Surbrooke had he ever spoken to her—Carolyn— of anything so suggestive. Nor had he employed that husky, intimate tone. Nor could she imagine him doing so. She wasn't the dazzling sort of woman to incite a man's passions, at least not a man in his position, who could have any woman he wanted, and according to rumor, did.

Emboldened by his words and her secret identity, she said, "Aphrodite was desired by all and had her choice of lovers."

"Yes. One of her favorites was Ares." He lifted his hand, and she noticed he'd removed his black gloves. Reaching out, he touched a single fingertip to her bare shoulder. Her breath caught at the whisper of contact then ceased altogether when he slowly dragged his finger along her collarbone. "Makes me wish I'd dressed as the god of war rather than a highwayman."

He lowered his hand to his side, and she had to press her lips together to contain the unexpected groan of protest that rose in her throat at the sudden absence of his touch. She braced her knees, stunned at how they'd weakened at that brief, feathery caress.

She swallowed to find her voice. "Aphrodite caught Ares with another lover."

"He was a fool. Any man lucky enough to have you wouldn't want any other."

"You mean Aphrodite."

"You *are* Aphrodite."

"Actually, I'm Galatea," she reminded him.

"Ah, yes. The statue Pygmalion fell so in love with was so lifelike he often laid his hand upon it to assure himself whether his creation were alive or not." He reached out and curled his warm fingers around her bare upper arm, just above where her long satin ivory glove ended. "Unlike Galatea, you are very much real."

Coming February 2008

Priceless

the classic novel
by *New York Times* bestselling author

Christina Dodd

*One of the celebrated Sirens of Ireland, spirited Bron-
wyn Edana is known for stunning titled society with
her courageous exploits. But once betrothed to nobleman Adam Keane, she finds herself at the center of a
shocking conspiracy that could rock the British realm.
Now she faces her most daring adventure yet: risking
it all for the only man she would ever love. . . .*

Adam drew her outdoors, into the heated darkness.
A great bonfire leaped in the middle of the square,
answering the flames atop the hill, calling in the summer. On a platform, a swarm of instruments—violin,
flute, and harmonica—squalled. The players cajoled
off-key bits of melody, then whole bars of music, and
at last, inspired by the occasion, a rollicking song. Although Bronwyn had never heard it before, its concentrated rhythm set her foot to tapping.

With a tug of his hand, Adam had her in the center

of a circle of clapping villagers. "I don't know how to dance to this," she warned.

"Nor do I," he answered, placing his hands on her waist. "Have a care for your toes."

She had no need to care for her toes, for Adam led with a strength that compensated for his limp. He kept his hands on her waist as he lifted her, turned her, swung her in circles. Under his guidance, she relaxed and began to enjoy the leaping, foot-stomping gambol. The community cheered, not at all distressed by the innovative steps, and the whole village joined them around the bonfire.

Girls with their sweethearts, men with their wives, old folks with their grandchildren, all whisked by as Adam twirled Bronwyn around and around. Bronwyn laughed until she was out of breath, and when she was gasping, the music changed. The rhythm slowed, the frenetic pace dwindled.

She saw Adam's amused expression change as he drew her toward him. His heavy lids veiled his gaze, and she knew he'd done so to hide his intention. She wondered why, then felt only shock as their bodies collided.

Shutting her eyes against the buffet of his heated frame against hers, she breathed a long, slow breath. The incense of his skin mated with the scent of the burning wood, and beneath the shield of her eyelids fireworks exploded She groaned as her own body was licked by the flames.

Before she was scorched, he twirled her away, then back, in accordance to the rules of the dance.

There were people around, she knew, but she pretended they weren't watching their lord and lady. She pretended Adam and she were alone.

Ignoring the proper steps, Adam wrapped himself around her, one arm against her shoulders, one arm at her waist.

Her hands held his shoulders. Her fingers flexed, feeling the muscles hidden beneath the fine linen. She could hear his heart thudding, hear the rasp of his breath and his moan as she touched his neck with her tongue. She only wanted a taste of him, but he mistook it for interest, for he scooped her up.

Her eyes flew open. He'd ferried them to the edge of the dancing figures, planning their escape like a smuggler planning a landfall. A whirl and they were gone into the trees. Looking back, she could see the sparks of the bonfire, like a constellation of stars climbing to the sky.

This was what she wanted, what she dreaded, what she longed for. Since she'd met Adam, she didn't understand herself. His gaze scorched her, and she reveled in the discomfort. His hands massaged her as if he found pleasure in her shape; they wandered places no one had touched since she'd been an infant, and it excited her. Even now, as he pulled her into the darkest corner of the wood, she went on willing feet.

He pushed her against the trunk of a broad oak and murmured, "Bronwyn, give me your mouth."

She found his lips and marveled at their accuracy. His arm held her back, his hand clasped her waist; all along their length they grew together, like two fevered creatures of the night.

Coming March 2008

The Perfect Wife

the classic novel
by *New York Times* bestselling author

Victoria Alexander

When the Earl of Wyldewood decides he is looking for a proper wife, Sabrina Winfield bargains for the position of his convenient bride. This fiery beauty will do anything to protect her family, even if it means playing into Nicholas Harrington's arrogant ideas about how a woman should behave. But the passion in the infuriating earl's touch shatters any illusions Sabrina has of keeping her heart safe. . . .

Sabrina stepped forward and gazed up at him. The glittering heavens reflected in her eyes, and Nicholas had to stop himself from reaching for her.

She drew a steady breath. "Since this is to be a marriage of convenience only and privately we shall continue to live our separate lives, and since you already have an heir, I will expect you to respect my privacy."

"Respect your privacy." he blurted, stunned. "Do you

mean to say you will be my wife but you will not share my bed?"

"That's exactly what I mean," she said earnestly. "I shall be everything you want in a countess. I shall be the perfect wife. But I shall not share any man's bed with other women, and I shall not give my favors to a man I do not love."

She stepped back. "I suspect you would never wish the public spectacle of a divorce; therefore, if we do not suit, we can have the marriage annulled, or we can do what so many do and live completely apart from one another. If these terms are unacceptable to you . . ." Sabrina tilted her head in a questioning manner. "Well, Nicholas, what's it to be?"

He stared, the silence growing between them. He had thought she'd be the appropriate wife for his purposes the evening they first met. But now he wanted more. Much, much more. The light of the moon cast a shimmering halo about her hair, caressing her finely carved features, her classically sculpted form. She was a vision in the misty magic of the black and silver shades of the night. He could only remember one other time in his life when his desire for a woman had been this overpowering. Irrational, instinctual and, ultimately, undeniable. He would take her as his wife, terms, conditions and all.

"I have a condition of my own," he said softly. "If we decide we do not suit, it must be a joint decision. We must agree to separate."

"Is that all?"

The moonlight reflected the surprise on her face.

Nicholas smiled to himself. Obviously, she did not think he'd accept her outrageous proposition. He nodded.

"Then as acting captain of this vessel, Simon can marry us. Is tomorrow acceptable?"

"More than acceptable." He pulled her into his arms.

"Nicholas," she gasped, "I hardly think this is an auspicious start to a marriage of convenience."

"We are not yet wed," he murmured, "and at the moment I find this wonderfully convenient." He pressed his lips to hers.

The pressure of his touch stole her breath and sapped her will. She struggled to fight a sea of powerful sensations, flooding her veins, throbbing through her blood. How would she resist him? If he could do this to her with a mere kiss . . . she shuddered with anticipation and ignored the distant warning in the back of her mind; it was not to be.

He held her close, plundering her lips with his own. Instinctively, he sensed her surrender, knew the moment of her defeat. Satisfied, he released her. Lifting her chin with a gentle touch, he gazed into eyes aglow with the power of his passion.

"Until tomorrow."

It took but a moment. Nicholas noted Sabrina gathering her wits about her. Noted her transformation into the cool, collected Lady Stanford. She was good, his bride-to-be, very good.

"Tomorrow." She nodded politely, turned and walked into the darkness. He rested his back against the rail and watched her disappear into the night. Her scent lingered in the air, vaguely spicy, hinting of a long-forgotten memory. A smile grew on his lips and he considered the unexpected benefits of taking a wife.

Nicholas, Earl of Wyldewood, was a man of honor, and he would abide by their bargain, abide by their terms.

All, of course, except one.

Coming April 2008

The Seduction of an Unknown Lady

an exciting new novel
by *New York Times* bestselling author

Samantha James

Fionna Hawkes values her independence as much as she does her privacy. Which is why she must resist Lord Aidan McBride, despite his persistent desire to know her better. Fiona not only has her secret identity as horror writer F. J. Sparrow to protect, but her family as well. But who will protect her from this bold nobleman's charms?

*Y*ou are the talk of all the neighbors, Lord Aidan—"

"Please," he interrupted. "It's Aidan. Just Aidan. The formality is not necessary. After all, we've been in each other's company in the dark before."

Fionna gasped.

"Miss Hawkes, you surprise me. I didn't think you were a woman easily shocked."

His eyes were twinkling. Fionna's narrowed. "I think you meant to shock me."

He chuckled. "I do believe I did."

For a fraction of an instant, his gaze met hers with that boldness she found so disconcerting. Then, to her further shock, his eyes trickled down her features, settling on her mouth. Something sparked in those incredible blue eyes; it vanished by the time she recognized it. Yet that spark set her further off guard . . . and further on edge.

Fionna we her lips. If he could be bold, then so could she. Her chin tipped. "I should like to know what you're thinking, my lord."

His smile was slow-growing. "I'm not so sure you do, Miss Hawkes."

"I believe I know my own mind." Fionna was adamant.

"Very well then. I was thinking that I am a most fortunate man."

"Why?" she asked bluntly.

Again that slow smile—a breathtaking one, she discovered. All at once she felt oddly short of breath. And there it was again, that spark in his eyes, only now it appeared in the glint of his smile.

"Perhaps fortunate is not the best way to describe it." He pretended to ponder. "No, that is not it at all. Indeed, I must say, I relish my luck."

"Your luck, my lord? And why is that?"

"It's quite simple, really. I relish my luck . . . in that I have found you before my brother."

Fionna's cheeks heated. Oh, heavens, the man was outrageous! He was surely an accomplished flirt—but surely he wasn't flirting with her.

"And another thing, Miss Hawkes." He traced a fingertip around the shape of her mouth, sending her heart into such a cascade of rhythm that she could barely breathe.

Nor could she have moved if the earth had tumbled away beneath them both.

He dared still more, for the very tip of that daring finger breached her lips, running lightly along the line of her teeth. "I am immensely delighted," he said mildly, "to discover that you are most definitely *not* a vampire."

No, she was not. Still, Fionna didn't know whether to laugh or cry. Ah, she thought, if he only knew . . .